POIROT'S METHOD

"Come now, monsieur," said Inspector Japp of Scotland Yard, "you're not going to run down the value of details as clues."

"By no means. But it is the brain, the little gray cells"—Poirot tapped his forehead—"on which one must rely. One must seek the truth from within—not without."

"You don't mean to say, Monsieur Poirot, that you would attempt to solve a case without moving your chair, do you?"

"That is exactly what I do mean."

Japp slapped his knee. "Hanged if I don't take you at your word. Bet you a fiver that you can't . . ."

A foolish wager, Inspector Japp, when dealing with the amazing Hercule Poirot!

POIROT INVESTIGATES

"Capital collection of mystery stories . . . Ingeniously constructed."

—New York Post

AGATHA CHRISTIE

POIROT INVESTIGATES

BANTAM BOOKS
TORONTO · NEW YORK · LONDON

*This low-priced Bantam Book
has been completely reset in a type face
designed for easy reading, and was printed
from new plates. It contains the complete
text of the original hard-cover edition.*
NOT ONE WORD HAS BEEN OMITTED.

RLI: $\dfrac{\text{VLM 7 (VLR 6–8)}}{\text{IL 8–adult}}$

POIROT INVESTIGATES

*A Bantam Book / published by arrangement with
Dodd, Mead & Company, Inc.*

PRINTING HISTORY
Dodd, Mead edition published April 1925
American Mercury edition published September 1943

Bantam edition / November 1961

2nd printing .. December 1961	6th printing ... February 1967
3rd printing .... October 1962	7th printing ... February 1967
4th printing ... January 1964	8th printing .. September 1968
5th printing ... February 1967	9th printing .... July 1969

New Bantam edition / July 1970

2nd printing ...... May 1971	5th printing .... January 1973
3rd printing .. December 1971	6th printing .. September 1973
4th printing .... July 1972	7th printing .. September 1974

8th printing ... December 1975

Bantam Books are published by Bantam Books, Inc. Its trade-
mark, consisting of the words "Bantam Books" and the por-
trayal of a bantam, is registered in the United States Patent
Office and in other countries. Marca Registrada. Bantam
Books, Inc., 666 Fifth Avenue, New York, New York 10019.

PRINTED IN THE UNITED STATES OF AMERICA

CONTENTS

POIROT
INVESTIGATES

I
THE ADVENTURE OF
"THE WESTERN STAR"

I was standing at the window of Poirot's rooms looking out idly on the street below.

"That's queer," I ejaculated suddenly beneath my breath.

"What is, *mon ami?*" asked Poirot placidly, from the depths of his comfortable chair.

"Deduce, Poirot, from the following facts! Here is a young lady, richly dressed—fashionable hat, magnificent furs. She is coming along slowly, looking up at the houses as she goes. Unknown to her, she is being shadowed by three men and a middle-aged woman. They have just been joined by an errand boy who points after the girl, gesticulating as he does so. What drama is this being played? Is the girl a crook, and are the shadowers detectives preparing to arrest her? Or are *they* the scoundrels, and are they plotting to attack an innocent victim? What does the great detective say?"

"The great detective, *mon ami,* chooses, as ever, the simplest course. He rises to see for himself." And my friend joined me at the window.

In a minute he gave vent to an amused chuckle.

"As usual, your facts are tinged with your incurable romanticism. That is Miss Mary Marvell, the film star. She is being followed by a bevy of admirers who have recognized her. And, *en passant,* my dear Hastings, she is quite aware of the fact!"

I laughed.

"So all is explained! But you get no marks for that, Poirot. It was a mere matter of recognition."

"*En vérité!* And how many times have you seen Mary Marvell on the screen, *mon cher?*"

1

I thought.

"About a dozen times perhaps."

"And I—once! Yet *I* recognize her, and *you* do not."

"She looks so different," I replied rather feebly.

"Ah! *Sacré!*" cried Poirot. "Is it that you expect her to promenade herself in the streets of London in a cowboy hat, or with bare feet, and a bunch of curls, as an Irish colleen? Always with you it is the non-essentials! Remember the case of the dancer, Valerie Saintclair."

I shrugged my shoulders, slightly annoyed.

"But console yourself, *mon ami,*" said Poirot, calming down. "All cannot be as Hercule Poirot! I know it well."

"You really have the best opinion of yourself of anyone I ever knew!" I cried, divided between amusement and annoyance.

"What will you? When one is unique, one knows it! And others share that opinion—even, if I mistake not, Miss Mary Marvell."

"What?"

"Without doubt. She is coming here."

"How do you make that out?"

"Very simply. This street, it is not aristocratic, *mon ami!* In it there is no fashionable doctor, no fashionable dentist—still less is there a fashionable milliner! But there *is* a fashionable detective. *Oui,* my friend, it is true—I am become the mode, the *dernier cri!* One says to another: *Comment?* You have lost your gold pencil-case? You must go to the little Belgian. He is too marvellous! Every one goes! *Courez!* And they arrive! In flocks, *mon ami!* With problems of the most foolish!" A bell rang below. "What did I tell you? That is Miss Marvell."

As usual, Poirot was right. After a short interval, the American film star was ushered in, and we rose to our feet.

Mary Marvell was undoubtedly one of the most popular actresses on the screen. She had only lately arrived in England in company with her husband, Gregory B. Rolf, also a film actor. Their marriage had taken place about a year ago in the States and this was their first visit to England. They had been given a great reception.

Every one was prepared to go mad over Mary Marvell, her wonderful clothes, her furs, her jewels, above all one jewel, the great diamond which had been nicknamed, to match its owner, "the Western Star." Much, true and untrue, had been written about this famous stone which was reported to be insured for the enormous sum of fifty thousand pounds.

All these details passed rapidly through my mind as I joined with Poirot in greeting our fair client.

Miss Marvell was small and slender, very fair and girl-ish-looking, with the wide innocent blue eyes of a child.

Poirot drew forward a chair for her, and she commenced talking at once.

"You will probably think me very foolish, Monsieur Poirot, but Lord Cronshaw was telling me last night how wonderfully you cleared up the mystery of his nephew's death, and I felt that I just must have your advice. I dare say it's only a silly hoax—Gregory says so—but it's just worrying me to death."

She paused for breath. Poirot beamed encouragement.

"Proceed, Madame. You comprehend, I am still in the dark."

"It's these letters." Miss Marvell unclasped her handbag, and drew out three envelopes which she handed to Poirot.

The latter scrutinized them closely.

"Cheap paper—the name and address carefully printed. Let us see the inside." He drew out the enclosure.

I had joined him, and was leaning over his shoulder. The writing consisted of a single sentence, carefully printed like the envelope. It ran as follows:

"The great diamond which is the left eye of the god must return whence it came."

The second letter was couched in precisely the same terms, but the third was more explicit:

"You have been warned. You have not obeyed. Now the diamond will be taken from you. At the full of the moon, the two diamonds which are the left and right eye of the god shall return. So it is written."

"The first letter I treated as a joke," explained Miss Marvell. "When I got the second, I began to wonder.

The third one came yesterday, and it seemed to me that, after all, the matter might be more serious than I had imagined."

"I see they did not come by post, these letters."

"No; they were left by hand—by a *Chinaman*. That is what frightens me."

"Why?"

"Because it was from a Chink in San Francisco that Gregory bought the stone three years ago."

"I see, madame, that you believe the diamond referred to to be——"

" 'The Western Star,' " finished Miss Marvell. "That's so. At the same time, Gregory remembers that there was some story attached to the stone, but the Chink wasn't handing out any information. Gregory says he seemed just scared to death, and in a mortal hurry to get rid of the thing. He only asked about a tenth of its value. It was Greg's wedding present to me."

Poirot nodded thoughtfully.

"The story seems of an almost unbelievable romanticism. And yet—who knows? I pray of you, Hastings, hand me my little almanac."

I complied.

"Voyons!" said Poirot, turning the leaves. "When is the date of the full moon? Ah, Friday next. That is in three days' time. *Eh bien,* madame, you seek my advice —I give it to you. This *belle histoire* may be a hoax— but it may not! Therefore I counsel you to place the diamond in my keeping until after Friday next. Then we can take what steps we please."

A slight cloud passed over the actress's face, and she replied constrainedly:

"I'm afraid that's impossible."

"You have it with you—*hein?*" Poirot was watching her narrowly.

The girl hesitated a moment, then slipped her hand into the bosom of her gown, drawing out a long thin chain. She leaned forward, unclosing her hand. In the palm, a stone of fire, exquisitely set in platinum, lay and winked at us solemnly.

Poirot drew in his breath with a long hiss.

"*Épatant!*" he murmured. "You permit, madame?" He took the jewel in his own hand and scrutinized it keenly, then restored it to her with a little bow. "A magnificent stone—without a flaw. Ah, *cent tonnerres!* and you carry it about with you, *comme ça!*"

"No, no, I'm very careful really, Monsieur Poirot. As a rule it's locked up in my jewel-case, and left in the hotel safe deposit. We're staying at the *Magnificent,* you know. I just brought it along today for you to see."

"And you will leave it with me, *n'est-ce pas?* You will be advised by Papa Poirot?"

"Well, you see, it's this way, Monsieur Poirot. On Friday we're going down to Yardly Chase to spend a few days with Lord and Lady Yardly."

Her words awoke a vague echo of remembrance in my mind. Some gossip—what was it now? A few years ago Lord and Lady Yardly had paid a visit to the States, rumor had it that his lordship had rather gone the pace out there with the assistance of some lady friends—but surely there was something more, some gossip which coupled Lady Yardly's name with that of a "movie" star in California—why! it came to me in a flash! of course it was none other than Gregory B. Rolf.

"I'll let you into a little secret, Monsieur Poirot," Miss Marvell was continuing. "We've got a deal on with Lord Yardly. There's some chance of our arranging to film a play down there in his ancestral pile."

"At Yardly Chase?" I cried, interested. "Why, it's one of the show places of England."

Miss Marvell nodded.

"I guess it's the real old feudal stuff all right. But he wants a pretty stiff price, and of course I don't know yet whether the deal will go through, but Greg and I always like to combine business with pleasure."

"But—I demand pardon if I am dense, madame—surely it is possible to visit Yardly Chase without taking the diamond with you?"

A shrewd, hard look came into Miss Marvell's eyes which belied their childlike appearance. She looked suddenly a good deal older.

"I want to wear it down there."

"Surely," I said suddenly, "there are some very famous jewels in the Yardly collection, a large diamond amongst them?"

"That's so," said Miss Marvell briefly.

I heard Poirot murmur beneath his breath: "Ah, *c'est comme ça!*" Then he said aloud, with his usual uncanny luck in hitting the bull's-eye (he dignifies it by the name of psychology): "Then you are without doubt already acquainted with Lady Yardly, or perhaps your husband is?"

"Gregory knew her when she was out West three years ago," said Miss Marvell. She hesitated a moment, and then added abruptly: "Do either of you ever see *Society Gossip?*"

We both pleaded guilty rather shamefacedly.

"I asked because in this week's number there is an article on famous jewels, and it's really very curious——" She broke off.

I rose, went to the table at the other side of the room and returned with the paper in question in my hand. She took it from me, found the article, and began to read aloud:

". . . Amongst other famous stones may be included the Star of the East, a diamond in the possession of the Yardly family. An ancestor of the present Lord Yardly brought it back with him from China, and a romantic story is said to attach to it. According to this, the stone was once the right eye of a temple god. Another diamond, exactly similar in form and size, formed the left eye, and the story goes that this jewel, too, would in course of time be stolen. 'One eye shall go West, the other East, till they shall meet once more. Then, in triumph shall they return to the god.' It is a curious coincidence that there is at the present time a stone corresponding closely in description with this one, and known as 'the Star of the West,' or 'the Western Star.' It is the property of the celebrated film actress, Miss Mary Marvell. A comparison of the two stones would be interesting."

I stopped.

"*Épatant!*" murmured Poirot. "Without doubt a romance of the first water." He turned to Mary Marvell. "And you are not afraid, madame? You have no superstitious terrors? You do not fear to introduce these two Siamese twins to each other lest a Chinaman should appear and, hey presto! whisk them both back to China?"

His tone was mocking, but I fancied that an undercurrent of seriousness lay beneath it.

"I don't believe that Lady Yardly's diamond is anything like as good a stone as mine," said Miss Marvell. "Anyway, I'm going to see."

What more Poirot would have said I do not know, for at that moment the door flew open, and a splendid-looking man strode into the room. From his crisply curling black head, to the tips of his patent-leather boots, he was a hero fit for romance.

"I said I'd call round for you, Mary," said Gregory Rolf, "and here I am. Well, what does Monsieur Poirot say to our little problem? Just one big hoax, same as I do?"

Poirot smiled up at the big actor. They made a ridiculous contrast.

"Hoax or no hoax, Mr. Rolf," he said dryly, "I have advised madame your wife not to take the jewel with her to Yardly Chase on Friday."

"I'm with you there, sir. I've already said so to Mary. But there! She's a woman through and through, and I guess she can't bear to think of another woman outshining her in the jewel line."

"What nonsense, Gregory!" said Mary Marvell sharply. But she flushed angrily.

Poirot shrugged his shoulders.

"Madame, I have advised. I can do no more. *C'est fini.*" He bowed them both to the door.

"Ah! *la la,*" he observed, returning. "*Histoire de femmes!* The good husband, he hit the nail on the head—*tout de même,* he was not tactful! Assuredly not."

I imparted to him my vague remembrances, and he nodded vigorously.

"So I thought. All the same, there is something curious underneath all this. With your permission, *mon ami,* I will take the air. Await my return, I beg of you. I shall not be long."

I was half asleep in my chair when the landlady tapped on the door, and put her head in.

"It's another lady to see Mr. Poirot, sir. I've told her he was out, but she says as how she'll wait, seeing as she's come up from the country."

"Oh, show her in here, Mrs. Murchison. Perhaps I can do something for her."

In another moment the lady had been ushered in. My heart gave a leap as I recognized her. Lady Yardly's portrait had figured too often in the Society papers to allow her to remain unknown.

"Do sit down, Lady Yardly," I said, drawing forward a chair. "My friend Poirot is out, but I know for a fact that he'll be back very shortly."

She thanked me and sat down. A very different type, this, from Miss Mary Marvell. Tall, dark, with flashing eyes, and a pale proud face—yet something wistful in the curves of the mouth.

I felt a desire to rise to the occasion. Why not? In Poirot's presence I have frequently felt a difficulty—I do not appear at my best. And yet there is no doubt that I, too, possess the deductive sense in a marked degree. I leant forward on a sudden impulse.

"Lady Yardly," I said, "I know why you have come here. You have received blackmailing letters about the diamond."

There was no doubt as to my bolt having shot home. She stared at me open-mouthed, all color banished from her cheeks.

"You know?" she gasped. "How?"

I smiled.

"By a perfectly logical process. If Miss Marvell has had warning letters——"

"Miss Marvell? She has been here?"

"She has just left. As I was saying, if she, as the holder of one of the twin diamonds, has received a mysterious series of warnings, you, as the holder of the other stone, must necessarily have done the same. You see how simple it is? I am right, then, you have received these strange communications also?"

For a moment she hesitated, as though in doubt whether to trust me or not, then she bowed her head in assent with a little smile.

"That is so," she acknowledged.

"Were yours, too, left by hand—by a Chinaman?"

"No, they came by post; but, tell me, has Miss Marvell undergone the same experience, then?"

I recounted to her the events of the morning. She listened attentively.

"It all fits in. My letters are the duplicates of hers. It is true that they came by post, but there is a curious perfume impregnating them—something in the nature of joss-stick—that at once suggested the East to me. What does it all mean?"

I shook my head.

"That is what we must find out. You have the letters with you? We might learn something from the postmarks."

"Unfortunately I destroyed them. You understand, at the time I regarded it as some foolish joke. Can it be true that some Chinese gang are really trying to recover the diamonds? It seems too incredible."

We went over the facts again and again, but could get no further towards the elucidation of the mystery. At last Lady Yardly rose.

"I really don't think I need wait for Monsieur Poirot. You can tell him all this, can't you? Thank you so much, Mr.——"

She hesitated, her hand outstretched.

"Captain Hastings."

"Of course! How stupid of me. You're a friend of the Cavendishes, aren't you? It was Mary Cavendish who sent me to Monsieur Poirot."

When my friend returned, I enjoyed telling him the tale of what had occurred during his absence. He cross-questioned me rather sharply over the details of our conversation and I could read between the lines that he was not best pleased to have been absent. I also fancied that the dear old fellow was just the least inclined to be jealous.

It had become rather a pose with him to consistently belittle my abilities, and I think he was chagrined at finding no loophole for criticism. I was secretly rather pleased with myself, though I tried to conceal the fact for fear of irritating him. In spite of his idiosyncrasies, I was deeply attached to my quaint little friend.

"Bien!" he said at length, with a curious look on his face. "The plot develops. Pass me, I pray you, that 'Peerage' on the top shelf there." He turned the leaves. "Ah, here we are! 'Yardly . . . 10th viscount, served South African War' . . . *tout ça n'a pas d'importance* . . . 'mar. 1907 Hon. Maude Stopperton, fourth daughter of 3rd Baron Cotteril' . . . um, um, um, . . . 'has iss. two daughters, born 1908, 1910. . . . Clubs . . . residences.' . . . *Voilà,* that does not tell us much. But to-morrow morning we see this *milord!"*

"What?"

"Yes. I telegraphed him."

"I thought you had washed your hands of the case?"

"I am not acting for Miss Marvell since she refuses to be guided by my advice. What I do now is for my own satisfaction—the satisfaction of Hercule Poirot! Decidedly, I must have a finger in this pie."

"And you calmly wire Lord Yardly to dash up to town just to suit your convenience. He won't be pleased."

"Au contraire, if I preserve for him his family diamond, he ought to be very grateful."

"Then you really think there is a chance of its being stolen?" I asked eagerly.

"Almost a certainty," replied Poirot placidly. "Everything points that way."

"But how——"

Poirot stopped my eager questions with an airy gesture of the hand.

"Not now, I pray you. Let us not confuse the mind. And observe that 'Peerage'—how you have replaced him! See you not that the tallest books go in the top shelf, the next tallest in the row beneath, and so on. Thus we have order, *method,* which, as I have often told you, Hastings——"

"Exactly," I said hastily, and put the offending volume in its proper place.

Lord Yardly turned out to be a cheery, loud-voiced sportsman with a rather red face, but with a good-humored bonhomie about him that was distinctly attractive and made up for any lack of mentality.

"Extraordinary business this, Monsieur Poirot. Can't make head or tail of it. Seems my wife's been getting odd kinds of letters, and that this Miss Marvell's had 'em too. What does it all mean?"

Poirot handed him the copy of the *Society Gossip*.

"First, *milord*, I would ask if these facts are substantially correct?"

The peer took it. His face darkened with anger as he read.

"Damned nonsense!" he spluttered. "There's never been any romantic story attaching to the diamond. It came from India originally, I believe. I never heard of all this Chinese god stuff."

"Still, the stone *is* known as 'The Star of the East.' "

"Well what if it is?" he demanded wrathfully.

Poirot smiled a little, but made no direct reply.

"What I would ask you to do, *milord*, is to place yourself in my hands. If you do so unreservedly, I have great hopes of averting the catastrophe."

"Then you think there's actually something in these wildcat tales?"

"Will you do as I ask you?"

"Of course I will, but——"

"*Bien!* Then permit that I ask you a few questions. This affair of Yardly Chase, is it, as you say, all fixed up between you and Mr. Rolf?"

"Oh, he told you about it, did he? No, there's nothing settled." He hesitated, the brick-red color of his face deepening. "Might as well get the thing straight. I've made rather an ass of myself in many ways, Monsieur Poirot— and I'm head over ears in debt—but I want to pull up. I'm fond of the kids, and I want to straighten things up, and be able to live on at the old place. Gregory Rolf is offering me big money—enough to set me on my feet again. I don't want to do it—I hate the thought of all that crowd play-acting round the Chase—but I may have to, unless——" He broke off.

Poirot eyed him keenly. "You have, then, another string to your bow? Permit that I make a guess? It is to sell the Star of the East?"

Lord Yardly nodded. "That's it. It's been in the family for some generations, but it's not entailed. Still, it's not the easiest thing in the world to find a purchaser. Hoffberg, the Hatton Garden man, is on the look-out for a likely customer, but he'll have to find one soon, or it's a washout."

"One more question, *permettez*—Lady Yardly, which plan does she approve?"

"Oh, she's bitterly opposed to my selling the jewel. You know what women are. She's all for this film stunt."

"I comprehend," said Poirot. He remained a moment or so in thought, then rose briskly to his feet. "You return to Yardly Chase at once? *Bien!* Say no word to anyone—to *anyone*, mind—but expect us there this evening. We will arrive shortly after five."

"All right, but I don't see——"

"*Ça n'a pas d'importance*," said Poirot kindly. "You will find that I preserve for you your diamond, *n'est-ce pas?*"

"Yes, but——"

"Then do as I say."

A sadly bewildered nobleman left the room.

It was half-past five when we arrived at Yardly Chase, and followed the dignified butler to the old paneled hall with its fire of blazing logs. A pretty picture met our eyes: Lady Yardly and her two children, the mother's proud dark head bent down over the two fair ones. Lord Yardly stood near, smiling down on them.

"Monsieur Poirot and Captain Hastings," announced the butler.

Lady Yardly looked up with a start, her husband came forward uncertainly, his eyes seeking instruction from Poirot. The little man was equal to the occasion.

"All my excuses! It is that I investigate still this affair

of Miss Marvell's. She comes to you on Friday, does she not? I make a little tour first to make sure that all is secure. Also I wanted to ask of Lady Yardly if she recollected at all the postmarks on the letters she received?"

Lady Yardly shook her head regretfully. "I'm afraid I don't. It is stupid of me. But, you see, I never dreamt of taking them seriously."

"You'll stay the night?" said Lord Yardly.

"Oh, *milord,* I fear to incommode you. We have left our bags at the inn."

"That's all right." Lord Yardly had his cue. "We'll send down for them. No, no—no trouble, I assure you."

Poirot permitted himself to be persuaded, and sitting down by Lady Yardly, began to make friends with the children. In a short time they were all romping together, and had dragged me into the game.

"Vous êtes bonne mère," said Poirot, with a gallant little bow, as the children were removed reluctantly by a stern nurse.

Lady Yardly smoothed her ruffled hair.

"I adore them," she said with a little catch in her voice.

"And they you—with reason!" Poirot bowed again.

A dressing-gong sounded, and we rose to go up to our rooms. At that moment the butler entered with a telegram on a salver which he handed to Lord Yardly. The latter tore it open with a brief word of apology. As he read it he stiffened visibly.

With an ejaculation, he handed it to his wife. Then he glanced at my friend.

"Just a minute, Monsieur Poirot. I feel you ought to know about this. It's from Hoffberg. He thinks he's found a customer for the diamond—an American, sailing for the States to-morrow. They're sending down a chap to-night to vet the stone. By Jove, though, if this goes through—" Words failed him.

Lady Yardly had turned away. She still held the telegram in her hand.

"I wish you wouldn't sell it, George," she said, in a low voice. "It's been in the family so long." She waited, as though for a reply, but when none came her face hard-

ened. She shrugged her shoulders. "I must go and dress.
I suppose I had better display 'the goods.'" She turned
to Poirot with a slight grimace.

"It's one of the most hideous necklaces that was ever
designed! George has always promised to have the stones
reset for me, but it's never been done." She left the
room.

Half an hour later, we three were assembled in the
great drawing-room awaiting the lady. It was already a
few minutes past the dinner hour.

Suddenly there was a low rustle, and Lady Yardly appeared framed in the doorway, a radiant figure in a long
white shimmering dress. Round the column of her neck
was a rivulet of fire. She stood there with one hand just
touching the necklace.

"Behold the sacrifice," she said gaily. Her ill humor
seemed to have vanished. "Wait while I turn the big light
on and you shall feast your eyes on the ugliest necklace
in England."

The switches were just outside the door. As
she stretched out her hand to them, the incredible thing
happened. Suddenly without any warning, every light was
extinguished, the door banged, and from the other side
of it came a long-drawn piercing woman's scream.

"My God!" cried Lord Yardly. "That was Maude's
voice! What has happened?"

We rushed blindly for the door, cannoning into each
other in the darkness. It was some minutes before we
could find it. What a sight met our eyes! Lady Yardly
lay senseless on the marble floor, a crimson mark on her
white throat where the necklace had been wrenched from
her neck.

As we bent over her, uncertain for the moment whether
she were dead or alive, her eyelids opened.

"The Chinaman," she whispered painfully. "The Chinaman—the side door."

Lord Yardly sprang up with an oath. I accompanied
him, my heart beating wildly. The Chinaman again! The
side door in question was a small one in the angle of
the wall, not more than a dozen yards from the scene

of the tragedy. As we reached it, I gave a cry. There, just short of the threshold, lay the glittering necklace, evidently dropped by the thief in the panic of his flight. I swooped joyously down on it. Then I uttered another cry which Lord Yardly echoed. For in the middle of the necklace was a great gap. The Star of the East was missing!

"That settles it," I breathed. "These were no ordinary thieves. This one stone was all they wanted."

"But how did the fellow get in?"

"Through this door."

"But it's always locked."

I shook my head. "It's not locked now. See." I pulled it open as I spoke.

As I did so something fluttered to the ground. I picked it up. It was a piece of silk, and the embroidery was unmistakable. It had been torn from a Chinaman's robe.

"In his haste it caught in the door," I explained. "Come, hurry. He cannot have gone far as yet."

But in vain we hunted and searched. In the pitch darkness of the night, the thief had found it easy to make his getaway. We returned reluctantly, and Lord Yardly sent off one of the footmen post-haste to fetch the police.

Lady Yardly, aptly ministered to by Poirot, who is as good as a woman in these matters, was sufficiently recovered to be able to tell her story.

"I was just going to turn on the other light," she said, "when a man sprang on me from behind. He tore my necklace from my neck with such force that I fell headlong to the floor. As I fell I saw him disappearing through the side door. Then I realized by the pig-tail and the embroidered robe that he was a Chinaman." She stopped with a shudder.

The butler reappeared. He spoke in a low voice to Lord Yardly.

"A gentleman from Mr. Hoffberg's, m'lord. He says you expect him."

"Good heavens!" cried the distracted nobleman. "I must see him, I suppose. No, not here, Mullings, in the library."

I drew Poirot aside.

"Look here, my dear fellow, hadn't we better get back to London?"

"You think so, Hastings? Why?"

"Well,"—I coughed delicately—"things haven't gone very well, have they? I mean, you tell Lord Yardly to place himself in your hands and all will be well—and then the diamond vanishes from under your very nose!"

"True," said Poirot, rather crestfallen. "It was not one of my most striking triumphs."

This way of describing events almost caused me to smile, but I stuck to my guns.

"So, having—pardon the expression—rather made a mess of things, don't you think it would be more graceful to leave immediately?"

"And the dinner, the without doubt excellent dinner, that the *chef* of Lord Yardly has prepared?"

"Oh, what's dinner!" I said impatiently.

Poirot held up his hands in horror.

"Mon Dieu! It is that in this country you treat the affairs gastronomic with a criminal indifference."

"There's another reason why we should get back to London as soon as possible," I continued.

"What is that, my friend?"

"The other diamond," I said, lowering my voice. "Miss Marvell's."

"Eh bien, what of it?"

"Don't you see?" His unusual obtuseness annoyed me. What had happened to his usually keen wits? "They've got one, now they'll go for the other."

"Tiens!" cried Poirot, stepping back a pace and regarding me with admiration. "But your brain marches to a marvel, my friend! Figure to yourself that for the moment I had not thought of that! But there is plenty of time. The full of the moon, it is not until Friday."

I shook my head dubiously. The full of the moon theory left me entirely cold. I had my way with Poirot, however, and we departed immediately, leaving behind us a note of explanation and apology for Lord Yardly.

My idea was to go at once to the *Magnificent,* and relate to Miss Marvell what had occurred, but Poirot vetoed the plan, and insisted that the morning would be time enough. I gave in rather grudgingly.

In the morning Poirot seemed strangely disinclined to stir out. I began to suspect that, having made a mistake to start with, he was singularly loath to proceed with the case. In answer to my persuasions, he pointed out, with admirable common sense, that as the details of the affair at Yardly Chase were already in the morning papers the Rolfs would know quite as much as we could tell them. I gave way unwillingly.

Events proved my forebodings to be justified. About two o'clock, the telephone rang. Poirot answered it. He listened for some moments, then with a brief *"Bien, j'y serai"* he rang off, and turned to me.

"What do you think, *mon ami?*" He looked half ashamed, half excited. "The diamond of Miss Marvell, it has been stolen."

"What?" I cried, springing up. "And what about the 'full of the moon' now?" Poirot hung his head. "When did this happen?"

"This morning, I understand."

I shook my head sadly. "If only you had listened to me. You see I was right."

"It appears so, *mon ami,*" said Poirot cautiously. "Appearances are deceptive, they say, but it certainly appears so."

As we hurried in a taxi to the *Magnificent,* I puzzled out the true inwardness of the scheme.

"That 'full of the moon' idea was clever. The whole point of it was to get us to concentrate on the Friday, and so be off our guard beforehand. It is a pity you did not realize that."

"Ma foi!" said Poirot airily, his nonchalance quite restored after its brief eclipse. "One cannot think of everything!"

I felt sorry for him. He did so hate failure of any kind.

"Cheer up," I said consolingly. "Better luck next time."

At the *Magnificent,* we were ushered at once into the manager's office. Gregory Rolf was there with two men from Scotland Yard. A pale-faced clerk sat opposite them.

Rolf nodded as we entered.

"We're getting to the bottom of it," he said. "But it's almost unbelievable. How the guy had the nerve I can't think."

A very few minutes sufficed to give us the facts. Mr. Rolf had gone out of the hotel at 11.15. At 11.30, a gentleman, so like him in appearance as to pass muster, entered the hotel and demanded the jewel-case from the safe deposit. He duly signed the receipt, remarking carelessly as he did so: "Looks a bit different from my ordinary one, but I hurt my hand getting out of the taxi." The clerk merely smiled and remarked that he saw very little difference. Rolf laughed and said: "Well, don't run me in as a crook this time, anyway. I've been getting threatening letters from a Chinaman, and the worst of it is I look rather like a Chink myself—it's something about the eyes."

"I looked at him," said the clerk who was telling us this, "and I saw at once what he meant. The eyes slanted up at the corners like an Oriental's. I'd never noticed it before."

"Darn it all, man," roared Gregory Rolf, leaning forward, "do you notice it now?"

The man looked up at him and started.

"No, sir," he said. "I can't say that I do." And indeed there was nothing even remotely Oriental about the frank brown eyes that looked into ours.

The Scotland Yard man grunted. "Bold customer. Thought the eyes might be noticed, and took the bull by the horns to disarm suspicion. He must have watched you out of the hotel, sir, and nipped in as soon as you were well away."

"What about the jewel-case?" I asked.

"It was found in a corridor of the hotel. Only one thing had been taken—'the Western Star.'"

We stared at each other—the whole thing was so bizarre, so unreal.

Poirot hopped briskly to his feet. "I have not been of much use, I fear," he said regretfully. "Is it permitted to see Madame?"

"I guess she's prostrated with the shock," explained Rolf.

"Then perhaps I might have a few words alone with you, monsieur?"

"Certainly."

In about five minutes Poirot reappeared.

"Now, my friend," he said gaily. "To a post office. I have to send a telegram."

"Who to?"

"Lord Yardly." He discounted further inquiries by slipping his arm through mine. "Come, come, *mon ami*. I know all that you feel about this miserable business. I have not distinguished myself! You, in my place, might have distinguished yourself! *Bien!* All is admitted. Let us forget it and have lunch."

It was about four o'clock when we entered Poirot's rooms. A figure rose from a chair by the window. It was Lord Yardly. He looked haggard and distraught.

"I got your wire and came up at once. Look here, I've been round to Hoffberg, and they know nothing about that man of theirs last night, or the wire either. Do you think that——"

Poirot held up his hand.

"My excuses! I sent that wire, and hired the gentleman in question."

"*You*—but why? What?" The nobleman spluttered impotently.

"My little idea was to bring things to a head," explained Poirot placidly.

"Bring things to a head! Oh, my God!" cried Lord Yardly.

"And the ruse succeeded," said Poirot cheerfully. "Therefore, *milord,* I have much pleasure in returning you—this!" With a dramatic gesture he produced a glittering object. It was a great diamond.

"The Star of the East," gasped Lord Yardly. "But I don't understand——"

"No?" said Poirot. "It makes no matter. Believe me, it was necessary for the diamond to be stolen. I promised you that it should be preserved to you, and I have kept my word. You must permit me to keep my little secret. Convey, I beg of you, the assurances of my deepest respect to Lady Yardly, and tell her how pleased I am to be able to restore her jewel to her. What *beau temps,* is it not? Good day, *milord."*

And smiling and talking, the amazing little man conducted the bewildered nobleman to the door. He returned gently rubbing his hands.

"Poirot," I said. "Am I quite demented?"

"No, *mon ami,* but you are, as always, in a mental fog."

"How did you get the diamond?"

"From Mr. Rolf."

"Rolf?"

"Mais oui! The warning letters, the Chinaman, the article in *Society Gossip,* all sprang from the ingenious brain of Mr. Rolf! The two diamonds, supposed to be so miraculously alike—bah! they did not exist. There was only *one* diamond, my friend! Originally in the Yardly collection, for three years it has been in the possession of Mr. Rolf. He stole it this morning with the assistance of a touch of grease paint at the corner of each eye! Ah, I must see him on the film, he is indeed an artist, *celui-là!"*

"But why did he steal his own diamond?" I asked, puzzled.

"For many reasons. To begin with, Lady Yardly was getting restive."

"Lady Yardly?"

"You comprehend she was left much alone in California. Her husband was amusing himself elsewhere. Mr. Rolf was handsome, he had an air about him of romance. But *au fond,* he is very business-like, *ce monsieur!* He made love to Lady Yardly, and then he blackmailed her. I taxed the lady with the truth the other night, and she admitted it. She swore that she had only been indiscreet, and I believe her. But, undoubtedly, Rolf had letters of hers that could be twisted to bear a different interpretation. Terrified by the threat of a divorce, and the prospect of being separated from her children, she agreed to all he wished. She had no money of her own, and she was forced to permit him to substitute a paste replica for the real stone. The coincidence of the date of the appearance of 'the Western Star' struck me at once. All goes well. Lord Yardly prepares to range himself—to settle down. And then comes the menace of the possible sale of the diamond. The substitution will be discovered. Without doubt she writes off frantically to Gregory Rolf who has just arrived in England. He soothes her by promising to arrange all—and prepares for a double robbery. In this way he will quiet the lady, who might conceivably tell all to her husband, an affair which would not suit our blackmailer at all, he will have £50,000 insurance money (aha, you had forgotten that!), and he will still have the diamond! At this point I put my finger in the pie. The arrival of a diamond expert is announced. Lady Yardly, as I felt sure she would, immediately arranges a robbery—and does it very well too! But Hercule Poirot, he sees nothing but facts. What happens in actuality? The lady switches off the light, bangs the door, throws the necklace down the passage, and screams. She has already wrenched out the diamond with pliers upstairs——"

"But we saw the necklace round her neck!" I objected.

"I demand pardon, my friend. Her hand concealed the part of it where the gap would have shown. To place a piece of silk in the door beforehand is child's play! Of course, as soon as Rolf read of the robbery, he arranged his own little comedy. And very well he played it!"

"What did you say to him?" I asked with lively curiosity.

"I said to him that Lady Yardly had told her husband all, that I was empowered to recover the jewel, and that if it were not immediately handed over proceedings would be taken. Also a few more little lies which occurred to me. He was as wax in my hands!"

I pondered the matter.

"It seems a little unfair on Mary Marvell. She has lost her diamond through no fault of her own."

"Bah!" said Poirot brutally. "She has a magnificent advertisement. That is all she cares for, that one! Now the other, she is different. *Bonne mère, très femme!*"

"Yes," I said doubtfully, hardly sharing Poirot's views on femininity. "I suppose it was Rolf who sent her the duplicate letters."

"Pas du tout," said Poirot briskly. "She came by the advice of Mary Cavendish to seek my aid in her dilemma. Then she heard that Mary Marvell, whom she knew to be her enemy, had been here, and she changed her mind, jumping at a pretext that *you,* my friend, offered her. A very few questions sufficed to show me that *you* told her of the letters, not she you! She jumped at the chance your words offered."

"I don't believe it," I cried, stung.

"Si, si, mon ami, it is a pity that you study not the psychology. She told you that the letters were destroyed? Oh, la la, *never* does a woman destroy a letter if she can avoid it! Not even if it would be more prudent to do so!"

"It's all very well," I said, my anger rising, "but you've made a perfect fool of me! From beginning to end! No, it's all very well to try to explain it away afterwards. There really is a limit!"

"But you were so enjoying yourself, my friend. I had not the heart to shatter your illusions."

"It's no good. You've gone a bit too far this time."

"Mon Dieu! but how you enrage yourself for nothing, *mon ami!"*

"I'm fed up!" I went out, banging the door. Poirot had made an absolute laughing-stock of me. I decided he needed a sharp lesson. I would let some time elapse before I forgave him. He had encouraged me to make a perfect fool of myself!

II
THE TRAGEDY AT
MARSDON MANOR

I had been called away from town for a few days, and on my return found Poirot in the act of strapping up his small valise.

"A la bonne heure, Hastings. I feared you would not have returned in time to accompany me."

"You are called away on a case, then?"

"Yes, though I am bound to admit that, on the face of it, the affair does not seem promising. The Northern Union Insurance Company have asked me to investigate the death of a Mr. Maltravers who a few weeks ago insured his life with them for the large sum of fifty thousand pounds."

"Yes?" I said, much interested.

"There was, of course, the usual suicide clause in the policy. In the event of his committing suicide within a year the premiums would be forfeited. Mr. Maltravers was duly examined by the Company's own doctor, and although he was a man slightly past the prime of life was passed as being in quite sound health. However, on Wednesday last—the day before yesterday—the body of Mr. Maltravers was found in the grounds of his house in Essex, Marsdon Manor, and the cause of his death is described as some kind of internal hemorrhage. That in itself would be nothing remarkable, but sinister rumors as to Mr. Maltravers' financial position have been in the air of late, and the Northern Union have ascertained beyond any possible doubt that the deceased gentleman stood upon the verge of bankruptcy. Now that alters matters considerably. Maltravers had a beautiful young wife, and it is suggested that he got together all the ready money he could for the purpose of paying the premiums on a life

insurance for his wife's benefit, and then committed suicide. Such a thing is not uncommon. In any case, my
friend Alfred Wright, who is a director of the Northern
Union, has asked me to investigate the facts of the case,
but, as I told him, I am not very hopeful of success.
If the cause of the death had been heart failure, I should
have been more sanguine. Heart failure may always be
translated as the inability of the local G. P. to discover
what his patient really did die of, but a hemorrhage seems
fairly definite. Still, we can but make some necessary inquiries. Five minutes to pack your bag, Hastings, and
we will take a taxi to Liverpool Street."

About an hour later, we alighted from a Great Eastern
train at the little station of Marsdon Leigh. Inquiries at
the station yielded the information that Marsdon Manor
was about a mile distant. Poirot decided to walk, and we
betook ourselves along the main street.

"What is our plan of campaign?" I asked.

"First I will call upon the doctor. I have ascertained
that there is only one doctor in Marsdon Leigh, Dr. Ralph
Bernard. Ah, here we are at his house."

The house in question was a kind of superior cottage,
standing back a little from the road. A brass plate on
the gate bore the doctor's name. We passed up the path
and rang the bell.

We proved to be fortunate in our call. It was the doctor's consulting hour, and for the moment there were no
patients waiting for him. Dr. Bernard was an elderly
man, high-shouldered and stooping, with a pleasant
vagueness of manner.

Poirot introduced himself and explained the purpose of
our visit, adding that Insurance Companies were bound
to investigate fully in a case of this kind.

"Of course, of course," said Dr. Bernard vaguely. "I
suppose, as he was such a rich man, his life was insured
for a big sum?"

"You consider him a rich man, doctor?"

The doctor looked rather surprised.

"Was he not? He kept two cars, you know, and Marsdon
Manor is a pretty big place to keep up, although I believe he bought it very cheap."

"I understand that he had had considerable losses of late," said Poirot, watching the doctor narrowly.

The latter, however, merely shook his head sadly.

"Is that so? Indeed. It is fortunate for his wife, then, that there is this life insurance. A very beautiful and charming young creature, but terribly unstrung by this sad catastrophe. A mass of nerves, poor thing. I have tried to spare her all I can, but of course the shock was bound to be considerable."

"You have been attending Mr. Maltravers recently?"

"My dear sir, I never attended him."

"What?"

"I understand Mr. Maltravers was a Christian Scientist —or something of that kind."

"But you examined the body?"

"Certainly. I was fetched by one of the under-gardeners."

"And the cause of death was clear?"

"Absolutely. There was blood on the lips, but most of the bleeding must have been internal."

"Was he still lying where he had been found?"

"Yes, the body had not been touched. He was lying on the edge of a small plantation. He had evidently been out shooting rooks, a small rook rifle lay beside him. The hemorrhage must have occurred quite suddenly. Gastric ulcer, without a doubt."

"No question of his having been shot, eh?"

"My dear sir!"

"I demand pardon," said Poirot humbly. "But, if my memory is not at fault, in the case of a recent murder, the doctor first gave a verdict of heart failure—altering it when the local constable pointed out that there was a bullet wound through the head!"

"You will not find any bullet wounds on the body of Mr. Maltravers," said Dr. Bernard dryly. "Now, gentlemen, if there is nothing further——"

We took the hint.

"Good morning, and many thanks to you, doctor, for so kindly answering our questions. By the way, you saw no need for an autopsy?"

"Certainly not." The doctor became quite apoplectic.

"The cause of death was clear, and in my profession we see no need to distress unduly the relatives of a dead patient."

And, turning, the doctor slammed the door sharply in our faces.

"And what do you think of Dr. Bernard, Hastings?" inquired Poirot, as we proceeded on our way to the Manor.

"Rather an old ass."

"Exactly. Your judgments of character are always profound, my friend."

I glanced at him uneasily, but he seemed perfectly serious. A twinkle, however, came into his eye, and he added slyly:

"That is to say, when there is no question of a beautiful woman!"

I looked at him coldly.

On our arrival at the Manor-house, the door was opened to us by a middle-aged parlormaid. Poirot handed her his card, and a letter from the Insurance Company for Mrs. Maltravers. She showed us into a small morning-room, and retired to tell her mistress. About ten minutes elapsed, and then the door opened, and a slender figure in widow's weeds stood upon the threshold.

"Monsieur Poirot?" she faltered.

"Madame!" Poirot sprang gallantly to his feet and hastened towards her. "I cannot tell you how I regret to derange you in this way. But what will you? *Les affaires* —they know no mercy."

Mrs. Maltravers permitted him to lead her to a chair. Her eyes were red with weeping, but the temporary disfigurement could not conceal her extraordinary beauty. She was about twenty-seven or -eight, and very fair, with large blue eyes and a pretty pouting mouth.

"It is something about my husband's insurance, is it? But must I be bothered *now*—so soon?"

"Courage, my dear madame. Courage! You see, your late husband insured his life for rather a large sum, and in such a case the Company always has to satisfy itself as to a few details. They have empowered me to act for them. You can rest assured that I will do all in my power to render the matter not too unpleasant for you. Will you recount to me briefly the sad events of Wednesday?"

"I was changing for tea when my maid came up—one of the gardeners had just run to the house. He had found——"

Her voice trailed away. Poirot pressed her hand sympathetically.

"I comprehend. Enough! You had seen your husband earlier in the afternoon?"

"Not since lunch. I had walked down to the village for some stamps, and I believe he was out pottering round the grounds."

"Shooting rooks, eh?"

"Yes, he usually took his little rook rifle with him, and I heard one or two shots in the distance."

"Where is this little rook rifle now?"

"In the hall, I think."

She led the way out of the room and found and handed the little weapon to Poirot, who examined it cursorily.

"Two shots fired, I see," he observed, as he handed it back. "And now, madame, if I might see——"

He paused delicately.

"The servant shall take you," she murmured, averting her head.

The parlormaid, summoned, led Poirot upstairs. I remained with the lovely and unfortunate woman. It was hard to know whether to speak or remain silent. I essayed one or two general reflections to which she responded absently, and in a very few minutes Poirot rejoined us.

"I thank you for all your courtesy, madame. I do not think you need be troubled any further with this matter. By the way, do you know anything of your husband's financial position?"

She shook her head.

"Nothing whatever. I am very stupid over business things."

"I see. Then you can give us no clue as to why he suddenly decided to insure his life? He had not done so previously, I understand."

"Well, we had only been married a little over a year. But, as to why he insured his life, it was because he had absolutely made up his mind that he would not live long. He had a strong premonition of his own death. I gather that he had had one hemorrhage already, and that he knew that another one would prove fatal. I tried to dispel these gloomy fears of his, but without avail. Alas, he was only too right!"

Tears in her eyes, she bade us a dignified farewell. Poirot made a characteristic gesture as we walked down the drive together.

"*Eh bien,* that is that! Back to London, my friend, there appears to be no mouse in this mousehole. And yet——"

"Yet what?"

"A slight discrepancy, that is all! You noticed it? You did not? Still, life is full of discrepancies, and assuredly the man cannot have taken his own life—there is no poison that would fill his mouth with blood. No, no, I must resign myself to the fact that all here is clear and above-board—but who is this?"

A tall young man was striding up the drive towards us. He passed us without making any sign, but I noted that he was not ill-looking, with a lean, deeply bronzed face that spoke of life in a tropic clime. A gardener who was sweeping up leaves had paused for a minute in his task, and Poirot ran quickly up to him.

"Tell me, I pray you, who is that gentleman? Do you know him?"

"I don't remember his name, sir, though I did hear it. He was staying down here last week for a night. Tuesday, it was."

"Quick, *mon ami,* let us follow him."

We hastened up the drive after the retreating figure. A glimpse of a black-robed figure on the terrace at the side of the house, and our quarry swerved and we after him, so that we were witnesses of the meeting.

Mrs. Maltravers almost staggered where she stood, and her face blanched noticeably.

"You," she gasped. "I thought you were on the sea—on your way to East Africa?"

"I got some news from my lawyers that detained me," explained the young man. "My old uncle in Scotland died unexpectedly and left me some money. Under the circumstances I thought it better to cancel my passage. Then I saw this bad news in the paper and I came down to see if there was anything I could do. You'll want some one to look after things for you a bit perhaps."

At that moment they became aware of our presence. Poirot stepped forward, and with many apologies explained that he had left his stick in the hall. Rather reluctantly, it seemed to me, Mrs. Maltravers made the necessary introduction.

"Monsieur Poirot, Captain Black."

A few minutes' chat ensued, in the course of which Poirot elicited the fact that Captain Black was putting up at the Anchor Inn. The missing stick not having been discovered (which was not surprising), Poirot uttered more apologies and we withdrew.

We returned to the village at a great pace, and Poirot made a bee line for the Anchor Inn.

"Here we establish ourselves until our friend the Captain returns," he explained. "You notice that I emphasized the point that we were returning to London by the first train? Possibly you thought I meant it. But no—you observed Mrs. Maltravers' face when she caught sight of this young Black? She was clearly taken aback, and he—*eh bien,* he was very devoted, did you not think so? And he was here on Tuesday night—the day before Mr. Maltravers died. We must investigate the doings of Captain Black, Hastings."

In about half an hour we espied our quarry approaching the inn. Poirot went out and accosted him and presently brought him up to the room we had engaged.

"I have been telling Captain Black of the mission which brings us here," he explained. "You can understand, *monsieur le capitaine,* that I am anxious to arrive at Mr. Maltravers' state of mind immediately before his death, and that at the same time I do not wish to distress Mrs. Maltravers unduly by asking her painful questions. Now, you were here just before the occurrence, and can give us equally valuable information."

"I'll do anything I can to help you, I'm sure," replied the young soldier; "but I'm afraid I didn't notice anything out of the ordinary. You see, although Maltravers was an old friend of my people's, I didn't know him very well myself."

"You came down—when?"

"Tuesday afternoon. I went up to town early Wednesday morning, as my boat sailed from Tilbury about twelve o'clock. But some news I got made me alter my plans, as I dare say you heard me explain to Mrs. Maltravers."

"You were returning to East Africa, I understand?"

"Yes. I've been out there ever since the War—a great country."

"Exactly. Now what was the talk about at dinner on Tuesday night?"

"Oh, I don't know. The usual odd topics. Maltravers asked after my people, and then we discussed the question of German reparations, and then Mrs. Maltravers asked a lot of questions about East Africa, and I told them one or two yarns, that's about all, I think."

"Thank you."

Poirot was silent for a moment, then he said gently: "With your permission, I should like to try a little experiment. You have told us all that your conscious self knows, I want now to question your subconscious self."

"Psychoanalysis, what?" said Black, with visible alarm.

"Oh, no," said Poirot reassuringly. "You see, it is like this, I give you a word, you answer with another, and so on. Any word, the first one you think of. Shall we begin?"

"All right," said Black slowly, but he looked uneasy.

"Note down the words, please, Hastings," said Poirot. Then he took from his pocket his big turnip-faced watch and laid it on the table beside him. "We will commence. Day."

There was a moment's pause, and then Black replied: "*Night.*"

As Poirot proceeded, his answers came quicker.

"Name," said Poirot.

"*Place.*"

"Bernard."

"*Shaw.*"

"Tuesday."

"Dinner."

"Journey."

"Ship."

"Country."

"Uganda."

"Story."

"Lions."

"Rook Rifle."

"Farm."

"Shot."

"Suicide."

"Elephant."

"Tusks."

"Money."

"Lawyers."

"Thank you, Captain Black. Perhaps you could spare me a few minutes in about half an hour's time?"

"Certainly." The young soldier looked at him curiously and wiped his brow as he got up.

"And now, Hastings," said Poirot, smiling at me as the door closed behind him. "You see it all, do you not?"

"I don't know what you mean."

"Does that list of words tell you nothing?"

I scrutinized it, but was forced to shake my head.

"I will assist you. To begin with, Black answered well within the normal time limit, with no pauses, so we can take it that he himself has no guilty knowledge to conceal. 'Day' to 'Night' and 'Place' to 'Name' are normal associations. I began work with 'Bernard' which might have suggested the local doctor had he come across him at all. Evidently he had not. After our recent conversation, he gave 'Dinner' to my 'Tuesday,' but 'Journey' and 'Country' were answered by 'Ship' and 'Uganda,' showing clearly that it was his journey abroad that was important to him and not the one which brought him down here. 'Story' recalls to him one of the 'Lion' stories he told at dinner. I proceed to 'Rook Rifle' and he answered with the totally unexpected word 'Farm.' When I say 'Shot,' he answers at once 'Suicide.' The association seems clear. A man he knows committed suicide with a rook rifle on a farm somewhere. Remember, too, that his mind is still on the stories he told at dinner, and I think you will agree that I shall not be far from the truth if I recall Captain Black and ask him to repeat the particular suicide story which he told at the dinner-table on Tuesday evening."

Black was straightforward enough over the matter.

"Yes, I did tell them that story now that I come to think of it. Chap shot himself on a farm out there. Did it with a rook rifle through the roof of the mouth, bullet lodged in the brain. Doctors were no end puzzled over it —there was nothing to show except a little blood on the lips. But what——"

"What has it got to do with Mr. Maltravers? You did not know, I see, that he was found with a rook rifle by his side."

"You mean my story suggested to him—oh, but that is awful!"

"Do not distress yourself—it would have been one way or another. Well, I must get on the telephone to London."

Poirot had a lengthy conversation over the wire, and came back thoughtful. He went off by himself in the afternoon, and it was not till seven o'clock that he announced that he could put it off no longer, but must break the news to the young widow. My sympathy had already gone out to her unreservedly. To be left penniless, and with the knowledge that her husband had killed himself to assure her future was a hard burden for any woman to bear. I cherished a secret hope, however, that young Black might prove capable of consoling her after her first grief had passed. He evidently admired her enormously.

Our interview with the lady was painful. She refused vehemently to believe the facts that Poirot advanced, and when she was at last convinced broke down into bitter weeping. An examination of the body turned our suspicions into certainty. Poirot was very sorry for the poor lady, but, after all, he was employed by the Insurance Company, and what could he do? As he was preparing to leave he said gently to Mrs. Maltravers:

"Madame, you of all people should know that there are no dead!"

"What do you mean?" she faltered, her eyes growing wide.

"Have you never taken part in any spiritualistic séances? You are mediumistic, you know."

"I have been told so. But you do not believe in Spiritualism, surely?"

"Madame, I have seen some strange things. You know that they say in the village that this house is haunted?"

She nodded, and at that moment the parlormaid announced that dinner was ready.

"Won't you just stay and have something to eat?"

We accepted gratefully, and I felt that our presence could not but help distract her a little from her own griefs.

We had just finished our soup, when there was a scream outside the door, and the sound of breaking crockery. We jumped up. The parlormaid appeared, her hand to her heart.

"It was a man—standing in the passage."

Poirot rushed out, returning quickly.

"There is no one there."

"Isn't there, sir?" said the parlormaid weakly. "Oh, it did give me a start!"

"But why?"

She dropped her voice to a whisper.

"I thought—I thought it was the master—it looked like 'im."

I saw Mrs. Maltravers give a terrified start, and my mind flew to the old superstition that a suicide cannot rest. She thought of it too, I am sure, for a minute later, she caught Poirot's arm with a scream.

"Didn't you hear that? Those three taps on the window? That's how *he* always used to tap when he passed round the house."

"The ivy," I cried. "It was the ivy against the pane."

But a sort of terror was gaining on us all. The parlormaid was obviously unstrung, and when the meal was over Mrs. Maltravers besought Poirot not to go at once. She was clearly terrified to be left alone. We sat in the little morning-room. The wind was getting up, and moaning round the house in an eerie fashion. Twice the door

of the room came unlatched and the door slowly opened,
and each time she clung to me with a terrified gasp.

"Ah, but this door, it is bewitched!" cried Poirot
angrily at last. He got up and shut it once more, then
turned the key in the lock. "I shall lock it, so!"

"Don't do that," she gasped, "if it should come open
now——"

And even as she spoke the impossible happened. The
locked door slowly swung open. I could not see into the
passage from where I sat, but she and Poirot were facing
it. She gave one long shriek as she turned to him.

"You saw him—there in the passage?" she cried.

He was staring down at her with a puzzled face, then
shook his head.

"I saw him—my husband—you must have seen him
too?"

"Madame, I saw nothing. You are not well—unstrung——"

"I am perfectly well, I— Oh, God!"

Suddenly, without any warning, the lights quivered and
went out. Out of the darkness came three loud raps. I
could hear Mrs. Maltravers moaning.

And then—I saw!

The man I had seen on the bed upstairs stood there
facing us, gleaming with a faint ghostly light. There was
blood on his lips, and he held his right hand out, pointing.
Suddenly a brilliant light seemed to proceed from it. It
passed over Poirot and me, and fell on Mrs. Maltravers.
I saw her white terrified face, and something else!

"My God, Poirot!" I cried. "Look at her hand, her
right hand. It's all red!"

Her own eyes fell on it, and she collapsed in a heap on
the floor.

"Blood," she cried hysterically. "Yes, it's blood. I
killed him. I did it. He was showing me, and then I put
my hand on the trigger and pressed. Save me from him—
save me! he's come back!"

Her voice died away in a gurgle.

"Lights," said Poirot briskly.

The lights went on as if by magic.

"That's it," he continued. "You heard, Hastings? And

you, Everett? Oh, by the way, this is Mr. Everett, rather a fine member of the theatrical profession. I phoned to him this afternoon. His make-up is good, isn't it? Quite like the dead man, and with a pocket torch and the necessary phosphorescence he made the proper impression. I shouldn't touch her right hand if I were you, Hastings. Red paint marks so. When the lights went out I clasped her hand, you see. By the way, we mustn't miss our train. Inspector Japp is outside the window. A bad night—but he has been able to while away the time by tapping on the window every now and then."

"You see," continued Poirot, as we walked briskly through the wind and rain, "there was a little discrepancy. The doctor seemed to think the deceased was a Christian Scientist, and who could have given him that impression but Mrs. Maltravers? But to us she represented him as being in a grave state of apprehension about his own health. Again, why was she so taken aback by the reappearance of young Black? And lastly, although I know that convention decrees that a woman must make a decent pretense of mourning for her husband, I do not care for such heavily-rouged eyelids! You did not observe them, Hastings? No? As I always tell you, you see nothing!

"Well, there it was. There were the two possibilities. Did Black's story suggest an ingenious method of committing suicide to Mr. Maltravers, or did his other listener, the wife, see an equally ingenious method of committing murder? I inclined to the latter view. To shoot himself in the way indicated, he would probably have had to pull the trigger with his toe—or at least so I imagine. Now if Maltravers had been found with one boot off, we should almost certainly have heard of it from some one. An odd detail like that would have been remembered.

"No, as I say, I inclined to the view that it was a case of murder, not suicide, but I realized that I had not a shadow of proof in support of my theory. Hence the elaborate little comedy you saw played to-night."

"Even now I don't quite see all the details of the crime," I said.

"Let us start from the beginning. Here is a shrewd and scheming woman who, knowing of her husband's financial *débâcle* and tired of the elderly mate she has only married for his money, induces him to insure his life for a large sum, and then seeks for the means to accomplish her purpose. An accident gives her that—the young soldier's strange story. The next afternoon when *monsieur le capitaine,* as she thinks, is on the high seas, she and her husband are strolling round the grounds. 'What a curious story that was last night!' she observes. 'Could a man shoot himself in such a way? Do show me if it is possible!' The poor fool—he shows her. He places the end of the rifle in his mouth. She stoops down, and puts her finger on the trigger, laughing up at him. 'And now, sir,' she says saucily, 'supposing I pull the trigger?'

"And then—and then, Hastings—she pulls it!"

III
THE ADVENTURE OF
THE CHEAP FLAT

So far, in the cases which I have recorded, Poirot's investigations have started from the central fact, whether murder or robbery, and have proceeded from thence by a process of logical deduction to the final triumphant unravelling. In the events I am now about to chronicle, a remarkable chain of circumstances led from the apparently trivial incidents which first attracted Poirot's attention to the sinister happenings which completed a most unusual case.

I had been spending the evening with an old friend of mine, Gerald Parker. There had been, perhaps, about half a dozen people there beside my host and myself, and the talk fell, as it was bound to do sooner or later wherever Parker found himself, on the subject of house-hunting in London. Houses and flats were Parker's special hobby. Since the end of the War, he had occupied at least half a dozen different flats and maisonnettes. No sooner was he settled anywhere than he would light unexpectedly upon a new find, and would forthwith depart bag and baggage. His moves were nearly always accomplished at a slight pecuniary gain, for he had a shrewd business head, but it was sheer love of the sport that actuated him, and not a desire to make money at it. We listened to Parker for some time with the respect of the novice for the expert. Then it was our turn, and a perfect babel of tongues was let loose. Finally the floor was left to Mrs. Robinson, a charming little bride who was there with her husband. I had never met them before, as Robinson was only a recent acquaintance of Parker's.

"Talking of flats," she said, "have you heard of our

piece of luck, Mr. Parker? We've got a flat—at last! In Montagu Mansions."

"Well," said Parker, "I've always said there are plenty of flats—at a price!"

"Yes, but this isn't at a price. It's dirt cheap. Eighty pounds a year!"

"But—but Montagu Mansions is just off Knightsbridge, isn't it? Big handsome building. Or are you talking of a poor relation of the same name stuck in the slums somewhere?"

"No, it's the Knightsbridge one. That's what makes it so wonderful."

"Wonderful is the word! It's a blinking miracle. But there must be a catch somewhere. Big premium, I suppose?"

"No premium!"

"No prem—oh, hold my head, somebody!" groaned Parker.

"But we've got to buy the furniture," continued Mrs. Robinson.

"Ah!" Parker brisked up. "I knew there was a catch!"

"For fifty pounds. And it's beautifully furnished!"

"I give it up," said Parker. "The present occupants must be lunatics with a taste for philanthropy."

Mrs. Robinson was looking a little troubled. A little pucker appeared between her dainty brows.

"It *is* queer, isn't it? You don't think that—that—the place is *haunted?*"

"Never heard of a haunted flat," declared Parker decisively.

"N-o." Mrs. Robinson appeared far from convinced. "But there were several things about it all that struck me as—well, queer."

"For instance—" I suggested.

"Ah," said Parker, "our criminal expert's attention is aroused! Unburden yourself to him, Mrs. Robinson. Hastings is a great unraveler of mysteries."

I laughed, embarrassed but not wholly displeased with the rôle thrust upon me.

"Oh, not really queer, Captain Hastings, but when we went to the agents, Stosser and Paul—we hadn't tried

them before because they only have the expensive May-
fair flats, but we thought at any rate it would do no
harm—everything they offered us was four and five hundred a year, or else huge premiums, and then, just as we
were going, they mentioned that they had a flat at eighty,
but that they doubted if it would be any good our going
there, because it had been on their books some time and
they had sent so many people to see it that it was almost
sure to be taken—'snapped up' as the clerk put it—only
people were so tiresome in not letting them know, and
then they went on sending, and people get annoyed at
being sent to a place that had, perhaps, been let some
time."

Mrs. Robinson paused for some much needed breath,
and then continued:

"We thanked him, and said that we quite understood it
would probably be no good, but that we should like an
order all the same—just in case. And we went there
straightaway in a taxi, for, after all, you never know. No.
4 was on the second floor, and just as we were waiting
for the lift, Elsie Ferguson—she's a friend of mine, Captain Hastings, and they are looking for a flat too—came
hurrying down the stairs. 'Ahead of you for once, my
dear,' she said. 'But it's no good. It's already let.' That
seemed to finish it, but—well, as John said, the place
was very cheap, we could afford to give more, and perhaps if we offered a premium— A horrid thing to do, of
course, and I feel quite ashamed of telling you, but you
know what flat-hunting is."

I assured her that I was well aware that in the struggle
for house-room the baser side of human nature frequently
triumphed over the higher, and that the well-known rule
of dog eat dog always applied.

"So we went up and, would you believe it, the flat
wasn't let at all. We were shown over it by the maid, and
then we saw the mistress, and the thing was settled then
and there. Immediate possession and fifty pounds for the
furniture. We signed the agreement next day, and we are
to move in to-morrow!" Mrs. Robinson paused trium-
phantly.

"And what about Mrs. Ferguson?" asked Parker. "Let's have your deductions, Hastings."

" 'Obvious, my dear Watson,' " I quoted lightly. "She went to the wrong flat."

"Oh, Captain Hastings, how clever of you!" cried Mrs. Robinson admiringly.

I rather wished Poirot had been there. Some times I have the feeling that he rather underestimates my capabilities.

The whole thing was rather amusing, and I propounded the thing as a mock problem to Poirot on the following morning. He seemed interested, and questioned me rather narrowly as to the rents of flats in various localities.

"A curious story," he said thoughtfully. "Excuse me, Hastings, I must take a short stroll."

When he returned, about an hour later, his eyes were gleaming with a peculiar excitement. He laid his stick on the table, and brushed the nap of his hat with his usual tender care before he spoke.

"It is as well, *mon ami,* that we have no affairs of moment on hand. We can devote ourselves wholly to the present investigation."

"What investigation are you talking about?"

"The remarkable cheapness of your friend's, Mrs. Robinson's, new flat."

"Poirot, you are not serious!"

"I am most serious. Figure to yourself, my friend, that the real rent of those flats is £350. I have just ascertained that from the landlord's agents. And yet this particular flat is being sublet at eighty pounds! Why?"

"There must be something wrong with it. Perhaps it is haunted, as Mrs. Robinson suggested."

Poirot shook his head in a dissatisfied manner.

"Then again how curious it is that her friend tells her the flat is let, and, when she goes up, behold, it is not so at all!"

"But surely you agree with me that the other woman must have gone to the wrong flat. That is the only possible solution."

"You may or may not be right on that point, Hastings. The fact still remains that numerous other applicants were sent to see it, and yet, in spite of its remarkable cheapness, it was still in the market when Mrs. Robinson arrived."

"That shows that there *must* be something wrong about it."

"Mrs. Robinson did not seem to notice anything amiss. Very curious, is it not? Did she impress you as being a truthful woman, Hastings?"

"She was a delightful creature!"

"Évidemment! since she renders you incapable of replying to my question. Describe her to me, then."

"Well, she's tall and fair; her hair's really a beautiful shade of auburn——"

"Always you have had a penchant for auburn hair!" murmured Poirot. "But continue."

"Blue eyes and a very nice complexion and—well, that's all, I think," I concluded lamely.

"And her husband?"

"Oh, he's quite a nice fellow—nothing startling."

"Dark or fair?"

"I don't know—betwixt and between, and just an ordinary sort of face."

Poirot nodded.

"Yes, there are hundreds of these average men—and, anyway, you bring more sympathy and appreciation to your description of women. Do you know anything about these people? Does Parker know them well?"

"They are just recent acquaintances, I believe. But surely, Poirot, you don't think for an instant——"

Poirot raised his hand.

"Tout doucement, mon ami. Have I said that I think anything? All I say is—it is a curious story. And there is nothing to throw light upon it; except perhaps the lady's name, eh, Hastings?"

"Her name is Stella," I said stiffly, "but I don't see——"

Poirot interrupted me with a tremendous chuckle. Something seemed to be amusing him vastly.

"And Stella means a star, does it not? Famous!"

"What on earth——"

"And stars give light! *Voilà!* Calm yourself, Hastings. Do not put on that air of injured dignity. Come, we will go to Montagu Mansions and make a few inquiries."

I accompanied him, nothing loath. The Mansions were a handsome block of buildings in excellent repair. A uniformed porter was sunning himself on the threshold, and it was to him that Poirot addressed himself:

"Pardon, but could you tell me if a Mr. and Mrs. Robinson reside here?"

The porter was a man of few words and apparently of a sour or suspicious disposition. He hardly looked at us and grunted out:

"No. 4. Second floor."

"I thank you. Can you tell me how long they have been here?"

"Six months."

I started forward in amazement, conscious as I did so of Poirot's malicious grin.

"Impossible," I cried. "You must be making a mistake."

"Six months."

"Are you sure? The lady I mean is tall and fair with reddish gold hair and——"

"That's 'er," said the porter. "Come in the Michaelmas quarter, they did. Just six months ago."

He appeared to lose interest in us and retreated slowly up the hall. I followed Poirot outside.

"*Eh bien,* Hastings?" my friend demanded slyly. "Are you so sure now that delightful women always speak the truth?"

I did not reply.

Poirot had steered his way into Brompton Road before I asked him what he was going to do and where we were going.

"To the house agents, Hastings. I have a great desire to have a flat in Montagu Mansions. If I am not mistaken, several interesting things will take place there before long."

We were fortunate in our quest. No. 8, on the fourth floor, was to be let furnished at ten guineas a week.

Poirot promptly took it for a month. Outside in the street again, he silenced my protests:

"But I make money nowadays! Why should I not indulge a whim? By the way, Hastings, have you a revolver?"

"Yes—somewhere," I answered, slightly thrilled. "Do you think——"

"That you will need it? It is quite possible. The idea pleases you, I see. Always the spectacular and romantic appeal to you."

The following day saw us installed in our temporary home. The flat was pleasantly furnished. It occupied the same position in the building as that of the Robinsons, but was two floors higher.

The day after our installation was a Sunday. In the afternoon, Poirot left the front door ajar, and summoned me hastily as a bang reverberated from somewhere below.

"Look over the banisters. Are those your friends? Do not let them see you."

I craned my neck over the staircase.

"That's them," I declared in an ungrammatical whisper.

"Good. Wait awhile."

About half an hour later, a young woman emerged in brilliant and varied clothing. With a sigh of satisfaction, Poirot tiptoed back into the flat.

"*C'est ça.* After the master and mistress, the maid. The flat should now be empty."

"What are we going to do?" I asked uneasily.

Poirot had trotted briskly into the scullery and was hauling at the rope of the coal-lift.

"We are about to descend after the method of the dustbins," he explained cheerfully. "No one will observe us. The Sunday concert, the Sunday 'afternoon out,' and finally the Sunday nap after the Sunday dinner of England—*le rosbif*—all these will distract attention from the doings of Hercule Poirot. Come, my friend."

He stepped into the rough wooden contrivance and I followed him gingerly.

"Are we going to break into the flat?" I asked dubiously.

Poirot's answer was not too reassuring:

"Not precisely to-day," he replied.

Pulling on the rope, we descended slowly till we reached the second floor. Poirot uttered an exclamation of satisfaction as he perceived that the wooden door into the scullery was open.

"You observe? Never do they bolt these doors in the daytime. And yet anyone could mount or descend as we have done. At night yes—though not always then—and it is against that that we are going to make provision."

He had drawn some tools from his pocket as he spoke, and at once set deftly to work, his object being to arrange the bolt so that it could be pulled back from the lift. The operation only occupied about three minutes. Then Poirot returned the tools to his pocket, and we reascended once more to our own domain.

On Monday Poirot was out all day, but when he returned in the evening he flung himself into his chair with a sigh of satisfaction.

"Hastings, shall I recount to you a little history? A story after your own heart and which will remind you of your favorite cinema?"

"Go ahead," I laughed. "I presume that it is a true story, not one of your efforts of fancy."

"It is true enough. Inspector Japp of Scotland Yard will vouch for its accuracy, since it was through his kind offices that it came to my ears. Listen, Hastings. A little over six months ago some important Naval plans were stolen from an American Government department. They showed the position of some of the most important Harbor defenses, and would be worth a considerable sum to any foreign Government—that of Japan, for example. Suspicion fell upon a young man named Luigi Valdarno, an Italian by birth, who was employed in a minor capacity in the Department and who was missing at the same time as the papers. Whether Luigi Valdarno was the thief or not, he was found two days later on the East Side in New York, shot dead. The papers were not on him. Now for some time past Luigi Valdarno had been going about with a Miss Elsa Hardt, a young concert singer who had recently appeared and who lived with a brother in an apartment in Washington. Nothing was known of the antecedents of Miss Elsa Hardt, and she disappeared suddenly about the time of Valdarno's death. There are reasons for believing that she was in reality an accomplished international spy who has done much nefarious work under various *aliases*. The American Secret Service, whilst doing their best to trace her, also kept an eye upon certain insignificant Japanese gentlemen living in Washington. They felt pretty certain that, when Elsa Hardt had covered her tracks sufficiently, she would approach the gentlemen in question. One of them left suddenly for England a fortnight ago. On the face of it, therefore, it would seem that Elsa Hardt is in England." Poirot paused, and then added softly: "The official description of Elsa Hardt is: Height 5 ft. 7, eyes blue, hair auburn, fair complexion, nose straight, no special distinguishing marks."

"Mrs. Robinson!" I gasped.

"Well, there is a chance of it, anyhow," amended Poirot. "Also, I learn that a swarthy man, a foreigner of some kind, was inquiring about the occupants of No. 4 only this morning. Therefore, *mon ami*, I fear that you must forswear your beauty sleep to-night, and join me in my all-night vigil in the flat below—armed with that excellent revolver of yours, *bien entendu!*"

"Rather," I cried with enthusiasm. "When shall we start?"

"The hour of midnight is both solemn and suitable, I fancy. Nothing is likely to occur before then."

At twelve o'clock precisely, we crept cautiously into the coal-lift and lowered ourselves to the second floor. Under Poirot's manipulation, the wooden door quickly swung inwards, and we climbed into the flat. From the scullery we passed into the kitchen where we established ourselves comfortably in two chairs with the door into the hall ajar.

"Now we have but to wait," said Poirot contentedly, closing his eyes.

To me, the waiting appeared endless. I was terrified of

going to sleep. Just when it seemed to me that I had been there about eight hours—and had, as I found out afterwards, in reality been exactly one hour and twenty minutes—a faint scratching sound came to my ears. Poirot's hand touched mine. I rose, and together we moved carefully in the direction of the hall. The noise came from there. Poirot placed his lips to my ear.

"Outside the front door. They are cutting out the lock. When I give the word, not before, fall upon him from behind and hold him fast. Be careful, he will have a knife."

Presently there was a rending sound, and a little circle of light appeared through the door. It was extinguished immediately and then the door was slowly opened. Poirot and I flattened ourselves against the wall. I heard a man's breathing as he passed us. Then he flashed on his torch, and as he did so, Poirot hissed in my ear:

"*Allez.*"

We sprang together, Poirot with a quick movement enveloped the intruder's head with a light woolen scarf whilst I pinioned his arms. The whole affair was quick and noiseless. I twisted a dagger from his hand, and as Poirot brought down the scarf from his eyes, whilst keeping it wound tightly round his mouth, I jerked up my revolver where he could see it and understand that resistance was useless. As he ceased to struggle Poirot put his mouth close to his ear and began to whisper rapidly. After a minute the man nodded. Then enjoining silence with a movement of the hand, Poirot led the way out of the flat and down the stairs. Our captive followed, and I brought up the rear with the revolver. When we were out in the street, Poirot turned to me.

"There is a taxi waiting just round the corner. Give me the revolver. We shall not need it now."

"But if this fellow tries to escape?"

Poirot smiled.

"He will not."

I returned in a minute with the waiting taxi. The scarf had been unwound from the stranger's face, and I gave a start of surprise.

"He's not a Jap," I ejaculated in a whisper to Poirot.

"Observation was always your strong point, Hastings! Nothing escapes you. No, the man is not a Jap. He is an Italian."

We got into the taxi, and Poirot gave the driver an address in St. John's Wood. I was by now completely fogged. I did not like to ask Poirot where we were going in front of our captive, and strove in vain to obtain some light upon the proceedings.

We alighted at the door of a small house standing back from the road. A returning wayfarer, slightly drunk, was lurching along the pavement and almost collided with Poirot, who said something sharply to him which I did not catch. All three of us went up the steps of the house. Poirot rang the bell and motioned us to stand a little aside. There was no answer and he rang again and then seized the knocker which he plied for some minutes vigorously.

A light appeared suddenly above the fanlight, and the door was opened cautiously a little way.

"What the devil do you want?" a man's voice demanded harshly.

"I want the doctor. My wife is taken ill."

"There's no doctor here."

The man prepared to shut the door, but Poirot thrust his foot in adroitly. He became suddenly a perfect caricature of an infuriated Frenchman.

"What you say, there is no doctor? I will have the law on you. You must come! I will stay here and ring and knock all night."

"My dear sir—" The door was opened again, the man, clad in a dressing-gown and slippers, stepped forward to pacify Poirot with an uneasy glance round.

"I will call the police."

Poirot prepared to descend the steps.

"No, don't do that for Heaven's sake!" The man dashed after him.

With a neat push Poirot sent him staggering down the steps. In another minute all three of us were inside the door and it was pushed to and bolted.

"Quick—in here." Poirot led the way into the nearest room switching on the light as he did so. "And you—behind the curtain."

"Si, signor," said the Italian and slid rapidly behind the full folds of rose-colored velvet which draped the embrasure of the window.

Not a minute too soon. Just as he disappeared from view a woman rushed into the room. She was tall with reddish hair and held a scarlet kimono round her slender form.

"Where is my husband?" she cried, with a quick frightened glance. "Who are you?"

Poirot stepped forward with a bow.

"It is to be hoped your husband will not suffer from a chill. I observed that he had slippers on his feet, and that his dressing-gown was a warm one."

"Who are you? What are you doing in my house?"

"It is true that none of us have the pleasure of your acquaintance, madame. It is especially to be regretted as one of our number has come specially from New York in order to meet you."

The curtains parted and the Italian stepped out. To my horror I observed that he was brandishing my revolver, which Poirot must doubtless have put down through inadvertence in the cab.

The woman gave a piercing scream and turned to fly, but Poirot was standing in front of the closed door.

"Let me by," she shrieked. "He will murder me."

"Who was it dat croaked Luigi Valdarno?" asked the Italian hoarsely, brandishing the weapon, and sweeping each one of us with it. We dared not move.

"My God, Poirot, this is awful. What shall we do?" I cried.

"You will oblige me by refraining from talking so much, Hastings. I can assure you that our friend will not shoot until I give the word."

"Youse sure o' dat, eh?" said the Italian leering unpleasantly.

It was more than I was, but the woman turned to Poirot like a flash.

"What is it you want?"

Poirot bowed.

"I do not think it is necessary to insult Miss Elsa Hardt's intelligence by telling her."

With a swift movement, the woman snatched up a big black velvet cat which served as a cover for the telephone.

"They are stitched in the lining of that."

"Clever," murmured Poirot appreciatively. He stood aside from the door. "Good evening, madame. I will detain your friend from New York whilst you make your getaway."

"Whatta fool!" roared the big Italian, and raising the revolver he fired point-blank at the woman's retreating figure just as I flung myself upon him.

But the weapon merely clicked harmlessly and Poirot's voice rose in mild reproof.

"Never will you trust your old friend, Hastings. I do not care for my friends to carry loaded pistols about with them and never would I permit a mere acquaintance to do so. No, no, *mon ami.*" This to the Italian who was swearing hoarsely. Poirot continued to address him in a tone of mild reproof: "See now, what I have done for you. I have saved you from being hanged. And do not think that our beautiful lady will escape. No, no, the house is watched, back and front. Straight into the arms of the police they will go. Is not that a beautiful and consoling thought? Yes, you may leave the room now. But be careful—be very careful. I— Ah, he is gone! And my friend Hastings looks at me with eyes of reproach. But it was all so simple! It was clear, from the first, that out of several hundred, probably, applicants for No. 4, Montagu Mansions only the Robinsons were considered suitable. Why? What was there that singled them out from the rest—at practically a glance? Their appearance? Possibly, but it was not so unusual. Their name, then!"

"But there's nothing unusual about the name of Robinson," I cried. "It's quite a common name."

"Ah! *Sapristi,* but exactly! That was the point. Elsa Hardt and her husband, or brother or whatever he really is, come from New York, and take a flat in the name of Mr. and Mrs. Robinson. Suddenly they learn that one of these secret societies, the Mafia, or the Camorra, to which doubtless Luigi Valdarno belonged, is on their track. What do they do? They hit on a scheme of transparent simplicity. Evidently they knew that their pursuers were not personally acquainted with either of them. What then can be simpler? They offer the flat at an absurdly low rental. Of the thousands of young couples in London looking for flats, there cannot fail to be several Robinsons. It is only a matter of waiting. If you will look at the name of Robinson in the telephone directory, you will realize that a fair-haired Mrs. Robinson was pretty sure to come along sooner or later. Then what will happen? The avenger arrives. He knows the name, he knows the address. He strikes! All is over, vengeance is satisfied, and Miss Elsa Hardt has escaped by the skin of her teeth once more. By the way, Hastings, you must present me to the real Mrs. Robinson—that delightful and truthful creature! What will they think when they find their flat has been broken into! We must hurry back. Ah, that sounds like Japp and his friends arriving."

A mighty tattoo sounded on the knocker.

"How did you know this address?" I asked as I followed Poirot out into the hall. "Oh, of course, you had the first Mrs. Robinson followed when she left the other flat."

"*A la bonne heure,* Hastings. You use your gray cells at last. Now for a little surprise for Japp."

Softly unbolting the door, he stuck the cat's head round the edge and ejaculated a piercing "Miaow."

The Scotland Yard inspector, who was standing outside with another man, jumped in spite of himself.

"Oh, it's only Monsieur Poirot at one of his little jokes!" he exclaimed, as Poirot's head followed that of the cat. "Let us in, moosior."

"You have our friends safe and sound?"

"Yes, we've got the birds all right. But they hadn't got the goods with them."

"I see. So you come to search. Well, I am about to depart with Hastings, but I should like to give you a little lecture upon the history and habits of the domestic cat."

"For the Lord's sake, have you gone completely balmy?"

"The cat," declaimed Poirot, "was worshiped by the ancient Egyptians. It is still regarded as a symbol of good luck if a black cat crosses your path. This cat crossed your path to-night, Japp. To speak of the interior of any animal or any person is not, I know, considered polite in England. But the interior of this cat is perfectly delicate. I refer to the lining."

With a sudden grunt, the second man seized the cat from Poirot's hand.

"Oh, I forgot to introduce you," said Japp. "Mr. Poirot, this is Mr. Burt of the United States Secret Service."

The American's trained fingers had felt what he was looking for. He held out his hand, and for a moment speech failed him. Then he rose to the occasion.

"Pleased to meet you," said Mr. Burt.

IV
THE MYSTERY OF
HUNTER'S LODGE

"After all," murmured Poirot, "it is possible that I shall not die this time."

Coming from a convalescent influenza patient, I hailed the remark as showing a beneficial optimism. I myself had been the first sufferer from the disease. Poirot in his turn had gone down. He was now sitting up in bed, propped up with pillows, his head muffled in a woolen shawl, and was slowly sipping a particularly noxious *tisane* which I had prepared according to his directions. His eye rested with pleasure upon a neatly graduated row of medicine bottles which adorned the mantelpiece.

"Yes, yes," my little friend continued. "Once more shall I be myself again, the great Hercule Poirot, the terror of evil-doers! Figure to yourself, *mon ami,* that I have a little paragraph to myself in *Society Gossip*. But yes! Here it is! 'Go it—criminals—all out! Hercule Poirot—and believe me, girls, he's some Hercules!—our own pet society detective can't get a grip on you. 'Cause why? 'Cause he's got *la grippe* himself'!"

I laughed.

"Good for you, Poirot. You are becoming quite a public character. And fortunately you haven't missed anything of particular interest during this time."

"That is true. The few cases I have had to decline did not fill me with any regret."

Our landlady stuck her head in at the door.

"There's a gentleman downstairs. Says he must see Monsieur Poirot or you, Captain. Seeing as he was in a great to-do—and with all that quite the gentleman—I brought up 'is card."

She handed me the bit of pasteboard. "Mr. Roger Havering," I read.

Poirot motioned with his head towards the bookcase, and I obediently pulled forth "Who's Who." Poirot took it from me and scanned the pages rapidly.

"Second son of fifth Baron Windsor. Married 1913 Zoe, fourth daughter of William Crabb."

"H'm!" I said. "I rather fancy that's the girl who used to act at the Frivolity—only she called herself Zoe Carrisbrook. I remember she married some young man about town just before the War."

"Would it interest you, Hastings, to go down and hear what our visitor's particular little trouble is? Make him all my excuses."

Roger Havering was a man of about forty, well set up and of smart appearance. His face, however, was haggard, and he was evidently laboring under great agitation.

"Captain Hastings? You are Monsieur Poirot's partner, I understand. It is imperative that he should come with me to Derbyshire to-day."

"I'm afraid that's impossible," I responded. "Poirot is ill in bed—influenza."

His face fell.

"Dear me, that is a great blow to me."

"The matter on which you want to consult him is serious?"

"My God, yes! My uncle, the best friend I have in the world, was foully murdered last night."

"Here in London?"

"No, in Derbyshire. I was in town and received a telegram from my wife this morning. Immediately upon its receipt I determined to come round and beg Monsieur Poirot to undertake the case."

"If you will excuse me a minute," I said, struck by a sudden idea.

I rushed upstairs, and in a few brief words acquainted Poirot with the situation. He took any further words out of my mouth.

"I see. I see. You want to go yourself, is it not so? Well, why not? You should know my methods by now.

All I ask is that you should report to me fully every day, and follow implicitly any instructions I may wire you."

To this I willingly agreed.

An hour later I was sitting opposite Mr. Havering in a first-class carriage on the Midland Railway, speeding rapidly away from London.

"To begin with, Captain Hastings, you must understand that Hunter's Lodge, where we are going, and where the tragedy took place, is only a small shooting-box in the heart of the Derbyshire moors. Our real home is near Newmarket, and we usually rent a flat in town for the season. Hunter's Lodge is looked after by a housekeeper who is quite capable of doing all we need when we run down for an occasional week-end. Of course, during the shooting season, we take down some of our own servants from Newmarket. My uncle, Mr. Harrington Pace (as you may know, my mother was a Miss Pace of New York), has, for the last three years, made his home with us. He never got on well with my father, or my elder brother, and I suspect that my being somewhat of a prodigal son myself rather increased than diminished his affection towards me. Of course I am a poor man, and my uncle was a rich one—in other words, he paid the piper! But, though exacting in many ways, he was not really hard to get on with, and we all three lived very harmoniously together. Two days ago my uncle, rather wearied with some recent gayeties of ours in town, suggested that we should run down to Derbyshire for a day or two. My wife telegraphed to Mrs. Middleton, the housekeeper, and we went down that same afternoon. Yesterday evening I was forced to return to town, but my wife and my uncle remained on. This morning I received this telegram." He handed it over to me:

"Come at once uncle Harrington murdered last night bring good detective if you can but do come—Zoe."

"Then, as yet you know no details?"

"No, I suppose it will be in the evening papers. Without doubt the police are in charge."

It was about three o'clock when we arrived at the little station of Elmer's Dale. From there a five-mile drive brought us to a small gray stone building in the midst of the rugged moors.

"A lonely place," I observed with a shiver.

Havering nodded.

"I shall try and get rid of it. I could never live here again."

We unlatched the gate and were walking up the narrow path to the oak door when a familiar figure emerged and came to meet us.

"Japp!" I ejaculated.

The Scotland Yard inspector grinned at me in a friendly fashion before addressing my companion.

"Mr. Havering, I think? I've been sent down from London to take charge of this case, and I'd like a word with you, if I may, sir."

"My wife——"

"I've seen your good lady, sir—and the housekeeper. I won't keep you a moment, but I'm anxious to get back to the village now that I've seen all there is to see here."

"I know nothing as yet as to what——"

"Ex-actly," said Japp soothingly. "But there are just one or two little points I'd like your opinion about all the same. Captain Hastings here, he knows me, and he'll go on up to the house and tell them you're coming. What have you done with the little man, by the way, Captain Hastings?"

"He's ill in bed with influenza."

"Is he now? I'm sorry to hear that. Rather the case of the cart without the horse, your being here without him, isn't it?"

And on his rather ill-timed jest I went on to the house. I rang the bell, as Japp had closed the door behind him. After some moments it was opened to me by a middle-aged woman in black.

"Mr. Havering will be here in a moment," I explained. "He has been detained by the inspector. I have come down with him from London to look into the case. Perhaps you can tell me briefly what occurred last night."

"Come inside, sir." She closed the door behind me, and

we stood in the dimly-lighted hall. "It was after dinner last night, sir, that the man came. He asked to see Mr. Pace, sir, and, seeing that he spoke the same way, I thought it was an American gentleman friend of Mr. Pace's and I showed him into the gun-room, and then went to tell Mr. Pace. He wouldn't give any name, which, of course, was a bit odd, now I come to think of it. I told Mr. Pace, and he seemed puzzled like, but he said to the mistress: 'Excuse me, Zoe, while I just see what this fellow wants.' He went off to the gun-room, and I went back to the kitchen, but after a while I heard loud voices, as if they were quarrelling, and I came out into the hall. At the same time, the mistress she comes out too, and just then there was a shot and then a dreadful silence. We both ran to the gun-room door, but it was locked and we had to go round to the window. It was open, and there inside was Mr. Pace, all shot and bleeding."

"What became of the man?"

"He must have got away through the window, sir, before we got to it."

"And then?"

"Mrs. Havering sent me to fetch the police. Five miles to walk it was. They came back with me, and the constable he stayed all night, and this morning the police gentleman from London arrived."

"What was this man like who called to see Mr. Pace?"

The housekeeper reflected.

"He had a black beard, sir, and was about middle-aged, and had on a light overcoat. Beyond the fact that he spoke like an American I didn't notice much about him."

"I see. Now I wonder if I can see Mrs. Havering?"

"She's upstairs, sir. Shall I tell her?"

"If you please. Tell her that Mr. Havering is outside with Inspector Japp, and that the gentleman he has brought back with him from London is anxious to speak to her as soon as possible."

"Very good, sir."

I was in a fever of impatience to get at all the facts. Japp had two or three hours' start of me, and his anxiety to be gone made me keen to be close at his heels.

Mrs. Havering did not keep me waiting long. In a few

minutes I heard a light step descending the stairs, and looked up to see a very handsome young woman coming towards me. She wore a flame-colored jumper, that set off the slender boyishness of her figure. On her dark head was a little hat of flame-colored leather. Even the present tragedy could not dim the vitality of her personality.

I introduced myself, and she nodded in quick comprehension.

"Of course I have often heard of you and your colleague, Monsieur Poirot. You have done some wonderful things together, haven't you? It was very clever of my husband to get you so promptly. Now will you ask me questions? That is the easiest way, isn't it, of getting to know all you want to about this dreadful affair?"

"Thank you, Mrs. Havering. Now what time was it that this man arrived?"

"It must have been just before nine o'clock. We had finished dinner, and were sitting over our coffee and cigarettes."

"Your husband had already left for London?"

"Yes, he went up by the 6.15."

"Did he go by car to the station, or did he walk?"

"Our own car isn't down here. One came out from the garage in Elmer's Dale to fetch him in time for the train."

"Was Mr. Pace quite his usual self?"

"Absolutely. Most normal in every way."

"Now, can you describe this visitor at all?"

"I'm afraid not. I didn't see him. Mrs. Middleton showed him straight into the gun-room and then came to tell my uncle."

"What did your uncle say?"

"He seemed rather annoyed, but went off at once. It was about five minutes later that I heard the sound of raised voices. I ran out into the hall and almost collided with Mrs. Middleton. Then we heard the shot. The gun-room door was locked on the inside, and we had to go right round the house to the window. Of course that took some time, and the murderer had been able to get well away. My poor uncle"—her voice faltered—"had been shot through the head. I saw at once that he was dead. I sent Mrs. Middleton for the police. I was careful to touch nothing in the room but to leave it exactly as I found it."

I nodded approval.

"Now, as to the weapon?"

"Well, I can make a guess at it, Captain Hastings. A pair of revolvers of my husband's were mounted upon the wall. One of them is missing. I pointed this out to the police, and they took the other one away with them. When they have extracted the bullet, I suppose they will know for certain."

"May I go to the gun-room?"

"Certainly. The police have finished with it. But the body has been removed."

She accompanied me to the scene of the crime. At that moment Havering entered the hall, and with a quick apology his wife ran to him. I was left to undertake my investigations alone.

I may as well confess at once that they were rather disappointing. In detective novels clues abound, but here I could find nothing that struck me as out of the ordinary except a large bloodstain on the carpet where I judged the dead man had fallen. I examined everything with painstaking care and took a couple of pictures of the room with my little camera which I had brought with me. I also examined the ground outside the window, but it appeared to have been so heavily trampled underfoot that I judged it was useless to waste time over it. No, I had seen all that Hunter's Lodge had to show me. I must go back to Elmer's Dale and get into touch with Japp. Accordingly I took leave of the Haverings, and was driven off in the car that had brought us up from the station.

I found Japp at the Matlock Arms and he took me forthwith to see the body. Harrington Pace was a small, spare clean-shaven man, typically American in appearance. He had been shot through the back of the head, and the revolver had been discharged at close quarters.

"Turned away for a moment," remarked Japp, "and the other fellow snatched up a revolver and shot him. The one Mrs. Havering handed over to us was fully loaded and I suppose the other one was also. Curious what darn fool things people do. Fancy keeping two loaded revolvers hanging up on your wall."

"What do you think of the case?" I asked, as we left the gruesome chamber behind us.

"Well, I'd got my eye on Havering to begin with. Oh, yes!" noting my exclamation of astonishment. "Havering has one or two shady incidents in his past. When he was a boy at Oxford there was some funny business about the signature on one of his father's checks. All hushed up of course. Then, he's pretty heavily in debt now, and they're the kind of debts he wouldn't like to go to his uncle about, whereas you may be sure the uncle's will would be in his favor. Yes, I'd got my eye on him, and that's why I wanted to speak to him before he saw his wife, but their statements dovetail all right, and I've been to the station and there's no doubt whatever that he left by the 6.15. That gets up to London about 10.30. He went straight to his club, he says, and if that's confirmed all right—why, he couldn't have been shooting his uncle here at nine o'clock in a black beard!"

"Ah, yes, I was going to ask you what you thought about that beard?"

Japp winked.

"I think it grew pretty fast—grew in the five miles from Elmer's Dale to Hunter's Lodge. Americans that I've met are mostly clean-shaven. Yes, it's amongst Mr. Pace's American associates that we'll have to look for the murderer. I questioned the housekeeper first, and then her mistress, and their stories agree all right, but I'm sorry Mrs. Havering didn't get a look at the fellow. She's a smart woman, and she might have noticed something that would set us on the track."

I sat down and wrote a minute and lengthy account to Poirot. I was able to add various further items of information before I posted the letter.

The bullet had been extracted and was proved to have been fired from a revolver identical with the one held by the police. Furthermore, Mr. Havering's movements on the night in question had been checked and verified, and it was proved beyond doubt that he had actually arrived in London by the train in question. And, thirdly, a sensational development had occurred. A city gentleman, living at Ealing, on crossing Haven Green to get to the District Railway Station that morning, had observed a brown-paper parcel stuck between the railings. Opening it, he found that it contained a revolver. He handed the parcel over to the local police station, and before night it was proved to be the one we were in search of, the fellow to that given us by Mrs. Havering. One bullet had been fired from it.

All this I added to my report. A wire from Poirot arrived whilst I was at breakfast the following morning:

"Of course black bearded man was not Havering only you or Japp would have such an idea wire me description of housekeeper and what clothes she wore this morning same of Mrs. Havering do not waste time taking photographs of interiors they are underexposed and not in the least artistic."

It seemed to me that Poirot's style was unnecessarily facetious. I also fancied he was a shade jealous of my position on the spot with full facilities for handling the case. His request for a description of the clothes worn by the two women appeared to me to be simply ridiculous, but I complied as well as I, a mere man, was able to.

At eleven a reply wire came from Poirot:

"Advise Japp arrest housekeeper before it is too late."

Dumfounded, I took the wire to Japp. He swore softly under his breath.

"He's the goods, Monsieur Poirot! If he says so, there's something in it. And I hardly noticed the woman. I don't know that I can go so far as arresting her, but I'll have her watched. We'll go up right away, and take another look at her."

But it was too late. Mrs. Middleton, that quiet middle-aged woman, who had appeared so normal and respectable, had vanished into thin air. Her box had been left behind. It contained only ordinary wearing apparel.

There was no clue in it to her identity or as to her whereabouts.

From Mrs. Havering we elicited all the facts we could:

"I engaged her about three weeks ago when Mrs. Emery, our former housekeeper, left. She came to me from Mrs. Selbourne's Agency in Mount Street—a very well-known place. I get all my servants from there. They sent several women to see me, but this Mrs. Middleton seemed much the nicest, and had splendid references. I engaged her on the spot, and notified the Agency of the fact. I can't believe that there was anything wrong with her. She was such a nice quiet woman."

The thing was certainly a mystery. Whilst it was clear that the woman herself could not have committed the crime, since at the moment the shot was fired Mrs. Havering was with her in the hall, nevertheless she must have some connection with the murder, or why should she suddenly take to her heels and bolt?

I wired the latest development to Poirot and suggested returning to London and making inquiries at Selbourne's Agency.

Poirot's reply was prompt:

"Useless to inquire at agency they will never have heard of her find out what vehicle took her up to hunters lodge when she first arrived there."

Though mystified, I was obedient. The means of transport in Elmer's Dale were limited. The local garage had two battered Ford cars, and there were two station flies. None of these had been requisitioned on the date in question. Questioned, Mrs. Havering explained that she had given the woman the money for her fare down to Derbyshire and sufficient to hire a car of fly to take her up to Hunter's Lodge. There was usually one of the Fords at the station on the chance of its being required. Taking into consideration the further fact that nobody at the station had noticed the arrival of a stranger, blackbearded or otherwise, on the fatal evening, everything seemed to point to the conclusion that the murderer had come to the spot in a car, which had been waiting near at hand to aid his escape, and that the same car had brought the mysterious housekeeper to her new post. I may mention that inquiries at the Agency in London bore out Poirot's prognostication. No such woman as "Mrs. Middleton" had ever been on their books. They had received the Hon. Mrs. Havering's application for a housekeeper, and had sent her various applicants for the post. When she sent them the engagement fee, she omitted to mention which woman she had selected.

Somewhat crestfallen, I returned to London. I found Poirot established in an arm-chair by the fire in a garish silk dressing-gown. He greeted me with much affection.

"*Mon ami* Hastings! But how glad I am to see you. Veritably I have for you a great affection! And you have enjoyed yourself? You have run to and fro with the good Japp? You have interrogated and investigated to your heart's content?"

"Poirot," I cried, "the thing's a dark mystery! It will never be solved."

"It is true that we are not likely to cover ourselves with glory over it."

"No, indeed. It's a hard nut to crack."

"Oh, as far as that goes, I am very good at cracking the nuts! A veritable squirrel! It is not that which embarrasses me. I know well enough who killed Mr. Harrington Pace."

"You know? How did you find out?"

"Your illuminating answers to my wires supplied me with the truth. See here, Hastings, let us examine the facts methodically and in order. Mr. Harrington Pace is a man with a considerable fortune which at his death will doubtless pass to his nephew. Point No. 1. His nephew is known to be desperately hard up. Point No. 2. His nephew is also known to be—shall we say a man of rather loose moral fiber? Point No. 3."

"But Roger Havering is proved to have journeyed straight up to London."

"*Précisément*—and therefore, as Mr. Havering left Elmer's Dale at 6.15, and since Mr. Pace cannot have been killed before he left, or the doctor would have spotted the time of the crime as being given wrongly when he examined the body, we conclude quite rightly, that Mr. Havering did *not* shoot his uncle. But there is a Mrs. Havering, Hastings."

"Impossible! The housekeeper was with her when the shot was fired."

"Ah, yes, the housekeeper. But she has disappeared."

"She will be found."

"I think not. There is something peculiarly elusive about that housekeeper, don't you think so, Hastings? It struck me at once."

"She played her part, I suppose, and then got out in the nick of time."

"And what was her part."

"Well, presumably to admit her confederate, the black-bearded man."

"Oh, no, that was not her part! Her part was what you have just mentioned, to provide an alibi for Mrs. Havering at the moment the shot was fired. And no one will ever find her, *mon ami,* because she does not exist! 'There's no sech person,' as your so great Shakespeare says."

"It was Dickens," I murmured, unable to suppress a smile. "But what do you mean, Poirot?"

"I mean that Zoe Havering was an actress before her marriage, that you and Japp only saw the housekeeper in a dark hall, a dim middle-aged figure in black with a faint subdued voice, and finally that neither you nor Japp, nor the local police whom the housekeeper fetched, ever saw Mrs. Middleton and her mistress at one and the same time. It was child's play for that clever and daring woman. On the pretext of summoning her mistress, she runs upstairs, slips on a bright jumper and a hat with black curls attached which she jams down over the gray transformation. A few deft touches and the makeup is removed, a slight dusting of rouge, and the brilliant Zoe Havering comes down with her clear ringing voice. Nobody looks particularly at the housekeeper. Why should they? There is nothing to connect her with the crime. She, too, has an alibi."

"But the revolver that was found at Ealing? Mrs. Havering could not have placed it there?"

"No, that was Roger Havering's job—but it was a mistake on their part. It put me on the right track. A man who has committed a murder with a revolver which he found on the spot would fling it away at once, he would not carry it up to London with him. No, the motive was clear, the criminals wished to focus the interest of the police on a spot far removed from Derbyshire; they were anxious to get the police away as soon as possible from the vicinity of Hunter's Lodge. Of course the revolver found at Ealing was not the one with which Mr. Pace was shot. Roger Havering discharged one shot from it, brought it up to London, went straight to his club to establish his alibi, then went quickly out to Ealing by the district, a matter of about twenty minutes only, placed the parcel where it was found and so back to town. That charming creature, his wife, quietly shoots Mr. Pace after dinner—you remember he was shot from behind? Another significant point, that!—reloads the revolver and puts it back in its place, and then starts off with her desperate little comedy."

"It's incredible," I murmured, fascinated, "and yet——"

"And yet it is true. *Bien sur,* my friend, it is true. But to bring that precious pair to justice, that is another matter. Well, Japp must do what he can—I have written him fully—but I very much fear, Hastings, that we shall be obliged to leave them to Fate, or *le bon Dieu,* whichever you prefer."

"The wicked flourish like a green bay tree," I reminded him.

"But at a price, Hastings, always at a price, *croyez-moi!*"

Poirot's forebodings were confirmed. Japp, though convinced of the truth of his theory, was unable to get together the necessary evidence to ensure a conviction.

Mr. Pace's huge fortune passed into the hands of his murderers. Nevertheless, Nemesis did overtake them, and when I read in the paper that the Hon. Roger and Mrs. Havering were amongst those killed in the crashing of the Air Mail to Paris I knew that Justice was satisfied.

V
THE MILLION DOLLAR
BOND ROBBERY

"What a number of bond robberies there have been lately!" I observed one morning, laying aside the newspaper. "Poirot, let us forsake the science of detection, and take to crime instead!"

"You are on the—how do you say it?—get-rich-quick tack, eh, *mon ami?*"

"Well, look at this last *coup,* the million dollars' worth of Liberty Bonds which the London and Scottish Bank were sending to New York, and which disappeared in such a remarkable manner on board the *Olympia.*"

"If it were not for the *mal de mer,* and the difficulty of practicing the so excellent method of Laverguier for a longer time than the few hours of crossing the channel I should delight to voyage myself on one of these big liners," murmured Poirot dreamily.

"Yes, indeed," I said enthusiastically. "Some of them must be perfect palaces; the swimming-baths, the lounges, the restaurant, the palm courts—really, it must be hard to believe that one is on the sea."

"Me, I always know when I am on the sea," said Poirot sadly. "And all those bagatelles that you enumerate, they say nothing to me; but, my friend, consider for a moment the geniuses that travel as it were incognito! On board these floating palaces, as you so justly call them, one would meet the élite, the *haute noblesse* of the criminal world!"

I laughed.

"So that's the way your enthusiasm runs! You would have liked to cross swords with the man who sneaked the Liberty Bonds?"

The landlady interrupted us.

"A young lady as wants to see you, Mr. Poirot. Here's her card."

The card bore the inscription: Miss Esmée Farquhar, and Poirot, after diving under the table to retrieve a stray crumb, and putting it carefully in the waste-paper-basket, nodded to the landlady to admit her.

In another minute one of the most charming girls I have ever seen was ushered into the room. She was perhaps about five-and-twenty, with big brown eyes and a perfect figure. She was well-dressed and perfectly composed in manner.

"Sit down, I beg of you, mademoiselle. This is my friend, Captain Hastings, who aids me in my little problems."

"I am afraid it is a big problem I have brought you to-day, Monsieur Poirot," said the girl, giving me a pleasant bow as she seated herself. "I dare say you have read about it in the papers. I am referring to the theft of Liberty Bonds on the *Olympia*." Some astonishment must have shown itself in Poirot's face, for she continued quickly: "You are doubtless asking yourself what I have to do with a grave institution like the London and Scottish Bank. In one sense nothing, in another sense everything. You see, Monsieur Poirot, I am engaged to Mr. Philip Ridgeway."

"Aha! and Mr. Philip Ridgeway——"

"Was in charge of the bonds when they were stolen. Of course no actual blame can attach to him, it was not his fault in any way. Nevertheless, he is half distraught over the matter, and his uncle, I know, insists that he must carelessly have mentioned having them in his possession. It is a terrible set-back in his career."

"Who is his uncle?"

"Mr. Vavasour, joint general manager of the London and Scottish Bank."

"Suppose, Miss Farquhar, that you recount to me the whole story?"

"Very well. As you know, the Bank wished to extend their credits in America, and for this purpose decided to send over a million dollars in Liberty Bonds. Mr. Vavasour selected his nephew, who had occupied a position of

trust in the Bank for many years and who was conversant
with all the details of the Bank's dealings in New York,
to make the trip. The *Olympia* sailed from Liverpool on
the 23rd, and the bonds were handed over to Philip on
the morning of that day by Mr. Vavasour and Mr. Shaw,
the two joint general managers of the London and Scottish Bank. They were counted, enclosed in a package,
and sealed in his presence, and he then locked the package at once in his portmanteau."

"A portmanteau with an ordinary lock?"

"No, Mr. Shaw insisted on a special lock being fitted to
it by Hubbs's. Philip, as I say, placed the package at the
bottom of the trunk. It was stolen just a few hours before
reaching New York. A rigorous search of the whole ship
was made, but without result. The bonds seemed literally
to have vanished into thin air."

Poirot made a grimace.

"But they did not vanish absolutely, since I gather that
they were sold in small parcels within half an hour of the
docking of the *Olympia!* Well, undoubtedly the next
thing is for me to see Mr. Ridgeway."

"I was about to suggest that you should lunch with me
at the 'Cheshire Cheese.' Philip will be there. He is meeting me, but does not yet know that I have been consulting
you on his behalf."

We agreed to this suggestion readily enough, and drove
there in a taxi.

Mr. Philip Ridgeway was there before us, and looked
somewhat surprised to see his fiancée arriving with two
complete strangers. He was a nice-looking young fellow,
tall and spruce, with a touch of graying hair at the
temples, though he could not have been much over thirty.

Miss Farquhar went up to him and laid her hand on
his arm.

"You must forgive my acting without consulting you,
Philip," she said. "Let me introduce you to Monsieur
Hercule Poirot, of whom you must often have heard, and
his friend, Captain Hastings."

Ridgeway looked very astonished.

"Of course I have heard of you, Monsieur Poirot," he
said, as he shook hands. "But I had no idea that Esmée

was thinking of consulting you about my—our trouble."

"I was afraid you would not let me do it, Philip," said Miss Farquhar meekly.

"So you took care to be on the safe side," he observed, with a smile. "I hope Monsieur Poirot will be able to throw some light on this extraordinary puzzle, for I confess frankly that I am nearly out of my mind with worry and anxiety about it."

Indeed, his face looked drawn and haggard and showed only too clearly the strain under which he was laboring.

"Well, well," said Poirot. "Let us lunch, and over lunch we will put our heads together and see what can be done. I want to hear Mr. Ridgeway's story from his own lips."

Whilst we discussed the excellent steak and kidney pudding of the establishment, Philip Ridgeway narrated the circumstances leading to the disappearance of the bonds. His story agreed with that of Miss Farquhar in every particular. When he had finished, Poirot took up the thread with a question.

"What exactly led you to discover that the bonds had been stolen, Mr. Ridgeway?"

He laughed rather bitterly.

"The thing stared me in the face, Monsieur Poirot. I couldn't have missed it. My cabin trunk was half out from under the bunk and all scratched and cut about where they'd tried to force the lock."

"But I understood that it had been opened with a key?"

"That's so. They tried to force it, but couldn't. And, in the end, they must have got it unlocked somehow or other."

"Curious," said Poirot, his eyes beginning to flicker with the green light I knew so well. "Very curious! They waste much, much time trying to prise it open, and then— *sapristi!* they find that they have the key all the time— for each of Hubbs's locks are unique."

"That's just why they couldn't have had the key. It never left me day or night."

"You are sure of that?"

"I can swear to it, and besides, if they had had the key

or a duplicate, why should they waste time trying to force an obviously unforceable lock?"

"Ah! there is exactly the question we are asking ourselves! I venture to prophesy that the solution, if we ever find it, will hinge on that curious fact. I beg of you not to assault me if I ask you one more question: *Are you perfectly certain you did not leave the trunk unlocked?*"

Philip Ridgeway merely looked at him, and Poirot gesticulated apologetically.

"Ah, but these things can happen, I assure you! Very well, the bonds were stolen from the trunk. What did the thief do with them? How did he manage to get ashore with them?"

"Ah!" cried Ridgeway. "That's just it. How? Word was passed to the Customs authorities, and every soul that left the ship was gone over with a toothcomb!"

"And the bonds, I gather, made a bulky package?"

"Certainly they did. They could hardly have been hidden on board—and anyway we know they weren't because they were offered for sale within half an hour of the *Olympia*'s arrival, long before I got the cables going and the numbers sent out. One broker swears he bought some of them even before the *Olympia* got in. But you can't send bonds by wireless."

"Not by wireless, but did any tug come alongside?"

"Only the official ones, and that was after the alarm was given when every one was on the look-out. I was watching out myself for their being passed over to some one that way. My God, Monsieur Poirot, this thing will drive me mad! People are beginning to say I stole them myself."

"But you also were searched on landing, weren't you?" asked Poirot gently.

"Yes."

The young man stared at him in a puzzled manner.

"You do not catch my meaning, I see," said Poirot, smiling enigmatically. "Now I should like to make a few inquiries at the Bank."

Ridgeway produced a card and scribbled a few words on it.

"Send this in and my uncle will see you at once."

Poirot thanked him, bade farewell to Miss Farquhar, and together we started out for Threadneedle Street and the head office of the London and Scottish Bank. On production of Ridgeway's card, we were led through the labyrinth of counters and desks, skirting paying-in clerks and paying-out clerks and up to a small office on the first floor where the joint general managers received us. They were two grave gentlemen, who had grown gray in the service of the Bank. Mr. Vavasour had a short white beard, Mr. Shaw was clean shaven.

"I understand you are strictly a private inquiry agent?" said Mr. Vavasour. "Quite so, quite so. We have, of course, placed ourselves in the hands of Scotland Yard. Inspector McNeil has charge of the case. A very able officer, I believe."

"I am sure of it," said Poirot politely. "You will permit a few questions, on your nephew's behalf? About this lock, who ordered it from Hubbs's?"

"I ordered it myself," said Mr. Shaw. "I would not trust to any clerk in the matter. As to the keys, Mr. Ridgeway had one, and the other two are held by my colleague and myself."

"And no clerk has had access to them?"

Mr. Shaw turned inquiringly to Mr. Vavasour.

"I think I am correct in saying that they have remained in the safe where we placed them on the 23rd," said Mr. Vavasour. "My colleague was unfortunately taken ill a fortnight ago—in fact on the very day that Philip left us. He has only just recovered."

"Severe bronchitis is no joke to a man of my age," said Mr. Shaw ruefully. "But I am afraid Mr. Vavasour has suffered from the hard work entailed by my absence, especially with this unexpected worry coming on top of everything."

Poirot asked a few more questions. I judged that he was endeavoring to gauge the exact amount of intimacy between uncle and nephew. Mr. Vavasour's answers were brief and punctilious. His nephew was a trusted official of the Bank, and had no debts or money difficulties that he knew of. He had been entrusted with similar missions in the past. Finally we were politely bowed out.

"I am disappointed," said Poirot, as we emerged into the street.

"You hoped to discover more? They are such stodgy old men."

"It is not their stodginess which disappoints me, *mon ami*. I do not expect to find in a Bank manager a 'keen financier with an eagle glance' as your favorite works of fiction put it. No, I am disappointed in the case—it is too easy!"

"Easy?"

"Yes, do you not find it almost childishly simple?"

"You know who stole the bonds?"

"I do."

"But then—we must—why——"

"Do not confuse and fluster yourself, Hastings. We are not going to do anything at present."

"But why? What are you waiting for?"

"For the *Olympia*. She is due on her return trip from New York on Tuesday."

"But if you know who stole the bonds, why wait? He may escape."

"To a South Sea island where there is no extradition? No, *mon ami,* he would find life very uncongenial there. As to why I wait—*eh bien,* to the intelligence of Hercule Poirot the case is perfectly clear, but for the benefit of others, not so greatly gifted by the good God—the Inspector McNeil, for instance—it would be as well to make a few inquiries to establish the facts. One must have consideration for those less gifted than oneself."

"Good Lord, Poirot! Do you know, I'd give a considerable sum of money to see you make a thorough ass of yourself—just for once. You're so confoundedly conceited!"

"Do not enrage yourself, Hastings. In verity, I observe that there are times when you almost detest me! Alas, I suffer the penalties of greatness!"

The little man puffed out his chest, and sighed so comically that I was forced to laugh.

Tuesday saw us speeding to Liverpool in a first-class carriage of the L. & N. W. R. Poirot had obstinately refused to enlighten me as to his suspicions—or certain-

ties. He contented himself with expressing surprise that
I, too, was not equally *au fait* with the situation. I dis-
dained to argue, and intrenched my curiosity behind a
rampart of pretended indifference.

Once arrived at the quay alongside which lay the big
transatlantic liner, Poirot became brisk and alert. Our
proceedings consisted in interviewing four successive stew-
ards and inquiring after a friend of Poirot's who had
crossed to New York on the 23rd.

"An elderly gentleman, wearing glasses. A great invalid,
hardly moved out of his cabin."

The description appeared to tally with one Mr. Ventnor
who had occupied the cabin C 24 which was next to
that of Philip Ridgeway. Although unable to see how
Poirot had deduced Mr. Ventnor's existence and personal
appearance, I was keenly excited.

"Tell me," I cried, "was this gentleman one of the first
to land when you got to New York?"

The steward shook his head.

"No, indeed, sir, he was one of the last off the boat."

I retired crestfallen, and observed Poirot grinning at
me. He thanked the steward, a note changed hands, and
we took our departure.

"It's all very well," I remarked heatedly, "but that last
answer must have damped your precious theory, grin as
you please!"

"As usual, you see nothing, Hastings. That last answer is, on the contrary, the coping-stone of my theory."

I flung up my hands in despair.

"I give it up."

When we were in the train, speeding towards London,
Poirot wrote busily for a few minutes, sealing up the
result in an envelope.

"This is for the good Inspector McNeil. We will leave
it at Scotland Yard in passing, and then to the Rendezvous Restaurant, where I have asked Miss Esmée Farquhar to do us the honor of dining with us."

"What about Ridgeway?"

"What about him?" asked Poirot with a twinkle.

"Why, you surely don't think—you can't——"

"The habit of incoherence is growing upon you, Hastings. As a matter of fact I *did* think. If Ridgeway had been the thief—which was perfectly possible—the case would have been charming; a piece of neat methodical work."

"But not so charming for Miss Farquhar."

"Possibly you are right. Therefore all is for the best. Now, Hastings, let us review the case. I can see that you are dying to do so. The sealed package is removed from the trunk and vanishes, as Miss Farquhar puts it, into thin air. We will dismiss the thin air theory, which is not practicable at the present stage of science, and consider what is likely to have become of it. Every one asserts the incredibility of its being smuggled ashore——"

"Yes, but we know——"

"*You* may know, Hastings. I do not. I take the view that, since it seemed incredible, it *was* incredible. Two possibilities remain: it was hidden on board—also rather difficult—or it was thrown overboard."

"With a cork on it, do you mean?"

"Without a cork."

I stared.

"But if the bonds were thrown overboard, they couldn't have been sold in New York."

"I admire your logical mind, Hastings. The bonds were sold in New York, therefore they were not thrown overboard. You see where that leads us?"

"Where we were when we started."

"*Jamais de la vie!* If the package was thrown overboard, and the bonds were sold in New York, the package could not have contained the bonds. Is there any evidence that the package *did* contain the bonds? Remember, Mr. Ridgeway never opened it from the time it was placed in his hands in London."

"Yes, but then——"

Poirot waved an impatient hand.

"Permit me to continue. The last moment that the bonds are seen as bonds is in the office of the London and Scottish Bank on the morning of the 23rd. They reappear in New York half an hour after the *Olympia* gets in, and according to one man, whom nobody listens to, actually *before* she gets in. Supposing, then, that they have never been on the *Olympia* at all? Is there any other way they could get to New York? Yes. The *Gigantic* leaves Southampton on the same day as the *Olympia,* and she holds the record for the Atlantic. Mailed by the *Gigantic,* the bonds would be in New York the day before the *Olympia* arrived. All is clear, the case begins to explain itself. The sealed packet is only a dummy, and the moment of its substitution must be in the office in the Bank. It would be an easy matter for any of the three men present to have prepared a duplicate package which could be substituted for the genuine one. *Très bien,* the bonds are mailed to a confederate in New York, with instructions to sell as soon as the *Olympia* is in, but some one must travel on the *Olympia* to engineer the supposed moment of the robbery."

"But why?"

"Because if Ridgeway merely opens the packet and finds it a dummy, suspicion flies at once to London. No, the man on board in the cabin next door does his work, pretends to force the lock in an obvious manner so as to draw immediate attention to the theft, really unlocks the trunk with a duplicate key, throws the package overboard and waits until the last to leave the boat. Naturally he wears glasses to conceal his eyes, and is an invalid since he does not want to run the risk of meeting Ridgeway. He steps ashore in New York and returns by the first boat available."

"But who—which was he?"

"The man who had a duplicate key, the man who ordered the lock, the man who has *not* been severely ill with bronchitis at his home in the country—*enfin,* that 'stodgy' old man, Mr. Shaw! There are criminals in high places sometimes, my friend. Ah, here we are. Mademoiselle, I have succeeded! You permit?"

And, beaming, Poirot kissed the astonished girl lightly on either cheek!

VI
THE ADVENTURE OF
THE EGYPTIAN TOMB

I have always considered that one of the most thrilling and dramatic of the many adventures I have shared with Poirot was that of our investigation into the strange series of deaths which followed upon the discovery and opening of the Tomb of King Men-her-Ra.

Hard upon the discovery of the Tomb of Tut-ankh-Amen by Lord Carnarvon, Sir John Willard and Mr. Bleibner of New York, pursuing their excavations not far from Cairo, in the vicinity of the Pyramids of Gizeh, came unexpectedly on a series of funeral chambers. The greatest interest was aroused by their discovery. The Tomb appeared to be that of King Men-her-Ra, one of those shadowy kings of the Eighth Dynasty, when the Old Kingdom was falling to decay. Little was known about this period, and the discoveries were fully reported in the newspapers.

An event soon occurred which took a profound hold on the public mind. Sir John Willard died quite suddenly of heart failure.

The more sensational newspapers immediately took the opportunity of reviving all the old superstitious stories connected with the ill luck of certain Egyptian treasures. The unlucky Mummy at the British Museum, that hoary old chestnut, was dragged out with fresh zest, was quietly denied by the Museum, but nevertheless enjoyed all its usual vogue.

A fortnight later Mr. Bleibner died of acute blood poisoning, and a few days afterwards a nephew of his shot himself in New York. The "Curse of Men-her-Ra" was the talk of the day, and the magic power of dead and gone Egypt was exalted to a fetish point.

It was then that Poirot received a brief note from Lady Willard, widow of the dead archaeologist, asking him to go and see her at her house in Kensington Square. I accompanied him.

Lady Willard was a tall, thin woman, dressed in deep mourning. Her haggard face bore eloquent testimony to her recent grief.

"It is kind of you to have come so promptly, Monsieur Poirot."

"I am at your service, Lady Willard. You wished to consult me?"

"You are, I am aware, a detective, but it is not only as a detective that I wish to consult you. You are a man of original views, I know, you have imagination, experience of the world—tell me, Monsieur Poirot, what are your views on the supernatural?"

Poirot hesitated for a moment before he replied. He seemed to be considering. Finally he said:

"Let us not misunderstand each other, Lady Willard. It is not a general question that you are asking me there. It has a personal application, has it not? You are referring obliquely to the death of your late husband?"

"That is so," she admitted.

"You want me to investigate the circumstances of his death?"

"I want you to ascertain for me exactly how much is newspaper chatter, and how much may be said to be founded on fact. Three deaths, Monsieur Poirot—each one explicable taken by itself, but taken together surely an almost unbelievable coincidence, and all within a month of the opening of the tomb! It may be mere superstition, it may be some potent curse from the past that operates in ways undreamed of by modern science. The fact remains—three deaths! And I am afraid, Monsieur Poirot, horribly afraid. It may not yet be the end."

"For whom do you fear?"

"For my son. When the news of my husband's death came I was ill. My son, who has just come down from Oxford, went out there. He brought the—the body home, but now he has gone out again, in spite of my prayers and entreaties. He is so fascinated by the work that he ntends to take his father's place and carry on the system of excavations. You may think me a foolish, credulous woman, but, Monsieur Poirot, I am afraid. Supposing that the spirit of the dead King is not yet appeased? Perhaps to you I seem to be talking nonsense——"

"No, indeed, Lady Willard," said Poirot quickly. "I, too, believe in the force of superstition, one of the greatest forces the world has ever known."

I looked at him in surprise. I should never have credited Poirot with being superstitious. But the little man was obviously in earnest.

"What you really demand is that I shall protect your son? I will do my utmost to keep him from harm."

"Yes, in the ordinary way, but against an occult influence?"

"In volumes of the Middle Ages, Lady Willard, you will find many ways of counteracting black magic. Perhaps they knew more than we moderns with all our boasted science. Now let us come to facts, that I may have guidance. Your husband had always been a devoted Egyptologist, hadn't he?"

"Yes, from his youth upwards. He was one of the greatest living authorities upon the subject."

"But Mr. Bleibner, I understand, was more or less of an amateur?"

"Oh, quite. He was a very wealthy man who dabbled freely in any subject that happened to take his fancy. My husband managed to interest him in Egyptology, and it was his money that was so useful in financing the expedition."

"And the nephew? What do you know of his tastes? Was he with the party at all?"

"I do not think so. In fact I never knew of his existence till I read of his death in the paper. I do not think he and Mr. Bleibner can have been at all intimate. He never spoke of having any relations."

"Who are the other members of the party?"

"Well, there is Dr. Tosswill, minor official connected with the British Museum; Mr. Schneider of the Metropolitan Museum in New York; a young American secretary; Dr. Ames, who accompanies the expedition in his

professional capacity; and Hassan, my husband's devoted
native servant."

"Do you remember the name of the American secretary?"

"Harper, I think, but I cannot be sure. He had not
been with Mr. Bleibner very long, I know. He was a
very pleasant young fellow."

"Thank you, Lady Willard."

"If there is anything else———?"

"For the moment, nothing. Leave it now in my hands,
and be assured that I will do all that is humanly possible to protect your son."

They were not exactly reassuring words, and I observed Lady Willard wince as he uttered them. Yet, at
the same time, the fact that he had not pooh-poohed her
fears seemed in itself to be a relief to her.

For my part I had never before suspected that Poirot
had so deep a vein of superstition in his nature. I tackled
him on the subject as we went homewards. His manner
was grave and earnest.

"But yes, Hastings. I believe in these things. You must
not underrate the force of superstition."

"What are we going to do about it?"

"*Toujours pratique,* the good Hastings! *Eh bien,*
begin with we are going to cable to New York for fuller
details of young Mr. Bleibner's death."

He duly sent off his cable. The reply was full and precise. Young Rupert Bleibner had been in low water for
several years. He had been a beach-comber and a remit-
tance man in several South Sea islands, but had returned
to New York two years ago, where he had rapidly sunk
lower and lower. The most significant thing, to my mind,
was that he had recently managed to borrow enough
money to take him to Egypt. "I've a good friend there
I can borrow from," he had declared. Here, however, his
plans had gone awry. He had returned to New York
cursing his skinflint of an uncle who cared more for the
bones of dead and gone kings than his own flesh and
blood. It was during his sojourn in Egypt that the death
of Sir John Willard occurred. Rupert had plunged once
more into his life of dissipation in New York, and then,

without warning, he had committed suicide, leaving behind him a letter which contained some curious phrases. It seemed written in a sudden fit of remorse. He referred to himself as a leper and an outcast, and the letter ended by declaring that such as he were better dead.

A shadowy theory leapt into my brain. I had never really believed in the vengeance of a long dead Egyptian king. I saw here a more modern crime. Supposing this young man had decided to do away with his uncle —preferably by poison. By mistake, Sir John Willard receives the fatal dose. The young man returns to New York, haunted by his crime. The news of his uncle's death reaches him. He realizes how unnecessary his crime has been, and stricken with remorse takes his own life.

I outlined my solutions to Poirot. He was interested.

"It is ingenious what you have thought of there—decidedly it is ingenious. It may even be true. But you leave out of cou. † the fatal influence of the Tomb."

I shrugged my shoulders.

"You still think that has something to do with it?"

"So much so, *mon ami,* that we start for Egypt tomorrow."

"What?" I cried, astonished.

"I have said it." An expression of conscious heroism spread over Poirot's face. Then he groaned. "But, oh," he lamented, "the sea! The hateful sea!"

It was a week later. Beneath our feet was the golden sand of the desert. The hot sun poured down overhead. Poirot, the picture of misery, wilted by my side. The little man was not a good traveler. Our four days' voyage from Marseilles had been one long agony to him. He had landed at Alexandria the wraith of his former self, even his usual neatness had deserted him. We had arrived in Cairo and had driven out at once to the Mena House Hotel, right in the shadow of the Pyramids.

The charm of Egypt had laid hold of me. Not so Poirot. Dressed precisely the same as in London, he carried a small clothes-brush in his pocket and waged an unceasing war on the dust which accumulated on his dark apparel.

"And my boots," he wailed. "Regard them, Hastings.

My boots, of the neat patent leather, usually so smart and shining. See, the sand is inside them, which is painful, and outside them, which outrages the eyesight. Also the heat, it causes my mustaches to become limp—but limp!"

"Look at the Sphinx," I urged. "Even I can feel the mystery and the charm it exhales."

Poirot looked at it discontentedly.

"It has not the air happy," he declared. "How could it, half-buried in sand in that untidy fashion. Ah, this cursed sand!"

"Come, now, there's a lot of sand in Belgium," I reminded him, mindful of a holiday spent at Knocke-sur-mer in the midst of *"les dunes impeccables"* as the guide book had phrased it.

"Not in Brussels," declared Poirot. He gazed at the Pyramids thoughtfully. "It is true that they, at least, are of a shape solid and geometrical, but their surface is of an unevenness most unpleasing. And the palm-trees I like them not. Not even do they plant them in rows!"

I cut short his lamentations, by suggesting that we should start for the camp. We were to ride there on camels, and the beasts were patiently kneeling, waiting for us to mount, in charge of several picturesque boys headed by a voluble dragoman.

I pass over the spectacle of Poirot on a camel. He started by groans and lamentations and ended by shrieks, gesticulations and invocations to the Virgin Mary and every Saint in the calendar. In the end, he descended ignominiously and finished the journey on a diminutive donkey. I must admit that a trotting camel is no joke for the amateur. I was stiff for several days.

At last we neared the scene of the excavations. A sun-burnt man with a gray beard, in white clothes, and wearing a helmet, came to meet us.

"Monsieur Poirot and Captain Hastings? We received your cable. I'm sorry that there was no one to meet you in Cairo. An unforeseen event occurred which completely disorganized our plans."

Poirot paled. His hand, which had stolen to his clothes-brush, stayed its course.

"Not another death?" he breathed.

baby

baby will coo and sing to you like the perfect
ou'll have visitors galore to admire your seemingly
Not so cute when you want to go to bed, though,
able baby is not the best sleeper, I'm afraid, pre-
atch up on their sleep when the rest of us need to
y! They don't mind playing on their own, but their
their lack of confidence, which only their parents
to help them overcome. It is important that you
hem as much as possible.

ar-old Libran

rs of age this child becomes strong-willed and
they have an opinion on everything. Don't even
force-feeding them; you'll be wasting your time
It is easy for them to single out a member of the
make their special friend. They do this with the
f having influence on their side should Dad or
thinking about not letting them have that new
otball kit they've seen.

year-old Libran

ert kids with quick wit and are musical by nature,
surprised if they join the school choir. This child
xcel in one special subject at this age and more
ot it is art. They don't like to be told what to do,
their school report is bound to tell you that they
,o off on a tangent. They are the class clowns and
of friends, but they also tend to notice the
a little earlier than most.

year-old Libran

Libran usually adores their mum, and with their
ab you are sure to feel as if you are talking to a

themselves within weeks of birth. They are willing to amuse
themselves for longer than most babies. They love attention
too, though, and once they start talking, they find it hard to
stop.

The five-year-old Leo

Your child will by now be full of energy and raring to go.
Don't be surprised if they creep into your bed at 1 a.m. with
an array of books for you to read to them. Don't even think
about force-feeding them; they will let you know what they
want, and as long as you can wait out this somewhat difficult
phase, then you will have a loving child who will while away
their time singing songs they have made up.

The eleven-year-old Leo

Poor old Madonna's dad must have had his hands full with
this eleven-year-old living under his roof. When your child
tells you that they want singing lessons or football lessons, or
whatever their passion may be, you should get your wallet
out, for they're certain to repay you ten times over when they
turn it into a vocation. They will also remember your support
or lack of it, so bear this in mind when the half-an-hour
journey to a football match is becoming a chore! It won't be
a hardship in ten years' time when you're making longer
journeys by private jet while drinking champagne!

The sixteen-year-old Leo

It's hard to stop this child from talking, and they won't always
say the right thing. They are not afraid of hard work or of
working for a low wage if they know it will lead to the job of
their dreams.

Virgo

This is the perfectionist of the zodiac who wants things their way or not at all. I mean, just imagine poor old Liam Gallagher's mum trying to force-feed him brown bread instead of white and think of his reaction! Children of this sign also have a tendency to be hypochondriacs. They are really good at listening to friends' problems, but will want their home run as they like it from nine years old, if not younger. They will decide what you do and when you do it, and no matter how much you swear that you are the boss, I'm afraid you're fighting a losing battle. The advantage is that this child will actually enhance your life, as if they don't like that new face you have introduced them to, there is usually a very valid reason, so back them up. They deserve it.

The Virgo baby

This is a baby who usually starts out in life looking more like their father and taking on their mother's temperament and personality. Virgos are actually not the most patient of babies, and even a minor job such as heating up their milk will take seconds too long for their liking. After the first four months any tantrums and crying should stop and you will be left with a baby that is weighing up your every move. Keep them occupied or they will catnap during the day and keep you up most of the night.

The five-year-old Virgo

You should now start to see the determination that is associated with this sign. If you don't start to get their number, they will have you over a barrel for the next twenty years, so make sure you put plenty of time and energy into this phase. Virgo Prince Harry is sure to have kicked up a right royal

stink if he wasn't watched cl
now just from the twinkle in

The eleven-year-old Virgo

This child will make it clear t
the leader and are more than
second in command. They c
around this time and are mor
their age. They won't like goin
with loose buttons, so make su
well or they may end up report

The sixteen-year-old Virgo

They are still the golden child a
but what Mum and Dad don't I
they're concerned. They won't i
that they would be quick to rej
self-indulgence are their main
avoided. This is one teenager
education further.

Libra

Libran babies really do look as
mouths. Just look at Leo Mad
image of innocence but with a
to play devil's advocate, and i
say white. Don't think that Gu
frown lines on his forehead fo
child, then just make sure yc
embroiled in a heated discussic
them reasoning with you until
up losing, if they are typical o

The Libra
The Libra
child and
cute baby
for this s
ferring to
start our
downfall
will be al
encourag

The five-
At five
moody,
think ab
and their
family t
intention
Granny
Barbie o

The eleve
These are
so don't
is sure tc
often tha
though, s
frequentl
have ple
opposite

The sixte
The teena
gift of the

friend and not a child. They don't mind hard work and are attracted to figures, both on and off paper! Music is a passion and this is probably when famous Librans such as Bob Geldof and Danni Minogue started singing into their hairbrush. They're definitely not all innocence and light, though. In fact you're sure to catch them behind the bike sheds sooner than most of the zodiac. This kid is a natural flirt, as I'm afraid you will discover for yourself. Don't knock it – this is a talent that will open many important doors for them in the future!

Scorpio

This child will have a sixth sense from birth. You'll feel as if you are looking at the past, present and future all rolled into one. The timeless and penetrating gaze of this child can also lead you to believe that they can read your every thought. They probably can. This is the second most psychic sign in the zodiac, with Pisces being the first. They tend to mix with other water signs as friends and love the drama that life offers. Good job too, with acting stars such as Brittany Murphy, Matthew McConaughey, Katharine Hepburn, Burt Lancaster, Sally Field, Joaquin Phoenix and Richard Burton among the famous line-up of Scorpio stars.

The Scorpio baby
This is an endearing yet restless child who will not really be able to understand the word 'no'. They love to feel in charge and show dominance from an early age. This bossy attitude can shock new parents, especially if this is their first child. Whether they have siblings older or younger than them, they will have them eating out of their hand and you'll just know there's something special about this bundle of joy.

The five-year-old Scorpio

By now they will have moved on to driving their teachers crazy as well as their parents, and their mysterious behaviour will really keep people on their toes. They enjoy a bit of mischief and know just how to create a drama. Those tales that they tell about what happened at school are unlikely to be as dramatic as they sound, so check your facts before you go complaining to the head.

The eleven-year-old Scorpio

By now this child will be showing a real skill for writing and storytelling. They have the whole class under a spell and are probably capable of leading a revolution. They usually take a dislike to one teacher in particular and if they choose to can make their life hell. They do nothing by halves and excel at some subjects while bombing at others. They usually hate the opposite sex at this stage, because they despise all that they do not understand.

The sixteen-year-old Scorpio

They have a flair for acting by now, and if they decide not to use it in their professional life, they are sure to do so in their personal one. If they have a problem, they are not upset, they are devastated, and their strong sexual drive can turn out to be a parent's worst nightmare. They are extremists who when they are good are very very good, and when they are bad, you can only imagine what they may be getting up to. It has to be said that this sign is tempted by experimenting with drugs and the like, so keep them well informed and maintain the strong bond they will have established with you.

Sagittarius

Sagittarians are great at the things they focus on, but when they don't have ambitions, they can become very lazy, so it's imperative that their parents encourage them to find their niche in life. I wonder if Steven Spielberg or Beethoven's mother knew they had a producer or composer in their arms? If they looked at their stars, then they would have seen that no dream was too big and no mountain too tall for their boys. If you believe in your Sagittarian child and help them to keep going and stay focused, then who knows what you could add to the list of famous Archers' achievements!

The Sagittarian baby
This is a baby who will do what they want when they want, but they do it with such determination that they get *you* into a routine. Don't knock it – this is a formula that works for some strange reason and you'll soon end up napping when they've taught you to. Their sense of spirit is formidable and will have friends and family commenting on how they have obviously been here before.

The five-year-old Sagittarian
Young Sagittarians are like clockwork toys – they rush about like mad things, then collapse in a heap. You might want to supervise playtime carefully to avoid tears before bedtime. Watch out for a ferociously sweet tooth too and ration the chocolate. They speak their mind when they should be quiet, and at this age, when they are prone to repeating what they hear, you could lose quite a few friends if you've talked about them behind their backs.

The eleven-year-old Sagittarian

By this age Sagittarians should already have a firm set of ambitions in their sights. Woe betide the parent who doesn't share them, as they will set out to prove to both their elders and their equals that they are a force to be reckoned with. It's when they don't know what they want to do that they become a worry and grow vague and lazy. Support them, for with vision and direction they will excel and make a fortune, though that is not to say they won't still be a handful, albeit a rich one.

The sixteen-year-old Sagittarian

By this age all that energy will ensure that Sagittarians reign supreme on the sports field. They'll be captain of this and champion of that, and the first in the class to have a boyfriend or girlfriend. Flirting is second nature to Sagittarians. Here's a surprise: many teenage Sagittarians will spurn the romantic opportunities that come their way for the sake of study and brilliant exam results. The dedication that made them school sports champions will give them a flying start in their careers too.

Capricorn

Nicholas Cage and Jude Law may well be Hollywood heart-throbs, but I bet they are still mummy's boys. You see, earth signs love their home and their roots, and no matter how famous they get, they will always want to keep that family bond. But just how easy was life bringing up Capricorn stars such as Mel C. and David Bowie? These children don't take well to being moved about a lot when they are young. In fact they find it hard to move out of home when the time comes, and if the stars of this sign have to stay in a hotel, then they are sure to have the urge to take a favourite pillow with them to ensure they have sweet dreams.

The Capricorn baby

This baby is very little trouble and is in fact extremely perceptive. They even seem to know when their parents need a little peace and quiet – when they are in a happy frame of mind, that is. They do suffer from teething problems more than most, but fit family life very well. Sleep is not usually a problem for them. They are a delight to have around. In fact you may find yourself having to wake them up.

The five-year-old Capricorn

The placid Capricorn child is easily taken advantage of by their brothers and sisters. They are obedient and like to do as they are told. They wouldn't dare risk a telling-off for anything trivial; it would have to be something worthwhile. They are observers and like to watch what everyone else is doing. These clever little souls are learning by others' mistakes, and they will make their move when they are good and ready.

The eleven-year-old Capricorn

They finally come into their own around this time and develop a flair for various things. They can actually surprise their close ones, who have witnessed a slow start. They do what their parents tell them, but more slowly than most. They want to make sure it's just right. This can come across as laziness, but they are simply making sure, so don't be too hard on them. Conflict with fathers can occur at this age, but you'll be pleased to hear it's only a phase.

The sixteen-year-old Capricorn

They are now keen students of life, but will listen and learn rather than push themselves forward. The boys like football, and the girls analyze the opposite sex as a full-time occupation. A shy streak can stand in the way of having a relationship, but if they do find a partner at this age, they may well stick with them for life. They like to build on things and people, and this is the attitude that sets them up for the rest of their very successful lives.

Aquarius

You're going to find it hard to get this child to shut up, as they have much to say about life, love and anything else. Don't knock them for it, though, for it's the very trait that can set them and you up for life. Aquarians include Robbie Williams, Emma Bunton and Justin Timberlake – just imagine what the world would have missed out on had their mums told them to pipe down when they were singing at inopportune moments. People may think that Elvis's daughter Lisa Marie is quiet, but believe me, behind closed doors she's certain to have displayed a most colourful and vocal side indeed, which is probably the reason Capricorn Nicholas Cage felt so 'shook up' after their divorce.

The Aquarian baby
This is a baby who is destructive by nature and is sure to reject cuddly toys in favour of an old slipper or a blanket. Nonetheless this is a happy baby who is sure to bring joy into the life of any parent. Don't leave them on their own for long, though – they like company and would far rather you have a party around them than go out and leave them on their own with a babysitter.

The five-year-old Aquarian
These are the kids who put on shows in the front room, but the difference is that the forward-thinking Aquarian will actually have the brains to charge the audience and to put the other performers on wages depending on skill and age,

reserving a large percentage for themselves of course. Some people say that they have an old head on young shoulders, and I have to say that I agree.

The eleven-year-old Aquarian

This child is popular with friends of all ages, and although they probably have a best friend, they will also participate in numerous clubs and after-school activities. A natural on computers, they can probably work out your technology at home far better than you or your family can. They are only bad at subjects that they find dull. They don't like routine, but want to be able to act on their instincts and ideas.

The sixteen-year-old Aquarian

They have a keen business sense and a capacity for hard work. They can work for really long hours without feeling tired or fatigued. They are not very good at attending to detail, though, so if you ask them to take the teacups out of their room for the tenth time, they will probably tell you off for interrupting the new computer program they are designing to aid travel and communication across the world, and they're probably not lying!

Pisces

Brooklyn Joseph Beckham may have been born with a silver spoon in his mouth, but being born under the water sign of Pisces, he is sure to have given his famous parents a few sleepless nights. You see, Pisceans come alive at night and so if it's not his crying as a baby that kept them awake, then it will certainly be his key in the door at 3 a.m. when he's a teenager. You just know that there's something special about the Piscean baby, and they know you know. They can guess things about you that will astound you and are naturally gifted and psychic, as you're sure to know if you have one in the family.

The Piscean baby

This is a baby who will show their true self as soon as they emerge from the womb. That is the only time in fact when you will see the Pisceans without all the dramatics that they soon start to display. They will constantly surprise and please you with their exploits and joyful expressions. I would be astonished to hear of any parents who got a whole night's sleep during the first very entertaining yet endearing year. When they don't go to someone or don't like someone, then trust them; they have a hunch about people from day one!

The five-year-old Piscean

A selfish streak can develop here if you are not careful and it's important to suppress it early on. Sharing toys will be practically unheard of, and they are sure to have an array of imaginary friends whose names and likes you are supposed to remember. This is when you will start to see their very vivid imagination emerge.

The eleven-year-old Piscean

It's a bookworm you have in your home now. Your child wants to read every bit of information that they can about life so that they can decide which very dramatic path they are going to follow. Don't tell them no, though, or they will set out to prove you wrong. They also have a habit of changing their room at about this time, so if you can't find Piscean Penelope in her bed, then look in the kitchen cupboard, where she's sure to be camped out for her latest adventure!

The sixteen-year-old Piscean

When this sign does something, they go all the way. Barings Bank trader Nick Leeson obviously went too far, but Piscean Albert Einstein goes to prove what a dramatic effect this sign can have on the world. So whether you've got an inventor or an actor in your Piscean child, then back them to the hilt. Just don't let them handle your bank accounts!

Chapter 5

SCHOOL DAZE

In this chapter you'll find out what your children are really getting up to behind the bike sheds these days. And what about you? Did you tell them what an angel you were at school? You can even read about your own sign and admit if those after-school clubs were really a cover for the many detentions you got. Do names from your past search for you on Facebook? Are you first on the list at your school reunion, or are your schooldays something you'd rather forget? I wonder how many of us remember what we were really like in our schooldays. Maybe you gloat that you were the school prefect or teacher's pet. Read on and relive your schooldays.

Aries

This is the schoolchild who leads the way in the art of class disruption, although after they have started the class humming to annoy their teacher, they will be sitting with such an innocent face that even the wisest of teachers will not suspect them. They really do look as if butter wouldn't melt in their mouths. They are both artistic and sensitive souls who will excel in music, and more often than not are to be seen with an impressive music collection in their schoolbag. They are quick to learn and are not bothered about staying up all night before an exam to revise. They will have a quick read on the bus on the way home from school and another one in the morning, yet often these jammy little dodgers can pass with top marks.

They like to be the leader of the pack and are quite often class captain or organizer of discussions. They need to be able to have freedom of expression, so even if there is a strict uniform code, you can be sure that when you look closely, there is some symbol of rebellion lurking, such as red socks or the wrong-length skirt. They can't help but show the world that no matter how much they are made to conform, they are and always will be an individual in their exciting lives!

Taurus

This child has a really strong personality and is hard to miss in a classroom, no matter how many other children there are. They tend to have a voice that is not easy to forget. In fact they can often be found in the school choir, where they will of course expect to be picked to sing lead every time. They love their food too, so woe betide you if you try to push in front of them in the school dinner queue. This is a child who will have both a packed lunch and a school meal if they can get away with it. Their worst subjects are usually sport and mathematics – they are not lazy, but the only way you would get them to take part in a sports day is if you dangled a chocolate bar on the finishing line. They really do have a natural ear for music, though, and if possible should be encouraged to take after-school music lessons. You could have the next Cher, Janet Jackson, Joe Cocker or Bing Crosby on your hands, who were all Taureans! They are not afraid to strut their stuff around the classroom, and their parents may well find that this is one child whose uniform bill is above and beyond the average.

I'm afraid they can become bullies and this must be nipped in the bud. As they can be a little bigger than other children of their age, they learn early how to throw their weight around; but if they can resist this temptation, then they should find themselves one of the most popular signs, for their love of life really is contagious. Just remember to keep an eye on their extra-curricular activities. This is one schoolchild who knows just how to find their way to the back of the bike sheds, and I'm not talking about smoking behind them!

Gemini

This child will probably be the head of the drama club and will most definitely be prepared to do dastardly deeds to become the editor of the school paper. You see, Gemini children were born to be in the media and they can't help but be fascinated with such areas. Marketing and selling come naturally to them, so when they ask to look after the tuck shop, you'd better check the price list; those crisps are likely to have gone up fifty pence when they're in charge. They love new experiences and have plenty of friends around them – people can't help but find them fun to be with, and they mix well with any age, so you are just as likely to see them hanging around with sixteen-year-olds as with ten-year-olds. I wouldn't call them liars, but they certainly bend the truth when the mood takes them.

Geminis show an interest in the opposite sex from an early age, and the majority of these air signs tend to have a crush on one of their teachers, going to great lengths to make their feelings known. Oh yes, this sign will bring the teacher of their dreams an apple a day and they can sometimes take things a tad too far. So if you hear of their decision to run off with Mr Jones, it's probably more of an obsessive fantasy than reality. They are dreamers and excel at staring into space, yet their gift of the gab can make them front runners in any class discussions. So as long as a test requires spoken as well as written skills, they may just pass with flying colours.

Cancer

This child is really self-sufficient and can manage to get themselves up, dressed and off to school without a parent yelling their name ten times or physically dragging them out of bed. They usually have younger friends as they like to be cast in the role of teacher themselves, so if they are able to pass on any knowledge to those younger, all the better for them. They stick up for their friends and are not generally seen as the bullying type, although they get an A for emotional blackmail and that's a trait that they take with them to adulthood. They are able to give the impression that they are good at things they know nothing about, and French is likely to appeal to them. Parents must make sure they send this child on any school trips, as experience is essential to their growth. They will probably spend much of their time in the school sick bay, not because they are ill but because they have a fascination with playing doctors and nurses. Not so bad, as long as they don't take their experiments with young Joe or Joanna too far or you could have the headmaster on the phone.

They will look up to their teachers as role models and can do extremely well in their school years owing to the support that those with power feel obliged to give. Teachers don't mind explaining things properly to a Cancerian as they feel that their help and advice are really being taken in. Relationships too young can be their downfall, though, so when

Tommy tells you he's going to Russell's for after-school studying, just check he doesn't mean Rosie's house for a whole different kind of studying!

Leo

The Leo schoolchild will have a pencil case or a schoolbag with a picture of their favourite celebrity on, and they will tell everyone that they too will be as famous as their idol. Don't laugh – they probably will. They tend to develop a little too quickly, so when the aftershave or eye shadow starts to become part of their morning routine, you know it's time to rein them in before you have a horde of screaming admirers camped outside your front door every evening. They are not silly, though. They have a great deal of self-control and won't be forced to do anything that they don't want to.

They will want to wear something to school that breaks the rules and that makes them different, but if they start complaining that all of the other schoolchildren have got Gucci pencil cases, just turn a deaf ear. When they have their own money, I am sure they will be able to indulge their designer tendencies, but until then just take them down to the local shops like all their friends, or you may have to move town and schools when your next bank statement comes in.

Virgo

Don't be angry when this child comes home from school with their best friend and proceeds to get them a sandwich from the kitchen, make them their favourite drink and watch their favourite cartoons. Virgo, you see, likes to please and is one of nature's reliable second in commands. Don't underestimate them, though, as this child knows just what they want out of life and they prefer to learn from other people's mistakes. So when their best friend is trying out the latest fashions, they will be quietly watching from the sidelines to make sure that their classmates are not laughing at them. They are the sort of child whom the teacher likes to make their pet, but don't be fooled when they are asked to get the basketballs out for the sports coach, they will still make sure they do it in their own time. They are born organizers and are extremely intelligent. Once centred, they can excel in any subject that they turn their hand to.

They are more mature than most kids their age, and will usually have their eye firmly on one person whom they will admire from afar, rather than having tons of sweethearts. Their problem can often be that they make their feelings in love known too late and so by the time they speak out, the person concerned has become interested and intrigued, followed by confused and bewildered. On the other hand, you will find them in the playground counselling all their friends on their problems. Believe me, their advice is spot on, so seek them out – they could just help you turn your life round. Adults will have found they can confide in them, so their advice is worldly, even if it is second-hand.

Libra

The Libran child has a way of doing things that is highly artistic – even the way they wear their school uniform will make them appear different from other children. They are not afraid to be different in their musical tastes either, and a love of the arts could see this child asking their parents for tickets to the ballet or the opera rather than the local disco.

They are not the best eaters, so if you give them a packed lunch, make sure you don't find it stuffed down the back of the car seat after you've dropped them off. They will have plenty of admirers, but I'm afraid they tend to go for a bit of an age difference, so just make sure that the birthday party they go to when they are eleven is not full of seventeen-year-olds. Many Librans pick up their first musical instrument during their school years and don't put it down again until they are well into their eighties. Teachers will love this child but will also have to watch them like a hawk, as they tend to grow up just a little too quickly for their own good. However, once you see the sparkle in their eyes, even you will forgive them for putting that frog in your desk.

Scorpio

This schoolchild will bring home their new best friend on Monday and by Friday will have declared that they don't even know their name, as new and improved offers will have come their way from more intriguing characters. It is quite likely that they will be head of the drama club, but if they're not, then their theatrics in the classroom will be enough to keep both pupils and teachers amused through the most boring of lessons. They have the ability to make you think that they excel in subjects that they know nothing about, so when Scorpio Sophie or Simon offers you tutoring in French, then they are more than likely winging it. Bypass their offer and learn the hard way – it will save you a lot of bother in the long run.

The lucky thing is that they don't usually have much of an interest in sex during their school years. They are more interested in themselves and how they can best explore the intriguing world they find themselves living in. It's the later years when you have to worry about sex with this sign!

They do nothing by halves, and if they decide to study something, then you can be sure they will excel in it. They may even have a habit of changing their name or nicknames at various points, but don't worry – their experimental nature nearly always leads them to a life that most of us could only ever dream of, so let them be themselves. Don't try to change them; have faith.

Sagittarius

The Sagittarian child will be one of the most popular characters in the class. The children around him or her will just know that this is a person who is destined for success, and as the years ahead will prove, they are right. Sagittarians are one step ahead of their classmates in their clothes, fashions and in loving a band you have never heard of but will be the latest thing next month, so don't mock them; they remember who their friends and enemies are.

If they are not interested in a subject, then there is nothing you can do to force them to learn, but once they take aim and focus, then, like their sign of the Archer, anything is possible. They are good at sports, so don't be surprised to find them captain of the hockey or basketball team. They are competitive by nature and, luckily for their parents, are clean and neat by nature too. You should find them an asset to any class, except when they are not in the mood. Then they're the child you will see standing outside the classroom or the headmaster's office. They will talk their way out of trouble, but not as well as a water sign. This is a child who will make your school years both memorable and fun.

Capricorn

At first glance you may think that this is a lazy child, but they are anything but. They are just slow and meticulous in their work and will go to great lengths to make sure that they can be proud of their projects. They do their homework slowly. You may think that they have been playing on the computer, but check and you will soon see that they have been making sure that they can be happy with their efforts. To the Capricorn child, if a thing is worth doing, then it is worth doing well. They will have long-term plans from an early age and it is not unusual for a nine-year-old Capricorn to talk in great detail about which universities they intend applying to. As far as sports and games are concerned, they may not be first on your list to pick for your team, as by the time the teams are lining up, Capricorn is still tying his or her shoelaces.

They have quite a deep and dark sense of humour and so will be able to come out with a one-liner just when the teacher has had enough, but their sensible appearance can usually win the day and the heart of the teacher, because this sign usually knows how far is too far. Friends they make they tend to keep through their life and for good reason – this is a mate who will not let you down, even if they do take twice as long returning any favours.

Aquarius

Talk about the chatterbox of the class – this is one sign who is sure to get into trouble time and time again for speaking when they should be studying. Class discussions see them at their best and they are actually extremely bright and intelligent souls who will surprise their parents by passing exams with pretty impressive marks. They should excel in computers as this is a sign that is forward-thinking and quick to pick up anything that helps the world to move forward and communicate at a quicker pace. You might think that they aren't taking in what their teacher is saying, but how wrong you would be. They retain information like a sponge, which is a good job, given the speed with which their life moves along.

They are popular with people of all ages, and although they probably have a best friend, they will be members of numerous clubs and participate in many after-school activities. The relationships that they build up with their best friends last through thick and thin. They will not try hard in the subjects they find dull, and no amount of coaxing can talk them into studying something they don't want to follow. They don't take authority all that well and have been known to laugh at their teachers. However, get to know them and you will see there is no malice to their character, only fun. After all, to them, that is what life is about!

Pisces

Although the Piscean child is unlikely to share their games with you, they will share their packed lunch. This is a child who tends to have a selfish streak in some areas and an over-generous streak in others. They are born leaders who won't think twice about nominating themselves for prefect or class captain. They love their books too and probably frequent the library, but behind the rows of educational books they will be listening to friends' deep, dark secrets. They expect friends to remain loyal to the end, but woe betide you to ask anyone else home for tea before inviting them.

They are popular characters, but in rare instances they can be idle and arrogant, which must be nipped in the bud. They can bully too, but usually on behalf of someone else whom they feel is being picked on. They are more than aware of the opposite sex and know just how to wind them up. They are born dramatists, but don't be fooled, as that book on Shakespeare that they have under their arm is probably hiding the latest steamy novel. They are clever and business-minded, and if they can motivate themselves in business studies, they can earn the money they dream of. The key word for this water sign is dream, as they are capable of losing a whole afternoon thinking about their fantasies; but then again, some of the biggest success stories in the world chased merely a dream in the beginning, didn't they?

Chapter 6

MUMS AND DADS

Who is the person who brought us into the world, and who do we most commonly turn to when we have a problem? Our mum, of course. However, the relationship between mother and child is often a difficult one. The path is fraught with tensions and differences, which can eventually become a reversed relationship in which the mother becomes the child and the child becomes the mother. So here's your guide to getting the best from your mum through understanding her star sign.

We'll also take a look at Dad to see if you can find the man behind the boy. Just like mothers, fathers shape who we grow up to be, but the importance of Dad often doesn't hit home until our later years. While Mum teaches us the basics in life, a father's job can be more complex. Although many men raise their children and do just the same things that a mother does, for many of us it's not until we start getting involved in relationships that we look back to see what our own father did and didn't do. If our father treated our mother with respect, it can give us a sense of pride about who we are, while if a father was absent or a negative influence, it can leave us lost. By understanding how each sign deals with the role of being a dad, you can learn to appreciate why they did and didn't do certain things when you were growing up. It will hopefully allow you to form a better relationship with them.

Aries

Mum

Your Aries mother is quite a character. She has a strong and somewhat diverse personality and probably won't be averse to the odd tipple every now and then, although this is a fact she will not admit willingly to her children! Being ruled by Mars, the planet of change and unpredictability, she will constantly manage to surprise you. Red is her colour and one she will wear when she is going into battle. You'll know if she has this colour on that she means business. Let's just hope it's not you she's ordered a face-to-face with or you're likely to be in for a real tongue-lashing or dressing-down. You have to be aware that this is a mother who is expected to and is allowed to go over the top every now and then. You'll never be able to say that life with this woman is boring. Just be sure to let her know that you love her. She may not be able to admit it as readily as you would like, but she will expect loyalty from her children. What you may not have realized in the beginning, but will learn as life teaches you its lessons, is that this is one mother who would go to war for you. The world had better watch out, as she's likely to win too! Her advice will never be typical of the average mother, but she'll allow you to live your own life. She doesn't want to know all the finer details, though, so you'd be better off telling her the advice you want is for a friend. She'll know it's for you, but it's the only way she won't pull her punches. She is an asset to any child's life, even if the road is at times somewhat bumpy and unpredictable!

And what about Dad?

The Aries father is not like having a dad but is more like having a best friend. You see, he never grows up. This is all very well when you are young, but as you get older, it could become something of an embarrassment. He may think it's cool to join you on the dance floor; you, I think, will not. Be kind to him, as he really is only a child at heart. His life has never gone to plan but will always have been fun, and if he has raised his children, then he is sure to have made a lot of sacrifices in his personal freedom along the way. You are sure to hear him talking about the grand plans he had but never carried out. Whatever you want to do, he's sure to have done in his adventure days. The more time you spend with him, the more you will get to understand him. He doesn't mean to let you down, but his mouth runs away with him and he makes promises because he knows they make you happy. He is not always able to do what he wants to, as life and the adventures he is always finding seem to interfere. The best way to keep a positive relationship with him is to remember that he is really the child and you will always be the adult!

Taurus

Mum

Although your Taurean mother is more likely to give you beans on toast than cordon bleu cooking, you will never be able to say that you were not fed well. She knows how to make a home a home. Unlike some of the more fanatically clean signs, such as Virgo, the Taurean mum is only intent on making the abode a place you can relax in. She will put love and care into your life and is likely to favour pastel shades in her home, such as pale blues, greens and pinks, which all fall under her rulership's colours. She won't approve of the bright clothing you wear and will want you to promise to be honest with her about what is going on in your life. She wants you to feel comfortable and considers her belongings, pets and children her responsibility, especially when things go wrong. This is the kind of mother you will run home to for chicken soup and ice cream after a break-up, as she'll have the remedies to make you feel safe and secure again. You may want to tuck a bottle of wine under your arm if you're returning home, though, as mother Bulls like a drop or two of the old vino and that wine collection for cooking is likely to have seen the inside of more glasses than it will have cooking pans. She'll know that red wine goes with red meat and white wine with fish and white meat, so be sure to advise any suitors who may be coming round to pick the right colour – it's sure to be noted by Mum.

No matter how old you get, you will always be her child. Allow her this pleasure and indulge her; it's likely to have been her life's dream to raise a family, and being ruled by Venus she's sure to have had a few personal struggles on the way, so appreciate this gem of a woman. She really is an amazing asset to your life.

And what about Dad?

We've all seen those fathers who run for cover as soon as their kids' friends enter the house. That can't have been a Taurean dad, though, for he will go out of his way to show visitors how warm and welcoming his home is. Even if friends have eaten before they've come round, they'd better be prepared for seconds, as Taurus will be setting an extra place before they've managed to get their coats off. He is, however, very old-fashioned as far as values are concerned, so even though he may dance around with you to your favourite tunes, you can forget wearing the latest clothes if he deems them too short, too flashy or too garish. Others can dress like that, but not a child of his. Often red-faced from a little too much vino with his dinner, he's not averse to falling asleep in his favourite armchair. He will want to play sports with you, but would rather watch them and will flirt with friends without thinking. There's no harm in it, even if it can prove a little embarrassing; he just has a playful nature. Fantastic as a grandfather too and probably better, as he's had the chance to learn from mistakes he made the first time round!

Gemini

Mum

The Gemini mother is very individual to say the least, and you must not take offence if at some point she has given you the impression that you are standing in the way of her career, her love life or her dreams. You see, this is the woman who wants it all and is capable of having it all too. She is a clever soul who is able, when in the right state of mind, to juggle kids, career and numerous other responsibilities. Many women of this sign work from home and are able to do so very well. Buy her some daffodils – yellow is her colour and is sure to make her smile. She loves to travel, so expect to find yourself with more house moves than the average family if Mum has her way. She loves excitement and may even get excited about the prospect of a drama in your life, which she will try with the best of intentions to take over for you so that she can sort out what has gone wrong. She will by no means be your usual mother, but will have given you an alternative view of life that will equip you very well for life's unpredictabilities. Children of a Gemini mother are often only too happy to marry young and quickly, just to get a bit of peace and quiet and predictability, but what you don't realize is that she will instil in even the most staid of signs a thirst for excitement that will prove almost impossible not to chase every now and then.

And what about Dad?

I can't promise that you will like the way your Gemini dad dresses. In fact it's common for embarrassed children and partners of this sign to buy them clothes for birthdays, Christmas and in fact any occasion they can think of. This is a father who has really lived life, and what you know about him when you reach your thirties will shed a new light on him. He's not just a sign who has talked about travel and change but has most likely done it too. He made money and lost it, and he may even have had two marriages. When he's strict, he's a nightmare and to stand up against his wishes would be a foolish move indeed. When he's feeling liberal, then you can get away with more than any other sign of the zodiac would dream possible. Race him for the phone too – if he picks it up when your friends call, you're likely to get cramp holding out your arm waiting for him to stop talking and pass it to you. Word of warning: you may think that you can tell him everything and that he has an open mind, and he has, apart from when his children are taking unnecessary risks!

Cancer

Mum

The Cancerian mother may as well have been taken straight from *Little House on the Prairie*. She is a born carer and knows just how to speak to children and how to raise them with love and understanding. What better way to show her this than to buy her some of her favourite flowers? Acanthus, carnations, lilies, water lilies, geraniums, white roses and white flowers in general are all perfect for this mum. Her lucky colours are smoky grey and silvery blue, which will often form part of her make-up and clothing. She doesn't always dress like the average mum, though, and sometimes her choice in clothing can leave a little to be desired. Some of your friends may even whisper behind her back that she is mutton dressed up as lamb, but to me and to you she should just be called funky and very loving with it too. Cry and she will cry with you; be naughty and she will emotionally blackmail you, leaving you with a sense of guilt that you will take with you to future relationships and may well lead you to choose signs who are colder than the norm just to give yourself a break from the heavy-duty emotions that form part of life with a Cancerian mum. She will try to cook, but look in the bin and you're likely to see some ready-meal packages hidden there. Get used to pasta – it's probably a firm favourite if you are under her roof! Oh, and run for cover on full moons, as she's likely to say and do things that aren't pretty.

And what about Dad?

This is a father who doesn't need to raise a hand to make you see right from wrong. He uses emotional blackmail like a professional and can make you feel bad about things you haven't even done yet. His clothing can be a little old-fashioned, although he is sure to swear that what he dons has come back round. It has, but it's been and gone again too. He doesn't like getting older and will probably prefer for you to call him by his first name. When he was young, he wished his life away, and as he embarked on adulthood and parenthood he realized he had not taken the time to relish the joys of youth. He will love to hear what you've been up to and will take great joy in trying to make your dreams become a reality. He will invest his own savings and the family's finances into giving you the best start, even if it means going behind your mother's back! He expects his family to be a family and can't stand rifts or problems, even though there will be at least a dozen faces in his circle whom he can't stand due to one drama or another. Show him respect and he'll do anything for you, but don't laugh at him it's taken him a lot of self-confidence to get where he is, even though he pretends otherwise.

Leo

Mum

Being ruled by the sun, this is a woman who will know how to bring sunshine into her children's lives. Want to go and stay at your friend's house? Forget it – all your friends will want to come round to yours once they have met your mother. Reds, yellows and oranges are all colours that she will be attracted to, so you can bet her kitchen is a burst of colour and activity. Red walls are a favourite in this her most lived-in room. She is not, however, as confident as she makes out, so be sure to give her plenty of praise. She has struggled to get where she is, and no matter how well she has done, she will never feel that she has lived up to what she deems to be a perfect mother. Many women of this sign have problems with their relationship with their own mother and spend years comparing and questioning where they went wrong. Be careful they don't spend your childhood trying to correct your grandparents' failings. Let her know she's doing fine and work as a team. Family to her is a unit, and by working together you'll be able to take on the world. With her by your side there is no vision that is not attainable. She will also often talk about how she wanted one more baby – you see, Leos always feel that their family should be large, and no matter whether there's one child or several, her mind will be turning over what one more would have meant to her brood!

And what about Dad?

You're lucky enough to have a father who won't mind doing the things that a mum should do. In fact many Leo fathers are better housewives than their partners. They are perfectionists in many respects and firmly believe that if you want a job done well, then you should do it yourself. He has worked hard and will expect his children to do the same. You will be given jobs and responsibilities from an early age, though your pocket money will be among the lowest in your class. He will know where his own upbringing went wrong, and he is more open to talking about it than most fathers, as he probably spent so long trying to come to terms with it when he was your age. He wants to be fit and healthy, but it is not uncommon for men of this sign to have a sports injury that stops them from indulging in all they desire with their children. Although he will allow you to have friends, he will want to have a hand in choosing which ones you hang out with. You can tell who he approves and disapproves of as some friends are kept waiting on the doorstep and others are sitting watching TV with him when you are called down. Strict but caring are the key words for this father. You'll certainly always remember that he was there for you, but you may not like the way he did things. Nevertheless you'll have to agree that he got the family where they needed to be in the end!

Virgo

Mum

Your Virgo mother is incredibly picky, and no matter who your friends are and what their parents do, they are never going to be good enough for your mum. If something gets broken when your parents are away for the weekend and you confess it was you, then Mum will still decide it was one of your friends and ban them. You are expected to do brilliantly in life, and if she can afford private education, then she will. If you can have links with the medical profession, then even better. She loves her home and her family, and will have proud pictures dotted around showing your achievements. Greens and dark browns are what she favours in furniture – nothing bright and garish. She will expect you to behave well when she takes you out and to have manners. If you don't want to have the life that she has planned for you, then be prepared for confrontation. The key is to let her know what makes you happy rather than doing things to please her. By doing this, you can save years of arguments. You've got to love her, though; she'd sell her most prized possession to make you happy and has spent her whole life wanting you, so communication is the key to getting the best from this very special and individual union.

And what about Dad?

The poor old Virgo dad thinks he knows his children so well and will go out of his way to make sure their lives are successful. Due to the fact that children learn from an early age not to tell Dad everything, the Virgo dad never of course really knows what his children are up to. The crafty kids of this parent will have managed to blame friends for the things they got up to over the years, and if they are clever will have learnt to twist him round their little finger. You are expected to do well because he wants you to succeed where he failed. If he sends you for extra homework lessons, then dig out his old school report from the attic and you'll see your tuition is in the very subjects he failed at when he was a child. Communication is essential or you will end up making choices that he has bullied or emotionally manipulated you into making.

Family holidays are likely to become a little boring as he'll make you all stick to the places that he liked ten years ago. This can be embarrassing if you invite your boyfriend or girlfriend along on a family trip later in life, only to realize that the karaoke machine in the hotel bar already has your family's favourite song up and ready for you all to sing, just as other families are making for the door. He doesn't have to know everything; he only has to know you are happy. You just have to learn to let him think he's in control.

Libra

Mum

The lovely Libran mum makes one of the best parents in the zodiac and you can bet that every problem you have had in your life she has taken on as her own, even when you didn't want her to! Shades of blue, pale green and pink are the colours that come under her rulership, and one of these is more than likely to be the colour she chooses to paint her most important room in the house, which is more often than not the bedroom. Librans have style and class, so try to treat her with respect. Bad language doesn't impress her, nor does impulsive spending. You may think it's OK to spend all your money on an item you've only seen a few minutes ago in a shop window, but tell her you've been thinking about it for months and she'll be highly impressed. She is one of the few mums in the zodiac who likes to listen to music around the home more than she does the telly. She's also pretty good with plants, and roses in particular should be something she will be able to cultivate with expertise. There is always the exception to the rule of course, but it's part of her make-up to have a natural tendency to green fingers. Washing and ironing are not a problem for her. However, her personal life sees emotions running very deep indeed. Help her to find the comedic value of problems and life and you'll find a mum who becomes your best friend, who will always listen and never judge you but always support you.

And what about Dad?

There is no other dad like a Libran dad; in fact they don't come much better. Here is a man who will take on the role of mother, father and best friend. He will make sure that whatever problem you have in life he is there with the right words to get you through. No matter what comes your way in life, with a Libran dad to guide you through you will find the confidence to make a success of things. The only trouble comes when you find out as you get older that he didn't really know everything. This can be devastating for many children, until you decide to take him off his pedestal and allow him to become a human being in your eyes. If you want something from the Libran dad, all you need to do is hit an emotional chord. He will spend his life giving you what he never had and telling you about his adventures. They may sound like fun, but underneath there will always be a word of warning attached to these stories, as he finds it hard to get straight to the point about any really delicate issues. Don't be angry with him when you find out that he couldn't give you all he wanted to. He'd give his Lucy or Lenny the world on a silver platter if he had the power to, as I'm sure you'll realize by the time you have children of your own!

Scorpio

Mum

Scorpio mothers are like no other; in fact they really are one in a million. You will find her both your best friend and a major headache. Her colours are deep reds and maroons, and these are usually the colours of lipstick she will choose when she's feeling confident in the world. Her drawers at home are sure to be crammed full. Above all this is a woman who likes mystery, and even if she tells you she doesn't expect you to tell her what is going on in your life, she will do everything in her power to work out what makes you tick. Don't forget her birthday, and don't make alternative plans for Christmas. This is her time and she will pull out all the stops to make sure you have fun. She would rather you bring your friends round than not see you during these important dates. Think *Ab Fab* and you will conjure up a vision of your Scorpio mum. When she wants to make an effort, she can look like a movie star, but that odd combination of clothing she wears at the school gates, with designer handbag, flip-flops and a heavy coat, means she has left in a hurry as she was busy planning a surprise in your honour. Love has no boundaries for her; she will go to the ends of the earth for you, even if you are the one who is in the wrong. You may, if she is particularly eccentric, have to get her to wait round the corner for you to save embarrassment, but when you get there, expect to find your mates deep in conversation with her. They'll love her and wish she was their mum, and you'll be glad she's yours, as you'll have no doubt her heart is in the right place.

And what about Dad?

The Scorpio father is heaven and hell at the same time as he makes you feel proud yet embarrassed, free yet restricted. He gives with one hand and takes away with the other because he always stretches himself slightly further than he can afford. If he can send you to private school, he will. He will try to educate you in the matters he has managed to blag his way through all of his life. He understands that his children, unless they are of the same sign, are not as blessed with intuitive skills as he is. He can strike a bargain and will make sure the home is a home, albeit an unusual one. Holidays will be fun and to unexpected places, and arguments will not be uncommon, but the making-up will prove to you that he is never too embarrassed to say he was wrong. He's a good judge of character and will be able to predict accurately which of your friends will let you down. He will also be able to spot the perfect suitor for you. Don't be afraid to listen to his advice; many people would pay for such words of wisdom!

Sagittarius

Mum

The Archer of the zodiac is a very ambitious sign, so to have had children would have been a sacrifice in her life no matter how maternal she is. Appreciate this fact by letting her know how able she is not just as a mother but as a person too. Strong colours such as rich purples and dark blues suit her. She won't be a stay-at-home mum and will like to get out for at least one night a week if she has her way. Don't chastise her for it: she'll be a better mum for being able to go out and let off some steam.

She is not predictable, so don't expect to be able to second-guess what she will say or do, but she will make sure she finds out the right school and the right clubs for you to belong to, and with the contacts that she makes in life she will ensure you jump any waiting lists. You represent her and so it is imperative that you do well. The funny thing with the Sagittarian mum is that she's very protective of you up until your teenage years but then she seems to see you as more of an individual and will often allow you free rein to make choices that other mothers in the zodiac wouldn't dare give to their children. She may not spend twenty-four seven with you, but they do say quality is better than quantity and that's just what you'll get with this very beautiful and able sign who will talk to you as an equal from the minute you take your first breath.

And what about Dad?

The Sagittarian dad wants to spend more time with his family, but also knows that his career is essential to the financial stability of his loved ones. That is why he finds it so hard not to put work before his children, something that takes many children years to come to terms with. His reasoning is quite simple: he makes the money; the family do well. It is not until later in life, when he has realized that success doesn't taste as sweet as he had hoped, that he learns to value the simple things in life. He is not predictable and you can expect to move house more than the average family, but you're sure to learn a lot from this impulsive and very fun sign.

This is also one dad who is willing to play sports with his children, at any age. He is naturally fit and will probably go on to beat your friends and his grandchildren. Don't ask too many questions about his past, though – he tends to make up what hasn't happened as he wants his children to believe only the very best about him.

Capricorn

Mum

A Capricorn mother may have been hard going at times, but I bet that you appreciate it now, don't you? She likes a routine and will have set a bedtime that your other friends will have laughed at, but just look at where you are in your career now compared with them. The colours she usually likes around her are dark green, grey, brown and black. You may think this sounds boring, but the most unusual combination of clothing works for her. She's not great at talking and so if you've had a problem, you're more likely to find a note in your bedroom asking for a truce than you are to have a debate round the kitchen table. She loves her family so much that it's sometimes too much and she can't deal with the bigger issues. This is where a third family member usually comes in handy to be her go-between and pass messages back and forth. Don't expect always to get to school on time, as she can be a little slow at gathering herself together, although she does of course embrace a routine once it is established. She likes younger children, and the older you get, the harder it will be for her to let you go. The dummy in the five-year-old's mouth is probably there because the Capricorn mother allowed it to be, but show her that you'll still be home for the Sunday roast even when you've left home and she'll let you go. She just can't bear the thought of not seeing her nearest and dearest on a regular basis; they're what makes her whole.

And what about Dad?

This is a father who can be testing, as he speaks before he listens and tries too hard to be a dad before being a friend. This is all very well, but unless he knows who his child is as an individual, he is going to have a hard time working out what is right and what is wrong for them in life. It is not unusual for this sign to want to live in the town they were brought up in, and I have in fact known several clients who have raised their children in the same house where they grew up.

He loves his family deeply and wants you all to work as a unit. This can often mean giving up or changing arrangements to fit in with what he deems to be 'family time'. He's not great at playing the dual role if he is a single parent, as he needs a mother to balance out and play the parts he can't. This is a time when things can really break down and he should enlist the help of family or friends. Trying to do it all is a recipe for disaster for this loving and somewhat old-fashioned sign.

He will probably have hated the way his parents raised him and yet he will fall into the trap of following the same rules;

it's inbuilt in him. As you grow up, you're unlikely to be given freedom as early as your friends, but this is only because he knows from his youth what dangerous ground romance and relationships can lead you to. He was probably the worst culprit of the lot. Learn to love his dry humour; it's seen him and will see you through many a crisis in life!

Aquarius

Mum

Air-sign mothers talk too much and you may even have been embarrassed as a kid when she spent more time talking to your mates than you did. I bet you appreciate it now, though, as this is a woman who will be a mother and a friend all rolled into one. Her colours are electric blue and turquoise, and she can often have really piercing blue eyes. Spare some time to sit down and talk to your Aquarian mum. She tells the whole world how proud she is of you and probably even carries something in her handbag from your childhood. She lives her own life, but what you don't realize is that the base for her whole existence was and still is you. She was probably a little wild in her younger days and you were the saving grace that helped her to become a better person.

She will talk about the past as if she were talking about a third party and is sure to have embarked on some travels that even the most courageous of men would never have undertaken. She's also likely to be far fitter than the other mums around you, as she can't bear the thought of not feeling the air in her lungs and living life to the full.

And what about Dad?

He can walk the walk, but can he talk the talk? is a question many children end up asking themselves about the Aquarian dad. He loves you with all of his heart, but he has a hard time showing it. He's too busy trying to make the perfect life for his family, who mean the whole world to him. Part of his problem is that he tries to spread himself too thinly. He thinks of work when he's at home and he just wants to get home to his family when he's stuck in the office. He can't do a normal job and neither can he work regular hours. When he's at home, you'll be sick of him, and when he's away, you'll miss him.

As you grow up, the Aquarian dad can turn out to be one of the best friends you'll have in life. After all, he knows more about you than anybody else and he's shared some of your most important experiences too. He's always young at heart and will probably know more of the latest tunes than you do. Just don't lie to him: he can't stand a liar, and once you break the trust with the Aquarian father, it can take years to regain that closeness.

Pisces

Mum

This is the most intriguing of all the signs in the zodiac and is even more dramatic than Scorpio (if that's possible). This is one mother whom your schoolfriends will still be talking about years on – agony aunt, best friend, sparring partner, the lot. Soft shades of green are her colours, and may even be the colour of her favourite sofa. She hates not being acknowledged, so if you have friends round, make sure they knock on her door to say 'hi' or they will be out of favour and out of your life within the week. She has a heart of gold and will turn heads wherever she goes, even now. You admire her and are embarrassed by her but wouldn't change her for the world.

If you go shopping together, she will barter as if she is in a market, and that's just in Marks & Spencer. Tell her something doesn't fit and she'll have it bagged and in front of the manager within the hour. She expects quality and enjoys sitting round a dining-room table with family, but not necessarily to eat her home-cooked food. She won't mind ordering in – it's the social aspect that appeals to her. Arguments will be colourful and loud, but the good times will be the best of your life. Just get some earplugs; she's likely to have the TV volume up louder than any teenager you know, even when she's sleeping. She needs the distraction to stop her imagination working overtime and interfering with her sleep. Boring never, unpredictable always, loving guaranteed!

And what about Dad?

There will be times when you want to push your Piscean father into the room first to represent you, and there will be times when you want to run for cover and deny any family link whatsoever. He likes things the way he likes them and has an imagination that could win him a prize for storytelling. You will have to accept, though, that he has a life outside his family too, usually a career or a hobby. He has to, for this is a man with so much energy that he has to put some of it elsewhere or you'd all go stir-crazy. If he did well at school, it was through sheer cheek and through sticking at things, and he is likely to have excelled in subjects that surprise your friends. He's not afraid to argue in public, and if you find a friend no longer calls you, it's likely to be due to the fact that your father has let them know what he really thinks of them! You will love him and hate him throughout your life, but you will know deep down that he will always be there for you when it really counts.

Chapter 7

PERFECT PRESENTS

Just what should you be buying your partner this festive season, or at any time of the year for that matter? Well, find out how to stay in the good books of your loved ones and to receive praise and attention from your family or even those you fancy with my indispensable guide to gifts for the signs of the zodiac.

Aries

For him

This is a man who craves excitement and really loves the unexpected, so don't go for the predictable. The look on his face will let you know if he doesn't approve of what you've bought him. Words will not be necessary, believe me; in fact he will never say he doesn't like a gift – it's not in his kind nature – but his expression will reveal all.

He would probably prefer a night out to remember rather than a new pair of socks. Many musicians are born under this sign, so why not think about music lessons? You could well uncover a talent he never knew he had! If you want to go for an aftershave, then choose something slightly different; he will hate it if everyone can guess the scent he is wearing, as he likes to keep a certain air of mystique. His ruling planet, Mars, is the planet of change and unpredictability, so why not give him a ticket to a mystery destination? The guessing will drive him wild and he is such an easygoing character that it doesn't have to cost you the earth; it is simply the fun of not knowing that will impress him. Tank-driving or flying lessons or a day at Brands Hatch will also win you favour, so get thinking and planning, and remember, make it different – that's what counts!

For her

This woman will want you to do something that will prove to her how much she means to you and how she is different from the rest. To buy her something that a friend owns just because she said she liked it would simply be insulting. Instead you are going to have to come up with a gift that she wants but hasn't mentioned. An unusual piece of art by someone she admires would be good, but if you are thinking of jewellery, then I have a word of warning for you: don't even think about buying costume jewellery, as she'll be getting it valued within the week and will not take kindly to a gesture that makes her feel cheap. You would be far better off spending your hard-earned money on a dozen red roses rather than a cheap ring. She can't help but sneak a look at the price tag; it's part of her inquisitive nature.

Flowers are a success with this woman, but you may want to think long term and invest in a nice plant. Again, though, it would have to be something different, so that she can talk to friends about it and impress them when they come round for one of the many social occasions that this woman likes to hold. Don't go for anything too boring. If she needs a new set of knives or saucepans, then believe me, she will buy them herself, so don't even bother looking in the kitchen shops.

Taurus

For him

He may not be aware of it, but he has a thing for leather. The perfect present for him could be a leather belt, leather gloves, leather wallet or even a leather jacket. I must stress, however, that it should be real leather and nothing fake; this man will know the difference and will think you are showing your true feelings for him if you put anything fake his way. Arguments could follow. He is a very sexy soul and so a nice piece of underwear would be successful, but I am afraid that being an earth sign, it is going to have to be practical. If he says he won't wear boxers, then don't try to change him. Chances are that he will never be forced into them and he is sure to have some very logical reason as to why they are not for him. A nice address book would also be good to help organize his life, but choose a hard cover, not a soft one – he will plan on keeping it for years if he has taken the time to write all of his important numbers into it. Oh, and if you want to go for an aftershave, then choose something musky. It's the only smell he'll put on; any others will just be worn to please you.

For her

The Taurean woman is passionate, with a discerning eye for both the elegant and the beautiful, so it is leather for her. Why not go for a leather skirt or a nice leather purse that she can keep all of her essentials in? Make sure it's 100 per cent leather – no mixes or fakes for this woman. She will also appreciate anything that can help her keep up her beauty regime, so if you can find a foot spa or a massage machine, then get it. You too can share in the pleasures of a gift like this, and it could even lead to romance if you throw some candles into the shopping basket. She loves food but is prone to putting on weight, so if you go for chocolates or champagne, then choose quality over quantity. Even better, buy some chocolate body paint. It's sure to provide you both with some very interesting memories. If it's your auntie, mother or sister you're shopping for, then stick to slippers. These home bodies love their abode and will get plenty of use out of them. (Their old ones are sure to have holes in the soles!) Chanel No. 5 is the most popular perfume with a Taurean woman, so why not buy a bottle of this scent, and perhaps get the body lotion too? The Bull loves to spoil herself and body creams are a luxury that's sure to earn any extra Brownie points you may have been seeking.

Gemini

For him

This is the man who is known to be the biggest flirt in the zodiac and so you may be a little resistant to the idea of buying anything that will help him in his exploits. Believe me, though, there is nothing better than to show him you trust him, so don't be afraid of buying him the new shirt that he is likely to have dropped a million hints about owning. Bear in mind that he is dress-conscious and has a mind of his own, so don't choose things that he has not seen or commented on; it will only prove embarrassing for you when you have to march it back down to the shop and change it for him, which he will not hesitate to ask you to do. If you know he really needs clothing, it would be far better to give him a voucher so that he can choose for himself. The latest electric toothbrush would also be good for a Gemini man – he never stops talking so is unlikely to find the time to use a manual toothbrush. Music also appeals to him, but once again listen for the hints. His tastes are alternative to say the least and what you think he will love he may well hate!

For her

This is a woman who is likely to get some very varied gifts on birthdays and at Christmas, and this is because people see her in so many different lights. She loves to come across as businesslike and wouldn't mind something like a leather briefcase, or better still a designer one, so that those she meets will know she means business and is a professional woman. If you've got the cash, then go for a laptop; she'll love it and love you for buying it for her. A mobile phone could cost you a small fortune if you agree to foot the bill, so why not get right to her roots, because if she really values you she will prefer something personal and slightly sentimental. A small piece of antique jewellery would be a perfect choice. So would a diary or address book that you have somehow had personalized, or even a framed picture of a memory that you have shared together.

A word of warning: if you're married to the woman, don't just give her money; she won't appreciate it. You see, it's far too impersonal and she will also end up spending it on others instead of herself. The best present of all for a Gemini woman is to make the effort to get on with her friends, who are certain to be a mixed bunch, and give her a happy Christmas to remember.

Cancer

For him

He is romantic, so the thought counts far more than the gift for this man. It doesn't really have to be a big or expensive present, but it should be something that looks as if you have put a lot of time and thought into it. What you buy depends on what his interests and hobbies are. You see, the Cancer man will have hobbies that he discovered years ago that remain a passion. He doesn't discover a new interest every day, so you will have to try to find a gadget he hasn't yet got for a skill that he probably thinks he perfected long ago. Most men born under the sign of Cancer are DIY enthusiasts, or at least like to think they are. Many are keen gardeners too, so there should be an idea in that for you to look into. Fishing and golfing are another possibility, so why not arrange a holiday that has places for him to indulge in his favourite pastimes as well as the romance that is so important to anyone born under Cancer? This very emotional sign would also appreciate a picture of someone he cares for, but don't be fooled – you'll have to put it in a very expensive, top-class frame or you may find yourself getting the cold shoulder, as he will think you should surely know better than to give him something half done.

For her

This is a woman who loves to pamper herself and a set of expensive bath oils are sure to meet with her approval. Be careful about going for face masks, though; she may think you don't believe she is beautiful enough for you already. A gift for her house or flat would be appreciated, or anything decorative to hang on the wall; a clock would be good as she's always running late both personally and professionally. A new duvet cover should go down well, and you may even get the chance to experience your new gift with her for being so thoughtful!

If it is a family member that you are buying for, then why not have a piece of jewellery that has been handed down made into her size? This emotional sign reads deeply into everything and will know that you think the world of her to give her something with an important memory or meaning attached to it. Also choose a card with meaning, as she will read the words more than once.

You may want to buy her favourite song on CD or MP3.

She is not as free with her own money as she is with others'
and she will probably have a stack of albums she is dying to
hear again, so pick up a copy of her favourite hits. It's sure to
be an artist from yesteryear!

Leo

For him

This is a man who won't mind if you spend money on things
that other guys would deem feminine. You see, Leo men
really are in touch with their feminine side and are not afraid
to look after themselves. Some skin products by trusted companies such as Aveda or Clinique will go down very well
indeed. You may also want to consider a day out at a beauty
salon. This is a man who probably has very good skin, hair
and nails, and so he will show an interest in a gift that helps
keep him in tiptop condition. The Leo male is a natural flirt
and anything that helps him look better is sure to stroke that
ego of his. He often has a fetish for shoes, so why not invest
in a new pair that he has seen? A shoe-care kit or a quality
set of shoehorns will not be laughed at by the Lion. He also
loves his sleep, so pick up a nice pillow for him to dream
away on. There are plenty of good ones on the market that
are sure to do the job. If you choose an aftershave, make it
light and lemony. He won't like anything too heavy.

For her

This is a woman you don't want to upset, so think very
carefully before investing your money on just anything for
her. Lesson number one is that you shouldn't break the bank
on a present for her: she can't stand people who mishandle
their finances, even though she is probably lousy with money
herself. She loves to look good and will not turn her nose up

at a designer jumper to keep warm this winter. The latest hair products could be a good idea too. She will not want to part with her own cash for them but won't mind you doing so on her behalf. She loves to change her look, so don't choose anything that is dated.

She will not like anything that is too difficult to work out, so forget puzzles or presents that she has to put together herself. Keep life simple for her and she will keep you in laughter and joy with her infectious sense of humour. A funny video or a movie that she deems a classic would go down well, and if it's perfume you're wanting to buy, then pick something that is happy and summery to go with the image she likes to portray to the world. Make it a well-known and expensive brand, so she can tell all her friends!

Virgo

For him

This man will probably already have a list of the presents he would like, how much they are and what shops they are available from. Take it, but then throw it out of the window and take this one with you instead. These are men who like to think they are in control but really they need looking after, as they are only little boys at heart and need to be loved and nurtured. Buy the Virgo man something that will show him you are around for more than just a day: underneath that confident exterior he is actually a very fragile character and lacks self-confidence more than you would ever imagine.

He loves a good book, but preferably something based on fact so he can talk about it afterwards. Buy him stuff for the upkeep of his health and you'll be making a rod for your own back, as he is also a hypochondriac. You could go for vitamins so he knows you care. Satin bedcovers could be a winner if you've got the nerve, or maybe a throw or rug with an earthy pattern or animal design, but don't go too wild – he likes natural, not bizarre!

For her
Like the Virgo man, the Virgo woman thinks she knows what she wants, though she doesn't have a clue. You see, she really needs pampering but she will think she wants to be organized and so while the new Filofax or latest mobile could be on Santa's list, you may want to head instead for the lingerie department and pamper her rotten. She'll never do it herself. This earthy sign of the zodiac will want to know that you are serious about her and so you will need to buy something that you can both use over the years but that also signals coupledom or family values. If you do give in and buy her a phone, make sure it's pay as you go: this sign could run up a bill that could well bankrupt you – she is the agony aunt of the zodiac and will use any means possible to counsel and put the world to rights. She needs to learn to relax and so a weekend at a beauty spa would hit the right buttons. Just check her diary for free dates – this is a woman who has plans right up until 2012, but will never stick to them. She's a born organizer of others, but unfortunately not very good at organizing herself.

Libra

For him
This man is addictive and so rather than just buying one gift for him, you will feel like buying several. You'll need to make a plan so that you don't break the bank, and remember that you don't have to spend a fortune to show a Libran you love him. Invest, if you can afford it, in a piece of artwork; this is a sign that will love anything that is beautiful and they are

often budding artists themselves. Whatever you buy your Libran man must look good, so forget spending a fortune if you don't have wrapping paper to match. If he has shown any interest in music, then look to a guitar; he should have a natural talent for it. Don't go for anything louder, he may just have a contradictory aspect and could end up driving you round the bend playing the bongos badly!

The air elements love to talk to friends about the gifts they have received, so do yourself a favour and get something you and he can be proud of. If you don't buy him a present he can show off, he will sulk for days or even weeks. The Libran man likes to look and feel good, so go for a scent that is classy not cheap, or he may just decide to wear the image you've painted him with!

For her

The Libran woman is going to need something that epitomizes good style and taste. She loves to wear nice clothes. Why not go for a small item by her favourite designer? She will not tolerate anything that she deems tacky and would rather go without than be embarrassed by something that she believes to be so obviously not her. She will also appreciate a meal out at her favourite restaurant. Flowers are a good choice, or an unusual plant – unusual being the key word; don't let her think you see her in the same light as everyone else. Taking her to an exhibition by her favourite artist would also be good, or a concert, or buying her an album by her favourite band; this woman is no wallflower, at least not if you really know her.

Underwear is only worth getting if you are willing to spend the money, and forget about perfume unless you are prepared to go for the real thing. Eau de toilette is just that to her, as past friends and loves are sure to tell you. The sure winner for this very exhilarating air sign, though, has got to be a new coat. She never stays in for long and is bound to need a new one for the adventures her life takes her on.

Scorpio

For him

This man, you will have to admit, has alternative tastes. What he loved last year he will hate this year. You will know what he is into as it will dominate his life and you may have trouble finding something he has not already got, because when he does something, he gives it 100 per cent. He is not afraid to spend money, yours or his. Steady on the drink as a gift: he doesn't handle alcohol too well, and if you buy him champagne, it really is a gamble whether you'll end up with him laughing or crying on your shoulder. Your best bet for him is some new undies, but check his size; he'll be devastated if they're too small and insulted if they're too big. If you can find something different and unusual, then buy it; he will hate to be the same as others and you'll wish you'd got it when it's disappeared from the shelf, only to find he bought it himself on one of his many shopping trips.

For her

This woman will know what she wants you to buy her, but forget asking – she'll expect you to guess from the very confused signals she's been giving since January. The best idea is to take her away for Christmas and really blow her mind. You see, she will believe that you can't pull the wool over her eyes, so it is all or nothing if you want to surprise her. Don't drop hints: she'll only imagine something you can't afford or couldn't possibly have organized in time. This is a lovely woman but one who will expect the best, so go for a piece of jewellery that you know she will value. She'll keep it with her for life and it will be well worth the investment.

A word of warning: don't buy lots of little things. She already has cupboards full of rubbish she's been hoarding and meaning to throw out. Nice cushions that she can lie about on would be a good idea. If you imagine a harem or a den of iniquity, then you'd be thinking along the right lines – only in terms of colours of course! She will love you to buy her something that makes her feel sexy; the way that others view her is more important to her than you can imagine. If you want to go for alcohol, don't go for a case of red wine, just one good bottle. She doesn't know the word 'limit', but is all too familiar with the word 'excess'!

Sagittarius

For him

The latest computer program could be spot on for this man. If he doesn't have a computer, then think about sending him on a course. He will also appreciate anything that can help him speed his journey to success, and self-help books are something that he may be too embarrassed to buy himself but is sure to appreciate from you. In fact if you look at the latest novels, then you would be on the right track. Wrap up a range of the latest blockbusters, but be warned it will probably only take him a week to read the lot. This man adores life and loves to work and play hard.

Book a table at a nice restaurant, but make sure it's a social place so that he can see plenty of faces and do the networking that is second nature to him. Other quick-fix options are any gadgets that can make life at home a little easier for this modern sign. The keyword really is speed. If you can find a remote that flicks through channels more quickly, then get it. He'll love you for life, if he can find time to tell you!

For her

Look for the latest beauty creams and you will be on the right lines. Even better, though, would be a gadget that does something new. This woman is born ahead of her time, so she wants to be the first to learn about something that can improve her life, skin, nails or just about anything. She could probably do with a new purse. Even if she bought one last month, she is sure to have used it so much that it needs repairing. A good party is likely to be her first choice as a gift, so why not give her tickets to an event? She's sure to have told you of a dozen already. Her music taste is often wide and varied, so she is bound to appreciate some more CDs to top up her ever-increasing collection. If you have any extra money and are willing to splash out on her, then buy this woman a piece of exercise equipment; she has an excess of energy to burn off. Invest in a treadmill and give us all a break from her exciting but very demanding personality.

Capricorn

For him

This is a man who will be very offended if you buy the wrong thing and won't be afraid to get you to take it back. Keep away from gifts without meaning, as he will go on for years about how you deliberately chose something that reminded you of an ex. He loves to read, so books are always a good buy. He doesn't often splash out on hardbacks, so you can be sure that he won't have read the latest title by his favourite author. He will love nice smells, but don't bother going for a new scent, as he will have his favourite. A good idea would be to get the hair product or lotion to match the aftershave. He loves to smell good all over and this flirtatious sign will know just how to greet people, so will want his neck and hair to smell nice. Chocolates are also a good bet, but don't expect him to share them, and exercise equipment is only worth investing in if he has asked for it. Capricorn men don't mince their words and you could end up wasting a fortune if you don't check with them first.

For her

This woman will love things for the home, so why not offer to contribute to a new sofa for her or even a new bed? Like the male of this sign, she will tell you if your gift does not meet with her approval. You would be wise to buy something she has asked for, as she will be very surprised if her gift is something you haven't discussed. Don't even think about choosing a new outfit as a present without her. The best, and I think most obvious, present is to take her out for a day of shopping and dress her from head to toe. If she feels good, then so will you. Top it all off with a meal at her favourite restaurant. She'll have several regular food haunts.

A nice wooden box that she could keep all of her mementoes in is another idea and is perfect if you won't get the chance to see her before Christmas. At least she'll have another place to store all her junk – sorry, treasures. Good-quality glasses or cups will also be appreciated, preferably in the pattern she collects but has not got round to completing.

Aquarius

For him

He is nostalgic, romantic and slightly sentimental, so give him a gift to remember you by, like a framed photograph of the two of you together or a book that means something to you, with some heartfelt words written on the inside. Aquarians love words and will certainly remember yours. Why not browse the bookshops and find out what the latest best-sellers are? You may just be able to add them to his collection before he does.

A keepsake, say a small box to keep things in, or perhaps a print of a painting will be appreciated. A money clip or a pair of cufflinks will also be things he can use and treasure over the years, and he's sure to love showing off these gifts to friends. Remember, though, that the loving words you write on any card will be just as important to him as the gift itself, so make them count; they could be worth far more to your future together than you can imagine.

For her

A meaningful but flippant and slightly sexy gift is what the Aquarian woman needs to go with her outrageous yet seductive nature. Perfume is a sure-fire winner, but just make sure she doesn't have hundreds of bottles already sitting on her bathroom shelf; there's a good chance friends and close ones will have cottoned on to her love of scents over the years and you don't want to end up buying something she's already got. A set of underwear will also gain you a high score in the popularity stakes, or maybe even a daring nightie or an outrageous top or skirt, as Aquarian women like to be noticed when they walk into a room. Avoid a sensible or practical gift, though. She won't thank you for a cookbook, bathroom scales or a new work briefcase, so don't kid yourself. Go for what she really wants and who knows what rewards could await you in return!

Pisces

For him

The Pisces man just loves surprises and is a real practical joker. You can get away with buying him very little if you make a big enough presentation and laugh out of it. Any small gift wrapped in layers and layers of paper that take ages to unwrap will delight him, or even a comic motto that he can put on his desk. If you are not one for jokes, then try something artistic, such as a nice jumper, but it will have to be tasteful; these are men with an eye for style, so any tacky clothing will be taken straight back and you could end up being traded in in the process! Something small, delicate and beautiful in the antique line will appeal to him much more than you think. These are men who really do prefer quality to quantity. They usually have quite a sweet tooth too, so some chocolates from Switzerland could do the trick if you're looking to seduce.

For her

She is a clever, sensible and practical type who will appreciate a clever, sensible and practical gift, provided of course that it is different. To get her something that everyone else has got is a sure recipe for disaster. A cookery book would go down well, but it would have to be written by someone she admires or has commented on seeing on television, otherwise it will be thrown in the cupboard with the rest of them she is sure to have collected over the years. Something to wear is also a safe bet; like her male counterpart, she can never have too many clothes. You see, behind that practical manner lurks a party animal with a thousand places to go and people to see. An easel and paintbrushes, a knitting machine or even a dressmaker's dummy may sound as if you'd be insulting her, but think again – she is naturally a dab hand at making and designing things and so if she has not shown an interest in the past, you could well be opening up a whole new world to her.

Part 3

MONEY AND CAREER

Chapter 8

MONEY

'Money can't buy friends,
but you can get a better class of enemy.'
SPIKE MILLIGAN

Were you born to be the next Bill Gates, or are you destined to pay off loans for the rest of your life? Do you check the price on your grocery bill, or do you use your credit card more than your brain? Maybe you're one of the signs who can no longer get a credit card. It's no laughing matter when the debts have got so bad that you can't see a way out. I've had clients who were determined to hide their financial problems from their loved ones, for fear that it would mean the end of their relationship. Their partners often think they're having an affair before they contemplate that a financial worry is the thing that has come between them. Keeping secrets of whatever kind causes damage to a relationship, but don't be one of the signs who allows money to end it. Not when there is a way out, no matter how bad things have become.

Some of the greatest and most famous faces of our times have survived bankruptcy, a word that is scary to say let alone contemplate. Businessman Richard Branson, founder of the Disney empire Walt Disney, film director Francis Ford Coppola, composer George Frideric Handel, talk-show host Larry King, businessman Donald Trump and actor Ray Winstone all went through this very tough experience, but they came back bigger and better than before. My aim of course is to turn your life round before you reach bankruptcy, but if you follow my advice, I can get you back where you belong regardless of how far you've fallen.

Do you know what is one of the biggest causes of financial problems? Lack of communication. Taureans, Virgos, Capricorns, Cancerians, Scorpios and Pisceans are prime candidates for burying their heads in the sand when things start to go wrong. Aries, Leos, Sagittarians, Geminis, Librans and Aquarians continue as if their finances are getting better by the day. They think that if they continue at full speed, they may just have a miraculous change of fortune along the way. Let's have a look at your sign's strengths and weaknesses so we can get you into the black and out of the red for good.

Aries

Being ruled by Mars, the planet of change and unpredictability, life is never as you planned and the majority of the time you kind of like it that way. Unfortunately your tastes are more expensive than the average sign. You can't help it, really; you just know how to walk into a shop and pick the most expensive item. You were born to expect quality and could probably tell a cheap imitation from a famous label any day.

What some of us would regard as an expensive, non-essential item, you will see as a necessity. Your enthusiasm for life in general is, however, infectious and you are very good at encouraging your friends and family to spend money they should be saving. 'Come on, you only live once' is one of your favourite sayings, and if there's a sign to make you feel that a social outlay is essential to your career, then this would be you.

The thing about you, Aries, is that you may claim that you

are broke, but as your life is one big adventure you will always find the money from somewhere to splash out on a little luxury. My mother had an Aries client who was about to be made bankrupt and was most put out by the fact that the bailiffs called her on her mobile in the south of France and interrupted her afternoon cocktail session with a girl-friend! To this particular Aries, holidays really did come before sorting out her debts. We never found out what happened to her, but the lack of contact probably meant that she was off on another adventure. (I am not advising this, by the way!)

Indeed entertainment is your main outlay. You would rather keep the same clogged-up hoover for fifty years than miss a Saturday night out at that must-be-seen-at party. You have a habit of changing your mind as often as the wind changes direction. Halfway through an evening you can decide you want to do something different, and if you don't get your own way you can become really difficult. This is where your secret supply of credit or loans comes in handy. It may be worth your while warning any new partners not to hurry home after you if you rush off following an argument. You're more likely to be sipping cocktails at the latest wine bar than sulking on the sofa.

So you see, my friends, yours is an expensive lifestyle. You can be a bit of a snob in many ways and woe betide a loved one who buys you an inferior label. Items must be from a credible and preferably designer source. You also have a talent for getting your loved ones to pay for things.

So the big question is, can you keep hold of your funds? If you have surrounded yourself with people who have taught you the value of the pound, then yes, but if you have surrounded yourself with faces who encourage you as much as you encourage them, then you could already be in trouble. The sensible of your sign do actually have money saved away;

if you can afford it, you will try to invest it in property or some fund that doesn't allow your impulsive nature to withdraw it too quickly. You are a little slower than other signs at putting fabulous ideas into action. You need to stop talking the fabulous talk and walk the walk. You have a really good brain – use it!

You'll be pleased to hear there are some famous Aries with money, one of whom is Elton John. (We all know how he's supposed to have spent thousands on flowers, though, so just watch out that those weekly carnations don't turn into daily bouquets of roses.) Then there's Mariah Carey (who has managed to work out how to get other people to pay for her flowers!) and Sarah Jessica Parker, from the popular girlie series and film *Sex and the City*. Her character, Carrie, has to be held responsible for a legion of women spending their mortgage or rent money on Jimmy Choos.

Just remember to keep putting a little of your money away on a regular basis, and if you have financial worries, then read the Rules on page 178. Make sure you don't give in to your weakness for overspending in the name of a good time. The majority of you live a long and healthy life, so do make sure you don't burn your bridges.

Taurus

Being ruled by Venus, the planet of love, your passions usually cost you the bulk of your income. You also seem to spend more when you are in love and need to learn that you don't have to buy things all the time to assure others of your affections. Financial problems have often started for Taurean clients of mine when they have got into debt for their close ones. Know a Taurean well and you will know that there is always a way to manipulate them. I've seen the most professional and worldly of Bulls lend money to family members who obviously have no intention of paying it back, but being a sucker for a show of waterworks, Taurus has handed over wads of cash.

When you become focused on what you are doing, you are capable of making an absolute fortune, but when you lose sight of your goals, then finances can start to dwindle. Earth signs such as you can and should be very good at saving money. You know that life is about planning, and this is something you do well. I must say that you don't mind spending your cash on nice food and drink, though, and this can sometimes be your downfall when your income dictates otherwise. It is well known in the world of astrology that Taureans love three things in life: food, sex and money, and sometimes all three mixed together! Socializing, however, doesn't cost you as much as people would think, as you prefer to see friends at home, so that you can hold court in the manner to which you have become accustomed.

You do, in your defence, think before you act. You're not as impulsive as Aries, for example, but you are far more emotional and here your problems begin. You want life to be beautiful and perfect, but what appears picture-perfect is not always what will make you happy in the end. Learn not to listen to what others tell you is the ideal. You are an individual with individual needs and you must work out what feels right to you. Wouldn't life be boring if we all craved the same job and the same-looking house and the same number of children? Dare to be different. By being youself you'll have people admiring you for the glow that's sure to adorn your very gorgeous face.

You don't mind putting your money into the family, and if you can invest in the younger generation, then so much the better. Family values mean the world to you, and even though you're known to have a mean streak towards those who are not part of your 'inner circle', for blood relations you would usually go to the ends of the earth.

You love to buy things for the home and your abode is often a place of great comfort. If there is a new and better sofa about or a bigger TV, then you have to have it. This is how you can start to spend more than you can really afford, though. Typical is the Taurean who complains about an item they bought last year because a new and better model has come out. You can start to sound quite immature to friends who have less than you, and it's not uncommon for you to lose friends over money. It would be hard for you to fall out with people over much else in fact, as you're such an amiable and welcoming character when things are going well for you.

The best way for you to keep hold of and improve your funds is to plough them into your property, as not only does this give you pleasure but you can see just how much you have to spend should you need it. Money is no good to you sitting in a bank. You like to be in control. You're also not averse to a pension fund, which the air elements would probably run a mile from. They don't have the patience to wait for things to mature, but you do.

It can take a long time for you to tell someone you have got into debt, as it's hard for you to admit. They say that the bigger you are, the harder you fall, but some very famous Taurean faces have overcome their debt problems. Think about how much tax and VAT you pay when you are earning a fortune, and think how much scarier it must feel when the bill could wipe you out because you've had a bad year. I've helped well-known faces out of trouble and I can help you too. Turn to the Rules on page 178 and realize that life can and will be fun again.

You'll be pleased to hear that there are some famous Taureans with money, including David Beckham, who is known for buying his wife expensive gifts. His homes have definitely seen a large amount of his income too, so much so in fact that his home in England used to be called Beckingham Palace. Then there's Jack Nicholson, who did a typically bullish thing by sinking his money into his own restaurant.

Gemini

Mercury is your ruling planet and governs travel and communication. You love excitement, and for you it is essential to keep up with the latest trends and fads. Your finances are eaten up by your social life. If friends have done something, then you want to do it too. There is nothing you wouldn't do for a true mate either, which can unfortunately include lending them money. More often than not it's harder to get back than you'd thought. When the mood and timing are right, you'll lend sums that many signs would consider unthinkable. Some Geminis may well have had one too many drinks, which made them feel like the Bank of England. Certain friends will swear the money was a gift. (I won't say which signs, for fear of ruining several close friendships in your life!)

You are lucky enough to be able to enjoy yourself anywhere and you can easily adapt to others' plans, even if it means giving away the tickets you have just splashed out on. Many of your sign actually spend a lot of money on books too, as you like exploring life. Trying out foreign shores, foods and fashion are other outlets for your spending. Did you know that a large percentage of Geminis either think about or actively attempt to live overseas during their lifetime? Your dual nature is always thinking that the grass is greener on the other side.

I'm afraid that you're not the best sign when it comes to handling money, but the good news is that as fast as you have lost your multi-million-pound fortune, you can make it again. Your gift for being able to talk your way into and out of anything is more valuable than any Swiss bank account.

You love to relax during the day and let your hair down at night, which doesn't really leave a lot of time for work, does it, Gemini? What your sign is good at is delegating your responsibilities. Due to your element of air, you keep abreast of the latest things and so are the first with the inside scoop on where money can be made.

I used to have a best friend who was a Gemini. She always gave the impression when we went out together that she was rolling in money. We would walk into a restaurant and the waiters and the owner would gather round and ask what they could do to improve her experience with them. She didn't have a penny; she was broke. Somehow, though, she had an air of class and riches. She led a really good life because people gave her free meals, free drinks, even free holidays and flights because they thought she was wealthy and successful. Her clothes may have looked designer, but she knew how to mix cheap with an average or expensive item (complimentary of course) to make her look like a millionaire. She has ended up with a millionaire who is madly in love with her and is rapidly spending every penny he has. I'm not worried, though, and I don't feel any need to warn him, as I know with her by his side he'll always be able to get a good meal or a nice bottle of wine on the house. How could he not with her charisma? It's like having a celebrity on your arm.

This is not to say that you should go out asking for free things, or building up debt. Be cleverer than that. Turn your charm into a multi-million-pound industry and make enough money so that you can relax and slow down a little. Think of how good it will feel to know you are in control of what happens and that you have made the riches that your sign has the potential to produce.

You don't mind a gamble with your money, but your sign is also prone to be nervy and tense, leading to problems when you back out of deals just as you have signed on the dotted line. Your intellectual and very eloquent way of attracting new faces into your life always saves the day, though. And you know what I love most about you, Gemini? Your sense of humour. You can laugh through any situation and charm your way into new ones.

The Rules, on page 178, will show you how to get rid of debt and get your dream business off the ground. Your sign is very good at communicating, so you can overcome your financial worries and turn them into gold.

Some famous Geminis with money include Noel Gallagher, whose ability to write great songs took him to a life of riches and brought him to the height of London society during his heyday. Then there's Mel B. of Spice Girls fame, who has proved that comebacks are possible. She's got the cheque to prove it and was, incidentally, born on the same day as Noel! Both of these examples came from no money to an abundance of it and you can do the same.

Remember to keep putting your money in the bank and you'll be able to indulge your dreams in times to come.

Cancer

Your ruling planet, the moon, can at times make you a little too cautious, but it can also push you to the other extreme: when there is a full moon, you will do what you want when you want, even if it means putting your money or that of your close ones on the line, and if there is a new moon, then you are great at thinking of successful new ways to replenish your funds. Write down the full moons and new moons in your diary. You know what they say, forewarned is forearmed!

As your sign is that of a nurturer, you will tend to put your children first in the financial-needs department. You won't mind spending your last penny on the best schooling for them, but you'll agonize over installing a new heating system in the house. You are, it has to be said, Cancer, a little mean when it comes to paying for the things that you need. If close ones want money from you, however, then you are a push-over, provided they have learnt that emotional blackmail is the way into your purse or wallet. You love to help the disadvantaged and I have met many Cancerians who have signed away a large portion of their wages to humanitarian causes.

When things get really bad, you tend to go into hiding, and you even hide from your own emotions, pretending that everything is all right when it obviously isn't. You can't bear to let down your loved ones, and you feel that anything that has gone wrong in your life is a personal reflection on those you care for. This is silly of course, for your loved ones will want nothing more than to help you. The more you shut them out, the less they will think you need their assistance.

Communication can be somewhat of an issue for you. Some clients of mine born under the sign of Cancer would rather divorce than let their partners discover that they have got into debt. This is crazy, firstly because it would probably cost more to get divorced than it would to get out of debt, and secondly because if your partner loves you, they will want to help with problems, not be shut out. When the mists of depression descend, you find it hard to realize this fact and have the craziest of notions.

You love charm, history and beauty, and would rather buy an antique book than a new one. Most of all, though, you love good company. You are quite picky with your friends and don't like everyone; you suffer from a lack of self-confidence, although from some of the lovely clothes you wear one would never guess this. Your nature is such that not only are you capable of enjoying yourself without any money, but others are willing to pay to be in your company.

You have a generous nature and a sense of fun, and won't think twice about buying tequila sunrises for the whole bar, until you see the size of your bill. You also love culture, and if you do go away on a holiday, then you will make sure it is somewhere a bit different.

No matter how much you owe, it is not too late to take action. Think positive and make a start today by promising that you will face your worries, not hide from them. I know from experience with your sign that the first step is talking and the rest comes naturally. Trust me, I've seen it first hand and I've also watched the relief when you are able to talk with others instead of fretting alone. Debt can't kill you, but worry can. The Rules (see page 178) will show you the light at the end of the tunnel. Life will get better with every minute that passes; in fact it will taste sweeter and better than ever, my friend.

Some famous Cancerians with money include Richard Branson, who is certainly no Virgin when it comes to making a fortune, and George Michael, who fell out with his record company and lost money in order to maintain control over his songwriting. This shows how emotional this sign can get about their art, and rightly so too. Actor Harrison Ford doesn't need to raid the bank thanks to the adventure films he's worked on. Ex-Beatle Ringo Starr no longer has to have a hard day's night with the money he's earned, and Cancerian Barbara Cartland wrote her way to a cool amount with her novels.

So remember it's never too late, no matter how far into debt you've got. This is the beginning of a brand-new you!

Leo

You are ruled by the sun and usually have a very happy disposition. You are popular in many different kind of circles and are great fun to be around. If you can't afford to go out, then you would never admit it. You would much rather tell others that you have a more important meeting or place to be. You love nice clothes and can make a cheap suit look designer. You are capable of earning millions just from the way you can charm the coldest of hearts. It is a talent you are sure to have learnt at a very young age and will continue to use your whole life.

Your problem with money is that you never do anything by halves, so if you book a nice holiday, you like to have all the trimmings. Don't think for a minute that the champagne that Leo is drinking was free, or that the outfit they are wearing was in the sale; they don't usually know the meaning of the word cheap, unless they are really strapped for cash. You are a clever sign with very alternative ideas. It is difficult to keep you down for long, although when things do go wrong, you feel that there is no way out and don't find it easy to admit that you need help.

You are a born leader and can turn a struggling business into an overnight success. With these leadership abilities, you can talk yourself out of most problems. You are quick at catching on to things and can give the impression you speak a language even if you only know a few choice words.

The real problem for you, lovely Leo, is that you are more often than not too busy having a great time to realize when you've overspent. You also forget to read the small print on things unless you've got enough money to pay someone else to read it for you. You claim you don't have the time to do things that other signs in the zodiac would deem imperative to ensure you don't get conned, or that you're not paying too high a price or interest rate. You are busy, but often you're doing things that should come much further down the line in your list of priorities.

You love luxury and will want to have the best of everything in your home, even if it means getting it on the never-never. The problem with this of course is that by the time you have eventually paid it off, you think it is out of date and require another credit card to keep up with the Joneses or the Smiths. Beware that you don't try to keep up with everyone all the time.

Make sure that you seek help as soon as you realize there are problems. It's often by sticking your head in the sand that you find problems become insurmountable. You *are* capable and you can get out of debt. Don't think just because things have got difficult that you can close your eyes and keep on spending blindly. You are no fool, so don't pretend to be. Read the Rules on page 178 and change things *now*.

The Rules will help you learn to keep making money and not losing it. Try putting some money away for a rainy day. You know you want a designer brolly, Leo, which means you need to start saving right now! Be able to hold your head up high with the power that you will now possess to be a money-maker. That twinkle in your eye will be brighter than ever before.

Remember, life should be about quality, not quantity. With your sunny disposition, you often like to buy things for the character they possess rather than just the price tag. There's no enjoyment in being in debt, but believe me when I tell you that there is immense enjoyment in opening up your bank statement and seeing that you are in the black.

Some famous Leos with money include Madonna, who has managed to turn herself into a multi-million-pound industry. It all began many years ago when she started selling the boyish clothes that she wore on her first album and she hasn't looked back since. Take a leaf out of the material girl's book and start to build on the things you know you're good at. She's never allowed herself to get bored, and when there was a chance she might, then she explored new directions. You can do the same.

Ever wondered about Geri Halliwell's constantly changing style? Well, she is also a Leo and has shown that she knows how to make money from her image. Love her or hate her, this is one woman who will be making money for many years to come.

Virgo

Ruled by Mercury, the planet of travel and communication, you will plough a large amount of your funds into experimenting and exploring life. Although this isn't what you'll really be doing of course, as you find it impossible *not* to plan. You know that by having an agenda you can get what you want.

I've even seen one client go so far as to have a potential girlfriend checked out by a private investigator. As far as he was concerned, this was simply a way of covering his back and not wasting money on unnecessary dates. The way that other people deal with money is very important indeed to you. In fact this could be a deciding factor in whether or not you stay with someone and will certainly be a bone of contention in any relationship. The only problem is, Virgo, you seem to set one rule for others and a completely different one for yourself. You don't mean to be unfair, it's just that you see a risk in everything you do and have to weigh up the pros and cons; it's all part of your lovely nature.

If your Virgo partner tells you that they have stumbled upon a little house for sale by accident and asks you to come and see it, then check their bag. You're sure to find the estate agent's details with mortgage calculations written on the side. They like to research both personal and professional decisions before they go ahead with them.

You are not against putting money into property, but many of your sign are not overly keen on spending on clothes. This is not normally your Achilles heel. If you have bought an item of clothing, or a pair of sunglasses, that cost more than you deem a fair amount, then you will make sure that everyone you meet knows just what you paid, even though you are likely to have got it cheaper elsewhere. You will know the true value and will stick to your story that you paid top whack. Some Virgos may even go so far as to leave the price tag on if they have paid full price. Believe me, I've seen it!

You can enjoy almost any lifestyle, though, and don't need lots of money in the bank to have a smile on your face. Just a small nest egg will do nicely for you, and you will probably pay your money in on the same day every week. Don't get me wrong – yours is not a sign that is boring, but you can be a little predictable.

You hate to be taken for a ride and so naive friends or potential lovers who take you out for dinner and then tell you that they've forgotten their wallet are more likely to end up in McDonald's than in the little Italian they had in mind. You plan carefully and like your instructions to be carried out to the letter. This is because you have tried and tested experiences very early on and actually know what does and doesn't work. In fact when your head is on straight, close ones should go with the flow and follow your lead, as you're sure to have the recipe for success in the palms of your hands.

The wonder of your sign is that you can surprise a loved one with amazing gifts when they least expect it. They had just better remember to tell others who bought the gift and how much it cost! You're not mean; you just attach value to things and want finery to be appreciated and acknowledged.

Life can and should be really good for you, but the worry that you put yourself through over money and the way you are so self-critical about past mistakes can make you ill. Who cares how much you spent on dinner? Well, you do, especially when you've had indigestion just thinking about the price of the desserts.

What other people find hard to fathom about you and money is how you're willing to pay a lot for certain items and yet won't spend a penny on what the rest of us see as essentials. You learn lessons the hard way, and your biggest fear is people finding out you've got bad credit, which in turn affects your health and nervous system and so the downward spiral can begin. But it doesn't have to and I can help you get on the straight and narrow. Follow the advice in the Rules on page 178 and make a fresh attempt to analyze the positive instead of the negative. Half of the battle in life is looking at things from the right perspective. This is the key to your success.

Not a sign to easily admit you have money problems, it takes a lot for you to lay your financial cards on the table, let alone take steps to get help. If you have a friend who is a Virgo, then don't even bother questioning them about their finances; they'd rather run naked around Buckingham Palace than admit their problems to you.

Famous Virgos with money include Wall Street stockbroker and financial whizz Peter Lynch, who made his fortune with his Virgo know-how, Stephen King, who wrote his way into riches and the top of the book charts, and Agatha Christie, who used detective work to make great finances for herself.

If you have financial worries, don't forget to read the Rules. No matter how much you think you've lost, you've got everything to gain by educating yourself and turning your problems into opportunities.

Libra

With Venus as your ruling planet, you can actually be something of a pushover with money, Libra. This means that if any of your close ones want to part you from your cash, then all they have to do is subject you to a bit of emotional blackmail. If a daughter says to her Libran mum or dad how happy it would make her to have that trendy and very expensive pair of shoes, well, she only has to squeeze out a tear and, hey presto, she'll be walking down the street wearing said shoes before the week is out! You love your family and would spend your last penny on them if it made them happy. You know when you are spending more than you can afford, though, as you usually turn a lovely shade of crimson.

You wear your heart on your sleeve, and unfortunately for you, credit cards seem like free cash when you are feeling emotionally vulnerable. The happier you are, the more careful you are, unless of course it comes down to someone putting on the old waterworks and then it's a different story. Emotional blackmail and emotions in general are your downfall. See life, love and money for what they are and you will be one step ahead of the game.

You don't mind letting your loved ones look after your money for you, which depending on what sign you live with can be either a help or a hindrance in your life. You like to look nice and so will pick the best clothes and materials, not always needing to fork out the top prices. Perfumes can cost you more than most signs, as you have to smell good and you use more than most of us. You take for ever to spend money, though, as you will stand there for a good hour or so thinking, Should I or shouldn't I splash out? It's enough to drive your family round the bend. You don't like to be forced to spend your money. You like to do your own thing and tend to expect others to follow you.

You are in love with the idea of love, and romantic places and faces and objets d'art can soon part you and your cash, or your credit card, or any form of finance you can get your hands on. A rich client of mine who was a Libran even bought a beautiful car because he thought it was a work of art in its design. He told me what a great buy it was, but I had to remind him that he didn't have a driver's licence. An independent soul who refused to have a driver, his car sat in his garage at home for him to admire for many years to come. Luckily he was a man who could afford to fritter the green stuff. Nevertheless beware of those shoes you think you want but will never wear, that dress that doesn't fit you now but might and that food that you won't be in this weekend to eat. I find it hard to tell you off because your heart is in the right place, but let's get your finances in the right place too and then you will see what true happiness is.

It's hard for you to admit when you are short of money. You'd far rather try to think of some colourful story about why you couldn't make a party or gathering, as you'd hate to turn up without the right gift, the right outfit and enough money to buy everyone a drink. Your personality is infectious and you love indulging in conversation. It is indeed your love of beautiful objects and people that often breaks the bank for you.

You are one of the worst signs at acknowledging you have money problems, preferring to hide from them and bury your bank statements in a drawer. This is silly of course because problems only escalate if you hide from them, and one of the key ways of getting out of debt is by communicating with your creditors. Your sign is good at communication when the pressure's off. Now all you have to do is learn to do it when the pressure is on, and I'm sure you can. Read the Rules on page 178 for advice on handling your money problems. This will tell you how you can avoid the pitfalls and make up for any mistakes that currently see you in the red. Your life is one of the easiest to turn round. Just try and you'll see.

Famous Librans with money include Sir Bob Geldof, who made his money from his TV production company and then went on to create Live Aid and make money for the Third World, a typical dream of someone of this sign, which he so admirably carried out. Actress Kate Winslet made a *Titanic* amount from her hard work and determination. Anita Roddick, another Libran humanitarian, founded the Body Shop which supported people in developing countries, and she also made a fortune.

Scorpio

Ruled by Mars and Pluto, you can surprise those closest to you by turning any disaster to your favour. Good job too, with the dramas that tend to unfold in your life, Scorpio!

When you save, you're very good, and when you spend, you're awful. Yours is a sign that is notorious for letting your obsession with making money take you over. If you spend, then it is usually a very large amount, and it is only by focusing on your goals and dreams that you are truly able to see that you have control over your long-term security.

You will do your best to support your close ones, and if you make enough, then you will not hesitate to buy a property for those you love. If things don't work out or a loved one does something to hurt you, then they should watch their back, as they could find the joint bank account drained before they know it. You are very quick indeed and you have learnt, usually the hard way, to put your head before your heart.

You are determined and forceful enough to prove that you can make and spend money with the best of them. You are ambitious and hard to stop once you have made up your mind what and who you want. If you say you are going to save up for the house of your dreams, then you will, whatever the odds against you. This determination more often than not pays off. However, you should learn not to let arguments force you to spend money you don't have. Don't order the most expensive drink just to prove to an ex that you are better off without them, and don't make promises you can't deliver to family or you'll let yourself down as well as them. Over-emotional at times, you can over-analyze and put the cart before the horse. Remember what our grandparents used to say: 'Don't throw the baby out with the bathwater!'

I know you can make a fortune if you want to, but I also know you are the kind of sign who doesn't need money to make them happy. You need security, but you want love, security and excitement all at the same time. Not an easy sign to please, but one who will love their close ones until the end of time. As long as they don't betray you, that is!

You can be very secretive with finances in times of trouble, and you do a very good job of hiding credit-card statements from your partner. I even had a friend who was screaming in labour not because of the pain of childbirth, but because she wanted to make sure another friend would open the post before her husband, just in case her credit-card statement arrived before she got home. What an interesting form of pain relief!

You may want to hide your statements when they're in the red, but you will still insist on seeing every single one of your partner's outgoings. This is partly because you are suspicious by nature, but you are also just plain nosy! If you do well, then you will reach the top of your financial game, but you have to make sure you are in a job you love.

Your skill at acting can talk you into many a bank manager's good books, but just remember one of the lessons you will learn when you read the Rules on page 178, is that you're doing them a favour, and not the other way round, Scorpio!

Some famous Scorpios with money include Demi Moore, who at one time was listed as one of the highest-earning females in Hollywood, and actor Leonardo Di Caprio, who certainly knows how to throw himself into a role, so much so that it was reported he got a cut of the earnings from blockbuster *Titanic*, certainly a water sign who knew a winner when he saw one. Rolling Stone Bill Wyman made his fortune with his passion for music and has not stopped making money, and neither has Sir Tim Rice.

Sagittarius

Being ruled by Jupiter, the planet of self-expansion, you are a sign who should know how to invest money and how to get other people to help you. Your sign tends to go from strength to strength, and even if you lose every penny, you are able to rebuild your fortune from almost nothing. Many people watch and study those born under Sagittarius to try to discover just what the secret is to your magic with money. What a lot of people don't realize is that you will borrow as much as you are worth, which is where this feeling of moving two steps forward and one back can come from. Sports hold a fascination for you and you are not averse to the odd gamble. It's often more business debt than personal that Sagittarians build up.

You are a little too opinionated about other people's

incomings and outgoings, however, which can be really annoying. You see, you may be allowed to buy an expensive item, but as soon as others do you will label them frivolous and careless with their cash, unless of course you advised them to splash out in the first place.

I think that it is your optimism in life that really enables you to be such a success. I don't know many signs who are as capable as you are, Sagittarius, of seeing good in every situation, but you have this brilliant way of being able to take charge and come up with ideas just when the rest of us have given up.

Your sense of humour and fun makes you an ideal candidate to head a business and make a fortune. You are also a natural, albeit harmless flirt who won't hesitate to say the right thing to the right face.

You do well heading a team, and spending as one too: you don't enjoy spending your money as much when you are on your own. You are the kind of person who can go out for a washing machine and come back with a car, so keep your eye on your credit limit or you'll end up with a short, sharp shock when the statement lands on your mat. Overspending is appealing to you because you enjoy the rush and the buzz that goes with risk-taking.

So what if you're reading this and you don't feel that you are this Sagittarian at all? Well, that means, my friend, that we have to help make you what you're meant to be. You see, the downside of your sign is that when others don't believe in you, you can think of giving up, but it's when you're at your lowest that you are most capable of turning things to your advantage. You may not admit it out loud but others' opinions of you matter. What good is a million pounds if those around you don't think you're absolutely marvellous for being able to earn it? One of the first lottery winners that I read about turned out to be a Sagittarian and I just knew that this was a recipe for disaster. How could this poor man feel that he had the right to live in a grand house when he hadn't worked for the money himself? OK, I know you're thinking that you could, but you can't! I know this because my Sagittarian clients who have been given their parents' money have spent it quicker than Imelda Marcos in a new shoe shop! You need to feel you earned what people are admiring.

Others must not lack faith in you; they must support you in your hour of need. If close ones are true to you, then you will help them out in return.

Although optimistic in general, when you get into debt you can probably be the most depressed sign in the zodiac, which is why if you're hiding problems with money, I want you to follow the Rules on page 178 and I will help you turn your life round.

Some famous Sagittarians with money include Frank Sinatra, who did the Archer trick of taking something a small number of people were into and making it popular worldwide, as did Sagittarian Mike Stock of Stock, Aitken & Waterman fame, who had the ability to take a nobody and turn them into a somebody overnight. You may mock, but Kylie was originally in their stable – need I say more! Actress Teri Hatcher is no longer desperate for cash since she made it big playing a housewife on our screens for amounts that will have her sleeping like a baby for many years to come. Then there's director and producer, not to mention three-time Academy Award-winner, Steven Spielberg. Now if these people aren't inspiration enough to make it big, then I don't know who is.

Capricorn

Your ruling planet Saturn places more than a few restrictions on your life, but you'll be pleased to hear that you do manage to keep your funds slowly but surely coming in. Well, usually, anyway.

Even though you are slow to get your wallet or purse out, I must say that you always get there in the end, my friend. You don't mean to be tight, but you don't like spending your money unnecessarily. Like your fellow earth signs of Taurus and Virgo, you would prefer to put your money into your home rather than a bank. You like to be sitting on your funds.

You do have a tendency to miss the big deals due to the amount of time it can take you to make up your mind. You like to have stimulating company around you, but you're not always willing to travel far to get it. You have a natural affinity with the good things in life, which can mean the expensive things, but you have the wonderful talent of being able to tighten your belt in some areas to make allowances for the others. You think long term, but you give the impression you live for the moment.

You want to make sure your family are well provided for and will go out of your way to ensure their happiness, even at the cost of sacrificing your own. What Capricorn doesn't always do, though, is check that what they're working towards for their family is what their family really want. Communication is essential but sometimes lacking. This can be rather off-putting for your loved ones when they ask you for money for essentials and you explain to them that the latest car is more important to the children's education and will help them get to school on time and in comfort. Fortunately for you, your way with words means you can make those around you believe anything. Don't be too tight towards your close ones, though; they wouldn't be with you if they didn't love you.

Romance can make you spend more than you intend because when you are in love you tend to take on some of the characteristics of the one you admire. As long as you don't end up signing your whole life away, then this is fine, but Capricorns can lose track of reality when the old love bug bites. Some would say in fact that dear old Capricorn tries too hard and loved ones can be in for a shock when normality is restored. There can often be a confrontation when Capricorn has to placate close ones and confirm that they are still happy.

You must try to stop looking at money as if the glass is half empty or you will have a heart attack from the stress of buying even just a loaf of bread. Approach life and money head on and you will be fine. I want you to read the Rules on page 178 for advice on making sure you are always in the black and never in the red. You have the ability to have a fun life and there is no reason for financial worries to hold you back – not when your down-to-earth nature gives you the skills to face your debtors.

Some famous Capricorns with money include Jim Carrey, whose very Capricorn sense of humour has made him his millions, and supermodel Kate Moss, whose talent for looking good has seen her endorse her own clothing line as well as her own perfume. Carol Vorderman has a typical Capricorn talent for numbers and it's taken her straight to the bank, and Muhammad Ali boxed his way to a fortune, thanks to the earth signs' ability to use their body as well as their brain.

Aquarius

With Saturn as your ruling planet and Uranus as your co-ruler, you are pulled in two directions. You can talk yourself in and out of a fortune. You will have learnt you can do this from a very early age, but somehow can't remember how to make it tip in the right direction.

Try not to surround yourself with negative influences, as you tend to pick up and imitate those who are close to you. You can be easily influenced to be reckless with money by friends. Resist this and leave them to their own devices. You have a successful life to plan! You live for the future and so if there is a new gadget or a piece of equipment on the market, then you can bet that you will spend your money on it. Not really a person to wait for the cash to come to you, you have been known to take out credit too readily. You may say you are keeping it for a rainy day, but what others would call drizzle or simply overcast, you could claim to be a torrential downpour if a new gadget is in your sights.

You are a friendly character who will not mind buying friends a drink even if you are down to your last fiver. You are honest and loyal too, so if you can't afford something, it is not in your nature to play games; you like to play life a little straighter than most. You are versatile, fun-loving and very particular. You won't hesitate to complain if the service is bad in a restaurant, whether it's McDonald's or the Ritz. You love company and will pay more than most to be included in the events that are taking place. If money allows, you wouldn't even mind hiring a plane to take you to a glamorous party, wearing the latest designer must-have clothes.

Try to keep away from long-term service contracts. You tend not to read the fine print and more often than not sign blind, believing that adverts won't lead you too far from the straight and narrow. You learn pretty quickly and expensively that credit-card companies and store cards are not in fact your best friends, although that doesn't stop you forgetting the lesson when tempted again.

You are unpredictable with your finances and should learn to invest more. You're more likely to splash out on an impulsive holiday deal than put down a deposit on a house. The secret is to make you think that you are getting the best deal and to take money from you when the time is right. If close ones can do this, then they may just see you both living in splendour. It is not unknown for you to cut up credit cards as soon as you get them, for you know you can't trust yourself. Loved ones can never fully relax, though, as they can never be too sure you're not planning the next big splurge.

You have a heart of gold, but for now your partner should not allow you to control the money and bills. You can learn, though, and I'm going to teach you, so read the Rules on page 178 and let's make you some money.

Famous Aquarians with money include Lisa Marie Presley, the daughter of Elvis, who has obviously landed on her feet with finances and has continued to make money of her own by endorsing her father's legacy. Another successful Aquarius is Robbie Williams, whose cheeky nature is typical of his sign and who admits to spending his fortune first time round on the latest televisions and stereos, as well as on other things we shan't mention. Let's just hope he can hang on to it this time! Then there's John Travolta, who likes to spend his fortune on planes, which is typical of his sign and their thrill-seeking nature. Luckily for John, his career can fund this, but the rest of you shouldn't go looking at helicopters and the like just yet!

Pisces

With Jupiter as your ruling planet and Neptune as your co-ruler, it's no wonder you seem like a crazy person to the rest of the signs. Drifting in and out of your dream world, making a fortune and then losing it, only to make it again, you would no doubt throw a champagne party while filing for bankruptcy!

Being one of the most dramatic signs in the zodiac, you either have loads of money or not a bean. There really is no in between for you, is there, Pisces? When you have a lot of money, you will not hesitate to spend it on your nearest and dearest, but you can't possibly work out why it is that they won't do the same for you. In fact you think your loved ones are downright mean if they don't give you what you want, but then that's all part of your very dramatic nature.

Your imagination has a tendency to work overtime and so the things that you see as a necessity can raise eyebrows among the rest of us. You like to run away from life from time to time and this can mean taking holidays just when funds are at their lowest, but you really don't care – if you need to run, you need to run, and that is what you will do.

You are spontaneous, and when you feel like doing something, it is important that you are able to do so without interference from others. In fact you may even have broken up a relationship in the past due to the fact that your ex asked too many questions about your finances. Your need to keep an air of mystery requires you to be in charge. Your impatient nature causes you to get bored quickly and so the new designer wardrobe that you bought can often end up being given to the new friend you've just made. They won't complain, though; in fact they're sure to love it.

You love spending money, preferably other people's, and have a natural flair for arranging little surprises, which don't always go down well with those they were planned for. The diamond ring may look lovely on your loved one's hand, but they would much rather you had paid the mortgage!

Your impulsiveness and disregard for money often lead you into hot water, particularly when on holiday. You throw caution to the wind, but you always seem to enjoy yourself.

You love wining and dining and sampling exotic dishes. Gambling and competitive sports also consume a lot of your cash. You don't really like to get involved in anything too energetic, though; you enjoy the anticipation of a new experience far more than the achievement; by then you are bored and ready to move on to something new and probably more expensive.

I don't actually know a Piscean who hasn't at some point got themselves into debt. In fact if there is one out there reading this book, then please contact me – you'll change history. The amazing thing is that you *always* get out of situations by the skin of your teeth and often just in the nick of time. It really is as if you have a guardian angel on your shoulder making sure that your life is blessed.

If your finances seem bad, don't get down – I know you can, but there is never ever a reason to give up. No matter how bad things have got, you are a fantastic sign to be, with great potential. This is why you are going to read the Rules on page 178 for advice on how you can change your life, right now, for the better. You know you love excitement – I can assure you those trips you like to make are far more of a buzz when you're not expecting a knock on the door from a creditor when you get home.

Some famous Pisceans who have (or had) money are jailed Barings dealer Nick Leeson, who took the Piscean tendency to use other people's money more than a little too far, Jilly Cooper, the author whose vivid imagination earned her a fortune, and Beatle George Harrison, who showed his talent to make money with the Fab Four. Not a lot of people know that Michael Caine is a Pisces, but they know he made his mark in the acting industry.

The Rules

Here are the golden rules that will change your life *right now*. All you have to do is be honest with yourself and the true facts and figures and you can solve your problems, no matter how complex they may seem. It's a bit like homework, really, and it will help you digest the facts more easily and thoroughly if you put each point on a separate piece of paper so that you can tackle them one by one. Don't tell me that you haven't got time. I don't care where you are or what you're doing. Even if it means writing the first one on a piece of toilet paper, it's going to change your life!

1. Communication
Write a list of your debts. You cannot solve your problems if you are not totally honest with yourself about the amount you owe. Don't hide from yourself. Bringing things out into the open may sound scary, but you're sure to feel better once you've admitted what is going on.

Talk to your creditors. I know it's all too easy to hide from their phone calls. You believe that if you don't answer the phone, your problems might go away. This is not true, and if you ignore the people requesting their money back, they will think you don't want to solve the problem. I've talked to such creditors and every single one of them has said that if someone who owes money is willing to talk, then they are always willing to find a solution. Pick up the phone and make contact; they're willing to negotiate, no matter how little you can afford to pay back. Not facing up to your problem can cause so much stress, which will catapult you into a downward spiral. By talking you will find a resolution, and if you find you can't talk to them because you are too scared, I have a list of people who are willing to speak on your behalf. Don't ignore them and don't hide. Facing our fears head on will make us stronger.

You are not the first and will certainly not be the last person to get into debt, but you can get out of it by tackling your fears. If you don't, you are only putting off the inevitable and allowing things to get more out of control when you could be paying back a small amount every month and working your way towards a clean credit sheet.

2. Spreadsheet

Write down honestly what you earn and what you spend. It's only by knowing these numbers that you can work out what you can afford to pay back. There are free companies out there who are willing to help you and act as mediator. You don't have to wait until your creditors come knocking at your door asking for money or waving court orders. Even if you are in this situation, there will still be a way forward.

No one can help you if you can't give figures, so draw up a list now. Review the figures on a monthly basis to keep up with any changes that may take place to both your earnings and your spending.

3. Avoid loan sharks, debt-consolidation and debt-management companies

Instead turn to the free help available, companies who won't want more of your money. With companies such as Payplan, who will review the figures that you owe, listen to what you tell them you can afford, talk to your creditors for you, arrange a payment plan and review it until it's paid, then how can you say you can't cope?

Debt consolidation is a bad thing because in most cases it doesn't solve the problem. If the person's difficulty is that they don't have sufficient funds to pay their debts, they will end up taking out interest to pay interest. Fee-charging debt management companies are different from Payplan because they charge the person in debt. With Payplan every penny you pay goes towards reducing your debt. Payplan is free because it is funded by voluntary contributions from the credit industry, and whether or not a particular creditor gives them financial support, they will still help with all of your debt.

Payplan
Offers debt-management services for free. They will help you to set up a manageable repayment plan and review your affairs as time goes on. They won't take away their support until your debts are cleared.

www.payplan.com
0800 917 7823

Consumer Credit Counselling Service
This is a registered UK charity that gives free, impartial help. They will contact your creditors for you, can help freeze interest, stop penalties and get you more time to pay at reduced rates.

www.cccs.co.uk
0800 138 1111

National Debtline
This is a free, confidential helpline serving people in England, Scotland and Wales. They give advice over the phone and can help to set up a free debt-management plan for you.

www.nationaldebtline.co.uk
0808 808 4000

Citizens Advice Bureau (CAB)

Free help is on hand to sort out money issues and legal problems.

www.citizensadvice.org.uk

Equifax

Find out your credit rating through Equifax. This is essential if you have had bad credit and want to know if this is a good time for you to apply for a mortgage or a new bank account. Each time you apply for credit it appears on your record, so you don't want to be applying dozens of times only to be declined. Find out if you have a clean sheet, and if not, when you will have.

EquifaxCredit File Advice Centre
PO Box 1140
Bradford BD1 5US
www.equifax.co.uk

Advicenow

If you are scared that you don't know your legal rights, Advicenow can offer up-to-date advice on legal issues.

www.advicenow.org.uk

The Samaritans

And last but never least, if you just need to talk to someone about what you are going through, the Samaritans offers twenty-four-hour help if you are feeling you can't cope and you need some emotional support.

www.samaritans.org.uk
08457 90 90 90

4. Stop paying the minimum repayment on your credit card

Remember that credit-card companies and lenders are not doing you a favour; you are doing them one! It is a common myth to think that if you stop using your card and keep making the minimum payment every month, you will pay off your debt. Credit-card companies want you to pay off the minimum amount so you pay the highest interest charges. Start paying as much as you can afford until it is cleared. Make sure that if it is a loan, there's not a penalty for early repayment.

If possible, switch to a cheaper credit card and you may be able to get 0 per cent interest balance-transfer offers. Cut up the old card if you do this or there is no point, and avoid using a credit card altogether if you can. Once you have worked out your budget, you will know how much cash you have to spend. This is the way to start getting in the black. You must stop spending money you don't have, and in time you'll learn the pleasure of spending money you do have. Also remember to try and pay off the cards with the highest interest rate first, rather than thinking of what items you bought with the card. It's all too easy to pay off the card with the highest debt first – make the card that charges most interest your priority.

5. Move your mortgage if you are on a lender's standard variable rate and change energy supplier

Deals change and it's imperative you keep up with the times. This is where the free help on offer comes in handy again. Too many of us become lazy with our mortgages, but if you tell your mortgage lender what rate you can get elsewhere, they're sure to take steps to avoid losing you. Check penalty fees on your mortgage if you redeem it early. Regular reviews are essential.

uSwitch (www.uswitch.com) is a free comparison service

with impartial advice on energy suppliers. Make sure you're with the company that offers the best rate.

6. Involve loved ones

Talk to those close to you; don't ignore them. They're unlikely to abandon you due to your debt problems, but they will if you shut them out of your life. Once you have called the advice lines, at least you will have some solutions to tell your loved ones. They may just pleasantly surprise you with their support and understanding. After all, a problem shared is a problem halved, as I've often seen with clients and their families. You will feel like a weight has been lifted from your shoulders.

7. Avoid store cards

They may seem like a great opportunity with exclusive offers, and they may seem like an easy way of getting your favourite luxuries and fashionable gadgets and clothes, but they can carry an interest rate in excess of 29 per cent. Don't think that the smiling face at the till has your best interests at heart when they ask if you would be interested in a card. It's more than likely they're on commission. Just say 'no'. This is becoming one of the quickest ways for people to get into debt. Plastic doesn't seem like money, and shop staff can feel like your new best friends, but they're running a business. If you save up for the items you want and then go back and get them, you will feel proud of yourself.

8. Get used to using cash

Why take out a load of cards in case of an emergency? What kind of emergency could possibly require you to have to use a credit card there and then? Any holidays or purchases can wait a few hours while you calm down and decide if they are a necessity or an impulse-buy.

9. Stop hiding from your bank statements

Many mistakes happen in banking (especially when Mercury is in retrograde!). Fees are added incorrectly and most banks are only too happy to pay these back. You can also negotiate for certain charges to be deducted if you feel they are unfair. Too many of us still believe that banks are doing us a favour. They're not. It's a business, remember, and they make money out of us.

Don't be scared of your bank statements; keep them somewhere handy and regularly read and review them. It's the only way you can work out a realistic budget. I hope that you will get used to using cash and still write down your budget, but in the beginning you're going to need to turn to your statements to identify the leakages in your finances. Remember that credit isn't cash. Keep your budget under review and you will find a manageable solution. The companies that can help can only do so if you give them true figures of what you can afford. You don't want to jump out of the frying pan and into the fire by making promises you can't keep.

10. Keep your priorities in order

Life is for living and that means learning. Don't be embarrassed by your debts. Credit is pushed on us these days and it's often hard to refuse the very lucrative offers of more glamorous lifestyles or quick-fix solutions. Now you have woken up to the business that is giving credit, you have the power to win the game and to get back in the black. Honesty, courage and determination will help make your life more enjoyable and rewarding than ever before.

Remember, live life, enjoy it, be positive and disregard the negative. Those who have made a success out of life have persevered. Try and try again.

Chapter 9

CAREER

Many top politicians and world leaders have long realized the value of astrology. Winston Churchill discovered that Hitler had a team of astrologers working out prime times for him to invade. What did Churchill do? He hired his own astrologer, Louis de Wohl, to work out Hitler's chart. He discovered that Hitler would always try to invade on the seventh day, which he thought brought him luck. Not so, though, for Churchill was prepared. I'm not saying it won the war, but it certainly proved a case of star wars!

Ronald Reagan used an astrologer from San Francisco called Joan Quigley to clear every major move and decision he made during his time at the White House. According to former White House aide Donald Regan, Quigley drew up horoscopes to make certain that the planets were in favourable alignment for the president's enterprises, and on days when Mercury was in retrograde Reagan put a big cross in his diary and avoided travelling. Reagan also admitted reading horoscope columns and was a fan of, well-known astrologer Carroll Righter and his stars led him right to Washington – can't be bad! He was even introduced to his wife Nancy by an astrologer. You too can use the stars to aid your career.

Are you in the right job for your star sign? Maybe you've been selling clothes when you should have been selling shares. When we are young, it's not easy to know what is the right profession for us. We go through school being given tasters of different subjects and are then expected to decide what we want to spend the next forty years doing. It's never too late to change, though. We often spend more time at work than at home, so read on to find out where your true talents lie. My advice could even see some of you handing in your notice today, or pushing the boss aside for the position that you realize was destined to be yours.

Aries

Fortunately for you, people love you and you usually love people (or are very good at pretending to!). This is a great asset for you as you can make total strangers feel as if they have a bond within five minutes of meeting you. When you are in charge of people, you tend to take a personal interest in their well-being, going out of your way to make sure that they get your full help and support.

One of the biggest mistakes you are prone to making is having *too* many friends at work. You can't be a best friend one minute and then be reprimanding someone the next. All too often you try to play both sides and it can create difficulties in the workplace.

Your sense of humour is verging on the naughty and you may have been accused in the past of showing an unprofessional side. It is hard for you always to act like the ultimate professional as you have a cheeky glint in your eye and often come out with the wrong thing at the wrong time. Overall, though, your dry wit and sense of humour are likely to go down well with colleagues, and you won't be against taking the blame for something that was not your fault in order to help someone else save face.

As a boss you are an employee's dream as you will hand out a salary advance with great ease (as long as the money is not yours, that is), but you will expect anyone you employ to put their heart and soul into your business. You can take time off, but your workers have to keep the ship afloat for you. It is one rule for you and another for those you employ, but you do it with such charm and grace that somehow you manage to get away with it.

If you don't like someone, you can't do business with them, and you would rather go without and let your finances and career suffer than tolerate someone you deem to be a fool. This is why your sign can never work for someone you don't like. It would show and you'd end up giving the game away before your first day on the job was over. You are perfect in social jobs. You know how to make people feel at ease and can create a great atmosphere. You carry a joke well while still getting the job done and could, when the mood beset you, sell ice to the Eskimos.

Always full of great ideas, it would not be going too far to suggest that you would make a great inventor or innovator. You certainly have the ideas; the problem is whether you'd talk about them so much that someone else would patent them before you. Less talking, more doing is the best advice for you. If not, you could end up making a lot of money for other people. You see, dear Aries, the truth of the matter is that you really could do any job you put your mind to. You just seem to spend too much time planning; you should trust in your instincts and jump instead of just standing on the edge. Some of the richest Rams in history have made their money this way.

It is also not unusual to see lecturers born under the sign of Aries. After all, you could talk the hind leg off a donkey! A friend of mine once said they were an airline pilot when asked what job they did, when the truth was they just had a very strong interest in flying.

Motor mechanic is another good job for your sign, as you

are naturally mechanically minded, but by no means down at the local garage. It's Formula One all the way or nothing for you. You are far cleverer than you let on. You prefer to let people judge you and then you quietly set out to prove to them how talented you are. You are able to see through flattery and false praise and you know exactly who your real allies in business are. This is not to say that you won't be nice to those you know are waiting to watch you fall. In fact you believe firmly in the old adage: keep your friends close and your enemies closer.

When you make a mistake at work, you can guarantee it will be something silly. Often you are too busy looking at the bigger picture to take care of the finer details, which is why you need a second in command so someone else can finish what you've started.

You play every game in work to win. With your ability to understand and manipulate a situation with complete professionalism when the mood takes you, you're a force to be reckoned with. You have a combustible personality and can be an explosive employee. You are unintentionally insensitive from time to time.

Public-service jobs are popular with your sign, such as teaching, the armed forces, medicine and anything that can offer up an adventure or new challenge. You need a career that is not a nine-to-five; in fact the very thought bores you rigid. If you could, you would work hard when the mood takes you and party when your job is done, but unfortunately that's not always the way work pans out. It is more usual for your sign to find their perfect career after discovering what *doesn't* work. You realize slowly but surely that you have a natural ability as a leader and it can take five years or more to accept this fact and act on it.

The truth is, you can be the biggest asset or the biggest

liability for an employer, but you have to have your heart in what you do and this is the key to your success, my friend.

The best career for this sign would be anything that involves fast-moving action. A sports commentator or presenter would be great for them, or a lecturer, but the best has to be an inventor with the original ideas this sign comes up with.

Ideal careers for an Aries: entrepreneur, lecturer, property developer, teacher, inventor or sales manager.

Taurus

Well, seeing as we know that the three favourite things in a Taurean's life are food, sex and money, your career choices are interesting! You can bet that the owner of your favourite restaurant is likely to be a Bull, and it is more common than not that a Taurean will have a brush with the food trade or think about it at some point in their lifetime.

Seeing as you also love money, it's not unusual for younger Taureans to go into banking or dealing with money and cash registers in their late teens. When you feel confident in your surroundings, then you attract both luck and opportunity. However, if you have to go away to do business or feel that you are out of your depth or dealing with people who speak a different language, then you become easily unnerved and edgy. This is why some of the most successful meetings for you will be done over the phone rather than in someone else's office. It is also why a large percentage of Taureans choose at some point to run a business from home.

Taurean bosses can be like a best friend to their employees one day and a tyrant the next. Your mood can change in seconds, which makes you hard to work for and best kept at arm's length when there is a deadline to meet. You want respect; in fact you demand it. You want things done your way, or the highway, and you're not afraid of making enemies if it helps to get the job done. You may bark orders at people, but you'd seldom get physical. People often say that your bark is worse than your bite, although I'm sure you beg to differ. Work is important to you because it is the way you get your money, which is also important and which turns your dreams into a reality. If people mess with your dreams, they mess with you. You will, however, always offer an ear for people's troubles and it is this glimpse of humanity that earns you respect and loyalty. You are good at keeping hold of the reins and not losing control, unlike some of the more impulsive signs of the zodiac.

You are ambitious and will aim high in life, and if you have a successful team around you, then you will get there too. Your staff, if you have them, will love you one day and hate you the next and yet they'll still turn up for work because they'll know they're on a winning team.

As an employee, you are loyal, reliable and a great team player. You won't start on something until you are fully prepared and no one can rush you to start before you are ready. Your system of organized chaos works so those above you should not knock a plan of yours because you have probably already applied it to numerous things throughout your life. Your temper needs reining in, but your artistic streak needs encouraging further.

Your creativity and love of beautiful things could well take you into the world of fashion. You are notoriously strong-willed, so it's vital that you are given firm rules from the start in any new business partnership. You are practical and grounded and this will ensure that you are an asset to any company or project.

Singing and dancing appeal to some Bulls, as you're good with your voice and more often than not light on your feet.

Singers Bono and Joe Cocker are typical Taureans. You can't deny that Taurean footballer David Beckham is light on his feet, although we'd have to ask his Aries wife, Victoria, if his singing in the shower is up to scratch.

Ideal careers for a Taurean: clothing designer, chef or restaurant owner, banker, artist, builder or advertising director.

Gemini

You have your own way of going about a job, but it works, Gemini. Notorious in the media industry, it is guaranteed you will have a brush with someone famous in your lifetime. You attract attention and look like you should be someone even if you're not.

Your tendency to use people from time to time can get you a bit of a reputation. Someone who is your best friend in business one day can turn out to be your arch enemy the following week. Your reputation often precedes you and it's no surprise. You have made your way up the career ladder in a way that probably sounds a bit like a fairy tale. There will have been a social opportunity here, an accidental meeting there, and before you knew it the big boss was asking if they could personally groom you to take over their position.

You can draw a crowd with ease, which makes you perfect at selling people things that they don't really need. If you can work on commission, then all the better as you have a competitive edge and are willing to work hard to get what you want.

You are in your element in a busy office, surrounded by people and bustle. Variety really is the spice of life for you, and with a restless and quick mind you like to move on rapidly from one project to the next. Your biggest skill, which I'm sure you know by now, is communication. You would excel in any job in which you have to act as a go-between or convey an idea to an unwilling ear. You are also brilliant at using social occasions to better your career and it's not unusual for you to come away from a wedding or a gathering with several business cards in your hand and a promise or two of a deal or new job. You see, socializing is a vital part of any work to you. It's just as important in fact as the job. There has to be an element of fun to your career, as you more often than not take your work home with you and so you have to feel passionate about it.

People are what interest you, although sometimes you can be curious to a fault. Long social lunches at work suit you right down to the ground. Just beware that your gossiping doesn't become a problem. There is a fine line between intrigue and stirring trouble. You thrive as an active team member and don't always have to be the leader. You know you are an individual in your own right and don't feel the need to fight for the spotlight.

You do need constant pressure or you can become complacent about what you are doing. Jobs with a tight deadline work well for you, or any work linked to sweet-talking your way out of a jam. You need to be able to talk as often and as freely as you want. If you can't have your say, you would rather walk out; you don't see the point in letting your best assets go to waste. Life is for living as far as you're concerned. In fact if you could write a gossip column, you'd make a fortune!

You naturally take charge, though can also be accused of delegating but not actually doing. Once you become aware of this fact, you quickly learn the skill of looking like you're working, but be careful it doesn't take you too long to notice those who may have already guessed your game.

Also bear in mind that working with family or loved ones doesn't work for you, Gemini. You need to have compartments in your life and to pretend otherwise could prove disastrous.

Ideal careers for a Gemini: translator, PR officer, any job in the media or gigolo!

Cancer

Due to your low-key approach to work, you can give the impression that you're not overly ambitious. How wrong that would be, though, Cancer. You are in fact one of the most diligent signs in the zodiac, and with a friendly and approachable nature, you're a joy to work with.

If you become a boss, however, you can get far too wrapped up in the workings of the job to pay your employees on time, and you have to remember to delegate and not try to do everything on your own. Prone both to dishing out and falling for emotional blackmail, you must also be careful that you don't end up being taken in by sorry sob stories or giving away things for free, including your valuable time. It's all very well doing overtime, but if your boss is making a mint out of it, then you need to make sure you get a cut. You don't like to be ruled but often are, due to the fact that some of the stronger signs work out how to manipulate you.

Your home life will always have to come before work, but that doesn't mean that it isn't affected by your job. You take your work home with you and your home life into work, which is probably your biggest disadvantage. You are hardworking and are not afraid of giving up your spare time in order to work your way into the chosen profession you desire. You are sympathetic, tolerant and kind. You like to help people who you see struggling in business, rather than seeing their problems as an opportunity to engineer their downfall. You regard people that you have worked with for a long time as extended members of your family, but this can cause problems as often as it helps you.

It is important for you to care about your job, and to have a career that doesn't ignite a passion in you will seem as bad as a prison sentence. Your work has to be something you would do for free and getting paid for it is just a perk of the job. Life is too important for you to spend it doing something that merely pays the bills.

A BlackBerry is perfect for your sign, as you can pretend you're working and checking your emails when you're not. I'm not suggesting for a moment that you're lazy, Cancer, anything but. You do, however, have to do things your way. Look at Cancerian entrepreneur Richard Branson and you'll see a recipe for great success. Beware of drinking on the job at any social meetings, though: you can't drink much alcohol and probably shouldn't. It lets out a demon who crosses the line.

You are artistic and know the best words to use when the time is right. You are also brilliantly cautious when it comes to business dealings. You like to protect yourself and those around you with a non-confrontational approach that makes you the perfect candidate for sensitive negotiations. If a customer isn't satisfied, they will be by the time they've talked to you. You are the voice of reason.

Your love of family and nurturing makes you ideal for a career in a caring profession or in teaching. Any job you do has to be useful to society and allow you to come into contact with the public on a day-to-day basis. You would probably be happiest running your own small business, as this would give you a certain sense of autonomy and lots of contact with different people without having to be told when and how to deal with customers by a superior. Your most valuable asset is probably your memory; you have the ability to absorb facts and figures with great ease. Given your love of history, a job at a museum would be ideal. Wherever you work, your office is sure to be homely, with comfortable chairs and a picture of a loved one.

Ideal careers for a Cancerian: lecturer, doctor, nutritionist, historian, manager, publisher or retailer.

Leo

Proud, energetic and confident, it is not unusual for those of your sign to be able to speak more than one language. You look at life as a challenge and embrace every hurdle as an adventure and an opportunity to improve your skills. You can give the impression you are the boss just by your superior air. Unfortunately for you, your sign tends to attract a lot of jealousy and competition in business. You can make those around you feel inferior and a wise Lion quickly learns to go out of their way to put others at ease whenever possible. You can succeed in life through sheer arrogance and charm, two traits that you possess in abundance.

Usually one of the youngest signs to apply for their first job, you realize early on the importance of getting out there and making your professional mark on the world. You are a team leader who is not afraid to take risks once in a while or to put your own reputation on the line.

You have a positive attitude to work that is just plain infectious, and for this reason you end up being a role model for many. It is not unusual for a Leo to have a younger person who follows them around, hanging on their every word, while bringing them tea and hoping for a few crumbs of wisdom to help them on their way. Look at the way Leo Madonna turns her legion of dancers into family members when she goes on tour. They even call her 'mama' and emulate her every move, knowing she holds the key to a winning career path. Just take care that you don't fall into a state of complacency, otherwise everything you have worked for could be taken from you.

Ideally, Leo, you need a prestigious job. You cope well under stress and tight deadlines. You are not afraid of staying up all night in order to tie up an important project. Networking is one of your many loves and you are often found in all the right bars after work, meeting people just as powerful and influential as you. Your office will certainly convey your position within the company; an expensive, imposing desk would suit you, or a throne in which to give orders to your empire. Frequent trips to international destinations are just up your street, and only business-class tickets will do.

Any employees you have will certainly get to know their place quickly; you'll make sure of that. Your dedication and drive are contagious, even if your strict rules and discipline are not easy for some of the other signs to comply with. If you say that lunch is at a certain time, you mean it and lateness is not looked upon kindly. You are a good and trusting boss, but will not suffer fools gladly and will not put up with sloppy work. Some would call you a control freak, others a born leader. Only you know how far you have taken your very royal traits. The wonderful thing about you, Leo, is that you take your job seriously. You are the ultimate professional who will remember to give colleagues or staff a birthday card but may not remember to give them time off!

Partnerships don't usually work for you, I'm afraid. You have your own way of doing things and you don't like to share the reins. You are happy to poach staff and jobs from other people because to you this is just the name of the game and part of business fair and square. If you have a boss, they should beware: it's highly likely you've got your eye on their job and you're more than likely to get it too!

Anything of a revolutionary nature appeals to them, as do professions such as judge or police officer, and the girls of this sign make great catwalk models, with their striking and somewhat alternative looks.

Ideal careers for a Leo: politician, art dealer, performer, film director, presenter, architect or manager.

Virgo

You are clever, quick and have a great sense of fair play. You are the good guy in a pool of sharks, out for justice and quick to speak up for those being trodden on. You can't abide liars or lack of loyalty, and you will have planned out your career with great precision right down to which outfit you will wear when being offered your promotion.

You like colleagues to pull together and don't hesitate to point out the weakest link. Quick with words and ready with a solution to other people's problems, you don't always recognize that colleagues' ways can work well sometimes too. Beware that you don't simply become very good at making other people money: you have the talent to be making it for yourself.

You are kind but at the same time hard to work for and with. You can't sit still and you dish out orders, which annoys new colleagues who haven't yet seen the endearing side to your many foibles. With a work ethic that will make the more lazy signs of the zodiac tremble, you want things done your way or not a all. As a secretary, you're great, but the way you reorganize your boss's schedule without asking will make it seem like your boss is your employee. You love to analyze facts and figures, and have excellent problem-solving skills. You are highly organized with an excellent filing system and orderly database at your disposal. You are a realistic worker who knows how to set achievable goals for yourself and your team.

You are also a perfectionist and are liable to criticize instead of encouraging others. You see a glass all too often as half empty instead of half full, and it is important to reverse this outlook sooner rather than later. Believe in yourself and great things will happen. Lacking confidence and believing the negative can be your downfall. Your perfectionism can also lead to health problems if you're not careful, as your health is often a mirror image of your emotional state. Balance is needed if you are to stay happy in your job. Your sign is keen on healthy living and you are attracted to working in the health industry. A job as a personal trainer or a nutritionist would give you a platform to preach about the importance of a healthy lifestyle, as would a job in the medical profession. The more unconventional among you would be interested in alternative medicine, such as homeopathy and aromatherapy.

If you can overcome the temptation to constantly self-criticize and if you keep your eyes focused on your goals, then you can and will make it to the top. You need to like the people you work with and for. You are fair, considerate, loyal and sincere, and expect the same from those around you.

You don't and shouldn't mix business and pleasure. In fact when you have spare time, you should get as far away from work as possible. You're not a sign that should work from home; it will end up making you ill, and you'll never be able to decide whether you should be doing the housework or your actual work. Deliberating between the two will eventually become intolerable.

Time counts for everything for you and you use every minute that you have to put your plans into action. When you're not working, you're planning, and so the circle continues.

Ideal careers for a Virgo: doctor, civil servant, lawyer, copy-editor, personal assistant or chemist.

Libra

Although you look like the first choice to have in charge, you don't really have a clue what you're doing some of the time, do you, Libra? You get by on a wing and a prayer. Don't get me wrong, the brainwork is there, but your charm does most of the work and it's no surprise, as you carry it in abundance.

No one could ever accuse you of favouritism or partiality. You have a sense of justice and fair play that is hard to rival. Any decision you make in the workplace will have been carefully weighed up beforehand. You would be suited to legal work and politics, although you're probably a little too honest for the latter! You like to weigh up problems logically and proceed to give great advice to those around you, albeit a little too airy-fairy for the more serious signs.

You are a dreamer and, unfortunately for you, people don't always take you as seriously as you would like. People born under your sign like to work in a harmonious environment and in beautiful surroundings.

Your sign needs a job that allows you to converse and exchange ideas with a range of people. You are also the net-worker of the zodiac and the king of schmooze when it comes to any sort of social occasion. You can get away with murder as you really do look as if butter wouldn't melt. You have staff and bosses alike eating out of your hands. You dislike formality among colleagues and are usually on first-name terms with everyone. You make a great teacher and an even better storyteller! You have an approachable manner and find it easy to deal with the public, knowing at just a glance what kind of handling each person will require from you, or what kind of flirting. Dress-designing could be an option, as could writing poetry, following in the footsteps of fellow Libran T. S. Eliot.

Stay away from speculative or risky jobs on the stock exchange; they are bound to end in disaster for someone as emotionally involved as you. You like work that involves a degree of travel, and if something has an air of nostalgia or romance, then so much the better.

You must make more of an effort to finish one thing before starting another. To be quite good at a lot of things may make you attractive to new faces, but is unlikely to make you wealthy. You need to learn that work can't always be fun; sometimes you have to get down to the nitty-gritty. By making the extra effort you can excel as long as you remember when the time comes to listen and not talk, Libra. With your charm, though, you'll work your way to the top no matter how many obstacles you encounter.

Ideal careers for a Libran: judge, diplomat, psychologist, artist or musician.

Scorpio

You are a force to be reckoned with in the workplace – when you choose the right profession, that is. Find your niche in life and you will make a fortune. Get into the wrong job and you will make your boss's life, your employees' lives and your customers' lives a nightmare.

Big business deals are your thing. Once you have a goal in mind, you will stop at nothing to reach your target. You play to win and are determined to reach the top. It could be argued that people born under your sign are only out for themselves, but you are capable of helping others, just so long as it doesn't inconvenience you too much. You have no patience for anyone who displays weakness. This means you will have trouble working for anyone you don't respect. It shows in your eyes, Scorpio; they are, after all, the window to your soul. If you are required to be ruthless to close a business deal, you won't hesitate to pull out all the stops, even if it means a few casualties along the way. Business is business to you and you just hope those caught up don't take it personally.

You set exceptionally high standards for your colleagues and don't suffer fools gladly. More people get hired and fired by a Scorpio than any other sign. You are very particular. If people don't suit you, then you won't take the time to train them your way like many of the other signs would. You are a hard taskmaster who expects the best because you want to give the best. When things go wrong for you, then everyone else had better run for cover, as you will spread your bad mood like the flu. You can forgive mistakes as long as you're not losing money. You remember all who have helped you and all who have crossed you too.

You do know that you can sometimes be too aggressive and inflexible, so need to remember that no one is indispensable, even you! Many of your sign have a natural aptitude for things mechanical, so engineering may appeal.

You are not afraid to take chances and face with bravery things that other signs would run a mile from. Your career has probably involved you taking a few gambles, and speculation and ambition go hand in hand for you. As soon as you have achieved what you wanted, you are off looking for the next challenge. No one could ever say you were dull or uninteresting. They could say that you were unpredictable and obsessed, but these are traits that help you to get ahead of the game. More often than not your sign excels and surpasses their dreams just through sheer cheekiness. You are willing to do what others only dream about.

You work hard and play hard, and can make a success of the most unexpected things. You're a great public speaker, although you probably don't think so. It is this slightly out-of-character nervous disposition that gives you your charm. You can convince people you know everything about anything with the power and energy you exude, and those who doubted you are sure to receive an anonymous clipping about your success in the post, although I'm not daring to suggest you hold a grudge!

You don't usually work just to earn money; you need to do a job that you enjoy. If you can earn a fortune doing what you love, then that is usually an added bonus. As you are one of the most dramatic signs in the zodiac, the most natural thing for you to go into is acting. Scorpios love the arts, so it's no surprise that some of the top male and female earners in Hollywood and Britain are born under this, the second water sign of the zodiac. Julia Roberts, Jodie Foster, Meg Ryan, the list goes on . . .

Ideal careers for a Scorpio: private detective, scientist, manager, actor or engineer.

Sagittarius

Yours is the face that looks cheerful on the first day back at work, Sagittarius, although you may not realize you're wearing a silly smile; it just comes naturally to you. You have a positive outlook and can see opportunity in every setback. This makes you a born leader to whom others will naturally turn for advice and guidance. You are excellent for team morale and at boosting everyone's spirits.

The idea of working on your own does not appeal to you. You're a people person and need contact with others in order to fuel your ambition for work and life. You have a thirst for knowledge, and your inquisitive nature gives you an aptitude for research. You get bored easily, though, and if you swap jobs at the beginning of your career, it can become a hard habit to break.

Money, although important to you, is not the be-all and end-all. It is essentially the experience of a job or profession that you are looking for. It just so happens that you put so much of yourself into what you do that you end up making lots of money from it. You are an explorer, adventurer and traveller of the zodiac who is never happier than when out on the road, meeting people along the way. It would prove hard for you to stay in an office for long; you would feel stifled. You need fresh air to clear your head and bring new ideas, to blow the cobwebs away.

You promise people the earth and then expect everyone else to rake in the sun and moon in order to get it. That said, you'll give anything a go and when the mood takes you, you could achieve things many of the other signs only dream about. Just beware of expending your energy too soon. Work on getting someone to help you who can finish off the great ideas you have, otherwise you'll end up forever talking about what could have been.

You prefer to work odd hours and you get your best ideas at the most strange times. That's why the successful of this sign so often carry a notebook with them or can be found with writing on their hand. These scribblings mean nothing to us, but could be the makings of a grand master plan.

You speak as you find, which makes you plain rude in some people's books, but with your natural good looks and model physique, it's hard for anyone to stay mad at you for long!

Ideal careers for a Sagittarian: travel agent, photographer, ambassador, expedition leader, newspaper magnate or professor.

Capricorn

Status and prestige are very important factors to you when picking a career. You need, you demand in fact, to have respect, for without it life is not worth living. Whatever you do, you will make it sound impressive, though. The list of responsibilities you reel off will give those listening the impression that you have had years of training. If you're the post-boy, you tell your friends you're the head of circulation! A Capricorn without a job is not a happy Capricorn. You need to work to feel a sense of purpose, and luckily for you, your appetite for life will get you back on your feet.

Your ability to persevere, coupled with your practical nature, means that you get there in the end, even when many of the other signs may have given up, though sometimes at a slow pace. It's hard for you to delegate, as you naturally take on more than you should, feeling that everything is your responsibility and yours alone. Learning to delegate can help you find success and can also earn you some very loyal supporters and co-workers.

Think of the goats on top of the mountain and how hard it must have been for them to get there. Well, the same goes for Capricorn. You know that hard work is imperative for you to feel genuinely successful. Unlike some signs, who would take a fancy job without having done a day's work, you want to know you are worthy. You get stuck in where many other signs would shy away, and it is this very trait that gets you such support and admiration.

You have to keep work and home life separate if you are to handle either well. Having a personal phone call in the middle of a meeting can create all sorts of problems for you. Dealing with one thing at a time is how you like to do it.

The temptation to link work and love is your downfall. It's a slippery slope, but your libido finds it too much of a temptation to resist at times. Ask a Capricorn over forty if they've had or nearly had a relationship at work that caused problems and they're sure to look bashful.

You expect people to keep to their word, and if you have been promised something and it has not been delivered, you will not be backward in coming forwards about confronting the person concerned. You'll even go so far as to seek legal help in getting things put right.

You will make it to the top even if it's just through sheer persistence. Just remember to keep flirtations for after hours; you'll always regret it if you don't!

Ideal careers for a Capricorn: computer expert, manager, army general or CEO, travel agent, teacher or estate agent.

Aquarius

It doesn't take a brain surgeon to see that your idea of hell would be working in a cramped office full of people. You like to be surrounded by lots of people, but on your terms! You are a humanitarian who will stop at nothing to help your fellow man. Working for a charity or other non-profit organization would stimulate you immensely. How long you can keep doing this while family shout at you to help pay the bills is quite another matter.

Teaching is another great profession for you. You are bound to get job satisfaction from educating and inspiring a new generation, particularly because you love to be admired by younger people, who can't possibly know as much as you do!

Your profession needs to involve a sense of purpose and needs to be challenging. The corporate world holds no appeal for you and is totally unsuited to your righteous nature. You do, however, have a natural aptitude for all things technical and what you know on the computer is probably self-taught. Computers do often play a major role in your life, and you can bring the most prehistoric business into the twenty-first century. You love gadgets and probably own more office gizmos than you could ever need or use. You are constantly coming up with new ideas for things you can do, but it's rare for them to make it past the planning stage. Cutting-edge ideas and new developments come naturally to you, then just sit there. So what you have to do is learn to take them to the next phase and level. You don't lack ambition, but you do expect to see results a little too soon.

You like everyone around you to be happy in their work and try to make a friend of those you deal with in business, only to reprimand them when they don't do things as you had envisioned. You expect your orders, should you give them, to be carried out to the letter, but then neglect to make sure you have completed your own list of responsibilities. You can't stand moaners or people who are not team-players. You like to be around people in work who can get results. You want to make money and are no fool; you know that brains come before beauty, although if you can get the two together, then so much the better!

Aquarians can be pretty tight-fisted with money in business, which can get you a bit of a reputation, particularly when you do a million-pound deal but then send in the taxi receipt for the cab you took to the meeting in the first place!

You take offence when others tell you how to do your job. Even if you've only been doing it five minutes, you already know the way you want to conduct things. You barely listen, except to your own voice, and you need to learn the art of convincing other people that your new approach was their idea in the first place. Tact, Aquarius, tact.

The more you can travel as part of your job, the better. Travelling from one country to another would suit you right down to the ground, but as soon as family come into the picture, you often feel torn and reach a rather painful crossroads in your life. One of your biggest fears is branching out on your own, but you're a fool not to try. It's what you were born to do, and you're sure to find career success if you do.

Anything run of the mill or predictable is not suitable for you. Constant challenges stimulate you and give you a thirst for life and a desire to go on. A tied-down Aquarian, robbed of an outlet for your Water-Carrier's marvellous sense of humour quickly becomes hard to live with, so mix humanity with change and see if you can't make a fortune and help those less fortunate. One last word of warning: just remember to finish that work you've started this time in case someone actually checks!

Ideal careers for an Aquarian: inventor, scientist, politician, fund-raiser or charity worker.

Pisces

People may tell you to stop daydreaming, but you need to inform them that you actually have some of your best ideas when you drift off. Practicality does not know your name, nor would you recognize it. You are a contradictory sign who has highs and lows in your career that many signs would find absolutely terrifying but that are part of your everyday life. You enjoy giving people pleasure and showing how much fun you can make of things. A lot of artists and musicians are born under your sign, as you have a natural ability to perform.

Yours is the most psychic sign in the zodiac, and if you have a hunch about a good business deal, then you should go for it. It is rare that your instincts will let you down. However, where large amounts of money are concerned, you would be wise to seek a second opinion, lest you end up out of a job and in debt. Your instincts do let you down when you become too emotionally involved.

If you decide you don't like someone, then woe betide them if they cross you, as you will never forget. You need to feel rewarded and appreciated for your efforts, and if those you cross paths with at work fail to do so, there could be a high price to pay. Love and hate come close together for you, both in how you feel about those around you and how they feel about you.

If we're being honest, you do prefer to hear your own voice rather than listen to others, and this is where you tend to miss out on some golden opportunities at work. Your brain never stops working and you retain the most bizarre pieces of information while forgetting things a child could remember.

Creative professions suit you right down to the ground, but hard-nosed business doesn't scare you and your reputation will precede you. You have not usually learnt your skills at school but through life. You absorb every experience like a sponge. You may not live in the real world, but it certainly can be a successful one, if you put your mind to it. Who can resist wanting to do business with a sign that could promise such an unforgettable experience? Well, some would run a mile, but those who do choose to work with you will never forget it.

Some of you see money as the be-all and end-all, whereas the rest of you just want to do what you want to do when you want to do it and are laid back beyond belief one minute and wound up like a spring the next. You go to such extremes that you could be the tea boy one month and own the company the next.

When you get bored, you'd give it all up for the promise of excitement in far-flung shores without a moment's hesitation. My best advice for you, Pisces, is to invest in things that you can come back to, otherwise you'll miss your past achievements.

Yours is the sign who liked a business so much you bought the company. My mother is a typical example of this. She had been out for so many bad meals that my father said to her over another terrible dinner one night, 'Why don't you open up your own restaurant if you don't think anyone else can do it right?' She did indeed open up her own restaurant, called Eva's, which was a fabulous seafood and steak house with live jazz and a chef who would come out and talk to you. She sold it for a profit, but years later always reminisced about how she'd like to be back there listening to the jazz and being part of the hustle and bustle of a kitchen. I don't miss it. I used to come back from a twelve-hour shift of giving palm readings and constructing birth charts to be whisked off to the kitchens because the washer-up or the commis chef hadn't turned up. Still, being a water sign myself (Scorpio), I understood her passion and even laughed at the nightly dramas, and I'm grateful for the culinary skills it taught me!

I digress, my friends, but you get my point. Don't taunt a Piscean by saying they wouldn't be able to run your business. They may just do it, and better than you; in fact I don't doubt it – although for how long and at what cost remains to be seen. Staying true to their psychic intuition and knowing when to get out and make a change is half the battle to a successful career for this very individual and loving sign.

Ideal careers for a Piscean: artist, musician, psychologist, writer and of course restaurateur!

Part 4

HEALTH MATTERS

Chapter 10

HEALTH, DIET AND FITNESS

We all want to be in optimum health, both physically and mentally. What we don't realize, though, is that it's hard to be fit mentally if our bodies are not at their best physically. Skipping meals, eating too much, stress-eating and choosing the wrong types of foods for our bodies can all lead to problems. I can help to make you fighting fit. Life will seem better than ever before. No more being depressed, no more feeling out of control.

Let's look at what you're eating and where you're going wrong. We'll also discover the right foods and exercises for your star sign to ensure you have the energy and the health that you need to make the most of your life. Your tailor-made plan can help you turn your life round and reach your full potential.

No wonder we feel depressed when we're missing out on vital nutrients. How can we expect to function well when we can't think straight? Mothers spend time and care giving their children the right foods because they *know* that diet plays a key role in development, yet when our own lives are going out of control, many of the signs seem to punish themselves as a way of telling others that they are unhappy, though half the time close ones don't even notice! There are certain signs of the zodiac who choose to head straight for the bottle or the larder as soon as they confront a problem, while others abstain from food and see it as a hidden enemy. Virgos and Scorpios in particular under-eat if they become sad, while Taureans, Aries and Pisceans often head straight for the chocolate.

Our bodies are all too often trying to tell us that something is wrong weeks or even months before we're willing to admit it out loud. Many of us ignore the warning signs and wait until something shuts down before we give ourselves an MOT. However, by recognizing the clues your body is giving you, you can overcome your problems and obtain both the health and mental agility you need to make a success of your life. Without a healthy body you cannot find a healthy mind.

Everything has a place

We've all looked at photographs of celebrities in newspapers and magazines and wished we had their figures. However, looking good is not just about being super slim; it's about being healthy and being the right weight for your height. Being underweight can cause just as many problems as being overweight.

Good health is about mentally adapting to the changes we face in life, which many people don't make a priority. They're too busy making sure that everyone else in their life is happy to think about themselves, or they're too busy doing what looks right instead of what feels right. How will close ones feel if what you're doing makes them happy but you miserable? Putting others before yourself will have a knock-on effect on your relationships.

Let's start by taking a look at what your ideal weight should be for your height and age. Remember that if you do feel you

need to start a weight-reduction programme, you should aim
for a sensible weight loss. About a kilo a week is ideal, as otherwise you risk starving your body so that it stores fat when
you eat.

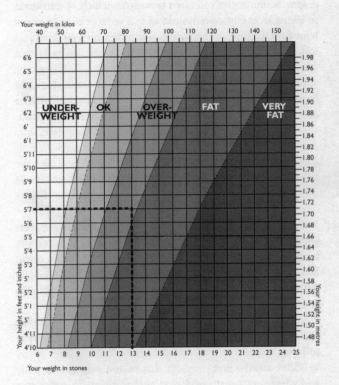

If you're using the BMI chart, you must be aware of your
body shape. The index doesn't take into account if you're an
apple, a pear, square, muscular and so on. You can use a BMI
chart as a base, but using a tape measure is the best way to
monitor changes. When you increase muscle mass through

exercise and lose fat through healthier eating, your shape can change rather than your weight, as muscle weighs more than fat.

Did you know that it is generally thought that the average person is about twelve kilos overweight, which, if you want to visualize it, is the equivalent of twelve large bags of sugar. Next time you are in the supermarket, pick up a bag and you will soon see how being just a little overweight can make you feel uncomfortable, awkward and off balance.

The majority of us are carrying around more weight than we should. That's why it's so important that we try to educate ourselves about exactly what we are putting into our bodies. When we reward ourselves with a piece of chocolate, why does it seem like a reward? Why should our five-a-day of fruit and vegetables be a chore? Relearn to value food for the energy it can give you. Why so many of us think we should stop learning when we leave school is crazy. As one chapter of your life closes, allow another one to begin.

An astonishing 60 per cent of people go to the supermarket when they are hungry. This means you're likely to buy more food than you would normally. Plan ahead and write a list. I'm sure the Virgos among you probably already do, and in aisle order too, but you Geminis and Aquarians don't. Librans get seduced by the beautiful colours and presentation of foods, and Scorpios go off on a tangent when one item they like the look of makes them decide to cook a completely different meal.

Did you know that your star sign rules a part of your body and when you get stressed, that part will start to suffer as a way of telling you that you need help? Let's take a look at the tell-tale signs you need to recognize and learn how you can get yourself in tip-top condition with your health, diet and fitness regime. It's the key to unlocking the real you and to reaching your full potential!

Aries

Aries rules the head, brain and face.

People may think you have a cool, calm exterior, but underneath that smile you're a bag of nerves. Even the way you hold yourself may seem like the height of coolness to some of the signs, but it is only a cover and inside you are fervently planning your next move so that you don't give the game away.

You need to be in charge and when you lose control, you lose your cool. Your very hectic lifestyle, along with your lack of planning, means you are more susceptible than some to stress. Problems that affect Aries people sign when life begins to take its toll are eye strain, insomnia and headaches ranging from mild to full-on migraines. This is linked to the fact that your sign often suppresses emotions. You must learn how to let off steam if you are to maintain the right physical and psychological health. The best advice is to try and treat headaches naturally first, rather than through medication. If you take away the stress, the headaches should disappear. Of course, getting rid of the stressful factors in our lives is easier said than done. Try getting plenty of fresh air. We spend far too much time indoors or in cars. You could also try drinking herbal teas instead of overdoing the caffeine. Infusions of valerian or lime flower made from a tea bag or one teaspoon of each herb per cup of hot water work well for your sign. Juniper oil diluted with two tablespoons of olive oil offers great results for you, and this treats nervous strain well too. Massage this oil into your temples to relieve migraine. Juniper berries are good for all kinds of Aries inflictions, including nervous strain, eye strain and stomach ailments. You can chew the berries raw or you can steep a dozen juniper berries in 900 millilitres of boiling water for ten minutes and drink, adding honey to taste. Most good herbalists and health-food stores will stock what you need. Some of the best solutions are the simplest, Aries.

Those typical of your sign are often too busy to remember to eat properly. A good breakfast, a light lunch and a light dinner usually work best for you. You are prone to a deficiency in potassium phosphate, which can contribute to the nervous problems you tend to suffer from – eat more fruit, pulses and cereals. You can boost your immune system and your all-round health by stocking up on tomatoes, lemons, celery and grapefruit, and resist the urge to opt for fast foods.

Because many fire signs such as you suffer from insomnia, you can develop a tendency to eat in the middle of the night. The fridge-raider at three in the morning is often an Aries. There you are, cheese sandwich in hand, denying you were ever on a proper diet or claiming that you are just having a well-earned night off. You are smooth talkers, so you can often convince your nearest and dearest that you are right, and that doesn't just apply to diet and exercise.

DIET

As I have mentioned before, your sign all too often runs on nervous energy. You also have trouble finishing what you have started, be it a diet plan or a business deal. If you have support, then you find it a lot easier, so joining an online diet club if you need to or a fitness group will help you to keep motivated. Watching other people's progress will also bring out the competitive streak in you, which will help you to keep up with any new regime. Try not to pitch yourself against others, though, as any threat of real competition from some-one who is losing more weight than you is a sure-fire way to knock your confidence and convince you to give up. You need a little leeway for the times when your very busy life has other areas that require your attention.

The secret to keeping weight off is to look out for the calorie and fat values usually found in the nutrition panel on food packets and read them carefully. Remember to note whether this is given by weight or by serving size. Know exactly what you are putting in your mouth, Aries.

If you go out to work, then taking a home-prepared meal can help you to shed any excess weight. Only you can decide to make this commitment to try to lose weight; you have to do it for yourself. It's your life and you must take control of it.

FITNESS

If you are an unfit Aries

You have probably failed in the past because you need change and get bored by routine. That's why you're best to try an exercise that can constantly stimulate you.

Start off with five to ten minutes of exercise twice a week if you have never done anything before, and then build up to twenty to thirty minutes three times a week. From here the sky is the limit, and your new fitness kick could lead you into many exciting sports. Try a boxercise class to get rid of all those pent-up emotions. Power-walking would be an ideal way to start. Just imagine you're walking towards your new future, and set yourself a distance as a goal, with a prize at the end of it – even if it's trying a new healthy dinner or buying a copy of your favourite magazine.

If you are a fairly fit Aries

I know you can excel because life is often one big competition to you, and I just know you're not going to take a challenge such as this lying down, are you, Aries? Start off with a celebrity fitness DVD from your favourite personality, but one which can take you to the next level. Once you feel confident with this, you should look at body-pump classes, which are sure to prove exciting and stress-relieving for your sign. You don't have to join a gym to do a class; you can often pay separately at your municipal gym. Running is also good for you, but short distances at a good speed will eventually turn out to be your best choice. It's important to use the right equipment to avoid injuries, so make sure you go to a proper running shop to buy the correct footwear. Hop on a treadmill and hit 'random' for a real challenge.

If you are a very fit Aries

You need variety, which is why a triathlon is ideal for you. Plenty of change and yet the ultimate challenge. Once you have started to become good at a sport, you can become complacent, which is why you always need to up the stakes. Fast sports attract you as you like to make an impact. There is no reason why you couldn't become a professional sportsperson; just look at motor racing's Mark Blundell, golf ace Sevvy Ballesteros, footballer Robbie Fowler, round-the-world yachtswoman Clare Francis and sprinter Linford Christie. If these Aries can do it, so can you!

Taurus

Taurus rules the throat.

The Bull is probably happiest when sitting down to eat. Nice food is a great love of yours, but you also know you have to be careful not to over-indulge. You can become fixated on a dish and eat nothing else for weeks on end. Just look at famous Taurean footballer David Beckham, who admitted that he used to have an addiction to SuperNoodles and on a supermarket trip would buy twenty at a time! It's not always good foods that your sign craves. As a result of this many of your sign suffer from acid indigestion and weight problems. Exercise is essential if you are to keep your body and mind fighting fit, but it's something that you either over-indulge in or under-indulge. You find it hard to reach a happy medium. Moderation *must* be your keyword. You have to learn to eat little and often. Hurrying meals is natural to you, but you need to remember to chew before you swallow and shovel in the next mouthful. Surely from the very romantic reputation you have you should know that it's not just love that can give you more pleasure when indulged in slowly, Taurus!

It is common for your sign to be deficient in sodium sulphate, which can lead to rheumatism, arthritis and stiffness. You should steer away from fat-laden foods and go instead for fruits. Strawberries and pomegranates are great for this deficiency, so make them a regular part of your diet. Remember that prevention is better than cure! Apples are also fantastic for your sign and ward off rheumatism, gout and bladder problems.

You Taurus types are also prone to sore throats and do not cope well with smoky atmospheres. Unfortunately for Taureans, products such as chocolate and cream exacerbate the problem of throat infections in that they are mucus-producing foods. Romanies have traditionally recommended that Taureans drink an infusion of blackcurrants, blackcurrant leaves and boiled water to soothe a sore throat.

DIET

Because moderation is an issue for your sign, it is often the amount of food you eat rather than the kind of food that is the problem. You must be careful that you don't turn to comfort-eating in times of stress or strain, particularly sweet foods. You love the home and you also love to entertain, so you always make sure you prepare plenty of food, which you usually end up eating yourself to make sure it doesn't go to waste.

Singer and actress Cher, who is a Taurean, once said that when she can't get her favourite jeans on, she knows it's time to diet. This is her guide, but many of us keep clothes we will never get into. Do a reality-check – look at the graph on page 215 and work out the healthy weight for you.

You, along with Virgo and Capricorn, have a tendency to go for the most fattening dish on a menu and so you will have to retrain your mind to get flavour without adding inches and the threat of heart disease. I don't write about health just so you can look good, it's about being healthy inside too, and I want you to be able to live long enough to see your dreams come true.

FITNESS

If you are an unfit Taurean

It's well known that many Taureans suffer from a slow metabolism. If you don't do any exercise at the moment, then find a passion that keeps you active, such as gardening. You could also always bring out the romantic in you and sign up for a dance class. You do have a brilliant sense of rhythm and you just have to look at the craze for dance programmes on television to see that they can transform someone's figure in a matter of weeks. Even just walking the children to school can be the perfect starting point.

If you are a fairly fit Taurean

If there is a social or family matter that calls, then you will more often than not be tempted to put your fitness routine second. However, if you're not fighting fit, then how can you help your close ones fight their battles in life? Yoga and Pilates can become a passion for you and will firm up all your best bits. These are also exercise forms that will become a way of life for a sign such as you, so should hopefully become a priority. Hatha yoga is one to look into, as it will suit your star sign. It concentrates on posture, something your sign doesn't usually make a priority.

If you are a very fit Taurean

Rock climbing and hiking are a must for the fittest of Bulls. Your love of the earth can see you excel, and even mountain-eering could be on your list of sports to conquer. There's an array of charity treks that you can sign up for, giving you the perfect inspiration to take sport to the next level. You share the same sign as famous cricketers Phil Tufnell and Brian Lara, footballers David Beckham and Neil Ruddock, and boxing legends Sonny Liston and Sugar Ray Leonard!

Gemini

Gemini rules the chest, shoulders, nervous system and lungs.

You are renowned for having an unpredictable, hectic and very exciting lifestyle. Unlike some of the other signs, at times you really seem to thrive on stress, Gemini! Active lifestyles such as yours deplete energy levels; therefore it is imperative that you get enough liquid into your body. Energy drinks are good, but you should also consider drinking the juice of a parsnip, a carrot and half a cucumber before you tackle the day. I promise you this simple but odd-sounding concoction is just what your sign needs to take on the world and start your day on a positive note.

You must learn to communicate with your body and stop and rest when you need to. Pushing through is second nature to you but doesn't always leave you fighting fit and ready for round two. I often think of you as a very good short-distance runner. Learn to be a long-distance runner and beat the competition. Your dreams are always big, and now it's time to make them attainable.

Geminis are prone to swollen glands, asthma and allergic reactions due to a deficiency in potassium chloride. Herbs such as comfrey, tansy and even sweet liquorice are rich in this mineral. Unlike Taurus, you Geminis should be guzzling more mucus-producing foods, such as organic milk. However, beware of fatty foods. You have a tendency to put on weight in certain areas, making your body look out of proportion.

Like Aries, you suffer from nervous strain, and juniper berries or juniper oil are the ideal remedy for this. See the advice for Aries on page 217. Yoga is the perfect way to unwind after a stressful day at work. Finding a new pace of life and slowing down when the body requires it are the best ways for you to maintain high levels of fitness and health.

You can always find the energy to go that extra mile if it's to impress someone. Well, now it's time to impress the most important person: yourself. Show the world that you put yourself first and then others will learn to treat you with the respect you deserve.

DIET

What I love about you is that you go into things with such a good heart, but air signs such as you don't always have a lot of willpower, which is why motivation is so very important for you. You could even think about starting your own diet group; it could certainly turn into a money-spinner with a sign as business-minded as you. You are good at getting other people motivated, you see, which in turn can help you to achieve your goals and dreams. You'll be pleased to hear that even though it's hard for you to start, once you get the initial weight off, you manage to keep it off. Your sign has also usually been vegetarian at some point in their lives. Fresh air and exercise are vital for Gemini. It should become an essential part of your diet regime and for the healthy life I know you really want to live.

FITNESS

If you are an unfit Gemini

I know that your social life has probably interfered with your gym life, but I'm also sure that at some point you have taken out a gym membership, so I know the good intention is there. Get down to the gym this week and discover how social the classes can be! A challenge such as the cross-trainer will give you a buzz, not to mention being great for fat loss and cardiovascular training.

If you are a fairly fit Gemini

Cycling is great for you – fresh air, speed, excitement and changing scenery. It will tone up your legs and your bum, and is brilliant for the front of your thighs too. Cycling to work can and should become a way of life for your sign, unless of course it's geographically impossible. If you have to take the bus to work or when you go out, then get off the bus two stops early. Within a month you'll feel the benefit in both your lungs and your mind.

If you've started something, then I know you can get to the top. Circuit training is great for you, as it gives you the chance to show off the natural skills your sign possesses, as Geminis are great at keeping up with constant change and pace. You could also try competing in a half-marathon, as you're more capable than most of raising the sponsorship money. As long as eyes are on you, then you will rise to the challenge. Make this the beginning of a new way of life and look up some alternative sports such as flying; there's an adventurer and explorer in you dying to get out.

If you are a very fit Gemini

Hang-gliding and extreme sports will call out to you once you know your mind and body are up to the challenge. You need to push the boundaries in order to deal with the stress that you all too often attract into your life. You could also try skiing or snowboarding, which you don't have to travel abroad to do. Join the ranks of famous fellow Geminis such as footballer Lee Sharpe, cricket's Mike Gatting and Ray Illingworth, fitness guru Diana Moran and tennis ace Steffi Graf.

Cancer

Cancer rules the stomach, breasts, digestive system and liver.

They don't call you crabby for no reason. You can be moody and irrational, and this is all too often reflected in your health, which is a mirror to your emotional state. When you get stressed, it is often the stomach that first shows signs of a breakdown. You always have so much going on in that head of yours, namely the past, present and future, that you forget to eat. In fact with the amount of emotion running through your body you probably already feel full! When you do eventually get round to looking after yourself, the temptation to over-indulge and to stuff yourself with the wrong foods is all too strong. You then spend the next few hours not relaxing but fretting over what you have put into your body. You are a perfect candidate for indigestion. This can be easily remedied by using peppermint oil. Place one or two drops in a small amount of warm water and sip. Do this three times daily, preferably with meals. Do not exceed this dose. You can also take peppermint in tablets, capsules and powder.

Make peppermint tea by infusing a tablespoon of the leaves in a cup of boiling water and drink two or three times a day. Those suffering from liver damage, inflammation of the gall bladder or obstruction of the bile ducts or gallstones should consult a doctor before using peppermint, as should anyone suffering from gastrointestinal upset. For children, chamomile is a better choice.

You can cleanse the liver with an infusion of fresh or dried sage in hot water. Take a handful of fresh sage, well washed, or a teaspoon of dried sage, and 600 millilitres of hot, not boiling, water. Place the herb in a jug, add the water, cover and leave for twenty-four hours. Keep in the fridge and drink one glass each morning. Don't strain it, though: it's essential you leave the sage in the water. You could also try milk thistle, which is available as a supplement from health-food shops.

A lack of calcium fluoride means that Cancerians suffer from nerve and muscle problems. You can ward these off by stocking up on plenty of organic milk, watercress and oily fish like sardines. You should stay away from sushi – raw foods can cause you all sorts of stomach problems, so you should make sure food is thoroughly cooked before eating.

Because of irregular eating patterns, you are also prone to migraines, so ensure you drink water throughout the day and avoid tea or coffee; if you are only 2 per cent dehydrated, you can lose up to 20 per cent of your concentration. Eating little and often, which will prevent blood sugar levels from dropping, can prevent migraine too, and incorporating more ginger into your diet also works a treat. Give yourself a schedule and plan ahead with your food. It can save you a lot of trouble (and stomach aches).

DIET

If you don't believe that you can lose weight, then you won't. Support, encouragement and self-belief are half the battle for you water signs. Even just having a phone number you can ring for support or a website address where you can chat to other people can be enough, but you do need to have some sort of network structure to be able to reach your goals.

One of the main reasons you tend to put on weight in the first place is contentment. Self-control is a crucial word for you to learn and one that you will come to know well in your lifetime, I'm sure. A healthy body gives a healthy mind, and water signs such as you always feel so much better when you are looking good. Your close ones will also be happier because you are happier, and arguments are less likely to ensue.

FITNESS

If you are an unfit Cancerian
Drink plenty of water when you exercise to keep your body well hydrated. No fizzy drinks, though: we want you to have a natural high! Look to cycling in the gym for ten minutes and then work up to changing machines every ten minutes, so that after a few weeks of just the bike you can alternate between rower and runner or stepper, leading up to twenty and then thirty minutes of cardio. Slowly but surely you will up your fitness and improve your mood, ready to take on the world. You've failed previously because you haven't believed you can succeed. Now believe you can and see what a difference it will make.

If you are a fairly fit Cancerian
I know you can excel, especially if you find a sport that you enjoy. With your often curvy figure, look to weights to make

a difference where it counts. You'll soon start to feel sexier, and before you know it, you can join in a body-pump or weights class and achieve the tone and confidence that will see you going for jobs and relationships you would previously have shied away from. Hiking is also therapeutic for you, my friend. Get your boots on and blow away those cobwebs. Nordic walking improves endurance, fitness, strengthens muscles, increases mobility and aids circulation, not to mention releasing pain and muscle tension in the neck and back. Get yourself some poles, find a group and get walking!

If you are a very fit Cancerian

Push the boundaries and try turning gentle swimming into a power swim. It's what your sign is made for and will give you the physique of your dreams. You can also look to kayaking and windsurfing. Your fitter body will open up a whole new world and can make all the difference. Team this with healthy eating instead of emotional eating and join famous Cancerian sports figures such as footballers Jamie Redknapp and Gianfranco Zola, cricket legend Sunil Gavaskar, golf ace Nick Faldo, boxer Steve Collins and even lord of the dance Michael Flatley.

Leo

Leo rules the back, spine and heart.

You love to live life to the full. If the mood takes you, then you will be open to a party at any time of the day or night. You often experience extremes, though. When you are happy, you are ecstatic, and when you are low, it's hard for close ones to know what to say to lift you up. Of course, these extreme characteristics are sure to take their toll on your health. Ease up on your schedule. Leos are all-or-nothing people, and while it is great to give everything 100 per cent, sometimes you need to say 'no' to things.

You are an ultimate professional when you're working, and even when you're partying. Over-exertion on your part links most commonly to back problems. Some astrologers argue that this is because you're naturally supposed to be on all fours, but whatever the reason back pain is very common for Leos. Massages can help this, as can making sure you've got the right sort of mattress. Avoid strain on the back by working to develop good posture. If you work sitting down, ensure your chair is correct for you.

You feel full of energy and vitality when the weather is good, but when it's cloudy and dark, you can become depressed. You love sunshine and good food, but when you get offered this, you often take it to the extreme and overindulge. You are prone to a deficiency of magnesium phosphate, which is needed for healthy lungs, muscles and nerves, not to mention the brain. This mineral can be found in plums, bran and even cocoa. You Leos are also lucky creatures – you rarely have alcohol problems and have mastered the trick of appearing sober, no matter how much you have had. In fact, you are more likely to get hooked on caffeine than alcohol, as Leos tend to be quite partial to cola and coffee. This doesn't mean you get the green light to over-indulge in the old vino either, though. Moderation is and must be the watchword for you, Leo.

Any foods that put a strain on the heart are not good for you. Make sure you eat meat in moderation and the best cuts only, and watch against over-indulgence once you hit fifty. Excess weight on a Leo is a lot harder to shift as you get older and yet that is precisely when we have more time to overindulge.

DIET

The big no-no for your sign is caffeine. It will keep you up all night and make you high as a kite. This is where your problems may start, as then you won't know or care what you are eating. Although caffeine is reputed to be good for you before a workout, if drunk afterwards it impedes your digestion, so cut down to reach your goal weight.

The majority of the time you are actually pretty good; it's just that when you have a bad day, you tend to go overboard. If you have eaten one thing that is bad, you see no reason to stop. Never go food-shopping when you are hungry. The people you see buying ten things that don't add up to a whole meal will be a fire sign such as you. Many Leo children find themselves underweight with all of the running around that they do, trying to find out what the world is all about. Why is it that as a child taking the stairs seems like a fun option to beat our family or friends who have taken the lift, yet as we get older we forget this? You always were a child at heart, Leo, so rediscover some of that enthusiasm for physical activity. It's the key to the body of your dreams.

FITNESS

If you are an unfit Leo

Now is the time to change. After all, your body is meant to be fit – you are a Lion, and without air in your lungs, your body and mind start to shut down. You need to tone your entire body and mind for a really dramatic change in the way you look. Don't overdo things; start by looking at simple measures if you are a really unfit Leo, such as carrying your basket at the supermarket instead of using a trolley. Doing speed housework could be fun, and when your confidence grows and we start to bring out the leader in you, head down to a tai chi class. Before you know it, you could be teaching it. Visualize your goals. Boxercise classes are great for you too. You have a great body, you just don't know it yet, so are already one step ahead.

If you are a fairly fit Leo

Up the tempo of any classes you have attended and take things to the next level. I know how much better you'll feel when you start to see a change in both your body and your mood. Even alternative sports such as archery and javelin-throwing will bring out the beast in you. You want excitement, so look up local places that can make your weekends alternative yet healthy. Ice-skating may seem like a chore but is sure to end up as a passion with the natural ability you will have for it.

If you are a very fit Leo

Long-distance running is something you are probably already good at. Keep going and make runs more interesting by heading somewhere new. Decathlons and even iron-man competitions could and should be on your list of things to do. Join the ranks of famous Leos such as cricketer Dominic Cork, boxer Chris Eubank, tennis players Anne Hobbs and Jim Courier, and racing driver Nigel Mansell.

Virgo

Virgo rules the intestines.

Your sign is reputed to be a hypochondriac and born worrier. Your cupboards are usually full of medicines, potions and lotions for things you've had or thought you were coming down with. The good side to all of this of course is that prevention is better than cure, and as you take your health very seriously, you are already likely to be a mine of information about it. You don't actually have many health problems, but when you do feel ill, the whole world gets to know about it.

It is normally work that affects your health, causing stomach and bowel problems. This is because you worry and get stressed a lot, and even if you don't work, there is always some drama in your personal life causing you anxiety. This can often be because you get involved too readily in the problems of your nearest and dearest. Having said that, you Virgos are usually very healthy, though you need to keep the digestive and nervous systems in good order. Juicing an apple with some strawberries, blackberries, raspberries and lemon can make a great stress-buster for your sign. Taken regularly, this will soothe the most frayed of nerves.

You are more likely to be vegetarian than any other sign in the zodiac and are fussy about what you eat. You can lack potassium sulphate, which causes colds and coughs – in fact Virgos catch colds more easily than other signs. You really need to eat more tomatoes, lemons, apples and grapefruit to ward off these ailments. Dress for the weather – you can still look good in a scarf, you know. If you think you've already picked something up, then go to bed, drink plenty of liquids to avoid fluid loss, caused by sweating, and to flush out those toxins, hug a hot-water bottle if you feel shivery and call your doctor for advice if your symptoms persist for more than a few days.

In addition you need to get more fresh air, and for an earth sign, walking or running are ideal exercises. Health-conscious Virgos find that alcohol gives them kidney problems, and they are far more sensible than the rest of us. You usually alternate drinks with water when you go out and suffer far less the next day. Those of you who do choose to be drinkers know it comes at a price and can suffer from kidney and liver problems more than the rest of the zodiac, so often learn the hard way.

DIET

The key for your sign has got to be quality, not quantity. Healthy foods are essential for earth signs for optimum results. You spend so much of your time worrying about your close ones that you get embarrassed when it comes to you because you know you have left it too late. It's never too late, though, and the beauty of your sign is that you more often than not like the healthy fruits and vegetables that the rest of the zodiac turn up their noses at.

The other good point is that if you promise yourself, you will stick at something. You are your own taskmaster and so can excel where others fail. My advice to you, my friend, is not to be quite so hard on yourself. Even the top diet experts treat themselves every now and then.

FITNESS

If you are an unfit Virgo

Pilates would be a nice start for you, Virgo. It's designed to tone and sculpt your entire body, strengthening core muscles and increasing flexibility, and can also help you lose weight. You can start off with a DVD at home if you like, but when you see the difference it can make, you'll want to pop down to a class and make a major change. It's great for improving the condition of your body. The trampoline could also be fun for your sign and is a great starting point to get the blood pumping round your body.

If you are a fairly fit Virgo

It's probably been hard for you to take things to the next level because you are scared of failure and of people laughing at you behind your back. You go about things in such a practical manner that there is no reason for you to be worried or scared. I'm sure you're among the best in the zodiac at preparing yourself for any challenge. The best activity for you now would be skiing either at a sports centre or on snow if you want to get on the piste. Another great exercise would be a spinning class, which is a stationary bike class to music, because this really gets the body working hard.

If you are a very fit Virgo

Find which sport is your passion and enter it professionally. It's a fantastic thing if someone of your sign can turn a hobby into a career. Fencing would appeal to you, as would kiting. With your sign, you've got to enjoy what you do and any sport must have a social aspect to it. Olympic gold-medal cyclist Chris Boardman did just that, as did fellow Virgos yachtswoman Tracey Edwards, tennis aces Tim Henman and Greg Rusedski, ex-motor-cycle champion Barry Sheene, footballer David Seaman and Grand Prix champion Damon Hill.

Libra

Libra rules the kidneys, lumbar region and skin.

Without balance and harmony in your life, you become a very unhappy Libran. You need to work, rest and play if you are to function at your best. You are a great social animal and are all too often the last to leave a party. You love rich foods and have a wickedly sweet tooth.

You should take care of your kidneys by going easy on the booze at those late-night parties you love to frequent. You handle beer better than spirits, though should beware of the effect this can have on your waistline. You poor Librans get worse hangovers than other signs. You should try juicing a bunch of grapes with a nectarine after over-indulging. You should also get into the habit of drinking plenty of water throughout the day to flush out any toxins from your system and cleanse the kidneys.

Your sign can have a deficiency of phosphate of soda, which means you should eat more spinach, lettuce, apples and strawberries to maintain the balance of fluids in the body. You seem to thrive on vegetables grown above the ground, like mushrooms and bamboo shoots, which make for delicious stir-fries.

Fresh air and exercise are vital for you, Libra, especially with your element of air. Blowing away the cobwebs after a stressful day can help sort out all manner of problems. You should join a gym so that you can exercise and socialize to your heart's content.

DIET

One of your main problems is that you don't like to stick to one method of dieting for too long. You would prefer to mix and match. That is why when someone asks a Libran which diet they're on, they often um and ah before they answer.

One of the main issues for those of your sign when trying to lose weight is that, like Taureans, you have a sweet tooth and cannot resist the chocolates. What you must learn, though, is that if you don't pick it up and put it in the trolley, you can't eat it! Fresh raw foods are good for your sign and can help you to maintain lasting weight loss. Anything that is grown in the open is good for your element. Explore the flavours and stop thinking that you are only prepared to pay a decent price for a pretty bottle or package. Look beyond the appealing packaging and go back to nature. Fresh fruit and vegetables can be just as exciting, and are worth the extra pennies too.

FITNESS

If you are an unfit Libran

Your health is often a mirror image of your emotional state. You know deep down that you need fresh air and exercise to think straight. Get outside, go sightseeing or walk and eventually jog around places that inspire you. It's important to avoid injuries, so make sure you go to a good running shop and buy the correct footwear. There are so many different intensities that you can jog at. Start today with walking and reveal a new you. Even just walking the dog (or a friend's dog) is a great way to start. Feel and see the benefits that the fresh air can have on your sign. With a beautiful view as inspiration, you're sure to want to take things to the next level.

If you are a fairly fit Libran

Jogging is something that your sign should really enjoy. It is a pursuit that is indulged in by people of all fitness levels. You are prone to dips in energy levels, so find the best time of the day to exercise and stick to it. Exercise at least three times a week.

Look to new classes to inspire you. The latest fads catch your attention, so opt for a class that's only just begun and you're sure to be top before the month is up. You should also try hot yoga, which is a series of poses (something you like to do) done in a hot room. The room is usually maintained at a temperature of about ninety-five degrees. As you can imagine, a vigorous yoga session at this temperature causes sweating, which rids the body of toxins. It also makes the body very warm and therefore more flexible.

If you are a very fit Libran

Then it's time to really tone up as well as hitting the cardio and getting hot under the collar. Don't be afraid to look to weights – they don't have to add pounds; they can define muscle and give shape. Your sign, the Scales, is all about balance, so you've got to make sure that as well as cardio you are toning. Perfection is but a step away. You could even get into power-plating, which with each vibration forces the body to perform reflexive muscle actions twenty-five to fifty times per second. This results in an improvement that doesn't take months to achieve, just regular commitment. How can you not want to join the likes of fellow Librans footballer Paul Warhurst, Olympic gold-medal rower Matthew Pinsent, rugby's David Campese and tennis aces Jana Novotna and Thomas Muster?

Scorpio

Scorpio rules the reproductive system.

You are intense and powerful, a real force to be reckoned with. You are full of energy and do not do anything by halves. Like Pisceans, you are the extremists of the zodiac – for example, Scorpios who smoke and drink will usually do so to excess. Your addictive personality can cause you lots of problems. Eating disorders are not uncommon among your sign and usually surface during the teenage years. Scorpio rules the reproductive organs and the womb, meaning people born under this sign are subject to menstrual pains, urinary infections and water retention. To combat water retention, you must eat foods rich in potassium such as potatoes, bananas and tuna (no more than three times a week if it's tinned tuna). Try a juice-booster of an orange, a pineapple, a plum and a tangerine. It's sure to put the spring back in your step and that glint in your eye.

Scorpios can lack calcium sulphate, which is needed to keep the lungs healthy and ulcers at bay. Many foods are full of calcium sulphate, including cabbage, kale, milk and onions. Contrary to popular belief, your sign does not thrive on stress; in fact it affects you badly, as you are an over-emotional sign. Wherever possible, you should try to avoid stressful situations, and when you do feel anxious, you should try relaxation techniques. A bath with aromatherapy oils is great for both body and soul, and will set you up for a good night's sleep. Scorpios are renowned for reacting unpredictably to alcohol – a drop of wine can leave you legless one night, whereas after drinking a bottle of whisky the next, you could still be sober as a judge. Focus is what's needed and then you can excel in whatever you put your mind to.

DIET

Your sign spends more time talking about what you're going to eat next than actually eating. It's not unusual for Scorpios to turn to their partner as they dish up that day's dinner to ask what they're going to be eating the following day.

Because water retention can be a problem for your sign, you need to be careful with your intake of both salt and alcohol. Sugary fizzy drinks, such as cola, can make you look far bigger than you are through bloating. You may want to avoid bloating foods such as beans, cabbage and onions three days before a big event. Just this simple deduction from your diet will offer you dramatic results. Drinking plenty of water is also important for you.

The problem for you, Scorpio, is that if anyone tells you that you can't have something, you want that food all the more. Fish is a key food to keeping you slim, as it suits your sign better than red meat.

FITNESS

If you are an unfit Scorpio

You have probably failed before because you have become obsessed with a particular exercise and have then grown so bored that you never want to go to that class or see that teacher again. Exercise can and will become a way of life for you. Start by treating yourself to something relaxing at the end of a workout. Get down to the gym and try a different class every week; you'll soon find which one becomes your new best friend.

If you have not done any exercise for a long time, then try a gentle aqua class. Don't take the car to the car wash; wash it yourself. Build up to a healthy active lifestyle. Promise to take the stairs, not the lift, and book a private swimming class. I promise it will be well worth it. Get some lessons on technique and before you know it you'll be beating everyone in the pool with your perfect front crawl.

If you are a fairly fit Scorpio

It's time to make sure you keep variety in your routine so you don't get bored. Naturally good at running, you should join a running club so that you can explore new places. It's important to avoid injury, so make sure you buy the correct footwear. Pilates would also help you to release your pent-up feelings and would probably save your close ones from an ear-bashing about the day's problems.

Variety is the key for you, as once you've mastered a sport, you'll need a new challenge. Cycling becomes mountain biking, swimming becomes competitive, and running turns into a marathon! Just make sure you plan something as a reward for yourself afterwards. Having an incentive will always see you go the extra mile. Make it a healthy treat, though, Scorpio!

If you are a very fit Scorpio

It's time to push the boundaries and enrol in a marathon in a foreign country. Run the five volcanoes in Italy, get on your bike and cycle the Nile or run the Great Wall! With a taste for excitement, you're sure to push yourself harder if you don't know what's round the corner. In fact with your determination it won't be long before Everest is on your agenda. You crave a challenge, just like fellow Scorpios top swimmer Sharon Davies, cricket's Courtney Walsh, rugby's Austin Healey, goalie Ian Walker and footballer Ian Wright.

Sagittarius

Sagittarius rules the hips, thighs, nerves and arteries.

Lust for life and optimism characterize your sign. You are extremely versatile and move quickly from one idea to the next, constantly needing to grow and expand. Adventurous Sagittarians relish a challenge and love exercise, sometimes to excess, so the poor body suffers. You are constantly on the move and often do not warm up before doing strenuous sports, meaning your body can be prone to sprains, thigh fractures and even hip dislocation. Swimming is the ideal exercise for helping pulled muscles and ligaments get back into shape.

When it comes to colds, you have a particularly weak resistance and only need to spend a short while in a smoky, crowded room before catching a nasty bug. I'm sure you were one of the signs who rejoiced when the no-smoking ban came into effect. Indeed more fresh air is the best preventative measure, and you must not forget to wrap up warm come winter. You could try to incorporate more onions, barley and cherries into your diet, which will help to boost your immune system and ward off colds.

Because you always have somewhere to go and people to

see, you are all too often impatient cooks. You frequently eat on the run and this almost always means that you eat fast food. It is very important that you take time out to ensure that you have a balanced diet. It is likely that you will suffer from a silica deficiency, which may well show itself in your appearance – brittle nails, poor skin and hair. You can remedy this by adding raw oats to a smoothie or eating parsnips, asparagus and the humble cucumber, which will give your health and appearance the boost they need.

DIET

Your sign is known as an initiator of action but not necessarily as a great stayer. You like constant change; it keeps you feeling alive. If you begin anything, it will be with a great deal of energy. People around you will believe you could make it to the stars and back again should you so desire. You inspire others, but don't always put as much effort into inspiring yourself. There is hope, though – you just have to want to change your life and you will find that you can. Many fire signs go on binges. They starve themselves for a couple of days and then go mad eating all the wrong things. Starving your body teaches it to store fat. Learn to eat the right foods and you won't need to calorie-count again.

FITNESS

If you are an unfit Sagittarian
Start off with your best asset: your legs. These are what give you an edge over the other signs. You already have a level of fitness to tap into of which you are unaware. Look to fun sports that will see you moving more on your feet, such as dancing, ice-skating, hockey and basketball, and take it from

there. Once you've got into the game, you'll get into the zone and you'll be looking for the next challenge.

If you are a fairly fit Sagittarian

Horse riding, tennis and archery are all things you'd be good at. Once you've begun any sort of exercise, you'll find that you have the kind of body that feels ill when you don't keep it up. You thrive when you are giving your body what it needs. Yoga is also good for you and can help you focus on the jobs you have ahead of you in life. Look to Ashtanga yoga if you want to take things up a level, as it is a vigorous and more athletic style of practice.

If you are a very fit Sagittarian

Rock on with rock climbing and discover the excitement that can come from taking risks. You do it in work and now you can do it in your spare time. Close ones will love the new you and I'm sure your love life will benefit too. Desert running and boxing should also be on your list of things to try. Join ranks with fellow Sagittarians at the top of their game, such as cricket legends Imran Khan and Craig White, squash ace Jahangir Khan, ski ace Alberto Tomba, footballer Ryan Giggs and boxer Gary Jacobs.

Capricorn

Capricorn rules the knees, skeleton, bones and skin.

With Saturn as your ruling planet, you are self-controlled and self-disciplined, and this is often reflected in your health. You are proud of your body and will be the first to notice when you have put on some weight.

You Capricorns need to watch your calcium level, as your joints and bones are particularly weak. Make sure you're eating plenty of green leafy vegetables and some nuts and seeds. Desk jobs exacerbate stiff joints: you really do need to keep moving! This does not necessarily mean to say you should go out and get a personal trainer to whip you into shape, though. Gentle exercise, like walking or swimming, is the best way to maintain fitness without putting too much strain on your joints. Knees are particularly weak and can be strengthened by adding more parsley to your food. Both parsley and devil's claw are good for aches and rheumatic pain, and can also help gastrointestinal problems. Sprinkle them over meat and vegetables for a quick and easy vitamin boost.

Like Sagittarians, Capricorns are vulnerable to chills. Glucosamine may help to relieve osteoarthritis of the knee, and studies even show the supplement can be good for mild to moderate arthritis. Do not take this if you are a diabetic or suffer from a seafood allergy, and always consult a qualified practitioner before you take any supplements. It can also help to slow down the progression of arthritis by helping to keep joint cartilage healthy.

You must remember to wrap up warm and get more fresh air. Your lungs are generally not as strong as those of people born under other signs, though a tea made with half a teaspoon of lungwort, half a teaspoon of ribwort (available from a good herbalist) and boiling water can work wonders on your respiratory system.

DIET

In general Capricorns are self-controlled, but eating can be an addiction for the earth sign such as you, just as smoking or drinking is for some of the other signs in the zodiac. You also spend a lot of time thinking about what you are going to eat or cook next. Many earth signs eat more food the more weight they gain. It is a kind of self-inflicted punishment for gaining weight in the first place. Change this habit now and work out a plan of action for yourself. Your sign naturally savours flavours and should really be able to stop eating when you are full. It is normally emotional pressures that tip you over the edge or that can see you reaching for foods you know make you lethargic. You are more aware of your body than many other signs, which is why it is so important you distinguish good foods from bad. You have an instinct for knowing what you should and shouldn't be eating and must rise above any emotional stress.

FITNESS

If you are an unfit Capricorn

Cycling is great for your calves, and if you're overweight, then it's perfect, as there is less pressure on the joints than in many forms of exercise. If you haven't cycled in years, then hop back on. Bikes now come in every shape and design you could imagine. Just call your nearest cycling school and get hooked up with some fellow enthusiasts. Make sure you have the saddle at the correct height or ask the professionals to show you. This is a sport that can help you lose the pounds without putting too much pressure on your body.

Rambling is also great for your sign; you get to see beautiful countryside while exercising your body. You are a sign that needs to stay hydrated, so make sure you take plenty of water with you. Up the intensity and make your trips longer each time. You'll soon be ready for the next level of fitness.

If you are a fairly fit Capricorn

You often drag yourself down with the belief that you can't do the things that lie ahead of you when in fact you could, if you took it in stages. You think of everything at once and need to learn only to worry about what is happening now and not what is round the corner. You are a natural climber, so get on the stepper at the gym; you'll find it soul-building to realize what a natural aptitude you have for exercises which the other signs find a struggle. Martial arts would also be great for your sign. You are a perfectionist and will rise through the ranks quicker than other less dedicated signs.

If you are a very fit Capricorn

Walking and climbing appeal to you, so take these to the next level and make your goals and destinations more extreme. Tobogganing, skiing or snowboarding should be on your list, and body-boarding is something you'd be a natural at. Weights are also something you can now incorporate into your regime to make your body the temple it should be. Meditation will allow you to focus on life and ensure that you are making the right decisions. With a good base of training, you can try any exercise you please. The sky's the limit. Join the leagues of high-achieving Capricorns like motor racing's Michael Schumacher, football's Lee Bowyer, rugby's Gavin Hastings, tennis ace Christine Truman, jockey Richard Dunwoody and soccer legend Eusébio da Silva Ferreira.

Aquarius

Aquarius rules the circulation and the ankles.

Those born under this sign are prone to ankle sprains and other leg problems. You often feel cold even when the weather is warm because of your poor circulation, and the fact that you love wearing skimpy clothing does not help matters. A tea made from angelica leaves will not only stimulate circulation but also blitz a stinking cold. Exercises like swimming and aqua aerobics are best for building up leg muscles and improving the circulation. Comfortable rather than impractical shoes are a must if you want to avoid those painful ankle strains. When it comes to fashion, you are all too often willing to pay a high price just to look good, but ill-fitting clothes can have disastrous consequences for a sign such as you, so be warned. Tight jeans, shoes or even just the wrong kind of products can cause skin problems. A high price tag doesn't always mean quality, Aquarius.

Like all air signs, you should have a light and nourishing diet. Fast foods can leave you feeling bloated and lethargic. Substituting them for something like a jacket potato with beans will see a slow release of energy that will last you throughout the day while still leaving you feeling full.

You really are sensitive creatures and can suffer from periods of nervous tension, which will affect the digestion. It is important you find a partner who can help you to lift yourself out of the depression you all too often find yourself in. Women are also prone to severe period pains. They should drink lots of water and avoid alcohol.

Although you are social animals, you should not and must not sacrifice your sleep. You need to make time for relaxation and pampering yourself. Valerian tea before bedtime is preferable to a stiff nightcap if you want a deep, satisfying sleep. Remember that you can't take on the whole world's problems yourself! Enjoy today and stop living for tomorrow.

DIET

You annoy the rest of the zodiac because there are parts of your body that look as if you have worked out even when you've been doing nothing. You are a great conversationalist, but you also have the ability to talk on subjects you know nothing about. Sensitive and impulsive, it's vital that the decision to do something about your diet and fitness must be one you have reached on your own and not one that you have made due to pressure from friends and family.

FITNESS

If you are an unfit Aquarian

Camping is an ideal way to get you into the idea of using your body and being at one with the elements. Just putting up the tent is sure to get the blood pumping. Outdoor exercises are ideal and bring out the adventurer in you. Rollerblading would be great for you, as you'd enjoy the social aspect. Why not team this with a competitive sport and look at ice hockey once you're ready to take things up a level?

If you are a fairly fit Aquarian

With your love of the outdoors you may want to start cycling. Work up to longer distances and even turn it into a weekend away. First of all I want you to aim for thirty minutes of continuous steady cycling and get used to the feel of the bike. Once you get used to this, you can incorporate some bursts of flat-out cycling and then continue at a lower intensity. Surfing or diving will fare well with you, as will parachuting. Do it for your favourite charity and feel extra good about your challenge. It should give you the incentive to actually do it instead of just thinking about it.

If you are a very fit Aquarian

Scuba-diving and gliding are exercises that allow your sign to express themselves and to experience some extremes. You need to get your circulation going and any sort of adrenalin rush is sure to keep you coming back for more. Don't rule out skiing either – you're sure to have a natural affinity with the sport. If fellow Aquarians boxer Nigel Benn, footballers David Ginola and Robbie Earle, ballet dancer Mikhail Baryshnikov, golfer Nick Price and boxer Prince Naseem Hamed can excel in their sports, then so can you!

Pisces

Pisces rules the feet.

Pisceans believe in suffering for their beauty, and strangely it is usually the feet that suffer. Your most common bad habit is buying shoes that look spectacular but are extremely bad for your feet. You must watch out for swollen ankles and water retention. Regular visits to the chiropodist are recommended, as is investing in a foot spa. If you can find a willing participant, a foot massage with essential oils will perk up the most tired and swollen of feet. Generally speaking, Pisceans create many of their own ailments by living life to the extreme. You love intense experiences, whether they are good for you or not. Moderation is not in your vocabulary! Pisceans are dreadful dieters; you are prone to snacking and have varied eating patterns, which results in digestive problems. You also tend to turn to food to make your worries go away instead of eating when you are actually hungry.

Pisceans are often lacking in phosphate of iron, which is needed to make red blood and increase good circulation. This can be found in most leafy green vegetables, raisins, dates, figs and nuts. When it comes to alcohol, Pisceans are extremely weak. You are not very good at judging when you have had enough, and those who over-indulge can suffer from liver ailments. Restraint should be the watchword for Pisceans everywhere, and that is in *all* aspects of their life.

DIET

We all know by now that you have an addictive nature. If I told you that you were not allowed my apple, you'd want it more than anything else. The problem is that it's not usually something as healthy as an apple that close ones are trying to keep away from you. It's probably that extra glass of wine or beer or that big dessert. Your figure can and should be fantastic. You have such a determined mind that you could easily excel in anything you put your mind to. Bananas are good for you, as they have a high potassium content and can take the place of sweet foods that are packed full of calories.

FITNESS

If you are an unfit Piscean

Dancing will appeal to you, as you are naturally good on your feet. Why not pick up one of the dance DVDs on the market? Or get down to a class and learn some new steps. The social aspect will appeal to you, and with your addictive nature it won't be long before you're ready to take things up a notch. It's never too late to start ballet either, you know. There are classes for all levels, so there's no reason not to start or to pick up where you left off as a child. You could also try Pilates, which involves rebalancing your body and stretching to build up muscle tone.

Besides burning calories and reducing your body fat, aerobic exercise is a fantastic stress-buster. It can help rid you of all the problems your day has heaped on you. Any class you do should give you plenty of variety, as you are prone to boredom. You can be sure that you will be working on lots of different muscles, ensuring an all-round programme.

If you are a fairly fit Piscean

Instead of swimming as a hobby, get into it as a sport and try alternating between the water sports. Scuba-diving would be good, especially as you'll get to visit some very exotic locations. You know you are good at whatever you decide to do, so make up your mind and increase the level and intensity. Challenge a friend and you're sure to find the inspiration to throw in a couple of extra sessions.

If you are a very fit Piscean

You want something with a hint of danger. Swimming with sharks, diving on the Great Barrier Reef or white-water rafting! You also want speed and action and would be great at a competitive sport, such as semi-professional or even professional football or boxing. Just remember not to take it too personally. Be inspired by fellow Pisceans motor-racing legend Alain Prost, soccer legend Denis Law, football's Ole Gunnar Solskjaer, boxer Barry McGuigan and basketball's Charles Barkley.

A new you will emerge

As your fitness levels increase and your body starts to take shape and become lean, your self-confidence will grow too. No longer will you be looking to other people for happiness; you will find what you need within yourself. You will, however, recognize who or what was dragging you down and then it will be 'Goodbye, past, and hello, new and improved future.' For example, I know many of you think you couldn't end a relationship that you rely on right now even though you know you should, but once you start to boost your self-confidence by becoming fit in body, the mind will follow and you will be able to sort out your life.

Quick health checklist for your shopping trolley

Coming from a Romany family, I have been brought up with the belief that herbs and vitamins are vital to our health. Further study over many years of writing books and working with health experts has only increased this belief. Of course, firstly we should all look to vitamins in our foods, and if we are not getting sufficient, then supplements are a good way to ensure we are mentally and physically able to tackle all that life throws at us. Read the checklist for your sign and see if you're getting enough of the right vitamins. It could turn out to be the key to the energy and vitality you've been looking for.

Aries

- Magnesium can help with tiredness.
- Try feverfew and evening primrose oil for headaches.
- Take B2 and B3 for the metabolism, nervous system, vital organs, eyes, muscles, skin and hair. These can be found in brewer's yeast, wholegrain cereals, liver, rice, nuts, milk, eggs, meat, fish, fruit and green leafy vegetables.
- For nervous problems and neuralgia, take B1 (thiamine). B1 is in brown rice, peas, beans, breakfast cereals and Marmite. It should aid your nervous system by releasing the energy you need.
- B6 can be found in wholemeal bread and wholegrains, liver, fish, bananas, wheat bran, yeast extract and brewer's yeast, and will promote healthy skin and nerves, and help hormone production by increasing antibodies.
- Drink peppermint tea for stomach problems.

Taurus

- For that vulnerable Taurean throat, baptisia or lachesis are fantastic and are what many of the top homeopaths recommend. They are also good for toxic intestinal conditions. Available from all good homeopaths and health-food stores.
- The best drink for a Taurean is water and plenty of it. This is the simplest and most effective health measure, and the cheapest. There is no excuse for not drinking lots of water, so give it a go. You will end up feeling and looking 100 per cent better.
- To reduce catarrh, turn to zinc, which can be found in seafood, beef, pork, dairy products, green vegetables and cereals, or take supplements if you must. The recommended daily intake is 15 milligrams.
- Vitamin C, which helps the body fight infection, can be found in blackcurrants, kiwi fruit, peas, potatoes, Brussels sprouts, broccoli and oranges. You can also take supplements. The recommended daily intake is 60 milligrams.
- Sniff tea-tree and eucalyptus oils, and take garlic supplements to ward off colds if you spot the symptoms in time.
- For digestion difficulties, try peppermint tea.
- If you've overeaten, try the herb centaury.

Gemini

You are one of the signs that can really benefit from taking vitamin supplements on a regular basis because no matter how much you try, you don't eat when you should.

- For eye strain, try bilberry extract and vitamin B-complex.
- vitamin B1 (thiamine) is good for nervous problems. Take a supplement or eat foods such as brown rice, peas, beans, breakfast cereals and Marmite.

- All the water-soluble vitamins (B-complex and C) are good to take on a regular basis. The body doesn't store these and they need constant replenishment, something Geminis need to bear in mind.

Cancer

- Honeysuckle is great to help a Cancerian who is having sleep problems. Fill a pillow with fresh honeysuckle and you can guarantee that your dreams will be sweet.
- The herb feverfew is great for migraines but needs to be taken regularly to get the best results. You can get feverfew in tablet form or tincture, but the fresh leaves are better. A couple of leaves a day eaten in between some bread work well. You can also soak a cloth in an infusion of feverfew and place it on your forehead to relieve headaches.
- For stomach problems, try taking digestive enzymes (extracted from pineapple and papaya) or peppermint oil.
- B2 detoxes the liver. For liver problems, get Bio Light liquid from your health-food store. It's a great detox and comes in several flavours.
- Nervous exhaustion can be tackled with vitamin B-complex and vitamin E. The nervous system depends on an adequate intake of those vitamins.
- Take vitamin B1 (thiamine) daily to help with muscle coordination and the nerves. It also acts as a general pick-me-up when energy is flagging or in times of stress, which can produce symptoms such as irritability, headaches, loss of appetite and indigestion.
- For the blues, 50 to 100 milligrams of vitamin B6 can help (but not if pregnant).

Leo

- If you suffer from strain on the heart, try co-enzyme Q10. This substance is found in all the body's cells, particularly its heart muscles, nerve tissue and blood. It aids the transfer of oxygen and energy between the blood and body's cells and between components of those cells. If you are deficient in Q10, often an affliction of athletes and the elderly, take a supplement of 10 to 30 milligrams daily. It is widely available in health-food shops and chemists. It occurs naturally in peanuts, spinach, bran, beef, sardines and mackerel.
- Antioxidants – for example, vitamins A, C and E, beta carotene and lecithin – are found in parsley, garlic, fruit and vegetables and fish oils, and should help fight free radicals, which are thought to damage the body's cells, making you prone to disease and the effects of ageing.
- Eat more fresh tuna, salmon, pilchards, sardines, herring and mackerel. They are all particularly good for you, as of course are fresh fruit and vegetables. Only have two to three portions of oily fish a week, preferably organic or wild.
- For over-exertion, rest! Restore your energy reserves with iron and good nutrition.
- Weak circulation can be treated with vitamin E or ginkgo biloba, which are especially good for those with cold hands and feet or poor memory and concentration.

Virgo

- Herbal remedies work well for Virgos and should always be tried. If you're not eating the diet you know you should, then take a one-a-day multivitamin and mineral tablet.
- Zinc lozenges are good for Virgo throat problems. Or try a horseradish throat remedy of half a teacup of fresh (and only fresh) horseradish soaked well in vinegar for twenty-four

hours, making sure the horseradish is immersed. Add a tablespoon of glycerine, mix well and take half a teaspoon in a glass of hot water when necessary. Sip very slowly.

- For stomach problems, look to the probiotics acidophilus and bifidus.
- A bout of flu means you may have to forget about work for at least a week. As a precaution or when winter looms, take echinacea, zinc and vitamin C.

Libra

- Cranberry is good for cystitis and kidney infections. Why not include cranberry juice in your shopping trolley? Make sure it's low in sugar and additives. Cantharis is a good homeo-pathic remedy for cystitis.
- If you are having problems with your skin, you need vitamins A and E. You can find vitamin A in cod-liver oil, liver, butter, cheese and eggs. Pregnant women must be careful about taking too much vitamin A. Vitamin E is found in vegetable oils, peanuts, eggs, wholemeal bread, wheatgerm and green leafy vegetables. Eat plenty of these and consider supple-ments. Evening primrose oil, vitamin C and beta carotene are also good for the skin. Aloe-vera lotion or gel is nice to apply to soothe and moisturize the skin.
- If you suffer from diabetes, ask your doctor about taking chromium.
- If you do take pills such as headache tablets, go for the lowest dose. Medicines affect Librans more quickly than most. You might find your headache is cured with just one tablet. Or try the herb feverfew, which is fantastic for headaches. Of course, if your problems persist, then consult your GP.

Scorpio

- If you want to ensure a healthy heart, make sure your diet includes essential fatty acids from either oily fish such as fresh tuna, salmon, pilchards, sardines, herring and mackerel or plant oils such as flaxseed. Also for the heart, co-enzyme Q10 is valuable. It can be absorbed by the body from peanuts, spinach, beans, bran, beef, sardines and mackerel. It helps to release the energy in food for use by the body's cells. Pregnant women should not take it as a supplement.

- For organ problems, make zinc a regular part of your diet. This is found in seafood, beef, pork, dairy products, green vegetables, seeds, nuts, pulses and cereals. It is particularly easy to add green vegetables to a dish or a meal, and there are so many different varieties around that you need never eat the same vegetable twice in a month, let alone a week.

- For nasal catarrh, take supplements of zinc, vitamin C and garlic. For relief, sniff tea-tree or eucalyptus oil.

Sagittarius

- For stress, try getting some fresh burdock root if you can track it down. Scrub the root clean, chop it up and then boil it in two pints of water for fifteen minutes. Strain and, when cooled, drink a glass three times a day. You can make up a new batch as and when necessary.

- Elderflower tea is good if you are recovering from a cough or a cold or are feeling a little run down.

- Fennel tea relieves indigestion, especially that caused by stressful mealtimes. Its lovely aniseed taste helps you digest food more easily, and it takes away that bloated feeling.

- Try peppermint tea if you have over-indulged in alcohol or are just feeling sickly. It will bring you nicely back down to earth.

- Camomile tea helps relieve anxiety attacks and should help you sleep more easily.
- For lack of sleep due to pain, try cowslip tea, available from all good health-food stores, which is fantastic.
- Rosehip tea contains vitamin C and has a pleasant taste.
- If you are pregnant, stick to camomile, lemon and lime or peppermint tea to be on the safe side.
- If you suffer from nervous exhaustion, improve your intake of the B vitamins. Good sources are brown rice, seeds, beans, breakfast cereals and Marmite.
- For blood disorders or anaemia, you need iron and vitamin B12. Please consult your doctor or a health professional, who can tell you the correct doses. Iron can be found in beef, pork, liver and kidneys, canned pilchards, sardines, eggs, fortified cereals, spinach, cocoa powder, tomato purée, apricots and green leafy vegetables. B12 can be found in meat, poultry, fish, eggs, cheese, milk, molasses and breakfast cereals.
- Rheumatism can be helped with evening primrose oil and starflower (borage) oil. Devil's claw also works well. Look to your local health-food store for supplies.

Capricorn

- For skin disorders, try zinc, which can be found in seafood, beef, pork, dairy products, green vegetables, seeds, nuts, pulses and cereals. Also try vitamin A, which can be found in cod-liver oil, liver, butter, cheese and eggs. Pregnant women must be careful not to take too much vitamin A. The B vitamins, vitamin E, antioxidants and evening primrose oil are also important for the skin.
- For chills, take ginkgo biloba.
- For rheumatism, ask your health-food store for devil's claw, evening primrose oil and starflower (borage) oil.

- Treat liver problems with Bio Light liquid, available from health-food shops.
- Make sure you get enough calcium. It helps to keep your teeth and bones strong.
- Magnesium, vitamin C (found in blackcurrants, kiwi fruit, peas, potatoes, Brussels sprouts, broccoli, guava, peppers and oranges) and vitamin D (found in kippers, mackerel, eggs, milk and some fortified margarines) are also important for you.

Aquarius

- If you suffer from bad nerves, try ginseng, a plant that has long been used as a nerve tonic. It is also a stimulant. B-complex is good for nerves too.
- For bad circulation, try ginkgo biloba (from your health-food store) or fish-oil supplements. Better still, add ginger to your cooking and eat plenty of tuna, salmon, pilchards, sardines, herring and mackerel. Only eat two to three portions of oily fish a week (and only one of tuna), and where possible, buy organic or wild. Vitamin E, found in vegetable oils, eggs, peanuts, wholemeal bread, wheatgerm and green leafy vegetables, is also good for the circulation.
- For cramps, look to magnesium supplements and eat more seafood, pasta, peas, soya beans, nuts and wholemeal bread. Try brewer's yeast too.
- For nervous indigestion, try peppermint tea.

Pisces

- For rheumatism, try evening primrose oil, devil's claw or starflower (borage) oil from your health-food store.
- For any chest problem, the essential fatty acid omega-3 is helpful. It can be found in oily fish and ground linseeds,

which you can try sprinkling over your cereal. Some of the other fats, especially too much saturated fat, can be harmful to the body, but omega-3s are beneficial and are especially good for the heart. Evening primrose oil is also good, as is antioxidant vitamin A, which is in cod-liver oil, butter, cheese and eggs. Pregnant women must avoid taking too much vitamin A. Avoid caffeine if you suffer chest pain.

- For chills or feet problems, try ginkgo biloba, as it helps to maintain healthy circulation.
- For gout, avoid meat and alcohol, and try zinc, vitamin B6 (found in wholemeal bread, liver, fish, bananas, wheat bran, yeast extract and brewer's yeast) or calcium and magnesium.

Health questionnaire

If you feel that all is not as it should be in your life, then ask yourself the questions below and answer with honesty. After you have written down your answers put them somewhere safe. When you have followed my health plan for a month, you can ask yourself the same questions. Keep answering them each month until the answers give you confidence and boost your self-esteem. If you follow my advice, it won't be long before *all* your answers are self-confident ones!

1. What or who is the main reason you want to get healthy and improve your diet?
2. What do you think will change about your life if you get healthy and improve your diet?
3. Do you like who you are?
4. Do you recognize the things and people you need to remove from your life that are bringing you down?

5. What are the goals and ambitions that you know will make you happy?

Remember that if you keep to an improved health and fitness regime, the answers to these questions will change as time goes on. You'll start to make the answers fit your life, instead of relying on those around you to affirm your identity and dictate your mood. You'll soon see that a healthy body does equal a healthy and happy mind. With this proven, there really will be no going back!

Chapter 11

HIGHS AND LOWS

We're only human and so we're bound to go wrong once in a while. Life is, after all, a learning curve. Remember that experience is what makes us wise, and without going through the hard times we wouldn't recognize the good times.

Did you know that some signs in the zodiac have more addictive personalities than others? Strange but very, very true. Scorpio and Pisces are actually two of the most addictive. In fact many famous stars born under these signs have fought problems with drink and drugs, but have also, you'll be pleased to know, won! Leos think life is a competition and get upset if they don't achieve things in the time they have allotted for themselves. Taureans and Virgos hate to let their loved ones down and blame themselves before others. Geminis think life is a race, while Capricorns give themselves too little time to complete what lies ahead. These signs can show addictive behaviour when they get stressed and must learn to recognize when they hit pressure points so that they can keep their lives from spiralling out of control.

Aries want to save the world and change it, Aquarians want to understand the universe before they've had a chance to understand who they are, while Cancerians and Librans want to solve the problems of people they don't even know. Sagittarians, meanwhile, want to excel in things they know nothing about. We're a confusing bunch, and that's before we start mixing together!

Whatever it is that you think you may be addicted to – drink, drugs, alcohol, bad relationships or overspending – you have to know that you are not alone. There are many people out there fighting the same battle as you, and there is far more help on hand than you think. If you want to go to a support group, that's great, but if you'd rather pick up the phone and talk to someone anonymously, then that's all right too. There is no hard and fast rule. If you embark on a road to recovery that makes you feel positive and good about yourself, then you know that it's the right route for you. If you don't feel that you're going in the right direction, then think about what and who isn't quite working. There are plenty of organizations out there to help you find your recipe for success and I have listed them later in this chapter.

The first step is believing in yourself. There is a whole future out there ready for the taking and anything is possible with just a little support and determination. If your partner or friends and family are not giving you the support you need, then move on and find someone who can. If you are with someone who has an addictive personality, then take the first step together. If they don't, then take it on your own. They should soon follow when they see what amazing progress you are making.

In this chapter we'll take a look at some of the traits that the various signs possess so you can recognize yourself at your lowest and embrace your highs. Addictions are often our way of saying that we need help, and it's important that we look at the root of the problem so that we don't solve one problem just to inherit another.

There is always a way to communicate, no matter what your sign. Some people like to sit and talk about their problems, while for others it's a personal journey they need to travel alone to discover what makes them happy. Years of experience have taught me that problems in our bodies and minds are warning us that something needs to change. I have seen clients who could not move for back pain and yet when they made a change in their life, the pain vanished virtually overnight.

We can blame a person or a situation, but we all hold the power to change, no matter what our sign or age. Taking action can and will help us move on to bigger and better things. Life is about balance. It's about making ourselves happy, giving something back to the people we love and acknowledging when there's a problem before that problem becomes bigger than us.

Aries

You know you are at your lowest when you feel totally irresponsible and become reckless. Aries such as Robert Downey Junior and Butch Cassidy allowed the negativity of their star sign to rule for a while.

Turn to your positive qualities and light up the lives of those around, like Aries Andrew Lloyd Webber, or create a more beautiful world like Aries Leonardo Da Vinci.

Taurus

You know you are at your lowest when you feel stuck in a rut and unable to think about tomorrow for worrying about the problems that today may bring.

Actor Al Pacino, star of *The Godfather*, is a Taurean and may have only been acting in many of his Mafia-style movies, but he's sure to have drawn on a few of his sign's traits for inspiration. Even the late, great actor Marlon Brando, who was also in *The Godfather*, was as famous for the controversy and excess in his personal life as he was for his on-screen success.

Turn to your positive qualities and be clever with your life and words, such as Taurean William Shakespeare. Be courageous and strong, like Pope John Paul II, who was always there for his faith and was deeply committed to the love of his life, God. Her Majesty the Queen has always followed her belief that life will and should go on, no matter what problems and dramas face her.

Gemini

You know you are at your lowest when you feel it impossible to let go of the past or of relationships that are not working. Gemini Marilyn Monroe had a string of lovers who were no good for her and who led to her decline.

Turn to your positive qualities, like Gemini Kylie Minogue, who faced the world when she became ill and fought her way back to health with the power of positive thinking.

Cancer

You know you are at your lowest when you feel emotionally empty and full of self-doubt and loathing.

Turn to your positive qualities, like Cancerian Helen Keller, who became blind and deaf at the age of nineteen months and went on to learn to read Braille. She graduated with honours and began a life of writing, lecturing and fundraising.

Leo

You know you are at your lowest when you feel that what you have is more important than who you are. Leo J. D.

Rockefeller allowed arrogance to prevail and take the limelight away from his best traits.

Turn to your positive qualities and reinvent yourself, just as Leo Madonna has done time after time. Know that life never has to be boring. Stay open to change; it's what your sign thrives on and what attracts success to you.

Virgo

You know you are at your lowest when you become self-critical. Virgo Nicole Richie may have come from a famous family, but she had her fair share of rehab before she realized that a simple life was not so hard to find. Actor River Phoenix died far too young, due to dabbling with narcotics.

Turn to your positive qualities and become a saint! The late Mother Teresa, who was a Virgo, certainly did a good job of showing off the best of this sign's traits.

Libra

You know you are at your lowest when you feel moody, lazy and unable to put others first. Rebel Tommy Lee, who is a Libran, had a reputation for this in the past.

Turn to your positive qualities and join the ranks of the late Linda McCartney, who was a typical Libra – charitable, animal-loving and a humanitarian.

Scorpio

You know you are at your lowest when you feel jealous, aggressive, ruthless and dangerous. The late Scorpio Ike Turner allowed these traits to come to the fore, so much so that he became known more for his turbulent relationship with his ex-wife, Tina Turner, than for anything else.

Martin Luther King and Gandhi certainly made the best of their positive Scorpio traits. Focus on your positive qualities and join the ranks of Scorpio Marie Curie. You can heal yourself and the world!

Sagittarius

You know you are at your lowest when you feel like taking gambles and living life in the fast lane. Sagittarian Frank Sinatra was no stranger in the night to this feeling in his heyday. Archer Britney Spears also went off the rails and lost control when success got too much for her to handle.

Turn to your positive qualities and join the ranks of Winston Churchill, the great prime minister. Walt Disney put a smile on children's faces, and still does with the most famous cartoon character in history, Mickey Mouse.

Capricorn

You know you are at your lowest when you feel your temper getting the better of you. The late, great Elvis Presley allowed his Capricorn addiction to food and drugs to take his life.

Turn to your positive qualities and become like Capricorn Isaac Newton. You too can change the world!

Aquarius

You know you are at your lowest when you feel unable to listen to advice and you do the opposite of what you know deep down to be right. The rebel in Aquarian Paris Hilton came into play when she featured in steamy videos on the Internet, and again when she ended up in jail for her illegal antics. Let's just hope she can manage to stay focused on her many winning attributes in the future!

Turn to your positive qualities and work to make the world a better place. You have a natural commitment to humanity, just like Aquarians Oprah Winfrey and Charles Darwin.

Pisces

You know you are at your lowest when you dice with drink or drugs. Piscean actress and director Drew Barrymore was on cocaine and alcohol before she reached her teens. She now talks openly about it and has certainly turned her life round.

Turn to your positive qualities. You are an artist with a natural ability to paint and draw. Be inspired by Piscean Michelangelo and his artwork in the Sistine Chapel.

Helplines

We all need a helping hand from time to time. If you do, then call today: the sooner you start, the sooner you can see results!

Alcoholics Anonymous
Get help with drinking problems.

www.alcoholics-anonymous.org.uk
0845 769 7555

Recover
Rehab and detox for getting off drink and drugs.

www.recovernow.co.uk
0845 603 6530

Frank
An honest website with information on drugs and help on
beating them.

www.talktofrank.com
0800 776 600

Shelter
Emergency access to refuge services.

www.shelter.org.uk
0808 800 4444

The Samaritans

www.samaritans.org.uk
08457 90 90 90

Women's Aid National Domestic Violence Helpline
Nationwide telephone support provided by highly trained
staff and volunteers backed up by a wide range of leaflets and
resources.

0808 200 0247

Man2Man
Abuse helpline for male victims only.

0208 698 9649

Gingerbread Lone-Parent Helpline
An information service for lone parents, organizations, local
authorities and the media.

0800 018 5026

NSPCC
Free confidential service for anyone concerned about children at risk. Offers counselling information and advice.

0808 800 5000

The Pink Practice
A counselling and psychotherapy practice for lesbian, gay, bisexual and transgender people in Leeds and London.

www.pinkpractice.co.uk
0207 060 4000

Refuge
Twenty-four-hour national crisis line that provides advice and support to those experiencing domestic violence. Refuge can also refer women and children to 250 refuges nationwide.

0990 995 443

Relate
Local Relate centres provide counselling for couples with relationship problems. They also offer psychosexual therapy and relationship and family education.

0300 100 1234

Chapter 12

FINDING YOUR CONFIDENCE

Each star sign is unique, and many of us can't see our good points for the many bad points that others all too often remind us about, so here is a little helping hand for those days when you're lacking inspiration or when tiredness and pressures make it impossible to see the wood for the trees.

Aries

Remember, no matter what anyone else thinks of you, you are living a life of which you can be proud. You are a person who is liked and who enjoys life, but your problem has all too often been that you've rushed into things. It's seemed to others that you've been callous when you've broken up a relationship or spent money that wasn't yours, but in my experience and knowledge of your sign, you have never, ever maliciously set out to hurt or upset anyone. Use your quick thinking to improve your life; it is an asset, not a failing. You are better than the other signs in the zodiac at coming up with a solution when things go wrong. You just need to stop looking to others for ways of turning something bad into something good and to trust in your own instincts. They may have got you into hot water, but they can get you out of it too. Don't run away from things any more either. Stop seeing the past through rose-tinted spectacles and allow your ruling planet, Mars, to help you get in touch with your inner self and your emotions.

You are dreadful at saying things you don't mean and then regret. Sometimes people of your sign spend their whole life making up for mistakes which only took them five minutes to make. Slow down and enjoy the view, and take a big breath before you make a commitment or a promise. What sounds good today may feel different after the sun has set. Read Chapter 15 and make tomorrow better today.

Taurus

If a relationship of yours has broken down, you know it's taken a long time and a lot of honesty to reach this sad point. Don't blame yourself: you don't give up on love easily, and your sign works harder at relationships than any other. You do, however, have a tendency to tell pointless lies, and this is something that can often spiral out of control and get you into a lot of trouble with your partner. You have a great sense of pride and this is what I hope will get you through any break-ups or problems. You know deep down that your loved ones want to see you get yourself together and strive for bigger and better things.

Just for the record, I have never known a Bull to repeat mistakes. You learn from every experience, so what you need to remember is that you've learnt your lesson and can now move on. People like you. You're popular, and you're funny and charismatic, so how can you not rise from the flames? Come on, think about it – don't you want to show that ex-partner or colleague how well you're doing without them? Your stubborn nature alone is reason enough not to give up. If you're feeling sad, you can shake it off with the power of your mind and by practising the Five-Step Plan in Chapter 15 daily. I know you will do just that!

Gemini

When you suffer a heartbreak or a disappointment, you can go to extremes. It is not unusual for Geminis to emigrate following a broken heart. You are a dual-natured sign whose instinct is to go to the opposite extreme in order to solve a situation, but that doesn't hide the fact that you are running away. You can move countries later, Gemini, when you've achieved enough for your friends, family, ex-lovers and ex-colleagues to attend your send-off with champagne at the ready. You need to be able to hold your head up high, and the Five-Step Plan in Chapter 15 will help you to do just that.

The great thing about you is that you're able to visualize, and with the power of your imagination you can sell yourself the ultimate game plan for your future. That plan has to start with sticking things out so you can clean up any mess that's been made. You do this by taking what went wrong and changing it into something that will work for you. Still living in the house you once shared with an ex? Don't move out and put it up for sale looking empty and unloved. Do it up and sell it for double the price, then show your ex how much you made. (After their name is off the paperwork of course!) If you've lost your sense of humour, then find it again. I know it's there somewhere and it really will be your saving grace, no matter how challenging the situation.

Cancer

When you're happy, you're ecstatic, and when you're down, you're inconsolable. You want friends and family to rally round, but the problem is that they can only do so for so long. It's not unknown for you to lock yourself away for a year after a relationship has broken down, even if it only consisted of a few dates! Think positive, as positivity is what will get your sign through any disaster. Read the Five-Step Plan in Chapter 15. It will give you the tips you need to see you through your problems.

If you begin the morning with a smile on your face, it will set you up for the rest of the day. It's when you start off your day with groans and gripes that things begin to go downhill. Remember that when there is a full moon, it affects you more than most, as the moon is your ruling planet. Luckily new moons also offer you inspiration, so note your ideas in a diary and use new moons to formulate plans. They're sure to be successful.

Get over that ex and don't fixate. One client of mine would still send her ex-partner pizzas and taxis that he didn't order a year after they broke up. Instead of ordering food for exes, go out yourself and eat. Don your party gear – you sparkle socially and it's time you realized it.

Leo

You are such a proud character that you hate to feel you've failed at anything, be it making a meal or losing a million. There is no difference, to you, between a minor and a major mistake, but it takes you a while to work out where the blame should lie. Why? Because pride is so strong in your character that you need to look elsewhere first. The problem is that even if you aren't to blame, you still end up shouldering some of the guilt. You don't let the past go and can't forget anything that has gone wrong. You carry the memory like a war wound but never really learn from it. Sometimes you can be like a child who walks into the same door time and time again. Read the Five-Step Plan in Chapter 15 and learn to watch for the warning signals.

Give yourself time to be happy without worrying if everyone else is happy first. Stop setting impossible standards and agree to disagree if you can't make a loved one or a colleague see sense. Stop worrying how your life looks to everyone else and start focusing on what makes *you* happy.

Virgo

You worry about things before they've even happened. It's not unusual for you to be angry with a loved one for something they might do but haven't yet done. Friends and lovers wouldn't be in your life if they didn't want to be and you should start enjoying them, rather than worrying about losing them. You give advice with the best intentions, but you should try taking your own. Stop right now and take in the view. Think about the things that are going on in your life and allow yourself to enjoy what you've done, where you are and what's on offer. You're allowed to have fun and must stop feeling guilty when you do.

Read the Five-Step Plan in Chapter 15, which can help you to appreciate who you are and value your many skills. After all, Virgo, if you don't put yourself first, then why should anyone else? You're worth more than you think. You are kind and compassionate to others, so start to show the same respect to yourself. You arrange things around what others might like, but all they really want is for you to be happy, so plan for yourself for a change, and that means dressing for yourself and not for an ex. The results will be tremendous.

Libra

It's awful to see a sign such as you broken-hearted or down on their luck because it affects you in every way. While some signs feel bad but put on a brave face, your every movement and word tells the tale of what you've been through. Because of your sign, you have no choice but to love completely and to give your heart and soul to any project you commit to. This is why you fall harder than most when things go wrong, but it is also your hidden strength. You see, Libra, even after a disappointment you don't lose faith. New projects don't scare you as much as they do many of the other signs. Where some see fear you see excitement, and this is the very strength that can carry you through any problem and on to better things.

Read the Five-Step Plan in Chapter 15 and allow yourself to grow as a person. You have so many attributes that I'm certain you can't yet have discovered every single one of them. Family often let your sign down, so promise yourself that you will learn and move on. It's all about focusing on the positive and not the negative, my friend. You'll always be a sign who can make new friends and you'll always be capable of carrying on, no matter how it may feel when you're going through a tough patch. Just remember that success will be all the sweeter if you've had to fight for it, so pick yourself up, brush yourself off and get going. There's a future waiting to be lived!

Scorpio

When things go wrong, you feel that life has never looked so bleak. Well, not until the next time, anyway. You see, a strange thing happens when you have a crisis: you forget that you've ever had a problem before. You are winded, shocked and deeply distressed. You have been through difficulties before, though, and you are probably one of the most able signs at coping with what's ahead. In fact turning disaster into opportunity is your talent. Don't be afraid to look to the past or to talk about it. Just remember not to wallow in what was. Take the lesson that's there to be learnt and move on. Don't go all out for revenge either, as there's nothing to be gained; you're just wasting time that could be spent enjoying a better future. Little do new partners realize that when you say you're ringing a friend, you're actually giving an ex nuisance calls.

Focus is the watchword for you. When you're in a constructive mood, you can change the world. When you're in a bad mood, you can ruin it. Read the Five-Step Plan in Chapter 15 and digest it. Make it your daily ritual and learn not to look back.

Sagittarius

When you know what you're doing with your life, you're one of the happiest signs around, but when you lose what you thought was going to be a staple in your life, it can be a really distressing time for you Archers. You love wholeheartedly, and you trust your loved ones implicitly. Actually, you don't have a choice: if you didn't trust them, you'd have a breakdown, as your life is so very busy that you just don't get the chance to watch your loved ones all the time. Work means the world to you and so if someone betrays you in your career, it can sometimes feel like adultery has been committed. Your sign will work with the same faces for years. You know you will go far and trust those you do business with to know this and offer you loyalty in return. The problem comes when people want a piece of the pie for themselves and undermine you because they want to try to be you. They can't and they won't, and that's what you have to realize. Follow my Five-Step Plan in Chapter 15. It will teach you that by simply carrying on you can walk out of the woods and back into the sunshine that is and should be the life of a Sagittarian.

Capricorn

It's hard for you to make a change for anyone, as you're quite a stubborn sign and it takes a very long time for people to earn your trust. When you're hurt or let down, it can often take you a few weeks to acknowledge to yourself what has happened. It's as if you've been winded, and deciding what the next move should be is usually something on which you have to seek advice and support. You fail to realize, though, that every setback is a learning experience that shows you where not to go next time and what not to do. I always advise your sign to take a holiday or a break after any shocking news or when you're feeling down. By changing the scenery, you can gain fresh inspiration and uncover new options. It is harder to do this if you stay at home, where you are reminded daily of what happened. The past haunts you, but it doesn't have to. The Five-Step Plan in Chapter 15 will help you turn every negative into a positive. There is nothing that has happened to you that hasn't made you stronger, and you are better off without anyone who has left your life. Time out, a fresh approach and on to a better footing for you, my friend.

Aquarius

You need to talk about what's gone wrong and find it hard when loved ones refuse to talk about a problem and just up and leave. You need answers and closure, and if you don't get them, then it's not unknown for you to choose the same types in love just so you can get the opportunity to work out what went wrong or even to right that wrong. You have an addictive personality and so you need to be careful that your behaviour doesn't become self-abusive. Remember that if something hasn't worked out, it wasn't meant to be. Blaming yourself is wrong. Lessons must and will be learnt in life, and you are a kind character who wants life to be full of laughter and fun. If someone has brought you down, then you weren't meant to be with them. They didn't bring out the best in you. Cut your losses, but don't cut off your nose to spite your face, not when there are so many signs out there who can help you turn your life into a spectacular one. Read the Five-Step Plan in Chapter 15 and make tomorrow better today. I know you are going to be tempted to skip through it, but don't. You are one of the signs who should read a step a day and do only one a day for five days. Armed with this plan, you need never look back again.

Pisces

The first indication that something is not going right in your life is when you start to let yourself go off the rails. All too often with your sign loved ones blame you for the breakdown of a relationship or for work problems, but what they've failed to realize is that the reason this has happened is because there was a problem there to begin with. You simmer and bubble, and when you are ready, your actions have even the hardiest signs in the zodiac running for cover. It's not surprising you've got a small circle of close friends: not many people can cope with your intensity. I'll tell you a secret, though – every other sign in the zodiac wants to be you and wishes they had your zest for life. They know you'll make it without the help of anybody else, no matter how down on your luck you are, how much money you've lost or how disastrous your love life. Within the year you'll have that ex begging for you to take them back, you'll have the bank willing to give you the account of your dreams, and you'll have achieved a dream. Read the Five-Step Plan in Chapter 15 for the future you know you deserve. It will help you navigate a less bumpy transition to the top and focus on the future instead of the past.

Steps to confidence

We've all had those days when we couldn't cope. Sometimes we blame it on others, and sometimes we blame ourselves. For some of us, it's the simple day-to-day things that can become too much – the school run, family pressures and financial worries. Some very powerful people cope very well with the daily pressures of their high-powered job and yet can't cope when it's time to come home and make their relationship work. What we need to know is that there are tools we can use that are individual to our star sign and personality that can help us to avoid the pitfalls and show us how to make our life a success.

Fire signs (Aries, Leo and Sagittarius)

You often fly off the handle and then regret what you have said but are too embarrassed to say you're sorry. Learn to count to ten before you react and promise yourself you will try to think before you speak. It could save you a lot of red faces, my friend.

Earth signs (Taurus, Virgo and Capricorn)

You often expect your close ones to know what you want. However, our loved ones are not all mind-readers (unless they're water signs, in which case they may have a hunch when you're unhappy!). Learn the skill of communication and try to keep others informed how you're feeling so that they can be there for you.

Air signs (Gemini, Libra and Aquarius)

You talk yourself in and out of a whole lot of trouble. You seem to spend too much time running away from your past and looking for a new future. You need to learn to put more time and energy into the here and now.

Water signs (Cancer, Scorpio and Pisces)

You don't have to stay in a situation that makes you unhappy. Don't wallow in self-pity and don't hold others responsible for your actions. Be assertive, and learn to love yourself. Depression doesn't suit you. Beat it and don't let it beat you. Think positive and life will be positive.

Pointers for bad days

Don't ever let anyone – no matter how important they are to you or how high up the career ladder or popularity stakes – tell you that you can't have a good life or that you won't ever be anything. Every time someone says 'can't', then come back with a 'can'. Every time others see failure, you must see opportunity. I want you to focus only on the positive. You hold the power to turn any experience to your advantage. See any problem as a challenge, not a failure. Look to the good points you have, not the bad points. They are a thing of the past, not the future.

If you're having a low day, then follow these helpful pointers:

1. Remember that experience is what makes us wise. Without the mistakes you have made how would you know not to go down that path again?

2. Learn to focus on your good points. We all have some, whether it's great teeth, a sense of humour or a listening ear. Acknowledge what yours are and say them out loud when you look in the mirror each morning.

3. Friends are there for a reason. If you're having a bad day, call up or text a friend and let them cheer you up. We all need a reserve team to keep us feeling good. Why not choose someone whom you can acknowledge as your feel-good buddy and offer to do the same for them? Know that when you hear from them, you will think of something great to say to them. Even have a codeword for these times. Spreading positivity can become infectious, you know!

4. Spring-clean your life. If you're unhappy, make it your goal for the day to rid yourself of one thing that is not working for you. It could be a top you don't like that it's time to give to the charity shop or deleting the phone number of someone who no longer makes you feel good about yourself.

5. Replay a memory in your head that you know makes you feel good. Sit with your eyes closed and play this moment in your mind as you would a DVD or a song. Let a smile wash over you and acknowledge that life can and will be good for you again.

6. Think of something you want to do. I don't care how extreme it is; it depends how wild you're feeling. I want you to do something to ensure that what you want is one step closer to happening. If you don't try, then how can a job you want be yours, how can a relationship you cherish improve, and how can financial problems disappear? You may need to call the bank today to arrange to see the manager about your financial troubles. You may need to pick up the paper to see what more interesting jobs are out there. You may need to call a friend to ask them to put the word out that you want more than friendship from someone. Taking a step towards one of your goals can make it happen. Doing nothing cannot.

Life Signs is here to give you the confidence to be the best your sign can be. I know from experience with my clients that part of the reason so many people don't obtain their dreams is because they don't try. Start today and you'll be amazed at the result.

Part 5

LIFESTYLE

———

Chapter 13

AT HOME AND ABROAD

We've looked at relationships, we've looked at finances, and we've looked at health, diet and fitness, but what about you? What about your surroundings and your things? Do you wonder why you can't think straight in your home but can find clarity in other places? Your star sign, your life sign, is not just about making things right in your head; it's about making sure that your surroundings work for you. Why is it that we need a holiday to recharge our batteries but when we come home we feel a sense of impending doom at opening our own front door? It needn't be like that.

With my help you will slowly but surely be able to tailor your life to make your home a happier place, to ensure that when you go away, you pick a destination that can give you what you need.

Are you stuck in the Eighties, or are you a Noughties guy or girl who should be heading back to the Swinging Sixties? We'll take a look at what you like to wear and what you should avoid. You can even learn how to look your best after a split. So let's start off with fashion signs to see what's really at the back of your wardrobe, what you should be carting down to the charity shop and what you need to invest in to make it to the top.

Fashion

Aries

With at least as many shoes as Imelda Marcos and a wardrobe most people would die for, you are the trendsetter of the zodiac. You aren't afraid to try new and daring outfits, safe in the knowledge that people around you will soon be following suit. When you see something that catches your eye, you don't hesitate to spend some of your hard-earned cash to look the part. You won't think twice about piercing your belly button or cutting up an expensive pair of jeans if that's what the fashion magazines deem to be cool.

Your wardrobe is a treasure trove, full of all shapes, sizes and colours, though you aren't the sort to go for a sharply tailored look. Male Aries tend to love clothes specially designed for sports or camping and are bound to have one phenomenally expensive pair of trainers in their collection. Accessories are another of your weaknesses – belts, bags and especially hat shops are your personal Mecca.

True to your fiery nature, if you want to knock them dead crimson is the only colour to wear – you'll make an impact that won't be forgotten.

Taurus

You are the typical designer diva who would never dream of rooting through a charity shop to find a funky outfit. You value the highest-quality fabrics and are willing to spend a small fortune on that perfect garment, even if it means you will be living on bread and butter for the rest of the month. Having said that, no one can deny that you have a great eye for style and colour, which means that you rarely appear in a fashion disaster.

People born under your sign never have the problem of knowing what to wear to a formal occasion. Dinner with the French ambassador? You will have at least five outfits that would be suitable. Your logic is that fashion fads come and go, whereas well-made clothes will last you a lifetime. Although you rarely have the confidence to wear something offbeat, when you do pluck up the courage, the effect is fantastic.

Taurean men love to wear blue, whereas Taurean women dress to impress in feminine colours such as pale pink and baby blue.

Gemini

When you open your wardrobe, the clothes probably all fall out into a crumpled mess on the floor! You can be incredibly fussy and indecisive about your clothes – in fact you probably only wear about 10 per cent of your wardrobe. This is because you tend to get bored with the latest fashions and embrace any new trends at the drop of a hat. Unlike Taureans, the label of a garment is the last thing you look at – how it looks and feels is more important than whether it says Gucci or Pucci.

You are one of the more experimental signs in the zodiac and are willing to try out all manner of new trends, though you do shy away from constricting clothes – Tom Jones with his leather trousers could never be your fashion icon. Clingy clothes are simply one of your worst fashion nightmares. Provided you get up early enough in the morning to decide on the day's outfit, you are generally pretty well dressed. Try being a bit more spontaneous when it comes to clothes and you will be surprised at the results.

Gemini colours are generally citrus tones like yellow and orange, which can be worn to brighten up a dark suit.

Cancer

It could be said that you are attached to certain items of clothing as much as you are to your loved ones and your pets. This is because you associate clothes with specific landmark events in your life. There is no doubt that you will have kept the jumper you got engaged in and the dress you wore to your graduation party because of their sentimental value.

Women born under Cancer are some of the most feminine in the zodiac. They manage to look womanly even wearing the most masculine of clothes – wellies and combat trousers make no difference to them. However, Cancerian women should really try to look as feminine as possible; it will give your confidence a boost. Invest in some silky lingerie to look your best.

Cancerian men don't tend to make much of an effort with their clothes unless there is a special occasion. When you do bother to dress up, you are bound to outshine those around you. You usually have a rule of thumb for dressing that dates back to a compliment you were given in your teens, and as the years go on you may need to reassess this rule in case it has become outdated or no longer flatters you. You are the sort of people who find a style you like, then stick to it throughout your life. Some experimentation is what's needed – wearing something a little more daring than you are used to could really pay off.

Silver, blue and green are the colours best suited to you.

Leo

No bargain-basement shopping for you, Leo. If it doesn't cost a small fortune, then you probably won't buy it. Fashion magazines are your bible and you tend to follow whatever they say. As for comfortable clothes, forget them. If the trend requires painting yourself blue and wearing sheepskin shoes, that's exactly what you'll be doing. You aren't afraid of wearing daring outfits and often customize a plain garment with funky accessories. If you weren't so attached to labels and designers, you could save a fortune by using your creativity to create fantastic outfits from garments picked up in thrift shops.

Male Leos tend to be a tad more conservative than the women, preferring expensive clothes that will stand the test of time. Leos have a weakness for costly, not to mention flashy, jewellery and love to show some skin. Don't forget your sign rules the back, so for women, going strapless or even backless is a great way to attract attention. So long as you keep your outfits dramatic, you won't fail to make a great impression.

Your best colours are those guaranteed to make you stand out – glitzy golds, oranges and bronzes teamed with black are the order of the day for either sex.

Virgo

Known as the perfectionists of the zodiac, woe betide you if you try to talk a Virgo into buying an outfit that doesn't match. They will know exactly what accessories go with the outfit they have chosen, right down to the correct scent to set it off. Usually seen going for greens and dark browns, true to their element of earth, they like to feel comfortable, practical and stylish all at the same time. Somehow, as if by magic, they manage to do this.

You will note that their homes are an organized mess, so their hanging space will consist of their wardrobe, the dressing table and the bed, but they will take great offence if you try to tell them this is not the norm.

Known more for telling friends how to dress, they believe

they are trendsetters, but they always manage to retain a certain amount of class as they don't go for fashions that are too OTT. Instead they look as if they have the secret style the rest of us are longing for.

Virgos won't spend more than they think is fair on an item of clothing, but if they do splash out, then they will go out of their way to let you know just how much they paid for it. The men of this sign get good use out of their suits, more so than the women, but at least they're in style when the cut comes back into fashion ten years later.

Libra

Librans are probably the most stylish dressers in the zodiac. They adore quality and beautiful-looking clothes. They wouldn't even be averse to planning a holiday around where all of the best clothes are to be found. Yes, this is the sign that will long for their coat to slip down so that the designer label shows. The secret they have is that they are also dab hands at tracking down designer goods in second-hand stores, and as they wear it so well, they make it look double the price it was to start with. The women of this sign are suckers for super handbags, and if it is a famous label, then so much the better.

Generous to the bitter end, clothing will be top of their list for friends and family too, so if you don't feel too pleased with the tie they've bought you, check again – it's likely to be top of the range and made in Italy, one of their favourite countries.

Blues, pale greens and pinks usually adorn their attractive bodies, and the males of this sign are likely to have a tie collection that other men would die for.

Scorpio

Scorpios love to look sexy, if you're trying to sell them a suit or an outfit that is designer but doesn't look sexy, then you may as well give up, for they have to look and feel a million pounds. Fabrics and the feel of a material are important to them, and if it comes in red or maroon, that's even better.

The women of this sign usually have enough nail varnishes to fill ten beauty salons, and they are not cheap brands either. These are, I'm afraid, all in dramatic colours. They love great shoes, and the higher the heel for the women, the better. Leather holds a great attraction, and Scorpio women also like to wear chokers, which may create a misleading impression as they will not be dominated. When wearing make-up, they concentrate mainly on the eyes, as they know these are their best feature, and they are not averse to large amounts of black eyeliner. Even the men don't mind a smudge or two to give their eyes definition – just look at Leonardo Di Caprio; at recent awards ceremonies, you may have noticed his eyes have been more defined than usual. Scorpios use fashion to give out a message, so read it and decide. But don't take too long, as they don't like people who can't make up their minds.

Sagittarius

The Archer has fantastic legs and will go to great lengths to show them off. One of the main problems they have with their dress sense is that they buy clothes in such a hurry they don't always have time to get a whole outfit, so they can end up dressing as if they represent every season. Fire signs are always in a hurry, but they do have this knack of being in vogue and turning more than a few heads with their clothes, whatever their age. Tina Turner is a typical Sagittarian dresser: her clothes are made to show off her fine muscles and yet give her the ability to run, dance, jump, whatever her energetic sign requires.

Just beware of catching them at home when they are not expecting you, though. Sagittarians hate being restricted and you may well find them wearing their birthday suit.

They prefer rich purples and dark blues. Rich is of course the operative word for this ambitious sign who always manages to dress like the boss, even if it's their very first day at work.

Capricorn

Capricorn is an earth sign who gives people the impression that they have been someone, are someone or will end up being someone. They have an air that makes it hard for you to be rude or cheeky to them, and this has as much to do with their dress sense as anything else. They can usually be seen in conservative colours – chiefly dark green, grey, brown and black. They are not avid followers of fashion but will have worked out their own style over the years. Even the young Capricorn will not feel the need to fit in with the rest of the crowd and will have their own sense of fashion, albeit strange at times. They worry about getting cold in winter, so even the good-looking eighteen-year-old will be found with thermals in their drawers ready for the chilly season.

They are practical and will want labels that are trusted. High-street stores are fine by them, but they will know the beauty of a designer piece too, usually jewellery. Look at their watch and you'll get my point. As they are slow to make up their mind, you may want to take a chair with you when going out shopping – you could have quite a wait if they haven't made a list!

Aquarius

Aquarians spend more of their time chatting about what they are going to buy than they do getting out there and buying it. When they do go shopping, they don't mind buying quantity over quality, and for the women of this sign, the smaller the item of clothing, the better. Remember, they have been known to suffer with circulation problems and this is no surprise considering the short skirts and the high heels they favour. This is usually only a phase, as when the first blister kicks in, they start to see the point of proper clothing and seek to wear things that scream comfort, with a sexy edge to it of course. They can usually be found going for electric blue and turquoise. The women like floaty skirts that you can see through, and the men love linen shirts. If a T-shirt has writing on it, then so much the better. After all, Aquarians don't have time to talk as much as they'd like, so they try to get their point across with their clothing.

They don't need designer clothes, but they do have to have trendy gear. They are forward-thinking and like to be at the front of any fashion revolution, even if it means going overdrawn. Bangles, peace beads and lots of necklaces appeal, and the child in them is fascinated by way-out hair dos, which often turn more heads than any item of clothing that can be seen adorning their beautiful bodies.

Pisces

Think Piscean and you must think of the sea and floaty materials, which for the men is often represented by linen trousers or even flares. Pisceans like to wear dramatic, over-the-top shoes or no shoes at all. They're accustomed to taking off their footwear to feel the earth under their feet. They believe that shoes are for looks, not comfort, so it's no surprise they want to kick them off after ten minutes.

Soft shades of green can often be seen adorning their attractive bodies, and they like to wear things that give them a slimline shape or that allow the light to catch them and show the contours of their bodies. Pisceans get obsessive about clothes, and if they choose a new fashion, they will throw out everything they have that represents their old style. They are true chameleons. Gypsy styles suit them, and that's probably because they spend most of their time counselling and giving readings to friends. They are, after all, the most psychic sign of the zodiac.

At home

The water signs, Cancer, Scorpio and Pisces, should live near the water if they can, but there are ways for them to find tranquillity if they can't get away from the city, whether it is walking in a park or sitting in a garden. Fire signs, Aries, Leo and Sagittarius, need a fast pace and hustle and bustle to feel alive, and earth signs, Taurus, Virgo and Capricorn, find living in temporary or rented accommodation can send them crazy as they need security. Air signs, Gemini, Libra and Aquarius, need a modern style of living, as they like to keep up with the times.

Clues you have entered a fire sign's home
The fire signs, Aries, Leo and Sagittarius, are always keen to make their homes look good, but all too often their enthusiasm wanes, leaving jobs half done and homes looking as if the builder has had to leave for an emergency call-out. They

mean well, but they need to be balanced by a sign who can finish what they've started. Bright colours suit them, but they can be a little too adventurous with fashion and style in the home, making the more old-fashioned and traditional signs feel uncomfortable. Chrome and glass will be a favourite choice for them, and they dislike clutter and gadgets, so their kitchen often has a minimalist feel.

Clues that you have entered an earth sign's home

The earth signs, Taurus, Virgo and Capricorn, can't help but keep belongings and objects that have personal meaning. The table or chair that they bought for their first flat will still be in their house twenty years on. It reminds them of where they came from and how far they've come. Don't get me wrong, though: this is a most fashion-conscious element. They have a flair for design and know how to make a home a home. Big armchairs and oversized items will be the perfect choice for them.

If your partner is an earth sign and you are not, then I'm afraid you are going to have to give in to their style, as they have a distinct idea of what will and will not work. This is one area where you should give them free rein, as they know what they're doing and are sure to make your home a place of comfort and relaxation.

Clues that you have entered an air sign's home

If it's new out, then the air signs, Gemini, Libra and Aquarius, have to have it. To be living with wooden floorboards when carpet is back in vogue would be enough to make these signs lose sleep. These are social creatures and so they need their home to be a place they can entertain in. They like to change the way their home looks but need to be careful that they don't invest large amounts of money in things they will want to change next year. These signs are not afraid to spend money to impress people. That funny-looking object on the wall is not a work of art; it's probably the latest phone, which they just had to acquire to bring them bang up to date with whatever the latest interiors magazines are raving about.

Clues that you have entered a water sign's home

The homes of water signs Cancer, Scorpio and Pisces will be full of things their loved ones have bought them. Dare to open a drawer and you must be prepared to find some oddity there. Water signs need a relaxing space; they will have to have a sofa that they can sleep on. Objects are not bought for how they look but for how they feel, although if they own an expensive item, you can bet it will be in prime view. The bedroom is a key room for them and should not contain anything to do with work. It has to be the place where they can recharge their batteries. To even think about having a shower instead of a bath is also a no-no. These signs need to soak their troubles away in order to plan their next big step in life. If you're invited into their home, you're lucky: they don't let people they don't like into their private space.

Holiday destinations

We often choose to vist places that please our loved ones, but are they right for us? Should you have been meditating when you were medicating with a Martini, or are you one of the signs who needs a glass of wine to wind down after a day at the office? This is your guide to holidays and relaxation. It could make all the difference between success and disaster when the going gets tough. A tired mind can make bad decisions, but with the right attitude there will be nothing to stop you from achieving all that your heart desires. You can even use this guide to plan a romantic trip for a loved one or a family member, to help a friend find a better path and clearer vision after a split, to recharge your batteries or just for some good old-fashioned fun!

Aries

People born under this sign are nomads at heart. Aries love exploring. They aren't afraid to go it alone and are stimulated by different cultures and people. The Ram is most likely to be found backpacking around the world, trying to cram as many countries into their itinerary as possible. A couple of weeks inter-railing around Europe and soaking up the architecture is just their cup of tea. They also have a great affection for the outdoors, so camping certainly appeals to this side of their nature. What about pitching a tent in a different place each night – the wilder and more remote the location, the better?

Although white-water rafting or rock climbing are not many people's idea of a holiday, the Ram will love the adrenalin rush. If it's not packed with excitement and stunning scenery, they just won't want to know. An athletic holiday on the ski slopes is just the thing for the Ram. A diving trip to the Great Barrier Reef would also be ideal – Aries would get high on the fact that they just might meet a shark in the depths of the ocean. Now wouldn't that be an adventure to tell the grandchildren!

Ideal destinations for an Aries: Austria, Nepal, Argentina and Spain.

Taurus

Taureans are not the sort of people to take a last-minute holiday. A trip away has to be planned as strategically as a military operation. The Bull will always do their research, poring over stacks of travel brochures before finally deciding on the appropriate destination. When they do go on holiday, they like to live the high life. Luxury is their middle name and top hotels or lavish meals are a must. Having said that, they don't need to travel far to get their fix. Taureans would appreciate the pleasures of French food, wine and cheese, not to mention the atmosphere of romantic Paris. Needless to say, their kind of holiday will do serious damage to their bank account. No camping in the great outdoors for them, thank you very much. Much more up the Bull's street is a grand tour of Europe, taking in all the beauty of Paris, followed by the architecture of Barcelona and a trip to the opera in Rome. Rest assured, after a hard day of sightseeing, they will retire to their high-class accommodation for some self-indulgence. Taureans certainly know how to travel in style and they try to avoid the cramped conditions of economy class at all costs.

Ideal destinations for a Taurean: France, Japan, the Netherlands and Thailand.

Gemini

People born under this sign are renowned for having a short attention span. The idea of a long holiday in one location would bore them senseless, as would two weeks of lazing on a tropical beach. Geminis prefer to keep on the go, travelling from place to place with no fixed route. The Twins are inquisitive people who are eager to learn as much as they can about destinations they visit. They would actually make excellent tour guides because there is nothing they like better than visiting all the sights.

Short breaks to large, vibrant cities like New York, Hong Kong and Tokyo are just up their street. They would be wide-eyed with wonder at the bustling markets and busy streets, not to mention the shopping in these huge urban jungles. The idea of a train trip through Spain, stopping at lots of towns along the way, would satisfy their desire to know a country inside and out. However, offer them a trip around the world and they are bound to politely decline – a whole year spent travelling would be pure torture for them. Remember, the grass is always greener to them and they could not bear missing out on what was happening back home. They aren't the sort of people who would enjoy the solitude of travelling alone and need someone with whom they can share the experience.

Ideal destinations for a Gemini: Spain, Greece and New York.

Cancer

Cancerians love the comfort and security of home. They lack the adventurous and pioneering spirit of the Ram and tend not to have a strong wanderlust. When the Crab does venture out, wherever they decide to go they need people around them to recreate a homely environment. They also aren't the sort of people to blow their savings on the trip of a lifetime – they'd rather watch a travel programme from the comfort of their settee.

So what kind of holiday could lure Cancerians away from their home comforts? As a water sign, the Crab would feel relaxed by a beach or a lake, where they are likely to indulge in a spot of sailing, surfing or diving. They love travelling with the family and so will visit all manner of theme and adventure parks. A rollercoaster ride is about as big a risk as they will take – the idea of rock climbing or abseiling would fill them with dread. When it comes to accommodation, the thrifty Crab will shy away from plush hotels in exclusive areas. They find all they need in a caravan and might even be persuaded into camping out for a few nights. This also gives them the opportunity to do their own cooking while on the road, and when they do have to eat out, they are bound to find the best of high-quality, good-value restaurants. Although being fair, they stay at the right places for the right price, while the rest of us are paying over the odds.

Ideal destinations for a Cancerian: Florida, Bahamas and Canada.

Leo

Leos like to sail through life with style, and the same is true when it comes to travelling. No bargain-basement, last-minute deals to the Costa del Sol for them. You'd never catch them making the most of cheap transport either – they're more likely to be found in the lap of luxury on *The Orient Express*. They are the people most likely to hire a driver to save them the inconvenience of getting from A to B. The Lion will always go to whatever country is trendy and 'the place' to visit that year, taking a multitude of friends along for the ride. Milan and Paris, with their reputation as centres of fashion, are a must, as are twenty-four-hour party cities like New York, Hong Kong and Miami. It is hard to envisage the Lion roughing it with a backpack in India and Africa. They like travelling to be a stress-free, easy experience and don't mind paying for the privilege. Leos are renowned for their love of gambling, so a trip to Monte Carlo would not go amiss, with a night at the casino followed by a stay at an exclusive hotel. If the urge to try their luck at roulette is particularly strong, a jaunt to Las Vegas will be firmly on the itinerary. The bright lights and excitement are a temptation Leos just won't be able to resist.

Ideal destinations for a Leo: Boston, New York, Singapore and Miami.

Virgo

Virgo's worst nightmare is for something to go slightly awry or not according to plan. Switzerland immediately comes to mind when thinking of ideal holiday destinations for them – they like clean streets, order and fresh air. This sign will rarely let the fact that they are on holiday affect their routine. Every day is bound to be organized down to the last detail, from where to eat to when they go to bed. Their intentions are good – they want to make the most of every minute and ensure they see everything on their list. Virgos enjoy culture and history. They will spend hours trailing around museums in their quest to learn.

They should avoid cities that are bound to cause them distress; Rio, with all its hustle and bustle, springs to mind. This does not mean that Virgos should only visit sanitized, rather dull parts of the world. They might enjoy more unusual destinations, like Scandinavia or even Tibet. Virgos are one of the most health-conscious signs in the zodiac, so a hiking holiday somewhere picturesque or perhaps a cycling holiday would give them pleasure.

Ideal destinations for a Virgo: Switzerland, Malta and Austria.

Libra

Ruled by Venus, goddess of love and all things beautiful, it is no wonder that Librans are drawn to places of luxury and beauty. Needless to say, thrift does not come into the equation when planning a Libran holiday. Plush hotels and only the best food and wine will do, but their biggest vice is souvenirs. They are liable to head straight for the most expensive shopping area in town to purchase mementoes of their travels. Shopping is an important factor when considering where to go on holiday, so New York and Hong Kong are always popular.

Librans generally do not enjoy travelling alone and have much more fun with a loved one beside them. Their desire for balance and harmony makes them great travelling partners because they will only be happy when their companion is too. Social animals that they are, Librans will be drawn to events like the Rio Carnival or New Orleans's Mardi Gras. Occasions like this will give them the chance to party and mingle in the most exotic of locations. Dressing up is important and you will rarely see Librans making a beeline for places without a dress code.

Ideal destinations for a Libran: Rome, Shanghai and Hong Kong.

Scorpio

Scorpios are the sort of people who love to try anything and everything – the more unusual, the better. They are not drawn to conventional destinations, but rather yearn to go further afield to experience as many weird and wonderful things as they can. Columbia or Algeria are appealing, as are the red-light districts of the world! People who come back from their travels having had a major personality change are most likely to be Scorpios – travel is an opportunity to get to know their inner self as well as different parts of the world. They are passionate about risky activities, from white-water rafting to bungee-jumping. When it comes to food, Scorpios are the kind of people who love to sample all the local delights, be it fried grasshoppers or snake soup. They will rarely plan where they are going to stay – half the fun is not knowing where they are going to end up. Whatever happens, they aren't bothered about luxurious restaurants and hotels. A chance encounter with one of the locals will give them much more pleasure!

Ideal destinations for a Scorpio: Angola, Egypt and Costa Rica.

Sagittarius

Think Sagittarius, think explorer. This is the sign of travel and Sagittarians belong on the road, searching for adventure and excitement. There aren't many places in the world that Sagittarians would not be willing to visit – every place is likely to stimulate them in some way.

Off-the-beaten-track locations are the best bet for a Sagittarian with itchy feet. A trip to China with a boat ride down the Yangtze would be ideal, as would an activity-packed holiday in the Himalayas. Sagittarians will get along with people they meet on their travels and are hungry to learn about the lifestyles of those from different cultures. Meeting up with street hawkers in Mozambique or praying with monks in Tibet is about as good as it gets for gregarious Sagittarians. For someone who is seeking 'the truth', issues such as accommodation or where to eat are mere trifles. In fact to the typical Sagittarian, eating is a waste of time, taking them away from more interesting activities.

Ideal destinations for a Sagittarian: Bangladesh, Lebanon and Kenya.

Capricorn

If you do manage to persuade a Capricorn to leave the office for long enough to go on holiday, rest assured it will be a very organized and carefully planned affair. Capricorns like to be comfortable when travelling, and holidays are sometimes all about social status. Cities with charm and elegance are high on the agenda, so Barcelona, Geneva and Madrid fit the bill. Like Leos, Capricorns are lured to the 'in' destinations. Luxury cruises are also a perfect choice because the Goat loves to see places but prefers not to have to walk too far. They don't shy away from travelling in a group and are happy to adopt the role of leader. They like to take their time when travelling and enjoy strolling around a museum at a leisurely pace. If you are looking for an adventurous holiday, then don't go away with this sign. Capricorns are more interested in eating and staying in the trendiest of places, though that does not extend to sampling the more exotic local delicacies.

Ideal destinations for a Capricorn: San Francisco, Australia and Spain.

Aquarius

When an Aquarian goes travelling, it is likely that they have saving the planet in mind. One of the more socially conscious signs in the zodiac, the Water-Bearer would love saving the rainforest in Brazil or rescuing endangered species in Malaysia. People born under this sign are usually surrounded by friends, so the idea of travelling in a group would appeal to them, as would taking on the role of leader. Because of their sociable natures, Aquarians feel at home in big, bustling cities, where they can hit the hotspots and party till dawn.

They are keen to collect fresh and exciting experiences, and will go anywhere, no matter how obscure and remote. They are extremely adaptable and are just as happy to sleep in a tent as in a five-star hotel, though their philosophy is usually to do as the locals do. This involves eating adventurously and trying all the local delicacies, whether shark's-fin soup or ostrich steaks.

Ideal destinations for an Aquarian: India, Mexico, Venezuela and New York.

Pisces

Pisceans are drawn to places where they feel they can do some good, for they are compassionate folk. They rarely travel without a particular purpose in mind – a trip to Guatemala will involve working with street kids and this is because they are one of the most charitable signs in the zodiac. They will make the utmost effort to get to know local people wherever they end up. Pisceans also tend to go through life in a dreamlike state. Their heads are always in the clouds and they sometimes need to be pulled back down to earth. They prefer not to be in charge of the more mundane aspects of travelling and will leave the job of booking tickets, making reservations and reading timetables to someone else.

Because of their yen for meditation and contemplation, Pisceans would feel most at home somewhere like Tibet or India, or even Lourdes, where they can continue on their spiritual journey. The Fish also have a strong artistic side to their nature and are stimulated by places rich in culture and art. A painting holiday or a trip to the opera in Italy is just the ticket for creative Pisceans.

Ideal destinations for a Piscean: Brazil, China and India.

Chapter 14

PARTIES

Are you a perfect dinner party host or a disaster waiting to happen? Do your friends secretly nickname you Porky Pete or Lady Lucy because of your table manners? Time to find out some home truths about your eating habits.

Guess who's coming to dinner

Aries

I'm afraid these people really are scoffers who would prefer to eat with a shovel rather than a knife and fork. If you see them nipping in and out of the kitchen, they are more likely to be sneaking an extra mouthful than washing dishes. They can drink quickly as well, so make sure you give them little and often if you want them to last the distance at a dinner party. They are usually pretty good cooks, so if you get an invite round to theirs, then go. They can whip up a delight in no time, as they have no fear about mixing the strangest of ingredients.

If you want to know the best dishes to serve and indeed even seduce an Aries, then make them spicy, the hotter the better; and if they down enough wine, they may even enter a chilli-eating competition. Just beware if they start mixing cocktails early on in the day, though, or you could have the hangover from hell. This is one sign who doesn't do anything by halves, but I'm sure you wouldn't have them any other way. They are both fun and unpredictable, as I'm sure you will have discovered by now if you have an Aries in your life.

Taurus

The funny thing with a Taurean is that they spend so much time talking about how they are looking forward to hosting a gathering and making sure that all of the fine details are perfect, but when it actually comes round, they are too busy in the kitchen to see the looks of joy on their guests' faces. Remember to thank them for the effort they have gone to; it's sure to have been a lot. Take them a gift if they are the host – something to eat or drink would be good. If they're coming to yours for food, then watch out, as they'll be opening the wine they've brought you as a thank-you gift quicker than you can say, 'Take your seats.' I have a brother who is a Taurean and a typical one at that. He used to stab his fork into my potato and say, 'Do you want that?' He's mellowed over the years and has taken on many traits of his Gemini girlfriend, so I no longer have to guard my plate.

The Bull will eat starters, main courses, the lot, but by far their favourite has got to be the dessert. No matter how much they've eaten, when pudding arrives they'll secretly loosen their waistband and tuck in, knowing full well they will be unable to move for an hour afterwards. They enjoy their food and like nothing better than sitting round a table drinking, eating and talking with their loved ones.

Don't give them second-rate food or drink – they're far cleverer than you can imagine and know the price of every-thing, so make it top quality, especially given the time and effort they are sure to have put into your gift, which they'll have already unwrapped for you!

Gemini

This is a sign who really will drive you round the bend. They say they are starving but by the time the food is put in front of them, they are busy talking and will have to be told at least a dozen times that their food is going cold. They don't mean to be rude, but they can come across that way, especially those of them who smoke and tell you that they really don't mind if you eat while they finish their fag. They are great socializers, though, and will invite all and sundry into their home, although I can't always guarantee what you are going to get. Any thank-you gifts are sure to be inventive, if they remember to bring these with them! Yours is sure to be just one of many gatherings to which the Gemini has been invited.

Their weight can go up and down over the course of the year depending on what is happening in their very active life. They may annoy you with the way they eat and talk at the same time, but don't tell them off, as I can assure you that you'll really want to hear the news they have to share with you, even if it has been embellished thanks to their very vivid imagination.

Cancer

Social gatherings round a dinner table are more important to the Crab than you can possibly imagine, as it gives them a chance to catch up with their nearest and dearest and to tell them for the hundredth time how much they love them. They have a habit of living in the past, so don't be surprised if they bake the biscuits you loved as a child. They will think they're doing good even if you grew sick of them years ago. Just smile and pretend to enjoy them.

Please be careful what you give this sign to drink, as they really do have a problem with handling alcohol. It will only take two shots of gin to have them crying into their pudding over a childhood sweetheart. They don't need a lot to get drunk; in fact for many of them, just the smell of alcohol is good enough.

As for food, Cancerians love certain foods and hate others. They put the same passion into food that they put into life. This is the character who will hate tomatoes but love tomato ketchup. The dishes they can do they will do well, so make sure you take up that invite to dinner – you're bound to find yourself having a ball.

Leo

Now this is a sign who is far more worried about what something looks like than the taste of it, so don't forget to sprinkle parsley over a dish before you serve it up to them. This fire sign goes through foods fads, and I don't think I'd be too far off the mark if I told you to look in magazines to see what the celebs are eating or what diet they are following, as Leos are sure to be hot on the heels of the latest trend.

They are very sociable souls who will go out of their way to make sure you aren't hungry and that your glass is never empty. You must praise them often, though, as omitting to mention every five minutes how fabulous the dessert was (even if it was bought and not made!) would devastate them. You will find the dinner-table conversation enchanting, as they talk about themselves and then ask you what you think of them; but you can't help but love them and the way they make you laugh and help you to forget the stresses of the day. It's all about effort with Leo, and they'll go to the ends of the earth for you, so make sure you remember to thank them. Their heart is always in the right place!

Virgo

I do love dear Virgo, but if things don't go exactly to plan, then don't we all know about it! This is a sign who will put name-cards on the table even if you have sat in exactly the same place for the last ten years. In their eyes this helps to avoid any confusion. You are sure to find all of your firm favourites on the dinner table as long as Virgos are around, which is bound to make you feel special. I don't know a sign who is more considerate of others' needs, even if it can drive you to the point of distraction sometimes – they will make you drive ten miles out of your way to buy the right ingredients for dessert. You have to know that they are doing so out of love.

If a Virgo is your dinner guest, they will have some pretty peculiar eating habits and the most unpredictable likes and dislikes when it comes to food. An evening with this sign will most certainly be unforgettable and fun!

Libra

Balance and harmony are vitally important to this air sign. They like to be able to follow their plans and their heart, which can often have some confusing results and some very late-running arrivals and departures, as they will do their famous disappearing act when they see fit. Librans are like children and expect a dinner party to be a little like a tea party with games and laughter on the agenda. You would be better to give them lots of fun foods rather than just one big meal; they want to be able to pick, to talk, to pick and then talk some more.

They like to drink, but start them off too early and they'll be the ones snoring in the corner while the rest of us are eating dessert. They also enjoy after-dinner games, but don't be put off by their childlike image: this is one sign who knows how to enjoy life, and you can be sure that if they're cooking for you, it will be a meal to remember with a setting right out of a storybook.

Scorpio

Scorpios look upon dinner parties with both excitement and dread. They love to gather round all the familiar faces, but they dread to think what past issues may be dragged up in the process. This sign has a lot of secrets and so they like to keep certain areas of their life private. You always find that one or two things come to light during any occasion that involves alcohol.

Scorpios are an extreme sign who will be either a great or a dreadful cook; there really is no in between. They give their heart and soul to everything they choose to do, so if they have decided to look into the world of cooking, they will have learnt properly and could probably cook a meal from every country in the world if asked. If the world of gastronomy has not appealed to them, then even beans on toast will be too much to expect. They either like alcohol or can't abide it, and if they do indulge, then they will throw it into their cooking too, so watch out – that fruit cocktail could well be all alcohol and no fruit. Dinner with a Scorpio is sure to prove unmissable, so get round there.

Sagittarius

The Archer will spend much time telling you with great excitement what they are going to cook when you come round, but by the time you get there they will have had a complete change of heart. They may even end up ordering a Chinese takeaway, so unpredictable are they. Fire signs make up their mind about something but don't have much patience, so a week later everything can change, although I'm sure they won't have had time to tell you. Don't believe them if they tell you it's fancy dress when they arrange a gathering: double-check if you want to avoid embarrassment.

Sagittarians like new and exciting foods, but can suffer from indigestion, so try to avoid cooking overly rich dishes for them. They will say they enjoyed the meal, but you may miss out on their very stimulating company when they spend the next hour in the bathroom. They like champagne and cocktails, and love to talk – or should I say gossip? You'll have great fun with this sign at any gathering, but with a Sagittarian you must expect the unexpected!

Capricorn

The earthy Capricorn adores having their loved ones around them, and although they are very kind souls, you may want to double-check with them if you are thinking of inviting friends to a gathering. You see, there are times in their life when they only want to be with their nearest and dearest, and they don't take too kindly to having their parade rained on without notice or without their written consent.

They can party with the best of them and don't mind donning a party hat; in fact, they probably brought them. They are children at heart and love to enjoy good food prepared by loving hands; they will even help you clean up if you get them on a good day. No dinner party is complete without a Capricorn, for they provide the party atmosphere that will bring smiles to the sternest of faces. Give them traditional food, though – they prefer their meat and two veg to anything you may have read about. If you go without pudding, then you may as well phone them a cab: some things are essential to them, and this, my friend, is one.

Aquarius

Aquarians just love the social side of dinner parties. They may promise to do something to help out, but they are usually so busy running around dishing the dirt and finding out what they can about the other faces who are attending that they forget the essentials. They can talk their way out of any problem, though, so don't even think about scolding them – they'll just laugh at you. The Aquarian will make your dinner party complete; they'll have you in stitches with laughter and will know all the latest jokes. They are not always on time, though, as they are too busy thinking about tomorrow to remember today. They make a party and can also make a great meal when they calm down and concentrate on the job at hand. They're sure to know all the latest dishes, their favourite being light bites so that they can keep going back for more in between the wine and fun but naughty stories.

Pisces

This is a sign who will go to extremes to make sure that your dinner party is all you dreamed. If they say that they will cook, then make sure you are hungry, as they are more likely to do ten courses than three or four. They want to create a dramatic impression, and they do. If you go round on a Friday, then you may not find yourself leaving until Sunday. If they like you, they love you and will have a dinner table laden with exotic and hard-to-find goods. They can drink you under the table, although that doesn't mean that they won't be completely and utterly sozzled; it just means that they refuse to give in. Drinking games are not an unusual suggestion from them either. Careful, though, as those ice cubes could well be full of gin or vodka. Those Pisceans who don't drink really don't drink, and those who do, well, they drink like a fish of course.

Treat them well and they will treat you even better. The conversation round the dinner table is sure to tantalize and surprise. This is one sign who knows how to enjoy a gathering to the full, even if there are a few casualties who will need to be attended to!

Downtime: party pooper or disco diva?

Will it be back to yours for a party, or are you aghast at the thought of anyone's dirty shoes even crossing your front door? Let's take a look at which of you signs are ready to party and which would rather turn in for an early night.

Aries

You Aries are a masculine, fiery lot! Needless to say, your life is a series of competitions and you play every game to win. This makes for a stressful life and there is no better way of forgetting about the pressures and strains of everyday life than having a party. You are the sort of person who is full of combustible energy begging to be burnt off. There should be no half-measures when it comes to planning your ideal party. You are very home-loving and probably would not be able to relax enough to enjoy a party at your place. Hiring out a hot nightclub for the evening is more up your street – you won't need to worry about people dropping food on the floor and wine stains on the sofa. Many of you Aries have excellent singing voices and are good dancers, so maybe a spot of karaoke wouldn't go amiss. Let's not forget party food, Aries! Variety is definitely the spice of life for you, so lots of appetizers are in order. Cheese and pineapple or sausages on sticks must be banned from your party – you hate bland things and like it hot and spicy. Salsa, chilli dips and samosas should be on the menu. When it comes to music, to say you are cutting edge does not do you justice. Only the most up-to-date, loudest tunes will have you hitting the dance floor, and once there, you are bound to party till dawn.

Taurus

Your sign is one of the most conventional and practical in the zodiac – as an earth sign, your feet are planted firmly on the ground. Of course, this does not mean to say you don't know how to let your hair down. You are extremely sociable creatures and there is nothing you like better than being surrounded by friends and family. A nightclub is no good for you – frenetic dancing and loud music just leave you exhausted, not exhilarated, and besides, how can you hear yourself think? In order to relax, you need to be creative. Planning an elaborate dinner party is nothing but stress to many people, but not you. You relish the opportunity to nurture the ones you love in a comfortable and relaxed environment.

Slow and steady is how you like your music. Thrash metal is out of the question, as is anything harsh and grating; you prefer music to be in the background, setting the mood of the party, be it classical or country. If you do decide to hold your party outside the home, a posh location with a great menu is essential. You like to be in beautiful surroundings and eat sumptuous food – anything remotely resembling a fast-food joint is not even an option!

Gemini

Organizing a fantastic party is always a difficult task for you Geminis. You get bored at the drop of a hat and are liable to switch off unless there's enough variety in your life. You thrive on doing ten things at once and are only happy when surrounded by stimuli. As the festive season draws closer, Geminis are in a prime party position. Your best bet would be to go to as many different parties as possible. This is because you are sociable creatures with a genuine interest in other people. Your idea of bliss is a huge room full of people to mingle with, talk to and find out their life stories. Sometimes you are given an undeserved reputation as a flirt (how dare they!), but this is only because you are in your element chatting to different people – if they happen to be gorgeous, then all the better!

Your music tastes are eclectic to say the least, and your CD collection is bound to span a good few decades. When it comes to party food, you aren't too fussy – fast food is sometimes your thing, though you aren't afraid to be adventurous and sample something new. A night spent flitting between people and parties should give you enough of the variety you desire.

Cancer

Homebodies that you Cancerians are, a house party is your best bet. You love being close to friends and family, though tend not to venture out of your social circle very much as you are extremely suspicious of outsiders. Sending out invites will eliminate the problem of gatecrashers! As you are highly unlikely to be a glutton or a heavy drinker yourself, any party of yours is bound to be extremely civilized.

Because of your interest in the past and all things historical, a theme party would be right up your street. Pick a decade and let your imagination run riot creating costumes and decorations to match. An Eighties party could also feature some typical Eighties food – chicken in a basket and prawn cocktail, anyone? However, with your delicate tummy, steer away from anything too spicy and exotic.

Your music taste reflects your passion for the past; sentimental music from the good old days will make your party go with a swing. James Brown, Otis Redding and Frank Sinatra should feature in your CD collection. You'll have trouble hiring a DJ to play the kind of things you want to hear, so maybe your dad or uncle will do the job just as well.

Leo

You are about as masculine and as fiery as it gets! You do everything to the best of your ability, and that includes throwing a party. No small, intimate soirées with simple food and wine for you; loud and proud is how you like things to be. You are renowned for your generosity and, rest assured, you won't skimp or take any short cuts with any party you throw.

You love food and good wine, and this has to be of the best quality. Spicy food from warm places should be on the menu, though you may well decide to hire a caterer to take some of the inconvenience out of planning the event.

Lions adore drama and action, so colourful personalities will be a welcome addition to one of your parties, though you can't abide wallflowers who don't contribute to the vibe.

You love listening to music and may well play an instrument yourself, though only the biggest and best of musical genres will do. Your extravagant streak will easily stretch to hiring a hot DJ or a band for the night. Yours are the sort of parties that everyone will talk about for weeks afterwards – lots of decadent goings-on are bound to be on the agenda, and the neighbours will almost certainly complain!

Virgo

Cool as a cucumber, with the ability to keep everything under control, is the hallmark of your sign. Your parties will rarely turn into the sort of chaos that leaves your garden destroyed and your carpets awash with wine, beer and whisky. A wild party is probably your idea of a nightmare – you are more suited to a small gathering in a pub or a club. And woe betide anyone mucking up your home! You hate to play the part of the host with the most, as you are happier in the background than the foreground. Some people misinterpret you as being unfriendly, though you are simply quite shy. When people get to know you, they will discover that you have a wicked sense of humour and that you can liven up any social gathering.

You will want a proper meal at one of your parties – this has to take the form of three courses, as you cannot abide finger food and buffets. You don't have strong musical tastes and probably won't notice what the background music is, so long as it doesn't distract too much. Easy listening music is best suited to any party of yours, so dig out those classic Andy Williams CDs and don't forget the jazz singer himself, Neil Diamond.

Libra

You Librans just hate making decisions, don't you? If you are planning a party, please do so at least eight weeks in advance, otherwise you will rush about madly organizing things. There's nothing you hate more than doing things at the last minute – it makes you irritable and sends you into a panic. However, you are excellent people to have at any party, as you are great conversationalists and very friendly.

Choosing the music is an integral part of your party: you love music and don't want anything you play to offend your guests. You are dying to strut your stuff, so make sure you have cleared a space for the dance floor, or choose to go to a club where you can boogie with style.

When it comes to food, you love ginger, mint and vanilla, so try to incorporate these flavours into the party buffet. Alternatively, stock up on some flavoured vodkas. Plan, plan, plan and your party is bound to go off with a bang!

Scorpio

Any party of yours will not be a low-key event. You have a high energy level and love to live life to the full. If you are holding a party, everyone will know about it and it's bound to be an event to remember.

Your sign is all about intensity and this should be reflected in the type of music you choose to play. Only sounds that get you dancing frenetically will do – you like the latest music with the loudest base line, and the louder and faster the music is, the better. As for the food, simple and bland should not feature. You love spices and concentrated flavours, so dips rich in herbs and garlic are ideal, though to be honest, there are many other things you would rather be doing at a party than eating. There are people to meet and flirting to be done!

You will definitely dress up at the drop of a hat in order to attract some attention – the more extreme the outfit, the more attention you will get. Extreme fashion that only you can carry off ought to achieve the desired result. Your party will be packed full of interesting and colourful personalities (not to mention yourself), and there's bound to be lots of gossip circulating the morning after!

Sagittarius

You are fiery and happy-go-lucky creatures who are always ready for a party. You enjoy keeping up with new trends, and this includes going to or holding fashionable parties. With your wanderlust, a party with a theme would be ideal. A Spanish-themed party would give you a chance to indulge the wilder, more sizzling side of your nature. Hot and spicy salsa with mounds of seafood paella are just the ticket, as are jugs of fruity sangria. You will love researching and getting your costume to look as authentic as possible, whether you choose to be a flamenco dancer or a matador.

You are passionate about world music and your own collection is bound to contain everything from reggae to calypso. Maybe you will have picked up some foreign dances on your travels and are ready to show off what you know. As for the location of your party, the more exotic, the better. If you have no choice but to hold your party at home, you'll probably decorate the place well to fit in with your theme. This will get everyone into the party spirit and dancing till dawn!

Capricorn

It is notoriously difficult to organize a party for people born under your sign. This is because Capricorns are such a varied bunch! Some are far too serious for their own good, whereas others know how to let their hair down and party the night away. Some of you are painfully shy and retiring, whereas others are outgoing to say the least and love a riotous time! Generally speaking, you are extremely cautious about spending money, but the thought of a party sends you into spendthrift mode!

An ideal event for you would involve going to a club – you love music and have a natural sense of rhythm – and let's not forget about the food! As a rule, you like simple foods that fill you up. You aren't a fan of garlic or spices, so delicate flavours like parsley and nutmeg are best for you. A trip to a restaurant followed by a club could be on your agenda. Pick the club carefully because you like listening to the music you were brought up on, so anything too up to date won't be your cup of tea. This doesn't mean to say that the only option open to you is ballroom dancing on Blackpool Pier – there are plenty of Seventies or Eighties nights on at discos around the country. Retro is your best bet!

Aquarius

Trying to categorize or pigeon-hole you Aquarians is a futile task. You are one of the most individual signs in the zodiac and each of you has your own way of going about things. Needless to say, any party you hold is bound to be out of the ordinary – no greatest-hits party album for you! The best thing for you would be to choose an unusual location for your get-together; hiring a barge or holding your party in a local swimming pool would be ideal. Your party does not have to be huge to be successful, as you will have a good time anywhere, provided you are surrounded by close friends. Food won't be the focal point of your party, as you would rather snack or get a takeaway than sit down for a traditional three-course meal. However, you do like bold flavours, such as garlic and basil, so maybe some Italian nibbles would go down well. When it comes to music, you are particularly fond of singalong classics, so long as they aren't too painful to listen to. Rest assured, with a bit of planning your party will be one of the most original to be held for a long time!

Pisces

You are the hopeless romantics and dreamers of the zodiac and let your hair down in a relaxing way. The atmosphere of an underground blues club would be perfect to transport you away from the drudgery of daily life. Jazz music will soothe your spirit and appeal to your artistic side – how could you possibly think creative thoughts with techno music pounding and strobe lights blinding you? If Miles Davis isn't your thing, then a night of salsa dancing will appeal to your saucy side.

Many people mistakenly think that you don't have the stamina to party along with the best of them. This is pure myth, though you need to be especially wary when it comes to alcohol. You don't handle booze very well and should remember to alternate your drinks with water if you are planning a big night out. A meal before the club is also important and, as a water sign, seafood is your best bet, be that smoked salmon or prawn piri piri. Invite lots of your friends and family along, but keep it fairly intimate – too many people you don't know very well can leave you retreating into a corner and your deep contemplations.

Chapter 15

THE PLAN

So here it is: the plan that will help you cope with whatever situations life throws your way. So far in *Life Signs* we've considered how your sign faces the challenges of relationships, health, finances and career. Hopefully you've come to know yourself better and worked out where you've been going wrong and how you can get on the right path.

Just remember that life will never be predictable. If it was, we would all be very bored (yes, even you Virgos and Librans!). By being armed with the right information, however, you can ensure that your journey through life is a fun one. It's all too easy to lean on our loved ones and to blame them when things go wrong. Think how good it would feel to know that you are the one in the driving seat and that you are responsible for the successes the future is going to bring.

A client whose husband had died came in to see me. She no longer knew how to go on with her life, having never paid a bill, used a credit card or even ordered anything for herself. She felt useless and, as she admitted, suicidal. Linda, as I shall call her now, didn't know how to take that first step. She was an Aquarian, so a bright spark, but enjoyed listening to other people speak. She had never had the chance to draw on her own strengths and I could see just by spending ten minutes with her that she was a flower waiting to bloom. I sat down with Linda and explained the basics of paying money in and out of an account, then sent her to the bank to open up her very own first account. She returned the following week, but this time with a spring in her step. I noticed there was a big change in her already and she proudly opened her purse to reveal a cheque book. She was like a kid in a sweetshop. She tried to pay me immediately, but I wanted to wait until I had asked her what else she'd been doing. Well, in seven days she'd bought a travel magazine and had been reading up on the destinations she'd often wondered about as a child. She was still a little scared, though, as she didn't have a passport and had never travelled outside England, let alone gone abroad on her own. I sent her away not with any advice, as she didn't need any, but with the instruction to go to the post office to obtain a passport form and have her photograph taken.

The story runs away with itself just as Linda ran away with her dreams. I often got postcards from her from the most obscure places. All I did was inform a very scared little bird that the cage door was not closed but open. If only she'd come to see me years ago, I could have told her that there was no lock on the door; she had chosen, as many clients do, to wait until some greater power took charge of her life.

The sad part to this story is that Linda's travels only lasted a year. She died very suddenly from cancer. At least she had a year to realize dreams, though she could have had more if she had been true to herself earlier on in life. Her husband would probably have happily travelled with her had he ever known her dreams, but she'd never uttered a word about them to him.

My point is, don't be another Linda. Don't bury your own needs. If you are content, others will be happy for you. As long as you are not purposely hurting anyone else, then what is stopping you? All of Linda's children had grown and left home, and when I met them at her funeral they told me that they wished she had lived her dreams. They had known something wasn't right but they hadn't dared question what their mother was doing when she had lived that way for so long. They even said they thought their father had never travelled because she had never asked.

Live the following plan every day and enjoy life to the full. Life is for living, remember, and as long as you help others as you go on your way, then who can blame you for doing what you enjoy? The most selfish act is to neglect yourself, as if you don't put yourself first, then why should anyone else?

The Five-Step Plan

Step one: time out

Take five minutes out of your day to recharge and concentrate on your body, breathing in through your nose and out through your mouth. Take in your surroundings, then focus on one thing that brings you pleasure, still breathing in through your nose and out through your mouth. Don't say that you can't see anything beautiful. There are a zillion things the minute you open your eyes and your mind. It could be the colour of the sky, the frost on the window pane, the softness of your sheets, cool water on your skin or the first mouthful of a delicious meal. Notice colours, let them come to you and wash over your mind. We often go through life without noticing the richness of colours. They were put there to give happiness, inspiration and pleasure. What we are doing here is making sure that we train our brains to focus on the positive, not the negative.

Step two: count your blessings

Think of five things that you are looking forward to. The first one could be a cup of tea or a morning orange juice. After all, remember that others won't ever have the pleasure of experiencing what we take for granted. Further things may range from a friend we are looking forward to seeing for lunch to a new project at work or even seeing the smile on our baby's face.

Step three: a lesson learnt

Think of what you have learnt from yesterday's experiences and appreciate whatever richness that has brought to your life. You may have had to return something to a shop, and in doing so you know not to buy from there again, or it could be that you've discovered you possess an untapped skill. Every day life's rich tapestry offers us a million lessons and I want you to pick out one of them. The braver you get, the more honest you can be with yourself. You may know you were short with a partner yesterday, but by acknowledging this fact you can use today to right that wrong. I promise that by saying you are sorry and acknowledging to your partner that you take responsibility, you will feel a million times better.

Step four: giving brings joy

Spread a little happiness. Do something positive for someone today, whether it's helping an old lady cross the road or giving a sad face your best smile. I want you to be able to end today with the knowledge that you've helped someone else. The sooner you do it, the happier you will feel. Spreading happiness will attract luck and love into your life like never before.

Step five: acknowledge yourself

You are who you are. Some may not like it but you have to live with it. You know you are going to make some mistakes, but you also know you are not a bad person. In fact sometimes you even quite like yourself. Let's pick one of your attributes, perhaps one you wouldn't normally talk about, and allow that thought to wash over you. Visualize your attribute moving through your body, starting in your toes and travelling up through your legs to your knees. Let it tingle. You may even get goose bumps as it moves to your bottom and pelvis and into your tummy, then up through your spine and into your hands and arms like an electric current. Eventually it reaches the top of your head. *You are a good person and you deserve a good life.* Today Step Five may feel different from other days, something more minor or more major, but you are going to carry this attribute with you all day. It is your golden ticket and will ensure that something good comes to you.

Key words for each sign

Don't give up on yourself or the ones you love. Look to your many attributes and remember that the glass is always half full, *never* half empty. Every problem brings opportunity, and every wrong turn shows you a new right way to go. Experience is what makes us wise. You must never regret what you've done, only what you haven't.

Use the following words to help each sign gain in confidence. These words encapsulate the heart of each person and will help them to become the best that they can be.

Aries

Personality. Help the Ram to have faith in who they are. Help them to accept themselves, faults and all. Teach them that any dents in their character add colour and definition. These are the lessons they need to build a better future.

Taurus

Finances. The Bull is a sign who is always worried about money and often leaves it too late to face financial dilemmas. However, their strength is that they are the most able sign in the zodiac when it comes to making money. Teach them to trust in the decisions they make with finances.

Gemini

Communication. This sign knows what it wants to say but often spends too much time talking about everyone else's problems before addressing their own. Keep bringing the focus back on to them and help them realize they deserve to put themselves first for once.

Cancer

Home and mother. Cancerians often have issues with their mother. They place great importance on the past and where they come from. Help them deal with this in a constructive way, even if it means seeing a counsellor. Their base is important, so help them make it secure.

Leo

Creativity. Teach the Lion to trust in their flair for knowing the right things to do in life. They are all too often held back by less inspirational signs and they need to be encouraged to break the mould and dare to be different. Great things will occur if they do.

Virgo

Work and health. The Virgo can really make their mark professionally, but their health often lets them down. A healthy mind leads to a healthy body, so Virgos need to address their emotional state. Get them into a routine; they'll love it and then the sky will be the limit.

Libra

Relationships. Let the Libran know that they are loved and that they have the faith and trust they need to build a really secure base. If they don't have someone to love them, they wilt like a flower without water. Support them and nourish them and they will bloom. They also need to learn to love themselves.

Scorpio

Interests and issues. Scorpios must do what they enjoy in life. To force them to pursue something their heart is not in can only lead to disaster. No matter how crazy an idea it may seem, support them. This is one sign who will surprise us all with the success they can achieve when focused.

Sagittarius

Spirituality. The Archer finds it hard to get in touch with their inner self. They spend so long trying to make money and find success in the rat race that they rarely pay attention to their spiritual and emotional needs. Encourage them to do so and then they can achieve anything.

Capricorn

Career and achievement. Allow the Capricorn to put their work first and you will see the other areas of their life just fall into place naturally. Support them and help them to put their dreams first and success will follow at lightning speed.

Aquarius

Aspirations and friendships. Allow them to dream and one day they will surprise you by turning their dreams into reality, not to mention a very large cheque. Believe in the impossible with them and you'll be in for a treat.

Pisces

Seclusion and the inner self. Give Pisceans the time out that they need to take stock of what is going on. Force their hand and they'll make bad and very dramatic decisions. Guide them gently and they will love you until the end of time.

Coping with stress

Stress is a word many of us know all too well. There are countless different areas of our life that can give us stress. It could be staying with a partner who is making us unhappy. It could be family problems, work problems or health problems. Whatever the issue there is always something you can do about it. You are not alone and you don't have to cope alone either.

No matter what our star sign, we will all face times of stress, but your sign will influence how you handle this stress and what triggers it for you.

Fire signs, which are Aries, Leo and Sagittarius, tend to let their problems run away with them and allow things to build up. They are rather like a pressure cooker whose lid is just about to blow. You can ask them if they are all right and they will say, 'Yes, I'm fine,' but you will know that's not true. Then one day things will unexpectedly come to a head. Think Sagittarian Britney Spears when she cracked under the pressure of fame! No one expected it; they just witnessed what appeared to be a crazed celebrity. Little did they know it had been building for a long time. Unfortunately fire signs often find it hard to talk when they should and so situations have a tendency to spiral out of control. If you have an Aries, Leo or Sagittarian in your life, then sit them down and talk to them. A regular check can uncover things that if left to fester, become impossible to address. Sometimes these signs have got something very small out of all proportion. More often than not the problem is money.

Taureans, Virgos and Capricorns are not usually the most stressed signs in the zodiac. They like to have their friends and family around them twenty-four seven. It is usually when their loved ones get problems that they start to get upset. They do tend to live part of their life through their family, which is not good, but is part of their make-up. It is something that those who know them well just have to come to understand. They must learn to take responsibility for their own lives, but not to feel as if they have to heal the whole world. If a child does something that is not right, it is not their fault. They are learning. Often an earth sign takes others' problems more to heart than those who are actually experiencing the difficulties.

Air signs, Libra, Gemini and Aquarius, talk their way into stress. They make promises they cannot keep and they want to make everyone happy. They often share problems with the wrong people. To get rid of stress, the key is not to stop talking but to learn who they can safely confide in. When you talk to a neighbour about your marriage problems and she comments on them to another neighbour, you will soon find the whole street is talking. Address the core of the problem and stress will slowly but surely start to drift away.

Cancerians, Scorpios and Pisceans need to learn not to jump head first into their problems. To say that they take things too much to heart would be an understatement. It is only by addressing a worry one stage at a time that they can ever find a viable solution. They give their heart and soul to whatever they are doing and would go to the ends of the earth to help out a friend or a family member. That involves digging into their own pocket. Problems can often arise when they take a stand for people who are not really their responsibility. They need to learn to save themselves and maybe one person at a time instead of the whole world.

If you want to know how best to handle the stress you are under, then you **fire signs** should simply talk about things as they happen and not ten years down the line. Aries, you are a leader and passionate about what you do, so choose a new path and soon your problems will be in the past. Leo, you are proud and generous, and impress others far more easily than you think, so just knock on the door you really want and see how quickly it will open for you. Sagittarius, you are honest and expansive, so take your seed of a dream and watch it grow as you take those first new and important steps.

If you want to know how best to handle the stress you are under, then you **earth signs** should live your own life and not keep sticking up for people who wouldn't do the same for you. Taurus, you are stubborn and loyal, so use these traits to create a new base. Before you know it, you will have a brighter and better future. Virgo, you are practical and intelligent, so do something you've always wanted to do but never dared try. You may just surprise yourself. Capricorn, you are ambitious and disciplined, so go back to your original dream and push aside the dead wood that's been holding you back.

If you want to know how best to handle the stress you are under, then you **air signs** should talk about the issues at hand instead of everything but. Gemini, you are generous and adaptable, so find some fresh faces to share in the many ideas you have and you will find new solutions. Libra, you are sociable and artistic, so don't pretend otherwise. Meet the people you have been admiring from afar. Aquarius, you are intelligent and funny, so use your charm and brains to look for new horizons and make new resolutions. Start from the top, where you belong.

If you want to know how best to handle the stress you are under, then you **water signs** should deal with a problem as it stands and not always imagine the worse-case scenario. Cancer, you are loving and caring so find something that will thrive on what you have to offer. This will give you the satisfaction you truly crave. Scorpio, you are determined and clever, so choose a goal and don't look back. Pisces, you are imaginative, talented and strong, so stop pretending to be weak to keep those around you happy. Show your true colours. The world is waiting.

Shining stars

I would like to leave you with a list of famous people of your star sign, so that you can see your true potential. Look up your star sign and you will see that these are people with the same qualities as you, the same foibles. They did it, and so can you.

Aries

Leonardo Da Vinci *painter*
Tennessee Williams *playwright*
Thomas Jefferson *politician*
Tom Clancy *writer*
John Major *Prime Minister*
Sarah Jessica Parker *actress*
Sir Alan Sugar *businessman*
Victoria 'Posh Spice' Beckham *singer*

Warren Beatty *actor*
Russell Crowe *actor*
Elton John *singer and songwriter*
Eddie Murphy *actor*
Quentin Tarantino *director and actor*
Mariah Carey *singer*

Taurus

Elizabeth II *Queen*
Charlotte Brontë *writer*
Catherine the Great *Russian royalty*
Irving Berlin *composer*
Michelle Pfeiffer *actress*
Naomi Campbell *supermodel*

Uma Thurman *actress*
Cher *singer and actress*
Janet Jackson *singer*
Craig David *singer*
George Clooney *actor*
Jack Nicholson *actor*
David Beckham *footballer*

Gemini

Lenny Kravitz *singer*
Paul Weller *singer*
Eric Cantona *footballer turned actor*
Denise Van Outen *presenter*
Liz Hurley *model and actress*
Elisabeth Shue *actress*
Kylie Minogue *singer*
Brooke Shields *actress and model*

Johnny Depp *actor*
Mel B. *singer*
Paul McCartney *singer and songwriter*
Courtney Cox *actress*
Bob Dylan *singer*
John F. Kennedy *President*
Angelina Jolie *actress*

Cancer

Princess Diana
His Holiness the Dalai Lama XIV
Meryl Streep *actress*
The Duke of Windsor
Nelson Mandela
George Bush *President*
Tom Cruise *actor*
Jamie Redknapp *footballer*

Chris O'Donnell *actor*
Pamela Anderson *actress*
Chris Isaak *singer*
Liv Tyler *actress*
George Michael *singer and songwriter*
Tom Hanks *actor*
Harrison Ford *actor*
Ernest Hemingway *writer*

Leo

The Queen Mother
Mick Jagger *singer*
Andy Warhol *artist*
Karl G. Jung *psychiatrist*
Dean Cain *actor*
Matt LeBlanc *actor*
Sandra Bullock *actress*
Matthew Perry *actor*

Gillian Anderson *actress*
Ulrika Jonsson *presenter*
Madonna *singer*
Geri Halliwell *singer*
Robert De Niro *actor*
Coco Chanel *designer*
T. E. Lawrence *adventurer*
Danielle Steel *novelist*

Virgo

Queen Elizabeth I
Shania Twain *singer*
Harry Connick Junior *singer*
Cameron Diaz *actress*
Sir Sean Connery *actor*
Hugh Grant *actor*

Michael Jackson *singer*
H. G. Wells *writer*
Prince Harry
Ray Charles *musician*
Sophia Loren *actress*

Libra

T. S. Eliot *poet*
Julie Andrews *actress*
John Lennon *Beatle*
Oscar Wilde *writer*
Luciano Pavarotti *opera singer*
Michael Douglas *actor*
Will Smith *actor and singer*

Keith Duffy *Boyzone member*
Jodie Kidd *model*
Bryan Ferry *singer*
Sting *singer*
Toni Braxton *singer*
Gwyneth Paltrow *actress*

Scorpio

Indira Gandhi *politician*
Martin Luther King *political
    leader*
Prince Charles
Pablo Picasso *artist*
Microsoft's Bill Gates
Winona Ryder *actress*
Julia Roberts *actress*

David Schwimmer *actor*
Bryan Adams *singer*
Meg Ryan *actress*
Ian Wright *footballer*
Louise *singer*
Demi Moore *actress*
Ralph Macchio *actor*
Davinia Murphy *actress*

Sagittarius

Charles de Gaulle *President and
    statesman*
George Eliot *writer*
Brad Pitt *actor*
Britney Spears *singer*
Denzel Washington *actor*
Teri Hatcher *actress*
Kim Basinger *actress*

Ray Liotta *actor*
Daryl Hannah *actress*
Sammy Davis Junior *singer and
    actor*
Mahara Ji *guru*
Ludwig van Beethoven *composer*
Jane Austin *writer*
Steven Spielberg *producer*

Capricorn

Louis Pasteur *scientist*
Henri Matisse *artist*
J. R. R. Tolkien *writer*
Joan of Arc *Saint*
Nostradamus *astrologer*
Nicholas Cage *actor*
Vinnie Jones *footballer turned
    actor*
Jim Carrey *actor*

Mel C. *singer*
Sade *singer*
Jude Law *actor*
Janis Joplin *singer*
Mel Gibson *actor*
Kate Moss *model*
Carol Vorderman *presenter*
Christy Turlington *model*

Aquarius

Edwin Aldrin *astronaut*
Christian Dior *designer*
Plácido Domingo *singer*
Lord Byron *poet*
Humphrey Bogart *actor*
Virginia Woolf *writer*
Paul Newman *actor*
Lewis Carroll *writer*
Franklin D. Roosevelt *President*
Vanessa Redgrave *actress*
Ronald Reagan *President*
Babe Ruth *sportsman*

Charles Dickens *writer*
Emma Bunton *singer*
Jennifer Aniston *actress*
Robbie Williams *singer*
John Travolta *actor*
Matt Dillon *actor*
David Ginola *footballer*
Natalie Imbruglia *singer and actress*
Bridget Fonda *actress*
Chris Rock *actor*
Sheryl Crow *singer*

Pisces

Prince Edward
Sydney Poitier *actor*
George Harrison *Beatle*
Elizabeth Taylor *actress*
Rex Harrison *actor*
Neville Chamberlain *Prime Minister*
Rudolf Nureyev *dancer*
Albert Einstein *scientist*
Michael Caine *actor*
Jack Kerouac *writer*
Dr Seuss *writer*

Bruce Willis *actor*
Rob Lowe *actor*
Drew Barrymore *actress*
Patsy Kensit *actress*
Cindy Crawford *model*
Melinda Messenger *model and presenter*
Billy Zane *actor*
Jon Bon Jovi *singer*
Niki Taylor *model*
Juliette Binoche *actress*
Sharon Stone *actress*

Never regret what you've done, only what you haven't done.

extracts reading groups
competitions books new
discounts extracts
competitions events
books extracts
new reading groups
discounts
events books
extracts
new titles reading groups
interviews
events extracts books
discounts
new books events
events new
discounts extracts discounts
www.panmacmillan.com
extracts events reading groups
competitions books extracts new

"Yes."

"Sir Guy Willard?" I cried.

"No, Captain Hastings. My American colleague, Mr. Schneider."

"And the cause?" demanded Poirot.

"Tetanus."

I blanched. All around me I seemed to feel an atmosphere of evil, subtle and menacing. A horrible thought flashed across me. Supposing I were the next?

"Mon Dieu," said Poirot, in a very low voice, "I do not understand this. It is horrible. Tell me, monsieur, there is no doubt that it was tetanus?"

"I believe not. But Dr. Ames will tell you more than I can do."

"Ah, of course, you are not the doctor."

"My name is Tosswill."

This, then, was the British expert described by Lady Willard as being a minor official at the British Museum. There was something at once grave and steadfast about him that took my fancy.

"If you will come with me," continued Dr. Tosswill, "I will take you to Sir Guy Willard. He was most anxious to be informed as soon as you should arrive."

We were taken across the camp to a large tent. Dr. Tosswill lifted up the flap and we entered. Three men were sitting inside.

"Monsieur Poirot and Captain Hastings have arrived, Sir Guy," said Tosswill.

The youngest of the three men jumped up and came forward to greet us. There was a certain impulsiveness in his manner which reminded me of his mother. He was not nearly so sunburnt as the others, and that fact, coupled with a certain haggardness round the eyes, made him look older than his twenty-two years. He was clearly endeavoring to bear up under a severe mental strain.

He introduced his two companions, Dr. Ames, a capable looking man of thirty odd, with a touch of graying hair at the temples, and Mr. Harper, the secretary, a pleasant lean young man wearing the national insignia of horn-rimmed spectacles.

After a few minutes' desultory conversation the latter

went out, and Dr. Tosswill followed him. We were left alone with Sir Guy and Dr. Ames.

"Please ask any questions you want to ask, Monsieur Poirot," said Willard. "We are utterly dumfounded at this strange series of disasters, but it isn't—it can't be, anything but coincidence."

There was a nervousness about his manner which rather belied the words. I saw that Poirot was studying him keenly.

"Your heart is really in this work, Sir Guy?"

"Rather. No matter what happens, or what comes of it, the work is going on. Make up your mind to that."

Poirot wheeled round on the other.

"What have you to say to that, *monsieur le docteur?*"

"Well," drawled the doctor, "I'm not for quitting myself."

Poirot made one of those expressive grimaces of his.

"Then, *évidemment,* we must find out just how we stand. When did Mr. Schneider's death take place?"

"Three days ago."

"You are sure it was tetanus?"

"Dead sure."

"It couldn't have been a case of strychnine poisoning, for instance?"

"No, Monsieur Poirot. I see what you're getting at. But it was a clear case of tetanus."

"Did you not inject anti-serum?"

"Certainly we did," said the doctor dryly. "Every conceivable thing that could be done was tried."

"Had you the anti-serum with you?"

"No. We procured it from Cairo."

"Have there been any other cases of tetanus in the camp?"

"No, not one."

"Are you certain that the death of Mr. Bleibner was not due to tetanus?"

"Absolutely plumb certain. He had a scratch upon his thumb which became poisoned, and septicæmia set in. It sounds pretty much the same to a layman, I dare say, but the two things are entirely different."

"Then we have four deaths—all totally dissimilar, one heart failure, one blood poisoning, one suicide and one tetanus."

"Exactly, Monsieur Poirot."

"Are you certain that there is nothing which might link the four together?"

"I don't quite understand you?"

"I will put it plainly. Was any act committed by those four men which might seem to denote disrespect to the spirit of Men-her-Ra?"

The doctor gazed at Poirot in astonishment.

"You're talking through your hat, Monsieur Poirot. Surely you've not been guyed into believing all that fool talk?"

"Absolute nonsense," muttered Willard angrily.

Poirot remained placidly immovable, blinking a little out of his green cat's eyes.

"So you do not believe it, *monsieur le docteur?*"

"No, sir, I do not," declared the doctor emphatically. "I am a scientific man, and I believe only what science teaches."

"Was there no science then in Ancient Egypt?" asked Poirot softly. He did not wait for a reply, and indeed Dr. Ames seemed rather at a loss for the moment. "No, no, do not answer me, but tell me this. What do the native workmen think?"

"I guess," said Dr. Ames, "that, where white folk lose their heads, natives aren't going to be far behind. I'll admit that they're getting what you might call scared—but they've no cause to be."

"I wonder," said Poirot non-committally.

Sir Guy leant forward.

"Surely," he cried incredulously, "you cannot believe in—oh, but the thing's absurd! You can know nothing of Ancient Egypt if you think that."

For answer Poirot produced a little book from his pocket—an ancient tattered volume. As he held it out I saw its title, *The Magic of the Egyptians and Chaldeans*. Then, wheeling round, he strode out of the tent. The doctor stared at me.

"What is his little idea?"

The phrase, so familiar on Poirot's lips, made me smile as it came from another.

"I don't know exactly," I confessed. "He's got some plan of exorcizing the evil spirits, I believe."

I went in search of Poirot, and found him talking to the lean-faced young man who had been the late Mr. Bleibner's secretary.

"No," Mr. Harper was saying, "I've only been six months with the expedition. Yes, I knew Mr. Bleibner's affairs pretty well."

"Can you recount to me anything concerning his nephew?"

"He turned up here one day, not a bad-looking fellow. I'd never met him before, but some of the others had— Ames, I think, and Schneider. The old man wasn't at all pleased to see him. They were at it in no time, hammer and tongs. 'Not a cent,' the old man shouted. 'Not one cent now or when I'm dead. I intend to leave my money to the furtherance of my life's work. I've been talking it over with Mr. Schneider to-day.' And a bit more of the same. Young Bleibner lit out for Cairo right away."

"Was he in perfectly good health at the time?"

"The old man?"

"No, the young one."

"I believe he did mention there was something wrong with him. But it couldn't have been anything serious, or I should have remembered."

"One thing more, has Mr. Bleibner left a will?"

"So far as we know, he has not."

"Are you remaining with the expedition, Mr. Harper?"

"No, sir, I am not. I'm for New York as soon as I can square up things here. You may laugh if you like, but I'm not going to be this blasted old Men-her-Ra's next victim. He'll get me if I stop here."

The young man wiped the perspiration from his brow.

Poirot turned away. Over his shoulder he said with a peculiar smile:

"Remember, he got one of his victims in New York."

"Oh, hell!" said Mr. Harper forcibly.

"That young man is nervous," said Poirot thoughtfully. "He is on the edge, but absolutely on the edge."

I glanced at Poirot curiously, but his enigmatical smile told me nothing. In company with Sir Guy Willard and Dr. Tosswill we were taken round the excavations. The principal finds had been removed to Cairo, but some of the tomb furniture was extremely interesting. The enthusiasm of the young baronet was obvious, but I fancied that I detected a shade of nervousness in his manner as though he could not quite escape from the feeling of menace in the air. As we entered the tent which had been assigned to us, for a wash before joining the evening meal, a tall dark figure in white robes stood aside to let us pass with a graceful gesture and a murmured greeting in Arabic. Poirot stopped.

"You are Hassan, the late Sir John Willard's servant?"

"I served my Lord Sir John, now I serve his son." He took a step nearer to us and lowered his voice. "You are a wise one, they say, learned in dealing with evil spirits. Let the young master depart from here. There is evil in the air around us."

And with an abrupt gesture, not waiting for a reply, he strode away.

"Evil in the air," muttered Poirot. "Yes, I feel it."

Our meal was hardly a cheerful one. The floor was left to Dr. Tosswill, who discoursed at length upon Egyptian antiquities. Just as we were preparing to retire to rest, Sir Guy caught Poirot by the arm and pointed. A shadowy figure was moving amidst the tents. It was no human one: I recognized distinctly the dog-headed figure I had seen carved on the walls of the tomb.

My blood literally froze at the sight.

"*Mon Dieu!*" murmured Poirot, crossing himself vigorously. "Anubis, the jackal-headed, the god of departing souls."

"Some one is hoaxing us," cried Dr. Tosswill, rising indignantly to his feet.

"It went into your tent, Harper," muttered Sir Guy, his face dreadfully pale.

"No," said Poirot, shaking his head, "into that of the Dr. Ames."

The doctor stared at him incredulously; then, repeating Dr. Tosswill's words, he cried:

"Some one is hoaxing us. Come, we'll soon catch the fellow."

He dashed energetically in pursuit of the shadowy apparition. I followed him, but, search as we would, we could find no trace of any living thing having passed that way. We returned, somewhat disturbed in mind, to find Poirot taking energetic measures, in his own way, to ensure his personal safety. He was busily surrounding our tent with various diagrams and inscriptions which he was drawing in the sand. I recognized the five-pointed star or Pentagon many times repeated. As was his wont, Poirot was at the same time delivering an impromptu lecture on witchcraft and magic in general, White Magic as opposed to Black, with various references to the Ka and the Book of the Dead thrown in.

It appeared to excite the liveliest contempt in Dr. Tosswill, who drew me aside, literally snorting with rage.

"Balderdash, sir," he exclaimed angrily. "Pure balderdash. The man's an impostor. He doesn't know the difference between the superstitions of the Middle Ages and the beliefs of Ancient Egypt. Never have I heard such a hotch-potch of ignorance and credulity."

I calmed the excited expert, and joined Poirot in the tent. My little friend was beaming cheerfully.

"We can now sleep in peace," he declared happily. "And I can do with some sleep. My head, it aches abominably. Ah, for a good *tisane!*"

As though in answer to prayer, the flap of the tent was lifted and Hassan appeared, bearing a steaming cup which he offered to Poirot. It proved to be camomile tea, a beverage of which he is inordinately fond. Having thanked Hassan and refused his offer of another cup for myself, we were left alone once more. I stood at the door of the tent some time after undressing, looking out over the desert.

"A wonderful place," I said aloud, "and a wonderful work. I can feel the fascination. This desert life, this probing into the heart of a vanished civilization. Surely, Poirot, you, too, must feel the charm?"

I got no answer, and I turned, a little annoyed. My annoyance was quickly changed to concern. Poirot was lying back across the rude couch, his face horribly convulsed. Beside him was the empty cup. I rushed to his side, then dashed out and across the camp to Dr. Ames's tent.

"Dr. Ames!" I cried. "Come at once."

"What's the matter?" said the doctor, appearing in pyjamas.

"My friend. He's ill. Dying. The camomile tea. Don't let Hassan leave the camp."

Like a flash the doctor ran to our tent. Poirot was lying as I left him.

"Extraordinary," cried Ames. "Looks like a seizure—or—what did you say about something he drank?" He picked up the empty cup.

"Only I did not drink it!" said a placid voice.

We turned in amazement. Poirot was sitting up on the bed. He was smiling.

"No," he said gently. "I did not drink it. While my good friend Hastings was apostrophizing the night, I took the opportunity of pouring it, not down my throat, but into a little bottle. That little bottle will go to the analytical chemist. No"—as the doctor made a sudden movement—"as a sensible man, you will understand that violence will be of no avail. During Hastings' brief absence to fetch you, I have had time to put the bottle in safe keeping. Ah, quick, Hastings, hold him!"

I misunderstood Poirot's anxiety. Eager to save my friend, I flung myself in front of him. But the doctor's swift movement had another meaning. His hand went to his mouth, a smell of bitter almonds filled the air, and he swayed forward and fell.

"Another victim," said Poirot gravely, "but the last. Perhaps it is the best way. He has three deaths on his head."

"Dr. Ames?" I cried, stupefied. "But I thought you believed in some occult influence?"

"You misunderstood me, Hastings. What I meant was that I believe in the terrific force of superstition. Once get it firmly established that a series of deaths are super-

natural, and you might almost stab a man in broad daylight, and it would still be put down to the curse, so
strongly is the instinct of the supernatural implanted in
the human race. I suspected from the first that a man
was taking advantage of that instinct. The idea came to
him, I imagine, with the death of Sir John Willard. A
fury of superstition arose at once. As far as I could see,
nobody could derive any particular profit from Sir John's
death. Mr. Bleibner was a different case. He was a man
of great wealth. The information I received from New
York contained several suggestive points. To begin with,
young Bleibner was reported to have said he had a good
friend in Egypt from whom he could borrow. It was
tacitly understood that he meant his uncle, but it seemed
to me that in that case he would have said so outright.
The words suggest some boon companion of his own.
Another thing, he scraped up enough money to take him
to Egypt, his uncle refused outright to advance him a
penny, yet he was able to pay the return passage to New
York. Some one must have lent him the money."

"All that was very thin," I objected.

"But the ... was more. Hastings, there occur often enough
words spoken metaphorically which are taken literally.
The opposite can happen too. In this case, words which
were meant literally were taken metaphorically. Young
Bleibner wrote plainly enough: 'I am a leper,' but nobody
realized that he shot himself because he believed that he
had contracted the dread disease of leprosy."

"What?" I ejaculated.

"It was the clever invention of a diabolical mind. Young
Bleibner was suffering from some minor skin trouble, he
had lived in the South Sea Islands, where the disease is
common enough. Ames was a former friend of his, and
a well-known medical man, he would never have dreamed
of doubting his word. When I arrived here, my suspicions
were divided between Harper and Dr. Ames, but I soon
realized that only the doctor could have perpetrated and
concealed the crimes, and I learnt from Harper that he
was previously acquainted with young Bleibner. Doubtless
the latter at some time or another had made a will or
had insured his life in favor of the doctor. The latter saw

his chance of acquiring wealth. It was easy for him to in-oculate Mr. Bleibner with the deadly germs. Then the nephew, overcome with despair at the dread news his friend had conveyed to him, shot himself. Mr. Bleibner, whatever his intentions, had made no will. His fortune would pass to his nephew and from him to the doctor."

"And Mr. Schneider?"

"We cannot be sure. He knew young Bleibner too, re-member, and may have suspected something, or, again, the doctor may have thought that a further death motive-less and purposeless would strengthen the coils of super-stition. Furthermore, I will tell you an interesting psy-chological fact, Hastings. A murderer has always a strong desire to repeat his successful crime, the performance of it grows upon him. Hence my fears for young Willard. The figure of Anubis you saw to-night was Hassan, dressed up by my orders. I wanted to see if I could fright-en the doctor. But it would take more than the super-natural to frighten him. I could see that he was not en-tirely taken in by my pretenses of belief in the occult. The little comedy I played for him did not deceive him. I suspected that he would endeavor to make me the next victim. Ah, but in spite of *la mer maudite,* the heat abom-nable, and the annoyances of the sand, the little gray cells still functioned!"

Poirot proved to be perfectly right in his premises. Young Bleibner, some years ago, in a fit of drunken merri-ment, had made a jocular will, leaving "my cigarette case you admire so much and everything else of which I die possessed which will be principally debts to my good friend Robert Ames who once saved my life from drown-ing."

The case was hushed up as far as possible, and, to this day, people talk of the remarkable series of deaths in connection with the Tomb of Men-her-Ra as a trimph-al proof of the vengeance of a bygone king upon the desecrators of his tomb—a belief which, as Poirot pointed out to me, is contrary to all Egyptian belief and thought.

VII
THE JEWEL ROBBERY
AT THE GRAND METROPOLITAN

"Poirot," I said, "a change of air would do you good."

"You think so, *mon ami?*"

"I am sure of it."

"Eh—eh?" said my friend, smiling. "It is all arranged, then?"

"You will come?"

"Where do you propose to take me?"

"Brighton. As a matter of fact, a friend of mine in the City put me on to a very good thing, and—well, I have money to burn, as the saying goes. I think a week-end at the *Grand Metropolitan* would do us all the good in the world."

"Thank you, I accept most gratefully. You have the good heart to think of an old man. And the good heart, it is in the end worth all the little gray cells. Yes, yes, I who speak to you am in danger of forgetting that sometimes."

I did not quite relish the implication. I fancy that Poirot is sometimes a little inclined to underestimate my mental capacities. But his pleasure was so evident that I put my slight annoyance aside.

"Then, that's all right," I said hastily.

Saturday evening saw us dining at the *Grand Metropolitan* in the midst of a gay throng. All the world and his wife seemed to be at Brighton. The dresses were marvellous, and the jewels—worn sometimes with more love of display than good taste—were something magnificent.

"*Hein,* it is a sight this!" murmured Poirot. "This is the home of the Profiteer, is it not so, Hastings?"

"Supposed to be," I replied. "But we'll hope they aren't all tarred with the profiteering brush."

Poirot gazed round him placidly.

"The sight of so many jewels makes me wish I had turned my brains to crime, instead of to its detection. What a magnificent opportunity for some thief of distinction! Regard, Hastings, that stout woman by the pillar. She is, as you would say, plastered with gems."

I followed his eyes.

"Why," I exclaimed, "it's Mrs. Opalsen."

"You know her?"

"Slightly. Her husband is a rich stockbroker who made a fortune in the recent Oil boom."

After dinner we ran across the Opalsens in the lounge, and I introduced Poirot to them. We chatted for a few minutes, and ended by having our coffee together.

Poirot said a few words in praise of some of the costlier gems displayed on the lady's ample bosom, and she brightened up at once.

"It's a perfect hobby of mine, Mr. Poirot. I just *love* jewelry. Ed knows my weakness, and every time things go well he brings me something new. You are interested in precious stones?"

"I have had a good deal to do with them one time and another, madame. My profession has brought me into contact with some of the most famous jewels in the world."

He went on to narrate, with discreet pseudonyms, the story of the historic jewels of a reigning house, and Mrs. Opalsen listened with bated breath.

"There now!" she exclaimed, as he ended. "If it isn't just like a play! You know, I've got some pearls of my own that have a history attached to them. I believe it's supposed to be one of the finest necklaces in the world—pearls so beautifully matched and so perfect in color. I declare I really must run up and get it!"

"Oh, madame," protested Poirot, "you are too amiable. Pray do not derange yourself!"

"Oh, but I'd like to show it to you."

The buxom dame waddled across to the lift briskly enough. Her husband, who had been talking to me, looked at Poirot inquiringly.

"Madame your wife is so amiable as to insist on showing me her pearl necklace," explained the latter.

"Oh, the pearls!" Opalsen smiled in a satisfied fashion. "Well, they are worth seeing. Cost a pretty penny too! Still, the money's there all right; I could get what I paid for them any day—perhaps more. May have to, too, if things go on as they are now. Money's confoundedly tight in the City. All this infernal E.P.D." He rambled on, launching into technicalities where I could not follow him.

He was interrupted by a small page-boy who approached and murmured something in his ear.

"Eh—what? I'll come at once. Not taken ill, is she? Excuse me, gentlemen."

He left us abruptly. Poirot leaned back and lit one of his tiny Russian cigarettes. Then, carefully and meticulously, he arranged the empty coffee-cups in a neat row, and beamed happily on the result.

The minutes passed. The Opalsens did not return.

"Curious," I remarked, at length. "I wonder when they will come back."

Poirot watched the ascending spirals of smoke, and then said thoughtfully:

"They will not come back."

"Why?"

"Because, my friend, something has happened."

"What sort of thing? How do you know?" I asked curiously.

Poirot smiled.

"A few moments ago the manager came hurriedly out of his office and ran upstairs. He was much agitated. The lift-boy is deep in talk with one of the pages. The lift-bell has rung three times, but he heeds it not. Thirdly, even the waiters are *distrait;* and to make a waiter *distrait—*" Poirot shook his head with an air of finality. "The affair must indeed be of the first magnitude. Ah, it is as I thought! Here come the police."

Two men had just entered the hotel—one in uniform, the other in plain clothes. They spoke to a page, and were immediately ushered upstairs. A few minutes later, the same boy descended and came up to where we were sitting.

"Mr. Opalsen's compliments, and would you step upstairs."

Poirot sprang nimbly to his feet. One would have said that he awaited the summons. I followed with no less alacrity.

The Opalsens' apartments were situated on the first floor. After knocking on the door, the page-boy retired, and we answered the summons, "Come in!" A strange scene met our eyes. The room was Mrs. Opalsen's bedroom, and in the center of it, lying back in an armchair, was the lady herself, weeping violently. She presented an extraordinary spectacle, with tears making great furrows in the powder with which her complexion was liberally coated. Mr. Opalsen was striding up and down angrily. The two police officials stood in the middle of the room, one with a notebook in hand. An hotel chambermaid, looking frightened to death, stood by the fireplace; and on the other side of the room a Frenchwoman, obviously Mrs. Opalsen's maid, was weeping and wringing her hands, with an intensity of grief that rivaled that of her mistress.

Into this pandemonium stepped Poirot, neat and smiling. Immediately, with an energy surprising in one of her bulk, Mrs. Opalsen sprang from her chair towards him.

"There now; Ed may say what he likes, but I believe in luck. I do. It was fated I should meet you the way I did this evening, and I've a feeling that if you can't get my pearls back for me nobody can."

"Calm yourself, I pray of you, madame." Poirot patted her hand soothingly. "Reassure yourself. All will be well. Hercule Poirot will aid you!"

Mr. Opalsen turned to the police inspector.

"There will be no objection to my—er—calling in this gentleman, I suppose?"

"None at all, sir," replied the man civilly, but with complete indifference. "Perhaps now your lady's feeling better she'll just let us have the facts?"

Mrs. Opalsen looked helplessly at Poirot. He led her back to her chair.

"Seat yourself, madame, and recount to us the whole history without agitating yourself."

Thus abjured, Mrs. Opalsen dried her eyes gingerly, and began.

"I came upstairs after dinner to fetch my pearls for Mr. Poirot here to see. The chambermaid and Célestine were both in the room as usual——"

"Excuse me, madame, but what do you mean by 'as usual'?"

Mr. Opalsen explained.

"I make it a rule that no one is to come into this room unless Célestine, the maid, is there also. The chambermaid does the room in the morning while Célestine is present, and comes in after dinner to turn down the beds under the same conditions; otherwise she never enters the room."

"Well, as I was saying," continued Mrs. Opalsen, "I came up. I went to the drawer here,"—she indicated the bottom right-hand drawer of the kneehole dressing-table —"took out my jewel-case and unlocked it. It seemed quite as usual—but the pearls were not there!"

The inspector had been busy with his notebook. "When had you last seen them?" he asked.

"They were there when I went down to dinner."

"You are sure?"

"Quite sure. I was uncertain whether to wear them or not, but in the end I decided on the emeralds, and put them back in the jewel-case."

"Who locked up the jewel-case?"

"I did. I wear the key on a chain round my neck." She held it up as she spoke.

The inspector examined it, and shrugged his shoulders.

"The thief must have had a duplicate key. No difficult matter. The lock is quite a simple one. What did you do after you'd locked the jewel-case?"

"I put it back in the bottom drawer where I always keep it."

"You didn't lock the drawer?"

"No, I never do. My maid remains in the room till I come up, so there's no need."

The inspector's face grew graver.

"Am I to understand that the jewels were there when you went down to dinner, and that since then *the maid has not left the room?*"

Suddenly, as though the horror of her own situation for the first time burst upon her, Célestine uttered a piercing shriek, and, flinging herself upon Poirot, poured out a torrent of incoherent French.

The suggestion was infamous! That she should be suspected of robbing Madame! The police were well known to be of a stupidity incredible! But Monsieur, who was a Frenchman——

"A Belgian," interjected Poirot, but Célestine paid no attention to the correction.

Monsieur would not stand by and see her falsely accused, while that infamous chambermaid was allowed to go scot-free. She had never liked her—a bold, red-faced thing—a born thief. She had said from the first that she was not honest. And had kept a sharp watch over her too, when she was doing Madame's room! Let those idiots of policemen search her, and if they did not find Madame's pearls on her it would be very surprising!

Although this harangue was uttered in rapid and virulent French, Célestine had interlarded it with a wealth of gesture, and the chambermaid realized at least a part of her meaning. She reddened angrily.

"If that foreign woman's saying I took the pearls, it's a lie!" she declared heatedly. "I never so much as saw them."

"Search her!" screamed the other. "You will find it as I say."

"You're a liar—do you hear?" said the chambermaid, advancing upon her. "Stole 'em yourself, and want to put it on me. Why, I was only in the room about three minutes before the lady come up, and then you were sitting here the whole time, as you always do, like a cat watching a mouse."

The inspector looked across inquiringly at Célestine. "Is that true? Didn't you leave the room at all?"

"I did not actually leave her alone," admitted Célestine reluctantly, "but I went into my own room through the door here twice—once to fetch a reel of cotton, and once for my scissors. She must have done it then."

"You wasn't gone a minute," retorted the chambermaid angrily. "Just popped out and in again. I'd be glad if the police *would* search me. *I've* nothing to be afraid of."

At this moment there was a tap at the door. The inspector went to it. His face brightened when he saw who it was.

"Ah!" he said. "That's rather fortunate. I sent for one of our female searchers, and she's just arrived. Perhaps if you wouldn't mind going into the room next door."

He looked at the chambermaid, who stepped across the threshold with a toss of her head, the searcher following her closely.

The French girl had sunk sobbing into a chair. Poirot was looking round the 1.... the main features of which I have made clear by a sketch.

"Where d.... that door lead?" he inquired, nodding his head towards the one by the window.

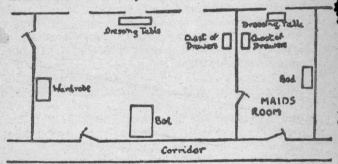

"Into the next apartment, I believe," said the inspector. "It's bolted, anyway, on this side."

Poirot walked across to it, tried it, then drew back the bolt and tried it again.

"And on the other side as well," he remarked. "Well, that seems to rule out that."

He walked over to the windows, examining each of them in turn.

"And again—nothing. Not even a balcony outside."

"Even if there were," said the inspector impatiently, "I don't see how that would help us, if the maid never left the room."

"*Évidemment*," said Poirot, not disconcerted. "As Mademoiselle is positive she did not leave the room——"

He was interrupted by the reappearance of the chambermaid and the police searcher.

"Nothing," said the latter laconically.

"I should hope not, indeed," said the chambermaid virtuously. "And that French hussy ought to be ashamed of herself taking away an honest girl's character!"

"There, there, my girl; that's all right," said the inspector, opening the door. "Nobody suspects you. You go along and get on with your work."

The chambermaid went unwillingly.

"Going to search *her?*" she demanded, pointing at Célestine.

"Yes, yes!" He shut the door on her and turned the key.

Célestine accompanied the searcher into the small room in her turn. A few minutes later she also returned. Nothing had been found on her.

The inspector's face grew graver.

"I'm afraid I'll have to ask you to come along with me all the same, miss." He turned to Mrs. Opalsen. "I'm sorry, madam, but all the evidence points that way. If she's not got them on her, they're hidden somewhere about the room."

Célestine uttered a piercing shriek, and clung to Poirot's arm. The latter bent and whispered something in the girl's ear. She looked up at him doubtfully.

"*Si, si, mon enfant*—I assure you it is better not to resist." Then he turned to the inspector. "You permit, monsieur? A little experiment—purely for my own satisfaction."

"Depends on what it is," replied the police officer noncommittally.

Poirot addressed Célestine once more.

"You have told us that you went into your room to fetch a reel of cotton. Whereabouts was it?"

"On the top of the chest of drawers, monsieur."

"And the scissors?"

"They also."

"Would it be troubling you too much, mademoiselle, to ask you to repeat those two actions? You were sitting here with your work, you say?"

Célestine sat down, and then, at a sign from Poirot, rose, passing into the adjoining room, took up an object from the chest of drawers, and returned.

Poirot divided his attention between her movements and a large turnip of a watch which he held in the palm of his hand.

"Again, if you please, mademoiselle."

At the conclusion of the second performance, he made a note in his pocket-book, and returned the watch to his pocket.

"Thank you, mademoiselle. And you, monsieur,"—he bowed to the inspector—"for your courtesy."

The inspector seemed somewhat entertained by this excessive politeness. Célestine departed in a flood of tears, accompanied by the woman and the plain-clothes official.

Then, with a brief apology to Mrs. Opalsen, the inspector set to work to ransack the room. He pulled out drawers, opened cupboards, completely unmade the bed, and tapped the floor. Mr. Opalsen looked on skeptically.

"You really think you will find them?"

"Yes, sir. It stands to reason. She hadn't time to take them out of the room. The lady's discovering the robbery so soon upset her plans. No, they're here right enough. One of the two must have hidden them—and it's very unlikely for the chambermaid to have done so."

"More than unlikely—impossible!" said Poirot quietly.

"Eh?" The inspector stared.

Poirot smiled modestly.

"I will demonstrate. Hastings, my good friend, take my watch in your hand—with care. It is a family heirloom! Just now I timed Mademoiselle's movements—her first absence from the room was of twelve seconds, her second of fifteen. Now observe my actions. Madame will have the kindness to give me the key of the jewel-case. I thank

you. My friend Hastings will have the kindness to say
'Go!' "

"Go!" I said.

With almost incredible swiftness, Poirot wrenched open
the drawer of the dressing-table, extracted the jewel-case,
fitted the key in the lock, opened the case, selected a piece
of jewelry, shut and locked the case, and returned it to
the drawer, which he pushed to again. His movements
were like lightning.

"Well, *mon ami?*" he demanded of me breathlessly.

"Forty-six seconds," I replied.

"You see?" He looked round. "There would not have
been time for the chambermaid even to take the necklace
out, far less hide it."

"Then that settles it on the maid," said the inspector
with satisfaction, and returned to his search. He passed
into the maid's bedroom next door.

Poirot was frowning thoughtfully. Suddenly he shot a
question at Mr. Opalsen.

"This necklace—it was, without doubt, insured?"

Mr. Opalsen looked a trifle surprised at the question.

"Yes," he said hesitatingly, "that is so."

"But what does that matter?" broke in Mrs. Opalsen
tearfully. "It's my necklace I want. It was unique. No
money could be the same."

"I comprehend, madame," said Poirot soothingly. "I
comprehend perfectly. To *la femme* sentiment is everything—is it not so? But monsieur, who has not the so fine
susceptibility, will doubtless find some slight consolation
in the fact."

"Of course, of course," said Mr. Opalsen rather uncertainly. "Still——"

He was interrupted by a shout of triumph from the
inspector. He came in dangling something from his fingers.

With a cry, Mrs. Opalsen heaved herself up from her
chair. She was a changed woman.

"Oh, oh, my necklace!"

She clasped it to her breast with both hands. We
crowded around.

"Where was it?" demanded Opalsen.

"Maid's bed. In among the springs of the wire mattress. She must have stolen it and hidden it there before the chambermaid arrived on the scene."

"You permit, madame?" said Poirot gently. He took the necklace from her and examined it closely; then handed it back with a bow.

"I'm afraid, madam, you'll have to hand it over to us for the time being," said the inspector. "We shall want it for the charge. But it shall be returned to you as soon as possible."

Mr. Opalsen frowned.

"Is that necessary?"

"I'm afraid so, sir. Just a formality."

"Oh, let him take it, Ed!" cried his wife. "I'd feel safer if he did. I shouldn't sleep a wink thinking someone else might try and get hold of it. That wretched girl! And I would never have believed it of her."

"There, there, my dear, don't take on so." I felt a gentle pressure on my arm. It was Poirot.

"Shall we slip away, my friend? I think our services are no longer needed."

Once outside, however, he hesitated, and then, much to my surprise, he remarked:

"I should rather like to see the room next door."

The door was not locked, and we entered. The room, which was a large double one, was unoccupied. Dust lay about rather noticeably, and my sensitive friend gave a characteristic grimace as he ran his finger round a rectangular mark on a table near the window.

"The service leaves to be desired," he observed dryly.

He was staring thoughtfully out of the window, and seemed to have fallen into a brown study.

"Well?" I demanded impatiently. "What did we come in here for?"

He stared.

"Je vous demande pardon, mon ami. I wished to see if the door was really bolted on this side also."

"Well," I said, glancing at the door which communicated with the room we had just left, "it is bolted."

Poirot nodded. He still seemed to be thinking.

"And, anyway," I continued, "what does it matter?

The case is over. I wish you'd had more chance of distinguishing yourself. But it was the kind of case that even a stiff-backed idiot like that inspector couldn't go wrong over."

Poirot shook his head.

"The case is not over, my friend. It will not be over until we find out who stole the pearls."

"But the maid did!"

"Why do you say that?"

"Why," I stammered, "they were found—actually in her mattress."

"Ta, ta, ta!" said Poirot impatiently. "Those were not the pearls."

"What?"

"Imitation, *mon ami.*"

The statement took my breath away. Poirot was smiling placidly.

"The good inspector obviously knows nothing of jewels. But presently there will be a fine hullabaloo!"

"Come!" I cried, dragging at his arm.

"Where?"

"We must tell the Opalsens at once."

"I think not."

"But that poor woman——"

"Eh bien; that poor woman, as you call her, will have a much better night believing the jewels to be safe."

"But the thief may escape with them!"

"As usual, my friend, you speak without reflection. How do you know that the pearls Mrs. Opalsen locked up so carefully to-night were not the false ones, and that the real robbery did not take place at a much earlier date?"

"Oh!" I said bewildered.

"Exactly," said Poirot, beaming. "We start again."

He led the way out of the room, paused a moment as though considering, and then walked down to the end of the corridor, stopping outside the small den where the chambermaids and valets of the respective floors congregated. Our particular chambermaid appeared to be holding a small court there, and to be retailing her late experiences to an appreciative audience. She stopped in the middle of a sentence. Poirot bowed with his usual politeness.

"Excuse that I derange you, but I shall be obliged if you will unlock for me the door of Mr. Opalsen's room."

The woman rose willingly, and we accompanied her down the passage again. Mr. Opalsen's room was on the other side of the corridor, its door facing that of his wife's room. The chambermaid unlocked it with her passkey, and we entered.

As she was about to depart Poirot detained her.

"One moment; have you ever seen among the effects of Mr. Opalsen a card like this?"

He held out a plain white card, rather highly glazed and uncommon in appearance. The maid took it and scrutinized it carefully.

"No, sir, I can't say I have. But, anyway, the valet has most to do with the gentlemen's rooms."

"I see. Thank you."

Poirot took back the card. The woman departed. Poirot appeared to reflect a little. Then he gave a short, sharp nod of the head.

"Ring the bell, I pray of you, Hastings. Three times, for the valet."

I obeyed, devoured with curiosity. Meanwhile Poirot had emptied the waste-paper basket on the floor, and was swiftly going through its contents.

In a few moments the valet answered the bell. To him Poirot put the same question, and handed him the card to examine. But the response was the same. The valet had never seen a card of that particular quality among Mr. Opalsen's belongings. Poirot thanked him, and he withdrew, somewhat unwillingly, with an inquisitive glance at the overturned waste-paper basket and the litter on the floor. He could hardly have helped overhearing Poirot's thoughtful remark as he bundled the torn papers back again:

"And the necklace was heavily insured. . . ."

"Poirot," I cried, "I see——"

"You see nothing, my friend," he replied quickly, "as

provided himself, extracts the necklace, and waits his time. Célestine leaves the room again, and—pst!—in a flash the case is passed back again and replaced in the drawer.

"Madame arrives, the theft is discovered. The chambermaid demands to be searched, with a good deal of righteous indignation, and leaves the room without a stain on her character. The imitation necklace with which they have provided themselves has been concealed in the French girl's bed that morning by the chambermaid—a master stroke, *ça!*"

"But what did you go to London for?"

"You remember the card?"

"Certainly. It puzzled me—and puzzles me still. I thought——"

I hesitated delicately, glancing at Mr. Opalsen.

Poirot laughed heartily.

"Une blague! For the benefit of the valet. The card was one with a specially prepared surface—for finger-prints. I went straight to Scotland Yard, asked for our old friend Inspector Japp, and laid the facts before him. As I had suspected, the finger-prints proved to be those of two well-known jewel thieves who have been 'wanted' for some time. Japp came down with me, the thieves were arrested, and the necklace was discovered in the valet's possession. A clever pair, but they failed in *method*. Have I not told you, Hastings, at least thirty-six times, that without method— —"

"At least thirty-six thousand times!" I interrupted. "But where did their 'method' break down?"

"Mon ami, it is a good plan to take a place as chambermaid or valet—but you must not shirk your work. They left an empty room undusted; and therefore, when the man put down the jewel-case on the little table near the communicating door, it left a square mark——"

"I remember," I cried.

"Before, I was undecided. Then—I *knew!*"

There was a moment's silence.

"And I've got my pearls," said Mrs. Opalsen as a sort of Greek chorus.

"Well," I said, "I'd better have some dinner."

Poirot accompanied me.

"This ought to mean kudos for you," I observed.

"Pas du tout," replied Poirot tranquilly. "Japp and the local inspector will divide the credit between them. But"—he tapped his pocket—"I have a check here, from Mr. Opalsen, and, how say you, my friend? This week-end has not gone according to plan. Shall we return here next week-end—at my expense this time?"

VIII
THE KIDNAPPED PRIME MINISTER

Now that war and the problems of war are things of the past, I think I may safely venture to reveal to the world the part which my friend Poirot played in a moment of national crisis. The secret has been well guarded. Not a whisper of it reached the Press. But, now that the need for secrecy has gone by, I feel it is only just that England should know the debt it owes to my quaint little friend, whose marvelous brain so ably averted a great catastrophe.

One evening after dinner—I will not particularize the date; it suffices to say that it was at the time when "Peace by negotiation" was the parrot-cry of England's enemies —my friend and I were sitting in his rooms. After being invalided out of the Army I had been given a recruiting job, and it had become my custom to drop in on Poirot in the evenings after dinner and talk with him of any cases of interest that he might have on hand.

I was attempting to discuss with him the sensational news of that day—no less than an attempted assassination of Mr. David MacAdam, England's Prime Minister The account in the papers had evidently been carefully censored. No details were given, save that the Prime Minister had had a marvelous escape, the bullet just grazing his cheek.

I considered that our police must have been shamefully careless for such an outrage to be possible. I could well understand that the German agents in England would be willing to risk much for such an achievement. "Fighting Mac," as his own party had nicknamed him, had strenuously and unequivocally combated the Pacifist influence which was becoming so prevalent.

He was more than England's Prime Minister—he *was* England; and to have removed him from his sphere of influence would have been a crushing and paralyzing blow to Britain.

Poirot was busy mopping a gray suit with a minute sponge. Never was there a dandy such as Hercule Poirot. Neatness and order were his passion. Now, with the odor of benzine filling the air, he was quite unable to give me his full attention.

"In a little minute I am with you, my friend. I have all but finished. The spot of grease—he is not good—I remove him—so!" He waved his sponge.

I smiled as I lit another cigarette.

"Anything interesting on?" I inquired, after a minute or two.

"I assist a—how do you call it?—'charlady' to find her husband. A difficult affair, needing the tact. For I have a little idea that when he is found he will not be pleased. What would you? For my part, I sympathize with him. He was a man of discrimination to lose himself."

I laughed.

"At last! The spot of grease, he is gone! I am at your disposal."

"I was asking you what you thought of this attempt to assassinate MacAdam?"

"Enfantillage!" replied Poirot promptly. "One can hardly take it seriously. To fire with the rifle—never does it succeed. It is a device of the past."

"It was very near succeeding this time," I reminded him.

Poirot shook his head impatiently. He was about to reply when the landlady thrust her head round the door and informed him that there were two gentlemen below who wanted to see him.

"They won't give their names, sir, but they says as it's very important."

"Let them mount," said Poirot, carefully folding his gray trousers.

In a few minutes the two visitors were ushered in, and my heart gave a leap as in the foremost I recognized no less a personage than Lord Estair, Leader of the House of Commons; whilst his companion, Mr. Bernard Dodge, was also a member of the War Cabinet, and, as I knew, a close personal friend of the Prime Minister.

"Monsieur Poirot?" said Lord Estair interrogatively. My friend bowed. The great man looked at me and hesitated. "My business is private."

"You may speak freely before Captain Hastings," said my friend, nodding to me to remain. "He has not all the gifts, no! But I answer for his discretion."

Lord Estair still hesitated, but Mr. Dodge broke in abruptly!

"Oh, come on—don't let's beat about the bush! As far as I can see, the whole of England will know the hole we're in soon enough! Time's everything."

"Pray be seated, messieurs," said Poirot politely. "Will you take the big chair, *milord?*"

Lord Estair started slightly. "You know me?"

Poirot smiled. "Certainly. I read the little papers with the pictures. How should I not know you?"

"Monsieur Poirot, I have come to consult you upon a matter of the most vital urgency. I must ask for absolute secrecy."

"You have the word of Hercule Poirot—I can say no more!" said my friend grandiloquently.

"It concerns the Prime Minister. We are in grave trouble."

"We're up a tree!" interposed Mr. Dodge.

"The injury is serious, then?" I asked.

"What injury?"

"The bullet wound."

"Oh, that!" cried Mr. Dodge contemptuously. "That's old history."

"As my colleague says," continued Lord Estair, "that affair is over and done with. Luckily, it failed. I wished I could say as much for the second attempt."

"There has been a second attempt, then?"

"Yes, though not of the same nature. Monsieur Poirot, the Prime Minister has disappeared."

"What?"

"He has been kidnapped!"

"Impossible!" I cried, stupefied.

Poirot threw a withering glance at me, which I knew enjoined me to keep my mouth shut.

"Unfortunately, impossible as it seems, it is only too true," continued his lordship.

Poirot looked at Mr. Dodge. "You said just now, monsieur, that time was everything. What did you mean by that?"

The two men exchanged glances, and then Lord Estair said:

"You have heard, Monsieur Poirot, of the approaching Allied Conference?"

My friend nodded.

"For obvious reasons, no details have been given of when and where it is to take place. But, although it has been kept out of the newspapers, the date is, of course, widely known in diplomatic circles. The Conference is to be held to-morrow—Thursday—evening at Versailles. Now you perceive the terrible gravity of the situation. I will not conceal from you that the Prime Minister's presence at the Conference is a vital necessity. The Pacifist propaganda, started and maintained by the German agents in our midst, has been very active. It is the universal opinion that the turning point of the Conference will be the strong personality of the Prime Minister. His absence may have the most serious results—possibly a premature and disastrous peace. And we have no one who can be sent in his place. He alone can represent England."

Poirot's face had grown very grave. "Then you regard the kidnapping of the Prime Minister as a direct attempt to prevent his being present at the Conference?"

"Most certainly I do. He was actually on his way to France at the time."

"And the Conference is to be held?"

"At nine o'clock to-morrow night."

Poirot drew an enormous watch from his pocket.

"It is now a quarter to nine."

"Twenty-four hours," said Mr. Dodge thoughtfully.

"And a quarter," amended Poirot. "Do not forget the quarter, monsieur—it may come in useful. Now for the details—the abduction, did it take place in England or in France?"

"In France. Mr. MacAdam crossed to France this morning. He was to stay to-night as the guest of the Commander-in-Chief, proceeding to-morrow to Paris. He was conveyed across the Channel by destroyer. At Boulogne he was met by a car from General Headquarters and one of the Commander-in-Chief's A.D.C.s."

"Eh bien?"

"Well, they started from Boulogne—but they never arrived."

"What?"

"Monsieur Poirot, it was a bogus car and a bogus A.D.C. The real car was found in a side road, with the chauffeur and the A.D.C. neatly gagged and bound."

"And the bogus car?"

"Is still at large."

Poirot made a gesture of impatience. "Incredible! Surely it cannot escape attention for long?"

"So we thought. It seemed merely a question of searching thoroughly. That part of France is under Military Law. We were convinced that the car could not go long unnoticed. The French police and our own Scotland Yard men, and the military are straining every nerve. It is, as you say, incredible—but nothing has been discovered!"

At that moment a tap came at the door, and a young officer entered with a heavily sealed envelope which he handed to Lord Estair.

"Just through from France, sir. I brought it on here, as you directed."

The minister tore it open eagerly, and uttered an exclamation. The officer withdrew.

"Here is news at last! This telegram has just been decoded. They have found the second car, also the secretary, Daniels, chloroformed, gagged, and bound, in an abandoned farm near C——. He remembers nothing, except something being pressed against his mouth and nose from behind, and struggling to free himself. The police are satisfied as to the genuineness of his statement."

"And they have found nothing else?"

"No."

"Not the Prime Minister's dead body? Then, there is hope. But it is strange. Why, after trying to shoot him this morning, are they now taking so much trouble to keep him alive?"

Dodge shook his head. "One thing's quite certain. They're determined at all costs to prevent his attending the Conference."

"If it is humanly possible, the Prime Minister shall be there. God grant it is not too late. Now, messieurs, recount to me everything—from the beginning. I must know about this shooting affair as well."

"Last night, the Prime Minister, accompanied by one of his secretaries, Captain Daniels——"

"The same who accompanied him to France?"

"Yes. As I was saying, they motored down to Windsor, where the Prime Minister was granted an Audience. Early this morning, he returned to town, and it was on the way that the attempted assassination took place."

"One moment, if you please. Who is this Captain Daniels? You have his dossier?"

Lord Estair smiled. "I thought you would ask me that. We do not know very much of him. He is of no particular family. He has served in the English Army, and is an extremely able secretary, being an exceptionally fine linguist. I believe he speaks seven languages. It is for that reason that the Prime Minister chose him to accompany him to France."

"Has he any relatives in England?"

"Two aunts. A Mrs. Everard, who lives at Hampstead, and a Miss Daniels, who lives near Ascot."

"Ascot? That is near to Windsor, is it not?"

"That point has not been overlooked. But it has led to nothing."

"You regard the Capitaine Daniels, then, as above suspicion?"

A shade of bitterness crept into Lord Estair's voice, as he replied:

"No, Monsieur Poirot. In these days, I should hesitate before I pronounced *anyone* above suspicion."

"*Très bien.* Now I understand, *milord,* that the Prime Minister would, as a matter of course, be under vigilant police protection, which ought to render any assault upon him an impossibility?"

Lord Estair bowed his head. "That is so. The Prime Minister's car was closely followed by another car containing detectives in plain clothes. Mr. MacAdam knew nothing of these precautions. He is personally a most fearless man, and would be inclined to sweep them away arbitrarily. But, naturally, the police make their own arrangements. In fact, the Premier's chauffeur, O'Murphy, is a C.I.D. man."

"O'Murphy? That is a name of Ireland, is it not so?"

"Yes, he is an Irishman."

"From what part of Ireland?"

"County Clare, I believe."

"*Tiens!* But proceed, *milord.*"

"The Premier started for London. The car was a closed one. He and Captain Daniels sat inside. The second car followed as usual. But, unluckily, for some unknown reason, the Prime Minister's car deviated from the main road——"

"At a point where the road curves?" interrupted Poirot.

"Yes—but how did you know?"

"Oh, *c'est évident!* Continue!"

"For some unknown reason," continued Lord Estair, "the Premier's car left the main road. The police car, unaware of the deviation, continued to keep to the high road. At a short distance down the unfrequented lane, the Prime Minister's car was suddenly held up by a band of masked men. The chauffeur——"

"That brave O'Murphy!" murmured Poirot thoughtfully.

"The chauffeur, momentarily taken aback, jammed on the brakes. The Prime Minister put his head out of the window. Instantly a shot rang out—then another. The first one grazed his cheek, the second, fortunately, went wide. The chauffeur, now realizing the danger, instantly forged straight ahead, scattering the band of men."

"A near escape," I ejaculated, with a shiver.

"Mr. MacAdam refused to make any fuss over the slight wound he had received. He declared it was only a scratch. He stopped at a local cottage hospital, where it was dressed and bound up—he did not, of course, reveal his identity. He then drove, as per schedule, straight to

Charing Cross, where a special train for Dover was awaiting him, and, after a brief account of what had happened
had been given to the anxious police by Captain Daniels,
he duly departed for France. At Dover, he went on board
the waiting destroyer. At Boulogne, as you know, the
bogus car was waiting for him, carrying the Union Jack,
and correct in every detail."

"That is all you have to tell me?"

"Yes."

"There is no other circumstance that you have omitted,
milord?"

"Well, there is one rather peculiar thing."

"Yes?"

"The Prime Minister's car did not return home after
leaving the Prime Minister at Charing Cross. The police
were anxious to interview O'Murphy, so a search was in-
stituted at once. The car was discovered standing outside
a certain unsavoury little restaurant in Soho, which is
well known as a meeting-place of German agents."

"And the chauffeur?"

"The chauffeur was nowhere to be found. He, too, had
disappeared."

"So," said Poirot thoughtfully, "there are two disap-
pearances: the Prime Minister in France, and O'Murphy
in London."

He looked keenly at Lord Estair, who made a gesture
of despair.

"I can only tell you, Monsieur Poirot, that, if anyone
had suggested to me yesterday that O'Murphy was a
traitor, I should have laughed in his face."

"And to-day?"

"To-day I do not know what to think."

Poirot nodded gravely. He looked at his turnip of a
watch again.

"I understand that I have carte blanche, messieurs—
in every way, I mean? I must be able to go where I
choose, and how I choose."

"Perfectly. There is a special train leaving for Dover
in an hour's time, with a further contingent from Scotland
Yard. You shall be accompanied by a Military officer and

a C.I.D. man, who will hold themselves at your disposal in every way. Is that satisfactory?"

"Quite. One more question before you leave, messieurs. What made you come to me? I am unknown, obscure, in this great London of yours."

"We sought you out on the express recommendation and wish of a very great man of your own country."

"*Comment?* My old friend the *Préfet*——?"

Lord Estair shook his head.

"Once higher than the *Préfet*. One whose word was once law in Belgium—and shall be again! That England has sworn!"

Poirot's hand flew swiftly to a dramatic salute. "Amen to that! Ah, but my Master does not forget. . . . Messieurs, I, Hercule Poirot, will serve you faithfully. Heaven only send that it will be in time. But this is dark—dark. . . . I cannot see."

"Well, Poirot," I cried impatiently, as the door closed behind the Ministers, "what do you think?"

My friend was busy packing a minute suitcase, with quick, deft movements. He shook his head thoughtfully.

"I do not know what to think. My brains desert me."

"Why, as you said, kidnap him, when a knock on the head would do as well?" I mused.

"Pardon me, *mon ami*, but I did not quite say that. It is undoubtedly far more their affair to kidnap him."

"But why?"

"Because uncertainty creates panic. That is one reason. Were the Prime Minister dead, it would be a terrible calamity, but the situation would have to be faced. But now you have paralysis. Will the Prime Minister reappear, or will he not? Is he dead or alive? Nobody knows, and until they know nothing definite can be done. And, as I tell you, uncertainty breeds panic, which is what *les Boches* are playing for. Then, again, if the kidnappers are holding him secretly somewhere, they have the advantage of being able to make terms with both sides. The German Government is not a liberal paymaster, as a rule, but no doubt they can be made to disgorge substantial remittances in such a case as this. Thirdly, they run no risk of the hangman's rope. Oh, decidedly, kidnapping is their affair."

"Then, if that is so, why should they first try to shoot him?"

Poirot made a gesture of anger. "Ah, that is just what I do not understand! It is inexplicable—stupid! They have all their arrangements made (and very good arrangements too!) for the abduction, and yet they imperil the whole affair by a melodramatic attack, worthy of a cinema, and quite as unreal. It is almost impossible to believe in it, with its band of masked men, not twenty miles from London!"

"Perhaps they were two quite separate attempts which happened irrespective of each other," I suggested.

"Ah, no, that would be too much of a coincidence! Then, further—who is the traitor? There must have been a traitor—in the first affair, anyway. But who was it— Daniels or O'Murphy? It must have been one of the two, or why did the car leave the main road? We cannot suppose that the Prime Minister connived at his own assassination! Did O'Murphy take that turning of his own accord, or was it Daniels who told him to do so?"

"Surely it must have been O'Murphy's doing."

"Yes, because if it was Daniels' the Prime Minister would have heard the order, and would have asked the reason. But there are altogether too many 'whys' in this affair, and they contradict each other. If O'Murphy is an honest man, *why* did he leave the main road? But if he was a dishonest man, *why* did he start the car again when only two shots had been fired—thereby, in all probability, saving the Prime Minister's life? And, again, if he was honest, why did he, immediately on leaving Charing Cross, drive to a well-known rendezvous of German spies?"

"It looks bad," I said.

"Let us look at the case with method. What have we for and against these two men? Take O'Murphy first. Against: that his conduct in leaving the main road was suspicious; that he is an Irishman from County Clare; that he has disappeared in a highly suggestive manner. For: that his promptness in restarting the car saved the

Premier's life; that he is a Scotland Yard man, and, obviously, from the post allotted to him, a trusted detective. Now for Daniels. There is not much against him, except the fact that nothing is known of his antecedents, and that he speaks too many languages for a good Englishman! (Pardon me, *mon ami,* but, as linguists, you are deplorable!) Now *for* him, we have the fact that he was found gagged, bound, and chloroformed—which does not look as though he had anything to do with the matter."

"He might have gagged and bound himself, to divert suspicion."

Poirot shook his head. "The French police would make no mistake of that kind. Besides, once he had attained his object, and the Prime Minister was safely abducted, there would not be much point in his remaining behind. His accomplices *could* have gagged' and chloroformed him, of course, but I fail to see what object they hoped to accomplish by it. He can be of little use to them now, for, until the circumstances concerning the Prime Minister have been cleared up, he is bound to be closely watched."

"Perhaps he hoped to start the police on a false scent?"

"Then why did he not do so? He merely says that something was pressed over his nose and mouth, and that he remembers nothing more. There is no false scent there. It sounds remarkably like the truth."

"Well," I said, glancing at the clock, "I suppose we'd better start for the station. You may find more clues in France."

"Possibly, *mon ami,* but I doubt it. It is still incredible to me that the Prime Minister has not been discovered in that limited area, where the difficulty of concealing him must be tremendous. If the military and the police of two countries have not found him, how shall I?"

At Charing Cross we were met by Mr. Dodge.

"This is Detective Barnes, of Scotland Yard, and Major Norman. They will hold themselves entirely at your disposal. Good luck to you. It's a bad business, but I've not given up hope. Must be off now." And the Minister strode rapidly away.

We chatted in a desultory fashion with Major Norman.

In the center of the little group of men on the platform I recognized a little ferret-faced fellow talking to a tall, fair man. He was an old acquaintance of Poirot's—Detective-Inspector Japp, supposed to be one of the smartest of Scotland Yard's officers. He came over and greeted my friend cheerfully.

"I heard you were on this job too. Smart bit of work. So far they've got away with the goods all right. But I can't believe they can keep him hidden long. Our people are going through France with a toothcomb. So are the French. I can't help feeling it's only a matter of hours now."

"That is, if he's still alive," remarked the tall detective gloomily.

Japp's face fell. "Yes. . . . But somehow I've got the feeling he's alive all right."

Poirot nodded. "Yes, yes; he's alive. But can he be found in time? I, like you, did not believe he could be hidden so long."

The whistle blew, and we all trooped up into the Pullman car. Then, with a slow, unwilling jerk, the train drew out of the station.

It was a curious journey. The Scotland Yard men crowded together. Maps of Northern France were spread out, and eager forefingers traced the lines of roads and villages. Each man had his own pet theory. Poirot showed none of his usual loquacity, but sat staring in front of him, with an expression on his face that reminded me of a puzzled child. I talked to Norman, whom I found quite an amusing fellow. On arriving at Dover Poirot's behavior moved me to intense amusement. The little man, as he went on board the boat, clutched desperately at my arm. The wind was blowing lustily.

"Mon Dieu!" he murmured. "This is terrible!"

"Have courage, Poirot," I cried. "You will succeed. You will find him. I am sure of it."

"Ah, *mon ami,* you mistake my emotion. It is this villainous sea that troubles me! The *mal de mer*—it is horrible suffering!"

"Oh!" I said, rather taken aback.

The first throb of the engines was felt, and Poirot groaned and closed his eyes.

"Major Norman has a map of Northern France if you would like to study it?"

Poirot shook his head impatiently.

"But no, but no! Leave me, my friend. See you, to think, the stomach and the brain must be in harmony. Laverguier has a method most excellent for averting the *mal de mer*. You breathe in—and out—slowly, so—turning the head from left to right and counting six between each breath."

I left him to his gymnastic endeavors, and went on deck.

As we came slowly into Boulogne Harbor Poirot appeared, neat and smiling, and announced to me in a whisper that Laverguier's system had succeeded "to a marvel!"

Japp's forefinger was still tracing imaginary routes on his map. "Nonsense! The car started from Boulogne— here they branched off. Now, my idea is that they transferred the Prime Minister to another car. See?"

"Well," said the tall detective, "I shall make for the seaports. Ten to one, they've smuggled him on board a ship."

Japp shook his head. "Too obvious. The order went out at once to close all the ports."

The day was just breaking as we landed. Major Norman touched Poirot on the arm. "There's a military car here waiting for you, sir."

"Thank you, monsieur. But, for the moment, I do not propose to leave Boulogne."

"What?"

"No, we will enter this hotel here, by the quay."

He suited the action to the word, demanded and was accorded a private room. We three followed him, puzzled and uncomprehending.

He shot a quick glance at us. "It is not so that the good detective should act, eh? I perceived your thought. He must be full of energy. He must rush to and fro. He should prostrate himself on the dusty road and seek the marks of tires through a little glass. He must gather up the cigarette-end, the fallen match? That is your idea, is it not?"

His eyes challenged us. "But I—Hercule Poirot—tell you that it is not so! The true clues are within—*here!*" He tapped his forehead. "See you, I need not have left London. It would have been sufficient for me to sit quietly in my rooms there. All that matters is the little gray cells within. Secretly and silently they do their part, until suddenly I call for a map, and I lay my finger on a spot—so—and I say: the Prime Minister is *there!* And it is so! With method and logic one can accomplish anything! This frantic rushing to France was a mistake—it is playing a child's game of hide-and-seek. But now, though it may be too late, I will set to work the right way, from within. Silence, my friends, I beg of you."

And for five long hours the little man sat motionless, blinking his eyelids like a cat, his green eyes flickering and becoming steadily greener and greener. The Scotland Yard man was obviously contemptuous, Major Norman was bored and impatient, and I myself found the time pass with wearisome slowness.

Finally, I got up, and strolled as noiselessly as I could to the window. The matter was becoming a farce. I was secretly concerned for my friend. If he failed, I would have preferred him to fail in a less ridiculous manner. Out of the window I idly watched the daily leave boat, belching forth columns of smoke, as she lay alongside the quay.

Suddenly I was aroused by Poirot's voice close to my elbow.

"*Mes amis,* let us start!"

I turned. An extraordinary transformation had come over my friend. His eyes were flickering with excitement, his chest was swelled to the uttermost.

"I have been an imbecile, my friends! But I see daylight at last."

Major Norman moved hastily to the door. "I'll order the car."

"There is no need. I shall not use it. Thank Heaven the wind has fallen."

"Do you mean you are going to walk, sir?"

"No, my young friend. I am no St. Peter. I prefer to cross the sea by boat."

"To cross the *sea?*"

"Yes. To work with method, one must begin from the beginning. And the beginning of this affair was in England. Therefore, we return to England."

At three o'clock, we stood once more upon Charing Cross platform. To all our expostulations, Poirot turned a deaf ear, and reiterated again and again that to start at the beginning was not a waste of time, but the only way. On the way over, he had conferred with Norman in a low voice, and the latter had dispatched a sheaf of telegrams from Dover.

Owing to the special passes held by Norman, we got through everywhere in record time. In London, a large police car was waiting for us, with some plain-clothes men, one of whom handed a typewritten sheet of paper to my friend. He answered my inquiring glance.

"A list of the cottage hospitals within a certain radius west of London. I wired for it from Dover."

We were whirled rapidly through the London streets. We were on the Bath Road. On we went, through Hammersmith, Chiswick and Brentford. I began to see our objective. Through Windsor and on to Ascot. My heart gave a leap. Ascot was where Daniels had an aunt living. We were after *him,* then, not O'Murphy.

We duly stopped at the gate of a trim villa. Poirot jumped out and rang the bell. I saw a perplexed frown dimming the radiance of his face. Plainly, he was not satisfied. The bell was answered. He was ushered inside. In a few moments he reappeared, and climbed into the car with a short, sharp shake of his head. My hopes began to die down. It was past four now. Even if he found certain evidence incriminating Daniels, what would be the good of it, unless he could wring from some one the exact spot in France where they were holding the Prime Minister?

Our return progress towards London was an interrupted one. We deviated from the main road more than once, and occasionally stopped at a small building, which

I had no difficulty in recognizing as a cottage hospital. Poirot only spent a few minutes at each, but at every halt his radiant assurance was more and more restored.

He whispered something to Norman, to which the latter replied:

"Yes, if you turn off to the left, you will find them waiting by the bridge."

We turned up a side road, and in the failing light I discerned a second car, waiting by the side of the road. It contained two men in plain clothes. Poirot got down and spoke to them, and then we started off in a northerly direction, the other car following close behind.

We drove for some time, our objective being obviously one of the northern suburbs of London. Finally, we drove up to the front door of a tall house, standing a little back from the road in its own grounds.

Norman and I were left with the car. Poirot and one of the detectives went up to the door and rang. A neat parlormaid opened it. The detective spoke.

"I am a police officer, and I have a warrant to search this house."

The girl gave a little scream, and a tall, handsome woman of middle age appeared behind her in the hall.

"Shut the door, Edith. They are burglars, I expect."

But Poirot swiftly inserted his foot in the door, and at the same moment blew a whistle. Instantly the other detectives ran up, and poured into the house, shutting the door behind them.

Norman and I spent about five minutes cursing our forced inactivity. Finally the door reopened, and the men emerged, escorting three prisoners—a woman and two men. The woman, and one of the men, were taken to the second car. The other man was placed in our car by Poirot himself.

"I must go with the others, my friend. But have great care of this gentleman. You do not know him, no? *Eh bien,* let me present to you, Monsieur O'Murphy!"

O'Murphy! I *gaped* at him open-mouthed as we started again. He was not handcuffed, but I did not fancy he would try to escape. He sat there staring in front of him as though dazed. Anyway, Norman and I would be more than a match for him.

To my surprise, we still kept a northerly route. We were not returning to London, then! I was much puzzled. Suddenly, as the car slowed down, I recognized that we were close to Hendon Aerodrome. Immediately I grasped Poirot's idea. He proposed to reach France by aeroplane.

It was a sporting idea, but, on the face of it, impracticable. A telegram would be far quicker. Time was everything. He must leave the personal glory of rescuing the Prime Minister to others.

As we drew up, Major Norman jumped out, and a plain-clothes man took his place. He conferred with Poirot for a few minutes, and then went off briskly.

I, too, jumped out, and caught Poirot by the arm.

"I congratulate you, old fellow! They have told you the hiding-place? But, look here, you must wire to France at once. You'll be too late if you go yourself."

Poirot looked at me curiously for a minute or two.

"Unfortunately, my friend, there are some things that cannot be sent by telegram."

At that moment Major Norman returned, accompanied by a young officer in the uniform of the Flying Corps.

"This is Captain Lyall, who will fly you over to France. He can start at once."

"Wrap up warmly, sir," said the young pilot. "I can lend you a coat, if you like."

Poirot was consulting his enormous watch. He murmured to himself: "Yes, there is time—just time." Then he looked up, and bowed politely to the young officer. "I thank you, monsieur. But it is not I who am your passenger. It is this gentleman here."

He moved a little aside as he spoke, and a figure came forward out of the darkness. It was the second male prisoner who had gone in the other car, and as the light fell on his face, I gave a gasp of surprise.

It was the Prime Minister!

"For heaven's sake, tell me all about it," I cried impatiently, as Poirot, Norman, and I motored back to London. "How in the world did they manage to smuggle him back to England?"

"There was no need to smuggle him back," replied Poirot dryly. "The Prime Minister has never left England. He was kidnapped on his way from Windsor to London."

"What?"

"I will make all clear. The Prime Minister was in his car, his secretary beside him. Suddenly a pad of chloroform is clapped on his face——"

"But by whom?"

"By the clever linguistic Captain Daniels. As soon as the Prime Minister is unconscious, Daniels picks up the speaking-tube, and directs O'Murphy to turn to the right, which the chauffeur, quite unsuspicious, does. A few yards down that unfrequented road, a large car is standing, apparently broken down. Its driver signals to O'Murphy to stop. O'Murphy slows up. The stranger approaches. Daniels leans out of the window, and, probably with the aid of an instantaneous anæsthetic, such as ..u ·lchloride, the chloroform trick is repeated. In a few secon~ the two helpless men are dragged out and transferred to the othe~ ~r. and a pair of substitutes take their places."

"Impossible!"

"Pas du tout! Have you not seen music-hall turns imitating celebrities with marvelous accuracy? Nothing is easier than to personate a public character. The Prime Minister of England is far easier to understudy than Mr. John Smith of Clapham, say. As for O'Murphy's 'double,' no one was going to take much notice of him until after the departure of the Prime Minister, and by then he would have made himself scarce. He drives straight from Charing Cross to the meeting-place of his friends. He goes in as O'Murphy, he emerges as some one quite different. O'Murphy has disappeared, leaving a conveniently suspicious trail behind him."

"But the man who personated the Prime Minister was seen by everyone!"

"He was not seen by anyone who knew him privately or intimately. And Daniels shielded him from contact with anyone as much as possible. Moreover, his face was bandaged up, and anything unusual in his manner would be put down to the fact that he was suffering from shock as a result of the attempt upon his life. Mr. MacAdam has a weak throat, and always spares his voice as much as possible before any great speech. The deception was perfectly easy to keep up as far as France. There it would be impracticable and impossible—so the Prime Minister disappears. The police of this country hurry across the Channel, and no one bothers to go into the details of the first attack. To sustain the illusion that the abduction has taken place in France, Daniels is gagged and chloroformed in a convincing manner."

"And the man who has enacted the part of the Prime Minister?"

"Rids himself of his disguise. He and the bogus chauffeur may be arrested as suspicous characters, but no one will dream of suspecting their real part in the drama, and they will eventually be released for lack of evidence."

"And the real Prime Minister?"

"He and O'Murphy were driven straight to the house of 'Mrs. Everard,' at Hampstead, Daniels' so-called 'aunt.' In reality, she is Frau Bertha Ebenthal, and the police have been looking for her for some time. It is a valuable little present that I have made to them—to say nothing of Daniels! Ah, it was a clever plan, but he did not reckon on the cleverness of Hercule Poirot!"

I think my friend might well be excused his moment of vanity.

"When did you first begin to suspect the truth of the matter?"

"When I began to work the right way—from *within!* I could not make that shooting affair fit in—but when I saw that the net result of it was that *the Prime Minister went to France with his face bound up,* I began to comprehend! And when I visited all the cottage hospitals between Windsor and London, and found that no one answering to my description had had his face bound up and dressed that morning, I was sure! After that, it was child's-play for a mind like mine!"

The following morning, Poirot showed me a telegram he had just received. It had no place of origin, and was unsigned. It ran:

"In time."

Later in the day the evening papers published an account of the Allied Conference. They laid particular stress on the magnificent ovation accorded to Mr. David MacAdam, whose inspiring speech had produced a deep and lasting impression.

overlook a footprint, or a cigar-ash, or a crumb even. He's got eyes that see everything."

"So, *mon ami,*" said Poirot, "has the London sparrow. But all the same, I should not ask the little brown bird to solve the problem of Mr. Davenheim."

"Come now, monsieur, you're not going to run down the value of details as clues?"

"By no means. These things are all good in their way. The danger is they may assume undue importance. Most details are insignificant; one or two are vital. It is the brain, the little gray cells"—he tapped his forehead—"on which one must rely. The senses mislead. One must seek the truth within—not without."

"You don't mean to say, Monsieur Poirot, that you would undertake to solve a case without moving from your chair, do you?"

"That is exactly what I do mean—granted the facts were placed before me. I regard myself as a consulting specialist."

Japp slapped his knee. "Hanged if I don't take you at your word. Bet you a fiver that you can't lay your hand—or rather tell me where to lay my hand—on Mr. Davenheim, dead or alive, before a week is o᠎ ."

Poirot considered. *"Eh bien, mon am᠎ I accept. Le sport,* it is the passion of you English. Now— -the facts."

"On Saturday last, as is his usual custom, Mr. Davenheim took the 12.40 train from Victoria to Chingside, where his palatial country place, The Cedars, is situated. After lunch, he strolled round the grounds, and gave various directions to the gardeners. Everybody agrees that his manner was absolutely normal and as usual. After tea he put his head into his wife's boudoir, saying that he was going to stroll down to the village and post some letters. He added that he was expecting a Mr. Lowen, on busi-ne᠎ . If Lowen should come before he himself returned, he was to be shown into the study and asked to wait. Mr. Davenheim then left the house by the front door, passed leisurely down the drive, and out at the gate, and—was never seen again. From that hour, he vanished com-pletely."

"Pretty—very pretty—altogether a charming little problem," murmured Poirot. "Proceed, my good friend."

"About a quarter of an hour later a tall, dark man with a thick black mustache rang the front-door bell, and explained that he had an appointment with Mr. Davenheim. He gave the name of Lowen, and in accordance with the banker's instructions was shown into the study. Nearly an hour passed. Mr. Davenheim did not return. Finally Mr. Lowen rang the bell, and explained that he was unable to wait any longer, as he must catch his train back to town. Mrs. Davenheim apologized for her husband's absence, which seemed unaccountable, as she knew him to have been expecting the visitor. Mr. Lowen reiterated his regrets and took his departure.

"Well, as everyone knows, Mr. Davenheim did *not* return. Early on Sunday morning the police were communicated with, but could make neither head nor tail of the matter. Mr. Davenheim seemed literally to have vanished into thin air. He had not been to the post office; nor had he been seen passing through the village. At the station they were positive he had not departed by any train. His own motor had not left the garage. If he had hired a car to meet him in some lonely spot, it seems almost certain that by this time, in view of the large reward offered for information, the driver of it would have come forward to tell what he knew. True, there was a small race-meeting at Entfield, five miles away, and if he had walked to that station he might have passed unnoticed in the crowd. But since then his photograph and a full description of him have been circulated in every newspaper, and nobody has been able to give any news of him. We have, of course, received many letters from all over England, but each clue, so far, has ended in disappointment.

"On Monday morning a further sensational discovery came to light. Behind a *portière* in Mr. Davenheim's study stands a safe, and that safe had been broken into and rifled. The windows were fastened securely on the inside, which seems to put an ordinary burglary out of court, unless, of course, an accomplice within the house fastened them again afterwards. On the other hand, Sunday having intervened, and the household being in a state of chaos, it is likely that the burglary was committed on the Saturday, and remained undetected until Monday."

"*Précisément*," said Poirot dryly. "Well, is he arrested, *ce pauvre* M. Lowen?"

Japp grinned. "Not yet. But he's under pretty close supervision."

Poirot nodded. "What was taken from the safe? Have you any idea?"

"We've been going into that with the junior partner of the firm and Mrs. Davenheim. Apparently there was a considerable amount in bearer bonds, and a very large sum in notes, owing to some large transaction having been just carried through. There was also a small fortune in jewelry. All Mrs. Davenheim's jewels were kept in the safe. The purchasing of them had become a passion with her husband of late years, and hardly a month passed that he did not make her a present of some rare and costly gem."

"Altogether a good haul," said Poirot thoughtfully. "Now, what about Lowen? Is it known what his business was with Davenheim that evening?"

"Well, the two men were apparently not on very good terms. Lowen is a speculator in quite a small way. Nevertheless, he has been able once or twice to score a *coup* off Davenheim in the market, though it seems, they seldom or never actually met. It was a matter concerning some South American shares which led the banker to make his appointment."

"Had Davenheim interests in South America, then?"

"I believe so. Mrs. Davenheim happened to mention that he spent all last autumn in Buenos Aires."

"Any trouble in his home life? Were the husband and wife on good terms?"

"I should say his domestic life was quite peaceful and uneventful. Mrs. Davenheim is a pleasant, rather unintelligent woman. Quite a nonentity, I think."

"Then we must not look for the solution of the mystery there. Had he any enemies?"

"He had plenty of financial rivals, and no doubt there are many people whom he has got the better of who bear him no particular good will. But there was no one likely to make away with him—and, if they had, where is the body?"

"Exactly. As Hastings says, bodies have a habit of coming to light with fatal persistency."

"By the way, one of the gardeners says he saw a figure going round to the side of the house toward the rose-garden. The long French window of the study opens on to the rose-garden, and Mr. Davenheim frequently entered and left the house that way. But the man was a good way off, at work on some cucumber frames, and cannot even say whether it was the figure of his master or not. Also, he cannot fix the time with any accuracy. It must have been before six, as the gardeners cease work at that time."

"And Mr. Davenheim left the house?"

"About half-past five or thereabouts."

"What lies beyond the rose-garden?"

"A lake."

"With a boathouse?"

"Yes, a couple of punts are kept there. I suppose you're thinking of suicide, Monsieur Poirot? Well, I don't mind telling you that Miller's going down to-morrow expressly to see that piece of water dragged. That's the kind of man he is!"

Poirot smiled faintly, and turned to me. "Hastings, I pray you, hand me that copy of the *Daily Megaphone*. If I remember rightly, there is an unusually clear photograph there of the missing man."

I rose, and found the sheet required. Poirot studied the features attentively.

"H'm!" he murmured. "Wears his hair rather long and wavy, full mustache and pointed beard, bushy eyebrows. Eyes dark?"

"Yes."

"Hair and beard turning gray?"

The detective nodded. "Well, Monsieur Poirot, what have you got to say to it all? Clear as daylight, eh?"

"On the contrary, most obscure."

The Scotland Yard man looked pleased.

"Which gives me great hopes of solving it," finished Poirot placidly.

"Eh?"

"I find it a good sign when a case is obscure. If a thing is clear as daylight—*eh bien,* mistrust it! Someone has made it so."

Japp shook his head almost pityingly. "Well, each to their fancy. But it's not a bad thing to see your way clear ahead."

"I do not see," murmured Poirot. "I shut my eyes—and think."

Japp sighed. "Well, you've got a clear week to think in."

"And you will bring me any fresh developments that arise—the result of the labors of the hard-working and lynx-eyed Inspector Miller, for instance?"

"Certainly. That's in the bargain."

"Seems a shame, doesn't it?" said Japp to me as I accompanied him to the door. "Like robbing a child!"

I could not help agreeing with a smile. I was still smiling as I re-entered the room.

"Eh bien!" said Poirot immediately. "You make fun of Papa Poirot, is it not so?" He shook his finger at me. "You do not trust his gray cells? Ah, do not be confused! Let us discuss this little problem—incomplete as yet, I admit, but already showing one or two points of interest."

"The lake!" I said significantly.

"And even more than the lake, the boathouse!"

I looked sidewise at Poirot. He was smiling in his most inscrutable fashion. I felt that, for the moment, it would be quite useless to question him further.

We heard nothing of Japp until the following evening, when he walked in about nine o'clock. I saw at once by his expression that he was bursting with news of some kind.

"Eh bien, my friend," remarked Poirot. "All goes well? But do not tell me that you have discovered the body of Mr. Davenheim in your lake, because I shall not believe you."

"We haven't found the body, but we did find his *clothes*—the identical clothes he was wearing that day. What do you say to that?"

"Any other clothes missing from the house?"

"No, his valet is quite positive on that point. The rest of his wardrobe is intact. There's more. We've arrested Lowen. One of the maids, whose business it is to fasten the bedroom windows, declares that she saw Lowen coming *towards* the study through the rose-garden about a quarter past six. That would be about ten minutes before he left the house."

"What does he himself say to that?"

"Denied first of all that he had ever left the study. But the maid was positive, and he pretended afterwards that he had forgotten just stepping out of the window to examine an unusual species of rose. Rather a weak story! And there's fresh evidence against him come to light. Mr. Davenheim always wore a thick gold ring set with a solitaire diamond on the little finger of his right hand. Well, that ring was pawned in London on Saturday night by a man called Billy Kellett! He's already known to the police—did three months last autumn for lifting an old gentleman's watch. It seems he tried to pawn the ring at no less than five different places, succeeded at the last one, got gloriously drunk on the proceeds, assaulted a policeman, and was run in in consequence. I went to Bow Street with Miller and saw him. He's sober enough now, and I don't mind admitting we pretty well frightened the life out of him, hinting he might be charged with murder. This is his yarn, and a very queer one it is.

"He was at Entfield races on Saturday, though I dare say scarfpins was his line of business, rather than betting. Anyway, he had a bad day, and was down on his luck. He was tramping along the road to Chingside, and sat down in a ditch to rest just before he got into the village. A few minutes later he noticed a man coming along the road to the village, 'dark-complexioned gent, with a big mustache, one of them city toffs,' is his description of the man.

"Kellett was half concealed from the road by a heap of stones. Just before he got abreast of him, the man looked quickly up and down the road, and seeing it apparently deserted he took a small object from his pocket and threw it over the hedge. Then he went on towards the station.

Now, the object he had thrown over the hedge had fallen with a slight 'chink' which aroused the curiosity of the human derelict in the ditch. He investigated and, after a short search, discovered the ring! That is Kellett's story. It's only fair to say that Lowen denies it utterly, and of course the word of a man like Kellett can't be relied upon in the slightest. It's within the bounds of possibility that he met Davenheim in the lane and robbed and murdered him."

Poirot shook his head.

"Very improbable, *mon ami*. He had no means of disposing of the body. It would have been found by now. Secondly, the open way in which he pawned the ring makes it unlikely that he did murder to get it. Thirdly, your sneak-thief is rarely a murderer. Fourthly, as he has been in prison since Saturday, it would be too much of a coincidence that he is able to give so accurate a description of Lowen."

Japp nodded. "I don't say you're not right. But all the same, you won't get a jury to take much note of a jail-bird's evidence. What seems odd to me is that Lowen couldn't find a cleverer way of disposing of the ring."

Poirot shrugged his shoulders. "Well, after all, if it were found in the neighborhood, it might be argued that Davenheim himself had dropped it."

"But why remove it from the body at all?" I cried.

"There might be a reason for that," said Japp. "Do you know that just beyond the lake, a little gate leads out on to the hill, and not three minutes' walk brings you to— what do you think?—a *lime kiln*."

"Good heavens!" I cried. "You mean that the lime which destroyed the body would be powerless to affect the metal of the ring?"

"Exactly."

"It seems to me," I said, "that that explains everything. What a horrible crime!"

By common consent we both turned and looked at Poirot. He seemed lost in reflection, his brow knitted, as though with some supreme mental effort. I felt that at last his keen intellect was asserting itself. What would his first words be? We were not long left in doubt. With a sigh, the tension of his attitude relaxed, and turning to Japp, he asked:

"Have you any idea, my friend, whether Mr. and Mrs. Davenheim occupied the same bedroom?"

The question seemed so ludicrously inappropriate that for a moment we both stared in silence. Then Japp burst into a laugh. "Good Lord, Monsieur Poirot, I thought you were coming out with something startling. As to your question, I'm sure I don't know."

"You could find out?" asked Poirot with curious persistence.

"Oh, certainly—if you *really* want to know."

"*Merci, mon ami.* I should be obliged if you would make a point of it."

Japp stared at him a few minutes longer, but Poirot seemed to have forgotten us both. The detective shook his head sadly at me, and murmuring, "Poor old fellow! War's been too much for him!" gently withdrew from the room.

As Poirot still seemed sunk in a daydream, I took a sheet of paper, and amused myself by scribbling notes upon it. My friend's voice aroused me. He had come out of his reverie, and was looking brisk and alert.

"*Que faites vous là, mon ami?*"

"I was jotting down what occurred to me as the main points of interest in this affair."

"You become methodical—at last!" said Poirot approvingly.

I concealed my pleasure. "Shall I read them to you?"

"By all means."

I cleared my throat.

" 'One: All the evidence points to Lowen having been the man who forced the safe.

" 'Two: He had a grudge against Davenheim.

" 'Three: He lied in his first statement that he had never left the study.

" 'Four: If you accept Billy Kellett's story as true, Lowen is unmistakably implicated.' "

I paused. "Well?" I asked, for I felt that I had put my finger on all the vital facts.

Poirot looked at me pityingly, shaking his head very

gently. *"Mon pauvre ami!* But it is that you have not the gift! The important detail, you appreciate him never! Also, your reasoning is false."

"How?"

"Let me take your four points.

"One: Mr. Lowen could not possibly know that he would have the chance to open the safe. He came for a business interview. He could not know beforehand that Mr. Davenheim would be absent posting a letter, and that he would consequently be alone in the study!"

"He might have seized his opportunity," I suggested.

"And the tools? City gentlemen do not carry round housebreaker's tools on the off chance! And one could not cut into that safe with a penknife, *bien entendu!"*

"Well, what about Number Two?"

"You say Lowen had a grudge against Mr. Davenheim. What you mean is that he had once or twice got the better of him. And presumably those transactions were entered into with the view of benefiting himself. In any case you do not as a rule bear a grudge against a man you have got the better of—it is more likely to be the other way about. Whatever grudge there might have been would have been on Mr. Davenheim's side."

"Well, you can't deny that he lied about never having left the study?"

"No. But he may have been frightened. Remember, the missing man's clothes had just been discovered in the lake. Of course, as usual, he would have done better to speak the truth."

"And the fourth point?"

"I grant you that. If Kellett's story is true, Lowen is undeniably implicated. That is what makes the affair so very interesting."

"Then I did appreciate *one* vital fact?"

"Perhaps—but you have entirely overlooked the two most important points, the ones which undoubtedly hold the clue to the whole matter."

"And pray, what are they?"

"One, the passion which has grown upon Mr. Davenheim in the last few years for buying jewelry. Two, his trip to Buenos Aires last autumn."

"Poirot, you are joking!"

"I am most serious. Ah, sacred thunder, but I hope Japp will not forget my little commission."

But the detective, entering into the spirit of the joke, had remembered it so well that a telegram was handed to Poirot about eleven o'clock the next day. At his request I opened it and read it out:

"'Husband and wife have occupied separate rooms since last winter.'"

"Aha!" cried Poirot. "And now we are in mid-June! All is solved!"

I stared at him.

"You have no moneys in the bank of Davenheim and Salmon, *mon ami?*"

"No," I said, wondering. "Why?"

"Because I should advise you to withdraw it—before it is too late."

"Why, what do you expect?"

"I expect a big smash in a few days—perhaps sooner. Which reminds me, we will return the compliment of a *dépêche* to Japp. A pencil, I pray you, and a form. *Voilà!* 'Advise you to withdraw any money deposited with firm in question.' That will intrigue him, the good Japp! His eyes will open wide—wide! He will not comprehend in the slightest—until to-morrow, or the next day!"

I remained skeptical, but the morrow forced me to render tribute to my friend's remarkable powers. In every paper was a huge headline telling of the sensational failure of the Davenheim bank. The disappearance of the famous financier took on a totally different aspect in the light of the revelation of the financial affairs of the bank.

Before we were half-way through breakfast, the door flew open and Japp rushed in. In his left hand was a paper; in his right was Poirot's telegram, which he banged down on the table in front of my friend.

"How did you know, Monsieur Poirot? How the blazes could you know?"

Poirot smiled placidly at him. "Ah, *mon ami,* after your wire, it was a certainty! From the commencement, see you, it struck me that the safe burglary was somewhat remarkable. Jewels, ready money, bearer bonds—all so conveniently arranged for—whom? Well, the good Monsieur Davenheim was of those who 'look after Number One' as your saying goes! It seemed almost certain that it was arranged for—himself! Then his passion of late years for buying jewelry! How simple! The funds he embezzled, he converted into jewels, very likely replacing them in turn with paste duplicates, and so he put away in a safe place, under another name, a considerable fortune to be enjoyed all in good time when everyone has been thrown off the track. His arrangements completed, he makes an appointment with Mr. Lowen (who has been imprudent enough in the past to cross the great man once or twice), drills a hole in the safe, leaves orders that the guest is to be shown into the study, and walks out of the house—where?" Poirot stopped, and stretched out his hand for another boiled egg. He frowned. "It is really insupportable," he murmured, "that every hen lays an egg of a different size! What symmetry can there be on the breakfast table? At least they should sort them in dozens at the shop!"

"Never mind the eggs," said Japp impatiently. "Let 'em lay 'em square if they like. Tell us where our customer went to when he left The Cedars—that is, if you know!"

"*Eh bien,* he went to his hiding-place. Ah, this Monsieur Davenheim, there may be some malformation in his gray cells, but they are of the first quality!"

"Do you know where he is hiding?"

"Certainly! It is most ingenious."

"For the Lord's sake, tell us, then!"

Poirot gently collected every fragment of shell from his plate, placed them in the egg-cup, and reversed the empty egg-shell on top of them. This little operation concluded, he smiled at the neat effect, and then beamed affectionately on us both.

"Come, my friends, you are men of intelligence. Ask

yourselves the question which I asked myself. 'If I were this man, where should *I* hide?' Hastings, what do you say?"

"Well," I said, "I'm rather inclined to think I'd not do a bolt at all. I'd stay in London—in the heart of things, travel by tubes and buses; ten to one I'd never be recognized. There's safety in a crowd."

Poirot turned inquiringly to Japp.

"I don't agree. Get clear away at once—that's the only chance. I would have had plenty of time to prepare things beforehand. I'd have a yacht waiting, with steam up, and I'd be off to one of the most out-of-the-way corners of the world before the hue and cry began!"

We both looked at Poirot. "What do *you* say, monsieur?"

For a moment he remained silent. Then a very curious smile flitted across his face.

"My friends, if *I* were hiding from the police, do you know *where* I should hide? *In a prison!*"

"What?"

"You are seeking Monsieur Davenheim in order to put him in prison, so you never dream of looking to see if he may not be already there!"

"What do you mean?"

"You tell me Madame Davenheim is not a very intelligent woman. Nevertheless I think that if you took her to Bow Street and confronted her with the man Billy Kellett, she would recognize him! In spite of the fact that he has shaved his beard and mustache and those bushy eyebrows, and has cropped his hair close. A woman nearly always knows her husband, though the rest of the world may be deceived!"

"Billy Kellett? But he's known to the police!"

"Did I not tell you Davenheim was a clever man? He prepared his alibi long beforehand. He was not in Buenos Aires last autumn—he was creating the character of Billy Kellett, 'doing three months,' so that the police should have no suspicions when the time came. He was playing, remember, for a large fortune, as well as liberty. It was worth while doing the thing thoroughly. Only——"

"Yes?"

"Eh bien, afterwards he had to wear a false beard and wig, had to *make up as himself* again, and to sleep with a false beard is not easy—it invites detection! He cannot risk continuing to share the chamber of madame his wife. You found out for me that for the last six months, or ever since his supposed return from Buenos Aires, he and Mrs. Davenheim occupied separate rooms. Then I was sure! Everything fitted in. The gardener who fancied he saw his master going round to the side of the house was quite right. He went to the boathouse, donned his 'tramp' clothes, which you may be sure had been safely hidden from the eyes of his valet, dropped the others in the lake, and proceeded to carry out his plan by pawning the ring in an obvious manner, and then assaulting a policeman, getting himself safely into the haven of Bow Street, where nobody would ever dream of looking for him!"

"It's impossible," murmured Japp.

"Ask Madame," said my friend, smiling.

The next day a registered letter lay beside Poirot's plate. He opened it, and a five-pound note fluttered out. My friend's brow puckered.

"Ah, sacré! But what shall I do with it? I have much remorse! *Ce pauvre Japp!* Ah an idea! We will have a little dinner, we three! That consoles me. It was really too easy. I am ashamed. I, who would not rob a child— *mille tonnerres! Mon ami,* what have you, that you laugh so heartily?"

X
THE ADVENTURE OF
THE ITALIAN NOBLEMAN

Poirot and I had many friends and acquaintances of a rather informal nature. Amongst these was to be numbered Dr. Hawker, a near neighbor of ours, and a member of the medical profession. It was the genial doctor's habit to drop in sometimes of an evening and have a chat with Poirot, of whose genius he was an ardent admirer. The doctor himself, frank and unsuspicious to the last degree, admired the talents so far removed from his own.

On one particular evening in early June, he arrived about half-past eight and settled down to a comfortable discussion on the cheery topic of the prevalence of arsenical poisoning in crimes. It must have been about a quarter of an hour later when the door of our sitting-room flew open, and a distracted female precipitated herself into the room.

"Oh, doctor, you're wanted! Such a terrible voice. It gave me a turn, it did indeed."

I recognized in our new visitor Dr. Hawker's housekeeper, Miss Rider. The doctor was a bachelor, and lived in a gloomy old house a few streets away. The usually placid Miss Rider was now in a state bordering on incoherence.

"What terrible voice? Who is it, and what's the trouble?"

"It was the telephone, doctor. I answered it—and a voice spoke. 'Help,' it said. 'Doctor—help. They've killed me!' Then it sort of trailed away. 'Who's speaking?' I said. 'Who's speaking?' Then I got a reply, just a whisper, it seemed, 'Foscatine'—something like that—'Regent's Court.' "

The doctor uttered an exclamation.

"Count Foscatini. He has a flat in Regent's Court. I must go at once. What can have happened?"

"A patient of yours?" asked Poirot.

"I attended him for some slight ailment a few weeks ago. An Italian, but he speaks English perfectly. Well, I must wish you good night, Monsieur Poirot, unless—" He hesitated.

"I perceive the thought in your mind," said Poirot, smiling. "I shall be delighted to accompany you. Hastings, run down and get hold of a taxi."

Taxis always make themselves sought for when one is particulary pressed for time, but I captured one at last, and we were soon bowling along in the direction of Regent's Park. Regent's Court was a new block of flats, situated just off St. John's Wood Road. They had only recently been built, and contained the latest service devices.

There was no one in the hall. The doctor pressed the lift-bell impatiently, and when the lift arrived questioned the uniformed attendant sharply.

"Flat 11. Count Foscatini. There's been an accident there, I understand."

The man stared at him.

"First I've heard of it. Mr. Graves—that's Count Foscatini's man—went out about half an hour ago, and he said nothing."

"Is the Count alone in the flat?"

"No, sir, he's got two gentlemen dining with him."

"What are they like?" I asked eagerly.

We were in the lift now, ascending rapidly to the second floor, on which Flat 11 was situated.

"I didn't see them myself, sir, but I understand that they were foreign gentlemen."

He pulled back the iron door, and we stepped out on the landing. No. 11 was opposite to us. The doctor rang the bell. There was no reply, and we could hear no sound from within. The doctor rang again and again; we could hear the bell trilling within, but no sign of life rewarded us.

"This is getting serious," muttered the doctor. He turned to the lift attendant.

"Is there any pass-key to this door?"

"There is one in the porter's office downstairs."

"Get it, then, and, look here, I think you'd better send for the police."

Poirot approved with a nod of the head.

The man returned shortly; with him came the manager.

"Will you tell me, gentlemen, what is the meaning of all this?"

"Certainly. I received a telephone message from Count Foscatini stating that he had been attacked and was dying. You can understand that we must lose no time— if we are not already too late."

The manager produced the key without more ado, and we all entered the flat.

We passed first into a small square lounge hall. A door on the right of it was half open. The manager indicated it with a nod.

"The dining-room."

Dr. Hawker led the way. We followed close on his heels. As we entered the room I gave a gasp. The round table in the center bore the remains of a meal; three chairs were pushed back, as though their occupants had just risen. In the corner, to the right of the fire-place, was a big writing-table, and sitting at it was a man—or what had been a man. His right hand still grasped the base of the telephone, but he had fallen forward, struck down by a terrific blow on the head from behind. The weapon was not far to seek. A marble statuette stood where it had been hurriedly put down, the base of it stained with blood.

The doctor's examination did not take a minute. "Stone dead. Must have been almost instantaneous. I wonder he even managed to telephone. It will be better not to move him until the police arrive."

On the manager's suggestion we searched the flat, but the result was a foregone conclusion. It was not likely that the murderers would be concealed there when all they had to do was to walk out.

We came back to the dining-room. Poirot had not accompanied us in our tour. I found him studying the center table with close attention. I joined him. It was a well-polished round mahogany table. A bowl of roses decorated the center, and white lace mats reposed on the gleaming surface. There was a dish of fruit, but the three dessert plates were untouched. There were three coffee-cups with remains of coffee in them—two black, one with milk. All three men had taken port, and the decanter, half-full, stood before the center plate. One of the men had smoked a cigar, the other two cigarettes. A tortoise shell-and-silver box, holding cigars and cigarettes, stood open upon the table.

I enumerated all these facts to myself, but I was forced to admit that they did not shed any brilliant light on the situation. I wondered what Poirot saw in them to make him so intent. I asked him.

"*Mon ami*," he replied, "you miss the point. I am looking for something that I do *not* see."

"What is that?"

"A mistake—even a little mistake—on the part of the murderer."

He stepped swiftly to the small adjoining kitchen, looked in, and shook his head.

"Monsieur," he said to the manager, "explain to me, I pray, your system of serving meals here."

The manager stepped to a small hatch in the wall.

"This is the service lift," he explained. "It runs to the kitchens at the top of the building. You order through this telephone, and the dishes are sent down in the lift, one course at a time. The dirty plates and dishes are sent up in the same manner. No domestic worries, you understand, and at the same time you avoid the wearying publicity of always dining in a restaurant."

Poirot nodded.

"Then the plates and dishes that were used tonight are on high in the kitchen. You permit that I mount there?"

"Oh, certainly, if you like! Roberts, the lift man, will take you up and introduce you; but I'm afraid you won't find anything that's of any use. They're handling hundreds of plates and dishes, and they'll be all lumped together."

Poirot remained firm, however, and together we visited

the kitchens and questioned the man who had taken the order from Flat 11.

"The order was given from the *à la carte menu*—for three," he explained. "Soup julienne, filet de sole norman-de, tournedos of beef, and a rice soufflé. What time? Just about eight o'clock, I should say. No, I'm afraid the plates and dishes have been all washed up by now. Un-fortunate. You were thinking of finger-prints, I suppose?"

"Not exactly," said Poirot, with an enigmatical smile. "I am more interested in Count Foscatini's appetite. Did he partake of every dish?"

"Yes; but of course I can't say how much of each he ate. The plates were all soiled, and the dishes empty— that is to say, with the exception of the rice soufflé. There was a fair amount of that left."

"Ah!" said Poirot, and seemed satisfied with the fact.

As we descended to the flat again he remarked in a low tone:

"We have decidedly to do with a man of method."

"Do you mean the murderer, or Count Foscatini?"

"The latter was undoubtedly an orderly gentleman. Af-ter imploring help and announcing his approaching de-mise, he carefully hung up the telephone receiver."

I stared at Poirot. His words now and his recent in-quiries gave me the glimmering of an idea.

"You suspect poison?" I breathed. "The blow on the head was a blind."

Poirot merely smiled.

We re-entered the flat to find the local inspector of police had arrived with two constables. He was inclined to resent our appearance, but Poirot calmed him with the mention of our Scotland Yard friend, Inspector Japp, and we were accorded a grudging permission to remain. It was a lucky thing we were, for we had not been back five minutes before an agitated middle-aged man came rushing into the room with every appearance of grief and agitation.

This was Graves, valet-butler to the late Count Fos-catini. The story he had to tell was a sensational one.

On the previous morning, two gentlemen had called to see his master. They were Italians, and the elder of the two, a man of about forty, gave his name as Signor Ascanio. The younger was a well-dressed lad of about twenty-four.

Count Foscatini was evidently prepared for their visit and immediately sent Graves out upon some trivial errand. Here the man paused and hesitated in his story. In the end, however, he admitted that, curious as to the purport of the interview, he had not obeyed immediately, but had lingered about endeavoring to hear something of what was going on.

The conversation was carried on in so low a tone that he was not as successful as he had hoped; but he gathered enough to make it clear that some kind of monetary proposition was being discussed, and that the basis of it was a threat. The discussion was anything but amicable. In the end, Count Foscatini raised his voice slightly, and the listener heard these words clearly:

"I have no time to argue further now, gentlemen. If you will dine with me to-morrow night at eight o'clock, we will resume the discussion."

Afraid of being discovered listening, Graves had then hurried out to do his master's errand. This evening the two men had arrived punctually at eight. During d⃨⃨⃨ they had talked of indifferent matters—politics, the weather, and the theatrical world. When Graves had plac⃨⃨ the port upon the table and brought in the coffee his master told him that he might have the evening off.

"Was that a usual proceeding of his when he had guests?" asked the inspector.

"No, sir; it wasn't. That's what made me think it must be some business of a very unusual kind that he was going to discuss with these gentlemen."

That finished Graves's story. He had gone out about 8.30, and, meeting a friend, had accompanied him to the Metropolitan Music Hall in Edgware Road.

Nobody had seen the two men leave, but the time of the murder was fixed clearly enough at 8.47. A small clock on the writing-table had been swept off by Foscatini's arm, and had stopped at that hour, which agreed with Miss Rider's telephone summons.

The police surgeon had made his examination of the

body, and it was now lying on the couch. I saw the face
for the first time—the olive complexion, the long nose,
the luxuriant black mustache, and the full red lips drawn
back from the dazzlingly white teeth. Not altogether a
pleasant face.

"Well," said the inspector, refastening his notebook.
"The case seems clear enough. The only difficulty will
be to lay our hands on this Signor Ascanio. I suppose
his address is not in the dead man's pocket-book by any
chance?"

As Poirot had said, the late Foscatini was an orderly
man. Neatly written in small, precise handwriting was the
inscription, "Signor Paolo Ascanio, Grosvenor Hotel."

The inspector busied himself with the telephone, then
turned to us with a grin.

"Just in time. Our fine gentleman was off to catch the
boat train to the Continong. Well, gentlemen, that's about
all we can do here. It's a bad business, but straightforward enough. One of these Italian vendetta things, as likely
as not."

Thus airily dismissed, we found our way downstairs.
Dr. Hawker was full of excitement.

"Like the beginning of a novel, eh? Real exciting stuff.
Wouldn't believe it if you read about it."

Poirot did not speak. He was very thoughtful. All the
evening he had hardly opened his lips.

"What says the master detective, eh?" asked Hawker,
clapping him on the back. "Nothing to work your gray
cells over this time."

"You think not?"

"What could there be?"

"Well, for example, there is the window."

"The window? But it was fastened. Nobody could have
got out or in that way. I noticed it specially."

"And why were you able to notice it?"

The doctor looked puzzled. Poirot hastened to explain.

"It is to the curtains I refer. They were not drawn. A
little odd, that. And then there was the coffee. It was
very black coffee."

"Well, what of it?"

"Very black," repeated Poirot. "In conjunction with

that let us remember that very little of the rice soufflé was eaten, and we get—what?"

"Moonshine," laughed the doctor. "You're pulling my leg."

"Never do I pull the leg. Hastings here knows that I am perfectly serious."

"I don't know what you are getting at, all the same," I confessed. "You don't suspect the manservant, do you? He might have been in with the gang, and put some dope in the coffee. I suppose they'll test his alibi?"

"Without doubt, my friend; but it is the alibi of Signor Ascanio that interests me."

"You think he has an alibi?"

"That is just what worries me. I have no doubt that we shall soon be enlightened on that point."

The *Daily Newsmonger* enabled us to become conversant with succeeding events.

Signor Ascanio was arrested and charged with the murder of Count Foscatini. When arrested, he denied knowing the Count, and declared he had never been near Regent's Court either on the evening of the crime or on the previous morning. The younger man had disappeared entirely. Signor Ascanio had arrived alone at the Grosvenor Hotel from the Continent two days before the murder. All efforts to trace the second man failed.

Ascanio, however, was not sent for trial. No less a personage than the Italian Ambassador himself came forward and testified at the police-court proceedings that Ascanio had been with him at the Embassy from eight till nine that evening. The prisoner was discharged. Naturally, a lot of people thought that the crime was a political one, and was being deliberately hushed up.

Poirot had taken a keen interest in all these points. Nevertheless, I was somewhat surprised when he suddenly informed me one morning that he was expecting a visitor at eleven o'clock, and that that visitor was none other than Ascanio himself.

"He wishes to consult you?"

"*Du tout,* Hastings. I wish to consult him."

"What about?"

"The Regent's Court murder."

"You are going to prove that he did it?"

"A man cannot be tried twice for murder, Hastings. Endeavor to have the common sense. Ah, that is our friend's ring."

A few minutes later Signor Ascanio was ushered in— a small, thin man with a secretive and furtive glance in his eyes. He remained standing, darting suspicious glances from one to the other of us.

"Monsieur Poirot?"

My little friend tapped himself gently on the chest.

"Be seated, signor. You received my note. I am determined to get to the bottom of this mystery. In some small measure you can aid me. Let us commence. You—in company with a friend—visited the late Count Foscatini on the morning of Tuesday the 9th——"

The Italian made an angry gesture.

"I did nothing of the sort. I have sworn in court——"

"*Précisément*—and I have a little idea that you have sworn falsely."

"You threaten me? Bah! I have nothing to fear from you. I have been acquitted."

"Exactly; and as I am not an imbecile, it is not with the gallows I threaten you—but with publicity. Publicity! I see that you do not like the word. I had an idea that you would not. My little ideas, you know, they are very valuable to me. Come, signor, your only chance is to be frank with me. I do not ask to know whose indiscretions brought you to England. I know this much, you came for the especial purpose of seeing Count Foscatini."

"He was not a count," growled the Italian.

"I have already noted the fact that his name does not appear in the *Almanach de Gotha*. Never mind, the title of count is often useful in the profession of blackmailing."

"I suppose I might as well be frank. You seem to know a great deal."

"I have employed my gray cells to some advantage. Come, Signor Ascanio, you visited the dead man on the Tuesday morning—that is so, is it not?"

"Yes; but I never went there on the following evening. There was no need. I will tell you all. Certain information concerning a man of great position in Italy had come into this scoundrel's possession. He demanded a big sum of money in return for the papers. I came over to England to arrange the matter. I called upon him by appointment that morning. One of the young secretaries of the Embassy was with me. The Count was more reasonable than I had hoped, although even then the sum of money I paid him was a huge one."

"Pardon, how was it paid?"

"In Italian notes of comparatively small denomination. I paid over the money then and there. He handed me the incriminating papers. I never saw him again."

"Why did you not say all this when you were arrested?"

"In my delicate position I was forced to deny any association with the man."

"And how do you account for the events of the evening, then?"

"I can only think that some one must have deliberately impersonated me. I understand that no money was found in the flat."

Poirot looked at him and shook his head.

"Strange," he murmured. "We all have the little gray cells. And so few of us know how to use them. Good morning, Signor Ascanio. I believe your story. It is very much as I had imagined. But I had to make sure."

After bowing his guest out, Poirot returned to his armchair and smiled at me.

"Let us hear M. le Capitaine Hastings on the case?"

"Well, I suppose Ascanio is right—somebody impersonated him."

"Never, never will you use the brains the good God has given you. Recall to yourself some words I uttered after leaving the flat that night. I referred to the window-curtains not being drawn. We are in the month of June. It is still light at eight o'clock. The light is failing by half-past. *Ça vous dit quelque chose?* I perceive a struggling impression that you will arrive some day. Now let us continue. The coffee was, as I said, very black. Count Foscatini's teeth were magnificently white. Coffee stains the teeth. We reason from that that Count Foscatini did not drink any coffee. Yet there was coffee in all three cups. Why should anyone pretend Count Foscatini had drunk coffee when he had not done so?"

I shook my head, utterly bewildered.

"Come, I will help you. What evidence have we that Ascanio and his friend, or two men posing as them, ever came to the flat that night? Nobody saw them go in; nobody saw them go out. We have the evidence of one man and of a host of inanimate objects."

"You mean?"

"I mean knives and forks and plates and empty dishes. Ah, but it was a clever idea! Graves is a thief and a scoundrel, but what a man of method! He overhears a portion of the conversation in the morning, enough to realize that Ascanio will be in an awkward position to defend himself. The following evening, about eight o'clock, he tells his master he is wanted at the telephone. Foscatini sits down, stretches out his hand to the telephone, and from behind Graves strikes him down with the marble figure. Then quickly to the service telephone—dinner for three! It comes, he lays the table, dirties the plates, knives, and forks, etc. But he has to get rid of the food too. Not only is he a man of brain; he has a resolute and capacious stomach! But after eating three tournedos, the rice soufflé is too much for him! He even smokes a cigar and two cigarettes to carry out the illusion. Ah, but it was magnificently thorough! Then, having moved on the hands of the clock to 8.47, he smashes it and stops it. The one thing he does not do is to draw the curtains. But if there had been a real dinner party the curtains would have been drawn as soon as the light began to fail. Then he hurries out, mentioning the guests to the lift man in passing. He hurries to a telephone box, and as near as possible to 8.47 rings up the doctor with his master's dying cry. So successful is his idea that no one ever inquires if a call was put through from Flat 11 at that time."

"Except Hercule Poirot, I suppose?" I said sarcastically.

"Not even Hercule Poirot," said my friend, with a smile. "I am about to inquire now. I had to prove my point to you first. But you will see, I shall be right; and then Japp, to whom I have already given a hint, will be able to arrest the respectable Graves. I wonder how much of the money he has spent."

Poirot *was* right. He always is, confound him!

XI
THE CASE OF
THE MISSING WILL

The problem presented to us by Miss Violet Marsh made rather a pleasant change from our usual routine work. Poirot had received a brisk and business-like note from the lady asking for an appointment, and he had replied asking her to call upon him at eleven o'clock the following day.

She arrived punctually—a tall, handsome young woman, plainly but neatly dressed, with an assured and business-like manner. Clearly a young woman who meant to get on in the world. I am not a great admirer of the so-called New Woman myself, and, in spite of her good looks, I was not particularly prepossessed in her favor.

"My business is of a somewhat unusual nature, Monsieur Poirot," she began, after she had accepted a chair. "I had better begin at the beginning and tell you the whole story."

"If you please, mademoiselle."

"I am an orphan. My father was one of two brothers, sons of a small yeoman farmer in Devonshire. The farm was a poor one, and the elder brother, Andrew, emigrated to Australia, where he did very well indeed, and by means of successful speculation in land became a very rich man. The younger brother, Roger (my father), had no leanings towards the agricultural life. He managed to educate himself a little, and obtained a post as a clerk with a small firm. He married slightly above him; my mother was the daughter of a poor artist. My father died when I was six years old. When I was fourteen, my mother followed him to the grave. My only living relation then was my Uncle Andrew, who had recently returned from Australia and bought a small place, Crab-

tree Manor, in his native county. He was exceedingly kind
to his brother's orphan child, took me to live with him,
and treated me in every way as though I was his own
daughter.

"Crabtree Manor, in spite of its name, is really only
an old farmhouse. Farming was in my uncle's blood, and
he was intensely interested in various modern farming
experiments. Although kindness itself to me, he had certain peculiar and deeply-rooted ideas as to the up-bring-
ing of women. Himself a man of little or no education,
though possessing remarkable shrewdness, he placed little value on what he called 'book knowledge.' He was
especially opposed to the education of women. In his
opinion, girls should learn practical housework and a dairy-
work, be useful about the home, and have as little to do
with book learning as possible. He proposed to bring me
up on these lines, to my bitter disappointment and annoyance. I rebelled frankly. I knew that I possessed a
good brain, and had absolutely no talent for domestic
duties. My uncle and I had many bitter arguments on
the subject, for, though much attached to each other,
we were both self-willed. I was lucky enough to win a
scholarship, and up to a certain point was successful in
getting my own way. The crisis arose when I resolved
to go to Girton. I had a little money of my own, left
me by my mother, and I was quite determined to make
the best use of the gifts God had given me. I had one
long, final argument with my uncle. He put the facts
plainly before me. He had no other relations, and he had
intended me to be his sole heiress. As I have told you,
he was a very rich man. If I persisted in these 'new-
fangled notions' of mine, however, I need look for nothing
from him. I remained polite, but firm. I should always
be deeply attached to him, I told him, but I must lead
my own life. We parted on that note. 'You fancy your
brain, my girl,' were his last words. 'I've no book learning, but for all that, I'll pit mine against yours any day.
We'll see what we shall see.'

"That was nine years ago. I have stayed with him for
a week-end occasionally, and our relations were perfectly
amicable, though his views remained unaltered. He never

referred to my having matriculated, nor to my B.Sc. For the last three years his health had been failing, and a month ago he died.

"I am now coming to the point of my visit. My uncle left a most extraordinary will. By its terms, Crabtree Manor and its contents are to be at my disposal for a year from his death—'during which time my clever niece may prove her wits,' the actual words run. At the end of that period, 'my wits having proved better than hers,' the house and all my uncle's large fortune pass to various charitable institutions."

"That is a little hard on you, mademoiselle, seeing that you were Mr. Marsh's only blood relation."

"I do not look on it in that way. Uncle Andrew warned me fairly, and I chose my own path. Since I would not fall in with his wishes, he was at perfect liberty to leave his money to whom he pleased."

"Was the will drawn up by a lawyer?"

"No; it was written on a printed will-form and witnessed by the man and his wife who live in the house and do for my uncle."

"There might be a possibility of upsetting such a will?"

"I would not even attempt to do such a thing."

"You regard it, then, as a sporting challenge on the part of your uncle?"

"That is exactly how I look upon it."

"It bears that interpretation, certainly," said Poirot thoughtfully. "Somewhere in this rambling old manor-house your uncle has concealed either a sum of money in notes or possibly a second will, and has given you a year in which to exercise your ingenuity to find it."

"Exactly, Monsieur Poirot; and I am paying you the compliment of assuming that your ingenuity will be greater than mine."

"Eh, eh! but that is very charming of you. My gray cells are at your disposal. You have made no search yourself?"

"Only a cursory one; but I have too much respect for my uncle's undoubted abilities to fancy that the task will be an easy one."

"Have you the will or a copy of it with you?"

Miss Marsh handed a document across the table. Poirot ran through it, nodding to himself.

"Made three years ago. Dated March 25; and the time is given also—11 A.M.—that is very suggestive. It narrows the field of search. Assuredly it is another will we have to seek for. A will made even half-an-hour later would upset this. *Eh bien,* mademoiselle, it is a problem charming and ingenious that you have presented to me here. I shall have all the pleasure in the world in solving it for you. Granted that your uncle was a man of ability, his gray cells cannot have been of the quality of Hercule Poirot's!"

(Really, Poirot's vanity is blatant!)

"Fortunately, I have nothing of moment on hand at the minute. Hastings and I will go down to Crabtree Manor to-night. The man and wife who attended on your uncle are still there, I presume?"

"Yes, their name is Baker."

The following morning saw us started on the hunt proper. We had arrived late the night before. Mr. and Mrs. Baker, having received a telegram from Miss Marsh, were expecting us. They were a pleasant couple, the man gnarled and pink-cheeked, like a shriveled pippin, and his wife a woman of vast proportions and true Devonshire calm.

Tired with our journey and the eight-mile drive from the station, we had retired at once to bed after a supper of roast chicken, apple pie, and Devonshire cream. We had now disposed of an excellent breakfast, and were sitting in a small paneled room which had been the late Mr. Marsh's study and living-room. A roll-top desk stuffed with papers, all neatly docketed, stood against the wall, and a big leather armchair showed plainly that it had been its owner's constant resting-place. A big chintz-covered settee ran along the opposite wall, and the deep low window seats were covered with the same faded chintz of an old-fashioned pattern.

"Eh bien, mon ami," said Poirot, lighting one of his tiny cigarettes, "we must map out our plan of campaign. Already I have made a rough survey of the house, but

I am of opinion that any clue will be found in this room. We shall have to go through the documents in the desk with meticulous care. Naturally, I do not expect to find the will amongst them; but it is likely that some apparently innocent paper may conceal the clue to its hiding-place. But first we must have a little information. Ring the bell, I pray of you."

I did so. While we were waiting for it to be answered, Poirot walked up and down, looking about him approvingly.

"A man of method this Mr. Marsh. See how neatly the packets of papers are docketed; then the key to each drawer has its ivory label—so has the key of the china cabinet on the wall; and see with what precision the china within is arranged. It rejoices the heart. Nothing here offends the eye——"

He came to an abrupt pause, as his eye was caught by the key of the desk itself, to which a dirty envelope was affixed. Poirot frowned at it and withdrew it from the lock. On it were scrawled the words: "Key of Roll Top Desk," in a crabbed handwriting, quite unlike the neat superscriptions on the other keys.

"An alien note," said Poirot, frowning. "I could swear that here we have no longer the personality of Mr. Marsh. But who else has been in the house? Only Miss Marsh, and she, if I mistake not, is also a young lady of method and order."

Baker came in answer to the bell.

"Will you fetch madame your wife, and answer a few questions?"

Baker departed, and in a few moments returned with Mrs. Baker, wiping her hands on her apron and beaming all over her face.

In a few clear words Poirot set forth the object of his mission. The Bakers were immediately sympathetic.

"Us don't want to see Miss Violet done out of what's hers," declared the woman. "Cruel hard 'twould be for hospitals to get it all."

Poirot proceeded with his questions. Yes, Mr. and Mrs. Baker remembered perfectly witnessing the will. Baker had previously been sent in to the neighboring town to get two printed will-forms.

"Two?" said Poirot sharply.

"Yes, sir, for safety like, I suppose, in case he should spoil one—and sure enough, so he did do. Us had signed one——"

"What time of day was that?"

Baker scratched his head, but his wife was quicker.

"Why, to be sure, I'd just put the milk on for the cocoa at eleven. Don't ee remember? It had all boilled over on the stove when us got back to kitchen."

"And afterwards?"

" 'Twould be about an hour later. Us had to go in again. 'I've made a mistake,' says old master, 'had to tear the whole thing up. I'll trouble you to sign again,' and us did. And afterwards master give us a tidy sum of money each. 'I've left you nothing in my will,' says he, 'but each year I live you'll have this to be a nest-egg when I'm gone'; and sure enough, so he did."

Poirot reflected.

"After you had signed the second time, what did Mr. Marsh do? Do you know?"

"Went out to the village to pay tradesmen's books."

That did not seem very promising. Poirot tried another tack. He held out the key of the desk.

"Is that your master's writing?"

I may have imagined it, but I fancied that a moment or two elapsed before Baker replied: "Yes, sir, it is."

"He's lying," I thought. "But why?"

"Has your master let the house?—have there been any strangers in it during the last three years?"

"No, sir."

"No visitors?"

"Only Miss Violet."

"No strangers of any kind been inside this room?"

"No, sir."

"You forget the workmen, Jim," his wife reminded him.

"Workmen?" Poirot wheeled round on her. "What workmen?"

The woman explained that about two years and a half ago workmen had been in the house to do certain repairs. She was quite vague as to what the repairs were. Her view seemed to be that the whole thing was a fad of her master's and quite unnecessary. Part of the time the workmen had been in the study; but what they had done there she could not say, as her master had not let either of them into the room whilst the work was in progress. Unfortunately, they could not remember the name of the firm employed, beyond the fact that it was a Plymouth one.

"We progress, Hastings," said Poirot, rubbing his hands as the Bakers left the room. "Clearly he made a second will and then had workmen from Plymouth in to make a suitable hiding-place. Instead of wasting time taking up the floor and tapping the walls, we will go to Plymouth."

With a little trouble, we were able to get the information we wanted. After one or two essays, we found the firm employed by Mr. Marsh.

Their employees had all been with them many years, and it was easy to find the two men who had worked under Mr. Marsh's orders. They remembered the job perfectly. Amongst various other minor jobs, they had taken up one of the bricks of the old-fashioned fireplace, made a cavity beneath, and so cut the brick that it was impossible to see the join. By pressing on the second brick from the end, the whole thing was raised. It had been quite a complicated piece of work, and the old gentleman had been very fussy about it. Our informant was a man called Coghan, a big, gaunt man with a grizzled mustache. He seemed an intelligent fellow.

We returned to Crabtree Manor in high spirits, and, locking the study door, proceeded to put our newly acquired knowledge into effect. It was impossible to see any sign on the bricks, but when we pressed in the manner indicated, a deep cavity was at once disclosed.

Eagerly Poirot plunged in his hand. Suddenly his face fell from complacent elation to consternation. All he held was a charred fragment of stiff paper. But for it, the cavity was empty.

"Sacré!" cried Poirot angrily. "Some one has been before us."

We examined the scrap of paper anxiously. Clearly it was a fragment of what we sought. A portion of Baker's signature remained, but no indication of what the terms of the will had been.

Poirot sat back on his heels. His expression would have been comical if we had not been so overcome.

"I understand it not," he growled. "Who destroyed this? And what was their object?"

"The Bakers?" I suggested.

"Pourquoi? Neither will makes any provision for them, and they are more likely to be kept on with Miss Marsh than if the place became the property of a hospital. How could it be to anyone's advantage to destroy the will? The hospitals benefit—yes; but one cannot suspect institutions."

"Perhaps the old man changed his mind and destroyed it himself," I suggested.

Poirot rose to his feet, dusting his knees with his usual care.

"That may be," he admitted. "One of your more sensible observations, Hastings. Well, we can do no more here. We have done all that mortal man can do. We have successfully pitted our wits against the late Andrew Marsh's; but, unfortunately, his niece is no better off for our success."

By driving to the station at once, we were just able to catch a train to London, though not the principal express. Poirot was sad and dissatisfied. For my part, I was tired and dozed in a corner. Suddenly, as we were just moving out of Taunton, Poirot uttered a piercing squeal.

"Vite, Hastings! Awake and jump! But jump I say!"

Before I knew where I was we were standing on the platform, bareheaded and minus our valises, whilst the train disappeared into the night. I was furious. But Poirot paid no attention.

"Imbecile that I have been!" he cried. "Triple imbecile! Not again will I vaunt my little gray cells!"

"That's a good job at any rate," I said grumpily. "But what is this all about?"

As usual, when following out his own ideas, Poirot paid absolutely no attention to me.

"The tradesmen's books—I have left them entirely out of account! Yes, but where? Where? Never mind, I cannot be mistaken. We must return at once."

Easier said than done. We managed to get a slow train to Exeter, and there Poirot hired a car. We arrived back at Crabtree Manor in the small hours of the morning. I pass over the bewilderment of the Bakers when we had at last aroused them. Paying no attention to anybody, Poirot strode at once to the study.

"I have been, not a triple imbecile, but thirty-six times one, my friend," he deigned to remark. "Now, behold!"

Going straight to the desk, he drew out the key, and detached the envelope from it. I stared at him stupidly. How could he possibly hope to find a big will-form in that tiny envelope? With great care he cut open the envelope, laying it out flat. Then he lighted the fire and held the plain inside surface of the envelope to the flame. In a few minutes faint characters began to appear.

"Look, *mon ami!*" cried Poirot in triumph.

I looked. There were just a few lines of faint writing stating briefly that he left everything to his niece, Violet Marsh. It was dated March 25, 12.30 P.M., and witnessed by Albert Pike, confectioner, and Jessie Pike, married woman.

"But is it legal?" I gasped.

"As far as I know, there is no law against writing your will in a blend of disappearing and sympathetic ink. The intention of the testator is clear, and the beneficiary is his only living relation. But the cleverness of him! He foresaw every step that a searcher would take—that I, miserable imbecile, took. He gets two will-forms, makes the servants sign twice, then sallies out with his will written on the inside of a dirty envelope and a fountain-pen containing his little ink mixture. On some excuse he gets the confectioner and his wife to sign their names under his own signature, then he ties it to the key of his desk and chuckles to himself. If his niece sees through his little ruse, she will have justified her choice of life and elaborate education, and be thoroughly welcome to his money."

"She didn't see through it, did she?" I said slowly. "It seems rather unfair. The old man really won."

"But no, Hastings. It is *your* wits that go astray. Miss Marsh proved the astuteness of her wits and the value of the higher education for women by at once putting the matter in *my* hands. Always employ the expert. She has amply proved her right to the money."

I wonder—I very much wonder—what old Andrew Marsh would have thought!

XII
THE VEILED LADY

I had noticed that for some time Poirot had been growing increasingly dissatisfied and restless. We had had no interesting cases of late, nothing on which my little friend could exercise his keen wits and remarkable powers of deduction. This morning he flung down the newspaper with an impatient *"Tchah!"*—a favorite exclamation of his which sounded exactly like a cat sneezing.

"They fear me, Hastings; the criminals of your England they fear me! When the cat is there, the little mice, they come no more to the cheese!"

"I don't suppose the greater part of them even know of your existence," I said, laughing.

Poirot looked at me reproachfully. He always imagines that the whole world is thinking and talking of Hercule Poirot. He had certainly made a name for himself in London, but I could hardly believe that his existence struck terror into the criminal world.

"What about that daylight robbery of jewels in Bond Street the other day?" I asked.

"A neat *coup*," said Poirot approvingly, "though not in my line. *Pas de finesse, seulment de l'audace!* A man with a loaded cane smashes the plate-glass window of a jeweler's shop and grabs a number of precious stones. Worthy citizens immediately seize him; a policeman arrives. He is caught red-handed with the jewels on him. He is marched off to the police station, and then it is discovered that the stones are paste. He has passed the real ones to a confederate—one of the aforementioned worthy citizens. He will go to prison—true; but when he comes out, there will be a nice little fortune awaiting him. Yes, not badly imagined. But I could do better than that. Sometimes,

Hastings, I regret that I am of such a moral disposition. To work against the law, it would be pleasing, for a change."

"Cheer up, Poirot; you know you are unique in your own line."

"But what is there on hand in my own line?"

I picked up the paper.

"Here's an Englishman mysteriously done to death in Holland," I said.

"They always say that—and later they find that he ate the tinned fish and that his death is perfectly natural."

"Well, if you're determined to grouse!"

"Tiens!" said Poirot, who had strolled across to the window. "Here in the street is what they call in novels a 'heavily veiled lady.' She mounts the steps; she rings the bell—she comes to consult us. Here is a possibility of something interesting. When one is as young and pretty as that one, one does not veil the face except for a big affair."

A minute later our visitor was ushered in. As Poirot had said, she was indeed heavily veiled. It was impossible to distinguish her features until she raised her veil of black Spanish lace. Then I saw that Poirot's intuition had been right; the lady was extremely pretty, with fair hair and large blue eyes. From the costly simplicity of her attire, I deduced at once that she belonged to the upper strata of society.

"Monsieur Poirot," said the lady in a soft, musical voice, "I am in great trouble. I can hardly believe that you can help me, but I have heard such wonderful things of you that I come literally as a last hope to beg you to do the impossible."

"The impossible, it pleases me always," said Poirot. "Continue, I beg of you, mademoiselle."

Our fair guest hesitated.

"But you must be frank," added Poirot. "You must not leave me in the dark on any point."

"I will trust you," said the girl suddenly. "You have heard of Lady Millicent Castle Vaughan?"

I looked up with keen interest. The announcement of Lady Millicent's engagement to the young Duke of South-

shire had appeared a few days previously. She was, I
knew, the fifth daughter of an impecunious Irish peer,
and the Duke of Southshire was one of the best matches
in England.

"I am Lady Millicent," continued the girl. "You may
have read of my engagement. I should be one of the happiest girls alive; but oh, M. Poirot, I am in terrible trouble! There is a man, a horrible man—his name is Lavington; and he—I hardly know how to tell you. There was
a letter I wrote—I was only sixteen at the time; and he—
he——"

"A letter that you wrote to this Mr. Lavington?"

"Oh, *no*—not to him! To a young soldier—I was very
fond of him—he was killed in the war."

"I understand," said Poirot kindly.

"It was a foolish letter, an indiscreet letter, but indeed,
M. Poirot, nothing more. But there are phrases in it
which—which might bear a different interpretation."

"I see," said Poirot. "And this letter has come into the
possession of Mr. Lavington?"

"Yes, and he threatens, unless I pay him an enormous
sum of money, a sum that it is quite impossible for me to
raise, to send it to the Duke."

"The dirty swine!" I ejaculated. "I beg your pardon,
Lady Millicent."

"Would it not be wiser to confess all to your future
husband?"

"I dare not, M. Poirot. The Duke is a rather peculiar
character, jealous and suspicious and prone to believe the
worst. I might as well break off my engagement at once."

"Dear, dear," said Poirot with an expressive grimace.
"And what do you want me to do, milady?"

"I thought perhaps that I might ask Mr. Lavington to
call upon you. I would tell him that you were empowered
by me to discuss the matter. Perhaps you could reduce
his demands."

"What sum does he mention?"

"Twenty thousand pounds—an impossibility. I doubt
if I could raise a thousand, even."

"You might perhaps borrow the money on the prospect of your approaching marriage—but I doubt if you

could get hold of half that sum. Besides—*eh bien,* it is repugnant to me that you should pay! No, the ingenuity of Hercule Poirot shall defeat your enemies! Send me this Mr. Lavington. Is he likely to bring the letter with him?"

The girl shook her head.

"I do not think so. He is very cautious."

"I suppose there is no doubt that he really has it?"

"He showed it to me when I went to his house."

"You went to his house? That was very imprudent, milady."

"Was it? I was so desperate. I hoped my entreaties might move him."

"Oh, *là là!* The Lavingtons of this world are not moved by entreaties! He would welcome them as showing how much importance you attached to the document. Where does he live, this fine gentleman?"

"At Buona Vista, Wimbledon. I went there after dark—" Poirot groaned. "I declared that I would inform the police in the end, but he only laughed in a horrid, sneering manner. 'By all means, my dear Lady Millicent, do so if you wish,' he said."

"Yes, it is hardly an affair for the police," murmured Poirot.

" 'But I think you will be wiser than that,' he continued. 'See, here is your letter—in this little Chinese puzzle box!' He held it so that I could see. I tried to snatch at it, but he was too quick for me. With a horrid smile he folded it up and replaced it in the little wooden box. 'It will be quite safe here, I assure you,' he said; 'and the box itself lives in such a clever place that you would never find it.' My eyes turned to the small wallsafe, and he shook his head and laughed. 'I have a better safe than that,' he said. Oh, he was odious! M. Poirot, do you think that you can help me?"

"Have faith in Papa Poirot. I will find a way."

These reassurances were all very well, I thought, as Poirot gallantly ushered his fair client down the stairs, but it seemed to me that we had a tough nut to crack. I said as much to Poirot when he returned. He nodded ruefully.

"Yes—the solution does not leap to the eye. He has

the whip hand, this M. Lavington. For the moment I do not see how we are to circumvent him."

Mr. Lavington duly called upon us that afternoon. Lady Millicent had spoken truly when she described him as an odious man. I felt a positive tingling in the end of my boot, so keen was I to kick him down the stairs. He was blustering and overbearing in manner, laughed Poirot's gentle suggestions to scorn, and generally showed himself as master of the situation. I could not help feeling that Poirot was hardly appearing at his best. He looked discouraged and crestfallen.

"Well, gentlemen," said Lavington, as he took up his hat, "we don't seem to be getting much farther. The case stands like this: I'll let the Lady Millicent off cheap, as she is such a charming young lady," he leered odiously. "We'll say eighteen thousand. I'm off to Paris to-day—a little piece of business to attend to over there. I shall be back on Tuesday. Unless the money is paid by Tuesday evening, the letter goes to the Duke. Don't tell me Lady Millicent can't raise the money. Some of her gentlemen friends would be only too willing to oblige such a pretty woman with a loan—if she goes the right way about it."

My face flushed, and I took a step forward, but Lavington had wheeled out of the room as he finished his sentence.

"My God!" I cried. "Something has got to be done. You seem to be taking this lying down, Poirot."

"You have an excellent heart, my friend—but your gray cells are in a deplorable condition. I have no wish to impress Mr. Lavington with my capabilities. The more pusillanimous he thinks me, the better."

"Why?"

"It is curious," murmured Poirot reminiscently, "that I should have uttered a wish to work against the law just before Lady Millicent arrived!"

"You are going to burgle his house while he is away?" I gasped.

"Sometimes, Hastings, your mental processes are amazingly quick."

"Suppose he takes the letter with him?"

Poirot shook his head.

"That is very unlikely. He has evidently a hiding-place in his house that he fancies to be pretty impregnable."

"When do we—er—do the deed?"

"To-morrow night. We will start from here about eleven o'clock."

At the time appointed I was ready to set off. I had donned a dark suit, and a soft dark hat. Poirot beamed kindly on me.

"You have dressed the part, I see," he observed. "Come let us take the underground to Wimbledon."

"Aren't we going to take anything with us? Tools to break in with?"

"My dear Hastings, Hercule Poirot does not adopt such crude methods."

I retired, snubbed, but my curiosity was alert.

It was just on midnight that we entered the small sub-urban garden of Buona Vista. The house was dark and silent. Poirot went straight to a window at the back of the house, raised the sash noiselessly and bade me enter.

"How did you know this window would be open?" I whispered, for really it seemed uncanny.

"Because I sawed through the catch this morning."

"What?"

"But yes, it was the most simple. I called, presented a fictitious card and one of Inspector Japp's official ones. I said I had been sent, recommended by Scotland Yard, to attend to some burglar-proof fastenings that Mr. Lavington wanted fixed while he was away. The housekeeper welcomed me with enthusiasm. It seems they have had two attempted burglaries here lately—evidently our little idea has occurred to other clients of Mr. Lavington's—with nothing of value taken. I examined all the windows, made my little arrangement, forbade the servants to touch the windows until to-morrow, as they were electrically connected up, and withdrew gracefully."

"Really, Poirot, you are wonderful."

"*Mon ami,* it was of the simplest. Now, to work! The servants sleep at the top of the house, so we will run little risk of disturbing them."

"I presume the safe is built into the wall somewhere?"

"Safe? Fiddlesticks! There is no safe. Mr. Lavington is an intelligent man. You will see, he will have devised a hiding-place much more intelligent than a safe. A safe is the first thing everyone looks for."

Whereupon we began a systematic search of the entire place. But after several hours' ransacking of the house, our search had been unavailing. I saw symptoms of anger gathering on Poirot's face.

"*Ah, sapristi,* is Hercule Poirot to be beaten? Never! Let us be calm. Let us reflect. Let us reason. Let us— *enfin!*—employ our little gray cells!"

He paused for some moments, bending his brows in concentration; then the green light I knew so well stole into his eyes.

"I have been an imbecile! The kitchen!"

"The kitchen," I cried. "But that's impossible. The servants!"

"Exactly. Just what ninety-nine people out of a hundred would say! And for that very reason the kitchen is the ideal place to choose. It is full of various homely objects. *En avant,* to the kitchen!"

I followed him, completely skeptical, and watched whilst he dived into bread-bins, tapped saucepans, and put his head into the gas-oven. In the end, tired of watching him, I strolled back to the study. I was convinced that there, and there only, would we find the *cache*. I made a further minute search, noted that it was now a quarter past four and that therefore it would soon be growing light, and then went back to the kitchen regions.

To my utter amazement, Poirot was now standing right inside the coal-bin, to the utter ruin of his neat light suit. He made a grimace.

"But yes, my friend, it is against all my instincts so to ruin my appearance, but what will you?"

"But Lavington can't have buried it under the coal?"

"If you would use your eyes, you would see that it is not the coal that I examine."

I then saw that on a shelf behind the coal-bunker some logs of wood were piled. Poirot was dexterously taking them down one by one. Suddenly he uttered a low exclamation.

"Your knife, Hastings!"

I handed it to him. He appeared to insert it in the wood, and suddenly the log split in two. It had been neatly sawn in half and a cavity hollowed out in the center. From this cavity Poirot took a little wooden box of Chinese make.

"Well done!" I cried, carried out of myself.

"Gently, Hastings! Do not raise your voice too much. Come, let us be off, before the daylight is upon us."

Slipping the box into his pocket, he leaped lightly out of the coal-bunker, brushed himself down as well as he could, and leaving the house by the same way as we had come, we walked rapidly in the direction of London.

"But what an extraordinary place!" I expostulated. "Anyone might have used the log."

"In July, Hastings? And it was at the bottom of the pile—a very ingenious hiding-place. Ah, here is a taxi! Now for home, a wash, and a refreshing sleep."

After the excitement of the night, I slept late. When I finally strolled into our sitting-room just before one o'clock, I was surprised to see Poirot, leaning back in an armchair, the Chinese box open beside him, calmly reading the letter he had taken from it.

He smiled at me affectionately, and tapped the sheet he held.

"She was right, the Lady Millicent; never would the Duke have pardoned this letter! It contains some of the most extravagant terms of affection I have ever come across."

"Really, Poirot," I said, rather disgustedly, "I don't think you should have read the letter. That's the sort of thing that isn't done."

"It is done by Hercule Poirot," replied my friend imperturbably.

"And another thing," I said. "I don't think using Japp's official card yesterday was quite playing the game."

"But I was not playing a game, Hastings. I was conducting a case."

I shrugged my shoulders. One can't argue with a point of view.

"A step on the stairs," said Poirot. "That will be Lady Millicent."

Our fair client came in with an anxious expression on her face which changed to one of delight on seeing the letter and box which Poirot held up.

"Oh M. Poirot. How wonderful of you! How did you do it?"

"By rather reprehensible methods, milady. But Mr. Lavington will not prosecute. This is your letter, is it not?"

She glanced through it.

"Yes. Oh, how can I ever thank you! You are a wonderful, wonderful man. Where was it hidden?"

Poirot told her.

"How very clever of you!" She took up the small box from the table. "I shall keep this as a souvenir."

"I had hoped, milady, that you would permit me to keep it—also as a souvenir."

"I hope to send you a better souvenir than that—on my wedding-day. You shall not find me ungrateful, M. Poirot."

"The pleasure of doing you a service will be more to me than a check—so you permit that I retain the box."

"Oh, no, M. Poirot, I simply must have that," she cried laughingly.

She stretched out her hand, but Poirot was before her. His hand closed over it.

"I think not." His voice had changed.

"What do you mean?" Her voice seemed to have grown sharper.

"At any rate, permit me to abstract its further contents. You observe that the original cavity has been reduced by half. In the top half, the compromising letter; in the bottom——"

He made a nimble gesture, then held out his hand. On

the palm were four large glittering stones, and two big milky white pearls.

"The jewels stolen in Bond Street the other day, I rather fancy," murmured Poirot. "Japp will tell us."

To my utter amazement, Japp himself stepped out from Poirot's bedroom.

"An old friend of yours, I believe," said Poirot politely to Lady Millicent.

"Nabbed, by the Lord!" said Lady Millicent, with a complete change of manner. "You nippy old devil!" She looked at Poirot with almost affectionate awe.

"Well, Gertie, my dear," said Japp, "the game's up this time, I fancy. Fancy seeing you again so soon! We've got your pal, too, the gentleman who called here the other day calling himself Lavington. As for Lavington himself, alias Croker, alias Reed, I wonder which of the gang it was who stuck a knife into him the other day in Holland? Thought he'd got the goods with him, didn't you? And he hadn't. He double-crossed you properly—hid 'em in his own house. You had two fellows looking for them, and then you tackled M. Poirot here, and by a piece of amazing luck he found them."

"You do like talking, don't you?" said the late Lady Millicent. "Easy there, now. I'll go quietly. You can't say that I'm not the perfect lady. *Ta-ta,* all!"

"The shoes were wrong," said Poirot dreamily, while I was still too stupefied to speak. "I have made my little observations of your English nation, and a lady, a born lady, is always particular about her shoes. She may have shabby clothes, but she will be well shod. Now, this Lady Millicent had smart, expensive clothes, and cheap shoes. It was not likely that either you or I should have seen the real Lady Millicent; she has been very little in London, and this girl had a certain superficial resemblance which would pass well enough. As I say, the shoes first awakened my suspicions, and then her story—and her veil—were a little melodramatic, eh? The Chinese box with a bogus compromising letter in the top must have been known to all the gang, but the log of wood was the late Mr. Lavington's own idea. *Eh, par exemple,* Hastings, I hope you will not again wound my feelings as you did yesterday by saying that I am unknown to the criminal classes. *Ma foi*, they even employ me when they themselves fail!"

XIII
THE LOST MINE

I laid down my bank-book with a sigh.

"It is a curious thing," I observed, "but my overdraft never seems to grow any less."

"And it perturbs you not? Me, if I had an overdraft, never should I close my eyes all night," declared Poirot.

"You deal in comfortable balances, I suppose!" I retorted.

"Four hundred and forty-four pounds, four and fourpence," said Poirot with some complacency. "A neat figure, is it not?"

"It must be tact on the part of your bank manager. He is evidently acquainted with your passion for symmetrical details. What about investing, say three hundred of it, in the Porcupine oil-fields? Their prospectus, which is advertised in the papers to-day says that they will pay one hundred per cent in dividends next year."

"Not for me," said Poirot, shaking his head. "I like not the sensational. For me the safe, the prudent investment—*les rentes,* the consols, the—how do you call it?— the conversion."

"Have you never made a speculative investment?"

"No, *mon ami,*" replied Poirot severely. "I have not. And the only shares I own which have not what you call the gilded edge are fourteen thousand shares in the Burma Mines, Ltd."

Poirot paused with an air of waiting to be encouraged to go on.

"Yes?" I prompted.

"And for them I paid no cash—no, they were the reward of the exercise of my little gray cells. You would like to hear the story? Yes?"

"Of course I would."

"These mines are situated in the interior of Burma about two hundred miles inland from Rangoon. They were discovered by the Chinese in the fifteenth century and worked down to the time of the Mohammedan Rebellion, being finally abandoned in the year 1868. The Chinese extracted the rich lead-silver ore from the upper part of the ore body, smelting it for the silver alone, and leaving large quantities of rich lead-bearing slag. This, of course, was soon discovered when prospecting work was carried out in Burma, but owing to the fact that the old workings had become full of loose filling and water, all attempts to find the source of the ore proved fruitless. Many parties were sent out by syndicates, and they dug over a large area, but this rich prize still eluded them. But a representative of one of the syndicates got on the track of a Chinese family who were supposed to have still kept a record of the situation of the mine. The present head of the family was one Wu Ling."

"What a fascinating page of commercial romance!" I exclaimed.

"Is it not? Ah, *mon ami,* one can have romance without golden-haired girls of matchless beauty—no, I am wrong; it is auburn hair that so excites you always. You remember——"

"Go on with the story," I said hastily.

"*Eh bien,* my friend, this Wu Ling was approached. He was an estimable merchant, much respected in the province where he lived. He admitted at once that he owned the documents in question, and was perfectly prepared to negotiate for this sale, but he objected to dealing with any other than principals. Finally it was arranged that he should journey to England and meet the directors of an important company.

"Wu Ling made the journey to England in the S.S. *Assunta,* and the *Assunta* docked at Southampton on a cold, foggy morning in November. One of the directors, Mr. Pearson, went down to Southampton to meet the boat, but owing to the fog, the train down was very much delayed, and by the time he arrived, Wu Ling had disembarked and left by special train for London. Mr. Pearson returned to town somewhat annoyed, as he had no idea where the Chinaman proposed to stay. Later in the day, however, the offices of the Company were rung up on the telephone. Wu Ling was staying at the Russell Square Hotel. He was feeling somewhat unwell after the voyage, but declared himself perfectly able to attend the Board meeting on the following day.

"The meeting of the Board took place at eleven o'clock. When half-past eleven came, and Wu Ling had not put in an appearance, the secretary rang up the Russell Hotel. In answer to his inquiries, he was told that the Chinaman had gone out with a friend about half-past ten. It seemed clear that he had started out with the intention of coming to the meeting, but the morning wore away, and he did not appear. It was, of course, possible that he had lost his way, being unacquainted with London, but at a late hour that night, he had not returned to the hotel. Thoroughly alarmed now, Mr. Pearson put matters in the hands of the police. On the following day, there was still no trace of the missing man, but towards evening of the day after that again, a body was found in the Thames which proved to be that of the ill-fated Chinaman. Neither on the body, nor in the luggage at the hotel, was there any trace of the papers relating to the mine.

"At this juncture, *mon ami,* I was brought into the affair. Mr. Pearson called upon me. While profoundly shocked by the death of Wu Ling, his chief anxiety was to recover the papers which were the object of the Chinaman's visit to England. The main anxiety of the police, of course, would be to track down the murderer—the recovery of the papers would be a secondary consideration. What he wanted me to do was to coöperate with the police while acting in the interests of the Company.

"I consented readily enough. It was clear that there were two fields of search open to me. On the one hand, I might look among the employees of the Company who knew of the Chinaman's coming; on the other, among the passengers on the boat who might have been acquainted with his mission. I started with the second, as being a narrower field of search. In this I coincided with

Inspector Miller, who was in charge of the case—a man altogether different to our friend Japp, conceited, ill-mannered and quite insufferable. Together we interviewed the officers of the ship. They had little to tell us. Wu Ling had kept much to himself on the voyage. He had been intimate with but two of the other passengers—one a broken-down European named Dyer who appeared to bear a somewhat unsavory reputation, the other a young bank-clerk named Charles Lester, who was returning from Hongkong. We were lucky enough to obtain snapshots of both these men. At the moment there seemed little doubt that if either of the two was implicated, Dyer was the man. He was known to be mixed up with a gang of Chinese crooks, and was altogether a most likely suspect.

"Our next step was to visit the Russell Square Hotel. Shown a snapshot of Wu Ling, they recognized him at once. We then showed them the snapshot of Dyer, but to our disappointment, the hall porter declared positively that that was not the man who had come to the hotel on the fatal morning. Almost as an afterthought, I produced the photograph of Lester, and to my surprise the man at once recognized it.

" 'Yes sir,' he asserted, 'that's the gentleman who came in at half-past ten and asked for Mr. Wu Ling, and afterwards went out with him.'

"The affair was progressing. Our next move was to interview Mr. Charles Lester. He met us with the utmost frankness, was desolated to hear of the Chinaman's untimely death, and put himself at our disposal in every way. His story was as follows: By arrangement with Wu Ling, he called for him at the hotel at ten-thirty. Wu Ling, however, did not appear. Instead, his servant came, explained that his master had had to go out, and offered to conduct the young man to where his master now was. Suspecting nothing, Lester agreed, and the Chinaman procured a taxi. They drove for some time in the direction of the docks. Suddenly becoming mistrustful, Lester stopped the taxi and got out, disregarding the servant's protests. That, he assured us, was all he knew.

"Apparently satisfied, we thanked him and took our leave. His story was soon proved to be a somewhat inaccurate one. To begin with, Wu Ling had had no servant with him, either on the boat or at the hotel. In the second place, the taxi-driver who had driven the two men on that morning came forward. Far from Lester's having left the taxi en route, he and the Chinese gentleman had driven to a certain unsavory dwelling-place in Limehouse, right in the heart of Chinatown. The place in question was more or less well known as an opium-den of the lowest description. The two gentlemen had gone in— about an hour later the English gentleman, whom he identified from the photograph, came out alone. He looked very pale and ill, and directed the taxi-man to take him to the nearest underground station.

"Inquiries were made about Charles Lester's standing, and it was found that, though bearing an excellent character, he was heavily in debt, and had a secret passion for gambling. Dyer, of course, was not lost sight of. It seemed just faintly possible that he might have impersonated the other man, but that idea was proved utterly groundless. His alibi for the whole of the day in question was absolutely unimpeachable. Of course, the proprietor of the opium-den denied everything with Oriental stolidity. He had never seen Wu Ling; he had never seen Charles Lester. No two gentlemen had been to the place that morning. In any case, the police were wrong: no opium was ever smoked there.

"His denials, however well meant, did little to help Charles Lester. He was arrested for the murder of Wu Ling. A search of his effects was made, but no papers relating to the mine were discovered. The proprietor of the opium-den was also taken into custody, but a cursory raid of his premises yielded nothing. Not even a stick of opium rewarded the zeal of the police.

"In the meantime my friend Mr. Pearson was in a great state of agitation. He strode up and down my room, uttering great lamentations.

" 'But you must have some ideas, M. Poirot!' he kept urging. 'Surely you must have some ideas?'

" 'Certainly I have ideas,' I replied cautiously. 'That is the trouble—one has too many; therefore they all lead in different directions.'

" 'For instance?' he suggested.

" 'For instance—the taxi-driver. We have only his word for it that he drove the two men to that house. That is one idea. Then—was it really that house they went to? Supposing that they left the taxi there, passed through the house and out by another entrance and went elsewhere?'

"Mr. Pearson seemed struck by that.

" 'But you do nothing but sit and think? Can't we *do* something?'

"He was of an impatient temperament, you comprehend.

" 'Monsieur,' I said with dignity, 'it is not for Hercule Poirot to run up and down the evil-smelling streets of Limehouse like a little dog of no breeding. Be calm. My agents are at work.'

"On the following day I had news for him. The two men had indeed passed through the house in question, but their real objective was a small eating-house close to the river. They were seen to pass in there, and Lester came out alone.

"And then, figure to yourself, Hastings, an idea of the most unreasonable seized this Mr. Pearson! Nothing would suit him but that we should go ourselves to this eating-house and make investigations. I argued and prayed, but he would not listen. He talked of disguising himself—he even suggested that I—*I* should—I hesitate to say it—should shave off my mustache! Yes, *rien que ça!* I pointed out to him that that was an idea ridiculous and absurd. One destroys not a thing of beauty wantonly. Besides, shall not a Belgian gentleman with a mustache desire to see life and smoke the opium just as readily as one without a mustache?

"*Eh bien,* he gave in on that, but he still insisted on his project. He turned up that evening—*Mon Dieu,* what a figure! He wore what he called the 'pea-jacket,' his chin, it was dirty and unshaved; he had a scarf of the vilest that offended the nose. And figure to yourself, he was enjoying himself! Truly, the English are mad! He made some changes in my own appearance. I permitted it. Can one argue with a maniac? We started out—after all, could I let him go alone, a child dressed up to act the charades?"

"Of course you couldn't," I replied.

"To continue—we arrived. Mr. Pearson talked English of the strangest. He represented himself to be a man of the sea. He talked of 'lubbers' and 'focselles' and I know not what. It was a low little room with many Chinese in it. We ate of peculiar dishes. *Ah, Dieu, mon estomac!*" Poirot clasped that portion of his anatomy tenderly before continuing. "Then there came to us the proprietor, a Chinaman with a face of evil smiles.

" 'You gentlemen no likee food here,' he said. 'You come for what you likee better. Piecee pipe, eh?'

"Mr. Pearson, he gave me the great kick under the table. (He had on the boots of the sea, too!) And he said: 'I don't mind if I do, John. Lead ahead.'

"The Chinaman smiled, and he took us through a door and to a cellar and through a trapdoor, and down some steps and up again into a room all full of divans and cushions of the most comfortable. We lay down and a Chinese boy took off our boots. It was the best moment of the evening. Then they brought us the opium-pipes and cooked the opium pills, and we pretended to smoke and then to sleep and dream. But when we were alone, Mr. Pearson called softly to me, and immediately he began crawling along the floor. We went into another room where other people were asleep, and so on, until we heard two men talking. We stayed behind a curtain and listened. They were speaking of Wu Ling.

" 'What about the papers?' said one.

" 'Mr. Lester, he takee those,' answered the other, who was a Chinaman. 'He say, puttee them allee in safee place—where pleeceman no lookee.'

" 'Ah, but he's nabbed,' said the first one.

" 'He gettee free. Pleeceman not sure he done it.'

"There was more of the same kind of thing, then apparently the two men were coming our way, and we scuttled back to our beds.

" 'We'd better get out of here,' said Pearson, after a few minutes had elapsed. 'This place isn't healthy.'

" 'You are right, monsieur,' I agreed. 'We have played the farce long enough.'

"We succeeded in getting away, all right, paying handsomely for our smoke. Once clear of Limehouse, Pearson drew a long breath.

" 'I'm glad to get out of that,' he said. 'But it's something to be sure.'

" 'It is indeed,' I agreed. 'And I fancy that we shall not have much difficulty in finding what we want—after this evening's masquerade.'

"And there was no difficulty whatsoever," finished Poirot suddenly.

This abrupt ending seemed so extraordinary that I stared at him.

"But—but where were they?" I asked.

"In his pocket—*tout simplement*."

"But in whose pocket?"

"Mr. Pearson's, *parbleu!*" Then, observing my look of bewilderment, he continued gently! "You do not yet see it? Mr. Pearson, like Charles Lester, was in debt. Mr. Pearson, like Charles Lester, was fond of gambling. And he conceived the idea of stealing the papers from the Chinaman. He met him all right at Southampton, came up to London with him, and took him straight to Limehouse. It was foggy that day; the Chinaman would not notice where he was going. I fancy Mr. Pearson smoked the opium fairly often down there and had some peculiar friends in consequence. I do not think he meant murder. His idea was that one of the Chinamen should impersonate Wu Ling and receive the money for the sale of the document. So far, so good! But, to the Oriental mind, it was infinitely simpler to kill Wu Ling and throw his body into the river, and Pearson's Chinese accomplices followed their own methods without consulting him. Imagine, then, what you would call the 'funk *bleu*' of M. Pearson. Some one may have seen him in the train with Wu Ling—murder is a very different thing to simple abduction.

"His salvation lies with the Chinaman who is personating Wu Ling at the Russell Square Hotel. If only the body is not discovered too soon! Probably Wu Ling had told him of the arrangement between him and Charles Lester whereby the latter was to call for him at the hotel. Pearson sees there an excellent way of diverting suspicion from himself. Charles Lester shall be the last person to be seen in company with Wu Ling. The impersonator has orders to represent himself to Lester as the servant of Wu Ling, and to bring him as speedily as possible to Limehouse. There, very likely, he was offered a drink. The drink would be suitably drugged, and when Lester emerged an hour later, he would have a very hazy impression of what had happened. So much was this the case, that as soon as Lester learned of Wu Ling's death, he loses his nerve, and denies that he ever reached Limehouse.

"By that, of course, he plays right into Pearson's hands. But is Pearson content? No—my manner disquiets him, and he determines to complete the case against Lester. So he arranges an elaborate masquerade. Me, I am to be gulled completely. Did I not say just now that he was as a child acting the charades? *Eh bien,* I play my part. He goes home rejoicing. But in the morning, Inspector Miller arrives on his doorstep. The papers are found on him; the game is up. Bitterly he regrets permitting himself to play the farce with Hercule Poirot! There was only one real difficulty in the affair."

"What was that?" I demanded curiously.

"Convincing Inspector Miller! What an animal, that! Both obstinate and imbecile. And in the end he took all the credit!"

"Too bad," I cried.

"Ah, well, I had my compensations. The other directors of the Burma Mines, Ltd., awarded me fourteen thousand shares as a small recompense for my services. Not so bad, eh? But when investing money, keep, I beg of you, Hastings, strictly to the conservative. The things you read in the paper, they may not be true. The directors of the Porcupine—they may be so many Mr. Pearsons!"

XIV
THE CHOCOLATE BOX

It was a wild night. Outside, the wind howled malevolently, and the rain beat against the windows in great gusts.

Poirot and I sat facing the hearth, our legs stretched out to the cheerful blaze. Between us was a small table. On my side of it stood some carefully brewed hot toddy; on Poirot's was a cup of thick, rich chocolate which I would not have drunk for a hundred pounds! Poirot sipped the thick brown mess in the pink china cup, and sighed with contentment.

"*Quelle belle vie!*" he murmured.

"Yes, it's a good old world," I agreed. "Here am I with a job, and a good job too! And here are you, famous——"

"Oh, *mon ami!*" protested Poirot.

"But you are. And rightly so! When I think back on your long line of successes, I am positively amazed. I don't believe you know what failure is!"

"He would be a droll kind of original who could say that!"

"No, but seriously, *have* you ever failed?"

"Innumerable times, my friend. What would you? *La bonne chance,* it cannot always be on your side. I have been called in too late. Very often another, working toward the same goal, has arrived there first. Twice have I been stricken down with illness just as I was on the point of success. One must take the downs with the ups, my friend."

"I didn't quite mean that," I said. "I meant, had you ever been completely down and out over a case through your own fault?"

184

"Ah, I comprehend! You ask if I have ever made the complete prize ass of myself, as you say over here? Once, my friend—" A slow, reflective smile hovered over his face. "Yes, once I made a fool of myself."

He sat up suddenly in his chair.

"See here, my friend, you have, I know, kept a record of my little successes. You shall add one more story to the collection, the story of a failure!"

He leaned forward and placed a log on the fire. Then, after carefully wiping his hands on a little duster that hung on a nail by the fireplace, he leaned back and commenced his story.

That of which I tell you, (said M. Poirot), took place in Belgium many years ago. It was at the time of the terrible struggle in France between church and state. M. Paul Déroulard was a French deputy of note. It was an open secret that the portfolio of a Minister awaited him. He was among the bitterest of the anti-Catholic party, and it was certain that on his accession to power, he would have to face violent enmity. He was in many ways a peculiar man. Though he neither drank nor smoked, he was nevertheless not so scrupulous in other ways. You comprehend, Hastings, c' etait des femmes—toujours des femmes!

He had married some years earlier a young lady from Brussels who had brought him a substantial dot. Undoubtedly the money was useful to him in his career, as his family was not rich, though on the other hand he was entitled to call himself M. le Baron if he chose. There were no children of the marriage, and his wife died after two years—the result of a fall downstairs. Among the property which she bequeathed to him was a house on the Avenue Louise in Brussels.

It was in this house that his sudden death took place, the event coinciding with the resignation of the Minister whose portfolio he was to inherit. All the papers printed long notices of his career. His death, which had taken place quite suddenly in the evening after dinner, was attributed to heart-failure.

At that time, mon ami, I was, as you know, a member of the Belgian detective force. The death of M. Paul

Déroulard was not particularly interesting to me. I am, as you also know, *bon catholique,* and his demise seemed to me fortunate.

It was some three days afterward, when my vacation had just begun, that I received a visitor at my own apartments—a lady, heavily veiled, but evidently quite young; and I perceived at once that she was a *jeune fille tout à fait comme il faut.*

"You are Monsieur Hercule Poirot?" she asked in a low sweet voice.

I bowed.

"Of the detective service?"

Again I bowed. "Be seated, I pray of you, mademoiselle," I said.

She accepted a chair and drew aside her veil. Her face was charming, though marred with tears, and haunted as though with some poignant anxiety.

"Monsieur," she said, "I understand that you are now taking a vacation. Therefore you will be free to take up a private case. You understand that I do not wish to call in the police."

I shook my head. "I fear what you ask is impossible, mademoiselle. Even though on vacation, I am still of the police."

She leaned forward. *"Ecoutez, monsieur.* All that I ask of you is to investigate. The result of your investigations you are at perfect liberty to report to the police. If what I believe to be true *is* true, we shall need all the machinery of the law."

That placed a somewhat different complexion on the matter, and I placed myself at her service without more ado.

A slight color rose in her cheeks. "I thank you, monsieur. It is the death of M. Paul Déroulard that I ask you to investigate."

"Comment?" I exclaimed, surprised.

"Monsieur, I have nothing to go upon—nothing but my woman's instinct, but I am convinced—*convinced,* I tell you—that M. Déroulard did not die a natural death!"

"But surely the doctors——"

"Doctors may be mistaken. He was so robust, so

strong. Ah, Monsieur Poirot, I beseech of you to help me——"

The poor child was almost beside herself. She would have knelt to me. I soothed her as best I could.

"I will help you, mademoiselle. I feel almost sure that your fears are unfounded, but we will see. First, I will ask you to describe to me the inmates of the house."

"There are the domestics, of course, Jeannette, Félicie, and Denise the cook. She has been there many years; the others are simple country girls. Also there is François, but he too is an old servant. Then there is Monsieur Déroulard's mother who lived with him, and myself. My name is Virginie Mesnard. I am a poor cousin of the late Madame Déroulard, M. Paul's wife, and I have been a member of their ménage for over three years. I have now described to you the household. There were also two guests staying in the house."

"And they were?"

"M. de Saint Alard, a neighbor of M. Déroulard's in France. Also an English friend, Mr. John Wilson."

"Are they still with you?"

"Mr. Wilson, yes, but M. de Saint Alard departed yesterday."

"And what is your plan, Mademoiselle Mesnard?"

"If you will present yourself at the house in half an hour's time, I will have arranged some story to account for your presence. I had better represent you to be connected with journalism in some way. I shall say you have come from Paris, and that you have brought a card of introduction from M. de Saint Alard. Madame Déroulard is very feeble in health, and will pay little attention to details."

On mademoiselle's ingenious pretext I was admitted to the house, and after a brief interview with the dead deputy's mother, who was a wonderfully imposing and aristocratic figure though obviously in failing health, I was made free of the premises.

I wonder, my friend (continued Poirot), whether you can possibly figure to yourself the difficulties of my task? Here was a man whose death had taken place three days previously. If there *had* been foul play, only one possibility was admittable—*poison!* And I had had no chance of seeing the body, and there was no possibility of examining, or analyzing, any medium in which the poison could have been administered. There were no clues, false or otherwise, to consider. Had the man been poisoned? Had he died a natural death? I, Hercule Poirot, with nothing to help me, had to decide.

First, I interviewed the domestics, and with their aid, I recapitulated the evening. I paid especial notice to the food at dinner, and the method of serving it. The soup had been served by M. Déroulard himself from a tureen. Next a dish of cutlets, then a chicken. Finally a compote of fruits. And all placed on the table, and served by Monsieur himself. The coffee was brought in a big pot to the dinner-table. Nothing there, *mon ami*—impossible to poison one without poisoning all!

After dinner Madame Déroulard had retired to her own apartments and Mademoiselle Virginie had accompanied her. The three men had adjourned to M. Déroulard's study. Here they had chatted amicably for some time, when suddenly, without any warning, the deputy had fallen heavily to the ground. M. de Saint Alard had rushed out and told François to fetch a doctor immediately. He said it was without doubt an apoplexy, explained the man. But when the doctor arrived, the patient was past help.

Mr. John Wilson, to whom I was presented by Mademoiselle Virginie, was what was known in those days as a regular John Bull Englishman, middle-aged and burly. His account, delivered in very British French, was substantially the same.

"Déroulard went very red in the face, and down he fell."

There was nothing further to be found out there. Next I went to the scene of the tragedy, the study, and was left alone there at my own request. So far there was nothing to support Mademoiselle Mesnard's theory. I could not but believe that it was a delusion on her part. Evidently she had entertained a romantic passion for the dead man which had not permitted her to take a normal view of the case. Nevertheless, I searched the study with meticulous care. It was just possible that a hypodermic needle might have been introduced into the dead man's chair in such a way as to allow of a fatal injection. The minute puncture it would cause was likely to remain unnoticed. But I could discover no sign to support that theory. I flung myself down in the chair with a gesture of despair.

"*Enfin,* I abandon it!" I said aloud. "There is not a clue anywhere! Everything is perfectly normal."

As I said the words, my eyes fell on a large box of chocolates standing on a table near by, and my heart gave a leap. It might not be a clue to M. Déroulard's death, but here at least was something that was *not* normal. I lifted the lid. The box was full, untouched; not a chocolate was missing—but that only made the peculiarity that had caught my eye more striking. For, see you, Hastings, while the box itself was pink, the lid was *blue*. Now, one often sees a blue ribbon on a pink box, and vice versa, but a box of one color, and a lid of another— no, decidedly—*ça ne se voit jamais!*

I did not as yet see that this little incident was of any use to me, yet I determined to investigate it as being out of the ordinary. I rang the bell for François, and asked him if his late master had been fond of sweets. A faint melancholy smile came to his lips.

"Passionately fond of them, monsieur. He would always have a box of chocolates in the house. He did not drink wine of any kind, you see."

"Yet this box has not been touched?" I lifted the lid to show him.

"Pardon, monsieur, but that was a new box purchased on the day of his death, the other being nearly finished."

"Then the other box was finished on the day of his death," I said slowly.

"Yes, monsieur, I found it empty in the morning and threw it away."

"Did M. Déroulard eat sweets at all hours of the day?"

"Usually after dinner, monsieur."

I began to see light.

"François," I said, "you can be discreet?"

"If there is need, monsieur."

"*Bon!* Know, then, that I am of the police. Can you find me that other box?"

"Without doubt, monsieur. It will be in the dustbin."

He departed, and returned in a few minutes with a dust-covered object. It was the duplicate of the box I held, save for the fact that this time the box was *blue* and the lid was *pink*. I thanked François, recommended him once more to be discreet, and left the house in the Avenue Louise without more ado.

Next I called upon the doctor who had attended M. Déroulard. With him I had a difficult task. He entrenched himself prettily behind a wall of learned phraseology, but I fancied that he was not quite as sure about the case as he would like to be.

"There have been many curious occurrences of the kind," he observed, when I had managed to disarm him somewhat. "A sudden fit of anger, a violent emotion,—after a heavy dinner, *c'est entendu,*—then, with an access of rage, the blood flies to the head, and *pst!*—there you are!"

"But M. Déroulard had had no violent emotion."

"No? I made sure that he had been having a stormy altercation with M. de Saint Alard."

"Why should he?"

"*C'est évident!*" The doctor shrugged his shoulders. "Was not M. de Saint Alard a Catholic of the most fanatical? Their friendship was being ruined by this question of church and state. Not a day passed without discussions. To M. de Saint Alard, Déroulard appeared almost as Antichrist."

This was unexpected, and gave me food for thought.

"One more question, Doctor: would it be possible to introduce a fatal dose of poison into a chocolate?"

"It would be possible, I suppose," said the doctor slowly. "Pure prussic acid would meet the case if there were no chance of evaporation, and a tiny globule of anything might be swallowed unnoticed—but it does not seem a very likely supposition. A chocolate full of morphine or strychnine—" He made a wry face. "You comprehend, M. Poirot—one bite would be enough! The unwary one would not stand upon ceremony."

"Thank you, M. le Docteur."

I withdrew. Next I made inquiries of the chemists, especially those in the neighborhood of the Avenue Louise. It is good to be of the police. I got the information I wanted without any trouble. Only in one case could I hear of any poison having been supplied to the house in question. This was some eye drops of atropine sulphate for Madame Déroulard. Atropine is a potent poison, and for the moment I was elated, but the symptoms of atropine poisoning are closely allied to those of ptomaine, and bear no resemblance to those I was studying. Besides, the prescription was an old one. Madame Déroulard had suffered from cataract in both eyes for many years.

I was turning away discouraged when the chemist's voice called me back.

"*Un moment,* M. Poirot. I remember, the girl who brought that prescription, she said something about having to go on to the *English* chemist. You might try there."

I did. Once more enforcing my official status, I got the information I wanted. On the day before M. Déroulard's death they had made up a prescription for Mr. John Wilson. Not that there was any making up about it. They were simply little tablets of trinitrin. I asked if I might see some. He showed me them, and my heart beat faster —for the tiny tablets were of *chocolate.*

"It is a poison?" I asked.

"No, monsieur."

"Can you describe to me its effect?"

"It lowers the blood-pressure. It is given for some forms of heart trouble—angina pectoris for instance. It relieves the arterial tension. In arteriosclerosis——"

I interrupted him. "*Ma foi!* This rigmarole says nothing to me. Does it cause the face to flush?"

"Certainly it does."

"And supposing I ate ten—twenty of your little tablets, what then?"

"I should not advise you to attempt it," he replied dryly.

"And yet you say it is not poison?"

"There are many things not called poison which can kill a man," he replied as before.

I left the shop elated. At last, things had begun to march!

I now knew that John Wilson held the means for the crime—but what about the motive? He had come to Belgium on business, and had asked M. Déroulard, whom he knew slightly, to put him up. There was apparently no way in which Déroulard's death could benefit him. Moreover, I discovered by inquiries in England that he had suffered for some years from that painful form of heart disease known as angina. Therefore he had a genuine right to have those tablets in his possession. Nevertheless, I was convinced that someone had gone to the chocolate box, opening the full one first by mistake, and had abstracted the contents of the last chocolate, cramming in instead as many little trinitrin tablets as it would hold. The chocolates were large ones. Between twenty or thirty tablets, I felt sure, could have been inserted. But who had done this?

There were two guests in the house. John Wilson had the means. Saint Alard had the motive. Remember, he was a fanatic, and there is no fanatic like a religious fanatic. Could he, by any means, have got hold of John Wilson's trinitrin?

Another little idea came to me. Ah! You smile at my little ideas! Why had Wilson run out of trinitrin? Surely he would bring an adequate supply from England. I called once more at the house in the Avenue Louise. Wilson was out, but I saw the girl who did his room, Félicie. I demanded of her immediately whether it was not true that M. Wilson had lost a bottle from his washstand some little time ago. The girl responded eagerly. It was quite true. She, Félicie, had been blamed for it. The English gentleman had evidently thought that she had broken it, and did not like to say so. Whereas she had never even touched it. Without doubt it was Jeannette—always nosing round where she had no business to be——

I calmed the flow of words, and took my leave. I knew now all that I wanted to know. It remained for me to prove my case. That, I felt, would not be easy. *I* might be sure that Saint Alard had removed the bottle of trinitrin from John Wilson's washstand, but to convince others, I would have to produce evidence. And I had none to produce!

Never mind. I *knew*—that was the great thing. You remember our difficulty in the Styles case, Hastings? There again, I *knew*—but it took me a long time to find the last link which made my chain of evidence against the murderer complete.

I asked for an interview with Mademoiselle Mesnard. She came at once. I demanded of her the address of M. de Saint Alard. A look of trouble came over her face.

"Why do you want it, monsieur?"

"Mademoiselle, it is necessary."

She seemed doubtful—troubled.

"He can tell you nothing. He is a man whose thoughts are not in this world. He hardly notices what goes on around him."

"Possibly, mademoiselle. Nevertheless, he was an old friend of M. Déroulard's. There may be things he can tell me—things of the past—old grudges—old love-affairs."

The girl flushed and bit her lip. "As you please—but —but—I feel sure now that I have been mistaken. It was good of you to accede to my demand, but I was upset— almost distraught at the time. I see now that there is no mystery to solve. Leave it, I beg of you, monsieur."

I eyed her closely.

"Mademoiselle," I said, "it is sometimes difficult for a dog to find a scent, but once he *has* found it, nothing on earth will make him leave it! That is if he is a good dog! And I, mademoiselle, I, Hercule Poirot, am a very good dog."

Without a word she turned away. A few minutes later she returned with the address written on a sheet of paper. I left the house. François was waiting for me outside. He looked at me anxiously.

"There is no news, monsieur?"

"None as yet, my friend."

"Ah! *Pauvre* Monsieur Déroulard!" he sighed. "I too was of his way of thinking. I do not care for priests. Not

that I would say so in the house. The women are all de-
vout—a good thing perhaps. *Madame est très pieuse—et
Mademoiselle Virginie aussi."*

Mademoiselle Virginie? Was she *"très pieuse?"* Thinking of the tear-stained passionate face I had seen that
first day, I wondered.

Having obtained the address of M. de Saint Alárd, I
wasted no time. I arrived in the neighborhood of his
château in the Ardennes but it was some days before I
could find a pretext for gaining admission to the house. In
the end I did—how do you think—as a plumber, *mon
ami!* It was the affair of a moment to arrange a neat little
gas leak in his bedroom. I departed for my tools, and
took care to return with them at an hour when I knew
I should have the field pretty well to myself. What I was
searching for, I hardly knew. The one thing needful, I
could not believe there was any chance of finding. He
would never have run the risk of keeping it.

Still when I found a little cupboard above the washstand locked, I could not resist the temptation of seeing
what was inside it. The lock was quite a simple one to
pick. The door swung open. It was full of old bottles. I
took them up one by one with a trembling hand. Suddenly, I uttered a cry. Figure to yourself, my friend, I
held in my hand a little phial with an English chemist's
label. On it were the words: *"Trinitrin Tablets. One to be
taken when required. Mr. John Wilson."*

I controlled my emotion, closed the little cupboard,
slipped the bottle into my pocket, and continued to repair the gas leak! One must be methodical. Then I left
the château, and took train for my own country as soon
as possible. I arrived in Brussels late that night. I was
writing out a report for the préfet in the morning, when a
note was brought to me. It was from old Madame Déroulard, and it summoned me to the house in the Avenue
Louise without delay.

François opened the door to me.

"Madame la Boronne is awaiting you."

He conducted me to her apartments. She sat in state
in a large armchair. There was no sign of Mademoiselle
Virginie.

"M. Poirot," said the old lady. "I have just learned that you are not what you pretend to be. You are a police officer."

"That is so, madame."

"You came here to inquire into the circumstances of my son's death?"

Again I replied: "That is so, madame."

"I should be glad if you would tell me what progress you have made."

I hesitated.

"First I would like to know how you have learned all this, madame."

"From one who is no longer of this world."

Her words, and the brooding way she uttered them, sent a chill to my heart. I was incapable of speech.

"Therefore, monsieur, I would beg of you most urgently to tell me exactly what progress you have made in your investigation."

"Madame, my investigation is finished."

"My son?"

"Was killed deliberately."

"You know by whom?"

"Yes, madame."

"Who, then?"

"M. de Saint Alard."

The old lady shook her head.

"You are wrong. M. de Saint Alard is incapable of such a crime."

"The proofs are in my hands."

"I beg of you once more to tell me all."

This time I obeyed, going over each step that had led me to the discovery of the truth. She listened attentively. At the end she nodded her head.

"Yes, yes, it is all as you say, all but one thing. It was not M. de Saint Alard who killed my son. It was I, his mother."

I stared at her. She continued to nod her head gently.

"It is well that I sent for you. It is the providence of the good God that Virginie told me before she departed for the convent, what she had done. Listen, M. Poirot! My son was an evil man. He persecuted the church. He led a life of mortal sin. He dragged down other souls beside his own. But there was worse than that. As I came out of my room in this house one morning, I saw my daughter-in-law standing at the head of the stairs. She was reading a letter. I saw my son steal up behind her. One swift push, and she fell, striking her head on the marble steps. When they picked her up she was dead. My son was a murderer, and only I, his mother, knew it."

She closed her eyes for a moment. "You cannot conceive, monsieur, of my agony, my despair. What was I to do? Denounce him to the police? I could not bring myself to do it. It was my duty, but my flesh was weak. Besides, would they believe me? My eyesight had been failing for some time—they would say I was mistaken. I kept silence. But my conscience gave me no peace. By keeping silence I too was a murderer. My son inherited his wife's money. He flourished as the green bay tree. And now he was to have a Minister's portfolio. His persecution of the church would be redoubled. And there was Virginie. She, poor child, beautiful, naturally pious, was fascinated by him. He had a strange and terrible power over women. I saw it coming. I was powerless to prevent it. He had no intention of marrying her. The time came when she was ready to yield everything to him.

"Then I saw my path clear. He was my son. I had given him life. I was responsible for him. He had killed one woman's body, now he would kill another's soul! I went to Mr. Wilson's room, and took the bottle of tablets. He had once said laughingly that there were enough in it to kill a man! I went into the study and opened the big box of chocolates that always stood on the table. I opened a new box by mistake. The other was on the table also. There was just one chocolate left in it. That simplified things. No one ate chocolates except my son and Virginie. I would keep her with me that night. All went as I had planned——"

She paused, closing her eyes a minute then opened them again.

"M. Poirot, I am in your hands. They tell me I have

not many days to live. I am willing to answer for my
action before the good God. Must I answer for it on
earth also?"

I hesitated. "But the empty bottle, madame," I said to
gain time. "How came that into M. de Saint Alard's possession?"

"When he came to say good-by to me, monsieur, I
slipped it into his pocket. I did not know how to get rid
of it. I am so infirm that I cannot move about much
without help, and finding it empty in my rooms might
have caused suspicion. You understand, monsieur,"—she
drew herself up to her full height,—"it was with no idea
of casting suspicion on M. de Saint Alard! I never
dreamed of such a thing. I thought his valet would find
an empty bottle and throw it away without question."

I bowed my head. "I comprehend, madame," I said.

"And your decision, monsieur?"

Her voice was firm and unfaltering, her head held as
high as ever.

I rose to my feet.

"Madame," I said, "I have the honor to wish you good
day. I have made my investigations—and failed! The
matter is closed."

He was silent for a moment, then said quietly: "She
died just a week later. Mademoiselle Virginie passed
through her novitiate, and duly took the veil. That, my
friend, is the story. I must admit that I do not make a
fine figure in it."

"But that was hardly a failure," I expostulated. "What
else could you have thought under the circumstances?"

"Ah, sacré, mon ami," cried Poirot, becoming suddenly
animated. "Is it that you do not see? But I was thirty-six
times an idiot! My gray cells, they functioned not at all.
The whole time I had the true clue in my hands."

"What clue?"

"The chocolate box! Do you not see? Would anyone
in possession of their full eyesight make such a mistake?
I knew Madame Déroulard had cataract—the atropine
drops told me that. There was only one person in the
household whose eyesight was such that she could not see

which lid to replace. It was the chocolate box that started
me on the track, and yet up to the end I failed consistently to perceive its real significance!

"Also my psychology was at fault. Had M. de Saint
Alard been the criminal, he would never have kept an
incriminating bottle. Finding it was a proof of his innocence. I had learned already from Mademoiselle Virginie
that he was absent-minded. Altogether it was a miserable
affair that I have recounted to you there! Only to you
have I told the story. You comprehend, I do not figure
well in it! An old lady commits a crime in such a simple
and clever fashion that I, Hercule Poirot, am completely
deceived. *Sapristi!* it does not bear thinking of! Forget it.
Or no—remember it, and if you think at any time that I
am growing conceited—it is not likely, but it might
arise."

I concealed a smile.

"Eh bien, my friend, you shall say to me, 'Chocolate
box.' Is it agreed?"

"It's a bargain!"

"After all," said Poirot reflectively, "it was an experience! I, who have undoubtedly the finest brain in Europe at present, can afford to be magnanimous!"

"Chocolate box," I murmured gently.

"Pardon, mon ami?"

I looked at Poirot's innocent face, as he bent forward
inquiringly, and my heart smote me. I had suffered often
at his hands, but I, too, though not possessing the finest
brain in Europe, could afford to be magnanimous!

"Nothing," I lied, and lit another pipe, smiling to myself.

ABOUT THE AUTHOR

AGATHA CHRISTIE, the great mystery story writer, was born in England. Since the publication of her first mystery in 1922, she has written over sixty-five books. She is one of the few writers of detective and mystery fiction whose books consistently appear on bestseller lists. In addition to her fiction, she has also written successful plays, including *Witness for the Prosecution*, and many of her books and plays have been made into movies.

Bantam Book Catalog

It lists over a thousand money-saving best-
sellers originally priced from $3.75 to $15.00
—bestsellers that are yours now for as little
as 50¢ to $2.95!

The catalog gives you a great opportunity to
build your own private library at huge savings!

So don't delay any longer—send us your
name and address and 25¢ (to help defray
postage and handling costs).